WITCH'S BLOOD

There had never before been a witch-burning in Dundee, so nobody in the town had known how to place the faggots. A man from the adjacent Monifieth parish had come to say that he had laid and lit witch-fires. Elspet Renkyne was tied upon the standing beam above the set wood and coals. She talked, writhing. The minister preached and his words were lost in the woman's words. The story of Dundee, she called, would be told in the story of her blood. The Monifieth man put his torch to the kindling.

'Ay,' she called out, 'the story of the town will be told in the story of my blood. The blood will go and go and go many times. The blood will return and return and return many times. In its returnings, the blood will sometimes bring back what's needed.'

William Blain

Witch's Blood

CORGI BOOKS

WITCH'S BLOOD
A CORGI BOOK : 0 552 14979 9

Originally published in Great Britain by
Hutchinson & Co. Ltd

PRINTING HISTORY
Hutchinson edition published 1946
Corgi edition published 1978

5 7 9 10 8 6 4

Set in Intertype Baskerville.

Corgi Books are published by Transworld Publishers,
61–63 Uxbridge Road, London W5 5SA,
a division of The Random House Group Ltd,
in Australia by Random House Australia (Pty) Ltd,
20 Alfred Street, Milsons Point, Sydney, NSW 2061, Australia,
in New Zealand by Random House New Zealand Ltd,
18 Poland Road, Glenfield, Auckland 10, New Zealand
and in South Africa by Random House (Pty) Ltd,
Endulini, 5a Jubilee Road, Parktown 2193, South Africa.

Printed and bound in Great Britain by
Cox & Wyman Ltd, Reading, Berkshire.

Papers used by Transworld Publishers are natural, recyclable
products made from wood grown in sustainable forests.
The manufacturing processes conform to the environmental
regulations of the country of origin.

Witch's Blood

Wild's Blood

WITCH'S BLOOD

This, the chronicle of the family surnamed English, is in
accordance with that family's much publicized 'contrariness'
in that it gives no account of the lives of those Englishes who
might be regarded as the reason for a chronicle being written, namely Lord Binnora, Mr. Robert English, and Miss
Elspet English, M.P. The explanation of why that is so is
best expressed in the words of the head of the family. When
Lord Binnora was asked to allow of himself and his brother
and sister being made the subject of biography, he said this:

'The story that is worth telling ends two years before I was
born. I am not interested in your desire to write about myself
and my present-day relatives. But I am interested in this –
that you, an author, have come to me, looking for a subject
to write. Especially am I interested to learn that you have an
intimate knowledge of that town where my forebears lived. I
am beginning to believe, in a way, that it was destined you
should come. . . . The subject I have in mind has long been
awaiting an author. For this writing I am suggesting to you,
there is a great deal of material already collected, the
legends and anecdotes of my family through more than two
hundred years. By writing it you will fulfil a prophecy!'

He smiled in the manner for which he and the other
members of the family are known.

'Well, maybe not a prophecy,' he added. 'It is difficult in
this age to believe in such things. Maybe only the gibberish
of a pain-crazed woman, but everything else in her gibbering
has been made to come true. She said that the story of a
town would be told in the story of her descendants. At any
rate, what she said has been given that meaning by her descendants. The town is that town you know so well.'

7

He dismissed all the objections that were at once raised.

'You say that only in my time has my family become a notable one, worthy of being written? I disagree. It is true that in the last sixty years or so, the family called the Englishes has moved out of provincial obscurity into rather a blaze of publicity, almost notoriety, but, really, the present-day Englishes are only an unimportant tag to what came before. An air of importance is rather easily gained in this era. We are all of us, myself, my brother Robert, my sister Elspet, only people in the news. An old family phrase that — people in the news! Our wealth? It came to us from the past. Whatever there is in it worth the writing is in its origins and its growth before our time. My brother's efforts to gather together the perfect symphony orchestra? His attempts to stage perfect opera? What would that be but a cataloguing of musicians' names and musical compositions? If you must have music to write, there is music in the subject I suggest, the origins of my brother's music. My sister's House of Commons career? Her scorn of town councils and other such local authorities? Her sacrilegious condemnation of that modern political demi-god, the small trader? All that is in the story of our past, more vitally there. These prejudices of Elspet's were hates once. My horses racing, my Derby winner, my two Oaks winners? The horse won, not I. I gave them intriguing names. I can claim only that, but for these names I am indebted as for everything else, to the past Englishes. Dirt Shoveller, Wee Humphy, Elspet Renkyne, Gallus Bailie, Nicol's One, Nicol's Two, Sidlaw Sorner, Townhouse Mason, Dargie's Flower, Bagpiping Orator — strange names for race-horses, names that have caused the raising of many an eyebrow, for the Turf is conservative about horse names. The contrary Englishes, the unorthodox Englishes, could scarcely be expected to have other than contrary, unorthodox names for their horses. The names are names in my family's story.'

He pointed into a small, glass-lidded cabinet.

'My filly, Red Tress, was named for that. Yes, it's hair, a

8

woman's hair. There were four tresses, but this is the only one now. The colour and the gleam are still in it. I wash it in brandy at times, a method of preserving the hair that has been passed down with the hair itself through nine generations.'

Lord Binnora produced the material he had mentioned, a leather-bound ledger more than half-filled with careful writing and pasted-in cuttings.

'My grandfather, Sir William English, he who was known among London city men as the Cripple, dictated most of this to a clerk in his employ. I was a youth then, and at times I sat by the bedside, looking up dates for him and sorting out these printed bits from newspapers and pamphlets. He was a dying man, no more than a mind for remembering and a mouth for speaking. There's little attention to chronological order. The legends and anecdotes were written down in the order in which they came, one recollection bringing to his mind another that was maybe fifty years on or fifty years back in point of time, but there is never dubiety about what period or person each anecdote relates to.'

He read a sentence or two as he turned over the pages.

'You can gather that an author who would make something of this would require a close knowledge of the locality and its traditions. That you have. But note that this is a vastly different view of the town and of its traditions from the view the town takes of itself. This is the unorthodox Englishes, the contrary Englishes, known for their cussedness. You would have to follow their line no matter how contrary it might seem. This is a town's history as seen by eyes that saw differently from most other eyes. There is love of the town here, but also hate of the town. There is what the Americans call debunking of some well-cherished national beliefs as well as of the local beliefs of that town. ... I am sure that once you have gone over this, you will want to do an author's writing of it.'

Later, Lord Binnora and the rest of the Englishes defined the other conditions on which the writing was to be undertaken. There was to be no whitewashing of the family. Their forefathers were not to be made to appear to have bourgeois virtues. Bourgeois – the word is that of Miss Elspet English, M.P.

'The family may have come by its money in queer ways,' she said, 'but we prefer that the truth be known rather than that anybody should imagine we gained it by shopkeeping. The love affairs of the family may not have been according to draper and grocer standards of morality, but write them as they were. If anybody blushes for them, it will not be us.'

Mr. Robert English stipulated that nothing be omitted of what he called the recurring theme of graveyards, that the tempo of the ledger account be not slowed down by too much writing, and that no attempt be made to put the dialogue into a local form.

'If you get the talk in dialect,' he said, 'you will make it incomprehensible for one person at least, namely myself. In the ledger the speech is all indirect and all in plain language. Our grandfather could have dictated the talk stuff in direct form and in dialect. That he didn't do so was obviously for the benefit of the clerk taking the dictation, but it has been a gain for everybody who has read this as well as for the clerk. Some of this indirect speech of the ledger might be useful to you as it stands. You'll know best yourself when to use it and when to translate to direct speech, but, remember, no dialect.'

Lord Binnora, himself, found the title for the chronicle he had proposed.

'We have a name for ourselves. We are "the blood". In the early pages of the ledger you will find the explanation. We are a witch's blood. A melodramatic phrase, yes, but we are a melodramatic family with its roots in a melodramatic town. I have never been there. Some day I'll have to visit it and walk in the streets called gaits – Overgait, Moraygait, Seagait, Cowgait, Wellgait. I'll have to look down upon Dundee from the summit of that hill called the Law.'

THE UNICORN ON THE SHAFT

It happened upon an August day in 1658, in Dundee market place, that a beheaded chicken laid an egg. A six-year-old boy saw that strange thing, and when he was seventy-five, with an aged man's vivid memory of childhood events, he talked about it to a hunchback girl of seven. She was over eighty when she talked, in her turn, to a boy of nine. He lived for seventy more years, and many times told about the chicken. His son, a helpless paralytic in 1902, was the London financier who dictated an account of the odd circumstance, for it to be written in the ledger, along with the many remarkable consequences that followed upon that first day of the history of the Englishes.

That August day of 1658, in Dundee, a woman named Elspet Renkyne had a seizure. She was about twenty-five years old, red-haired, a knitter of broad bonnets, and, in contrast to the raw hacked chilblained feet and legs of most women of the town, her feet and legs were white and smooth. Her child always remembered his mother's feet and legs. That morning, he wept in fear when he saw her writhing and rolling on the floor.

'A shawm will be blown,' she called out, 'but the tune will be one more suited for bagpipes.' Her voice had become deep and gruff. 'A bell will be rung for a tolling, but the beat will be too fast.'

She recovered from the fit, but was agitated and unfit for work. She took the boy's hand, and led him to one of the town gates. A year before it had been a stone archway with a door of oak, but the military governor of Scotland had ordered the demolition of all such fortifications, and now there were only the stumps of the arch's two piers. The woman and the boy sat upon one of these, and she told him about the battle that had been fought seven years before. Her account was a woman's account.

Around them were the ruins of that fight. She pointed to a single broken wall that stood in nettle clumps. She had lived in the tenement of which that wall was the one remaining fragment. She told the boy that when the sudden assault came, she had been in the street, to draw water at a well, and could not move for fright. Around her, she said, men were piking each other, and her eyes would not shut against the horrors. The attackers came in short rushes, and always they pointed and shouted 'There! Get that one!' A soldier crouched, to load his musket, in the cover of the steps on which she sat. 'Get within, mistress!' he said. 'Get within with that hair of yours!' He lifted her, and carried her up the stairs into the building, out of the firing. 'Hair like that shouldn't be sitting in a fight,' he said, laughing, and went back to his killing. The day after, when the tenement was bombarded because a few of the defenders of the town had taken possession of it for a last stand, that same soldier caught her as she ran, and carried her into shelter. 'It's you, with the hair!' he said. The soldier's own hair, Elspet Renkyne told her son, had been red, but not the same redness as hers. His nose had been flattened at the tip.

Elspet Renkyne cried for a long time when she had talked about the soldier. She examined her son's hair, comparing it with her own. She followed the line of his nose with her fingers.

'You have your father's flattened nose,' she said, 'but the redness of your hair is my redness, not your father's.'

She asked the boy by what name the neighbours called him, and when he said he was called the English brat, or often just English, her face was taut. She said, while sobbing, that she had never heard the soldier's second name, only the first, Adam, which name she had given to her son.

'If folks call you English,' she exclaimed, her look wild, 'put your head up and think to yourself that it's a better name than any in Dundee. You're as good as anybody!

You're not Dundee dirt!' These words stayed in his mind.

After that she babbled again, in the frightening voice, about the shawm that would play a tune more suited for bagpipes, and a bell's ringing too quickly for a tolling. There were no people about in that ruined part of the town. Nobody came to help the child while he struggled to quieten his mother. When she was composed again, he importuned her to tell him more about his father. Never before had she spoken about the soldier named Adam. The boy was pleased to be like other boys in having a father, and proud that he was different from others in that his father was of the winning army. He was thinking that he would know what to shout back at those who sneered after him.

She said that the soldier had taken her to a merchant's house where he was billeted. The merchant had complained of a lack of servants to attend the men forced upon him, and could not well refuse to have a servant whom a trooper brought. Adam the soldier could not marry her because, at that time, the army were forbidden to take up with townswomen. He was good to her, and gave her more than two years money at the bonnet-making, his loot from sackings. He had said he would come for her after his discharge. His company went from the town, and she never again heard of him. She had made it known that her child was a soldier's child, because she feared punishment for sinfulness, and guessed rightly that the bailies would not be eager to put into the pillory a woman for whom an enemy trooper, a frightening man to them, might return to a town still held by his comrades. She cried as she talked about these matters, and the boy cried with her, not knowing why he cried.

On the stair leading to their single-room home, she collapsed again. Women came out of the many doors in the tenement's corridors, and attended to her. Her babbling now was to the effect that a dead thing would do what a living thing should do.

That afternoon, the boy saw the chicken in the Marketgait. A country woman cut off its head, and laid the fowl upon a cabbage leaf, for sale, but it leaped from the stall and ran in circles, with children chasing after it. Coming upon straw in its blind running, it squatted there, quivered, and was still. When the woman picked it up, an egg was seen among the straw.

'It was the dead thing, and it did what a living thing should do,' Elspet Renkyne said, frightened, when he told her.

She held him, her eyes staring into his, and asked him to repeat what she had said in her fits. A shawm would play a tune that would be fitter for bagpipes? Could this refer to the town piper, who, with his reeded shawm playing, paraded the streets every morning to signal a new day of work and, with his bagpipes, sounded the curfew in the evenings? No, there was no meaning in the words. The piper had tunes which he blew upon both bagpipes and shawm. A bell's ringing would be too fast for a tolling? These words had even less sense in them. Elspet decided that her talk about shawm and bell and bagpipes was only the havers of a woman in a faint. She listened again to the boy's report of the chicken. She laughed then, and said that for a moment she had believed she might have the gifts which nobody would want to have.

The boy had seen the chicken that ran and laid an egg when dead. He had heard about his father. The day was memorable. Seventy years later, Adam English told his grand-daughter, Katherine, about that day. They were standing, aged man and little hunchback girl, on the spot where had been the stump of an archway, where the Wellgait of Dundee comes down its slope to the junction of Moraygait and Cowgait. There was no debris of battle, but still were gaps where cottages and tall houses and tenements had been, still an air of desolation, the Cowgait yet wasteland with weed-covered hillocks and hollows to hide the last relics of destruction, the Wellgait bearing the evidences of impoverished repairing. 'Here,' the old man said, 'she talked about the shawm and the bell, and it came true just as her talk about the chicken had come true, and just as other things that she said have come true in years not so long ago. Things that she said would come true have still to come. Mind!' And seventy more years after that, an ancient hunchback woman spoke to a red-haired boy whose nose was blunted, at the same place, the busiest part of a busy town, standing amid the carters' angry arguments against each other's slowness in the traffic-jammed Moraygait, amid the brisk walking and brisk talking of flax men's deals at the Cowgait–Wellgait corner, amid the shouts for a passage for rolls of linen and the spinners' appeals for attention to the even fineness of their spools. 'Here,' the old hunchback woman said, 'the soldier saved Elspet Renkyne from the guns, and here she said something that came true. There are things of her saying that have still to come true. Mind!'

Some weeks after that first day of the Englishes' history, in 1658, Cromwell died on Cromwell's day, September the third. Eight years before, on September the third, he had routed a Scotch army at Dunbar. Seven years before, on September the third, when he was winning his crowning victory against the Scotch at Worcester, his general, Monck, had stormed the last Scotch stronghold of resistance to Cromwell, the old Steeple of Dundee, moving his regiments through burning Dundee streets, past Dundee's slain on the cobble-stones.

Cromwell was dead, he was dead, he was dead! The news, four days in its coming to Dundee, was news that could not wait for formal announcement. The man who brought the news shouted it on his way to the tolbooth. The folks in the streets and the folks at the window-holes shouted it. A thousand came to the tolbooth with the news, bearing aloft the one who had ridden from Perth.

The council in the tolbooth debated, afraid that word of Dundee's reception of the tidings would be carried to Monck, Cromwell's Monck, military governor in Edinburgh.

These dancing folk in the Marketgait would not be called upon to answer to Monck, but the council might. Better to treat this news in the traditional manner for a king's death, the safe formality used for good kings and bad kings alike.

The traditional manner, what was it? Ten years ago a king had died, and for his death, blood-stirring news, riotous news, death by the axe, there had been no market cross announcement. The traditional manner? The oldest councillor thought long and, at last, remembered – a procession of the whole council, with the provost leading, a reading of the news by the day's watch-bailie, the knelling of the tolbooth bell, a lament played by the town-piper upon his shawm, a pause, and then from the provost the announcement of the accession of a new king. Today the last part must be omitted, but the remainder was well fitted to be reported to Monck. The crowd halted their singing and dancing, and made a way for the procession from the tolbooth to the cross on the other side of the Marketgait.

A bailie mounted to the parapet of the little tower, from which rose the long slender shaft with the unicorn upon it. His words were heard in silence, then someone shouted: 'We'll be hearing about the devil having his head cut off, and there'll be a Lord Protector of Hell.' Everybody laughed, the provost and bailies laughing with the crowd. The bell on the tolbooth wall started to ring. 'Faster, porter, faster!' the crowd yelled. 'One-two and a one and two, rum-tum tumity tum! Let it swing, porter!' The porter's shoulders moved with the crowd's timing. In the merry jangle of the bell, the shawm started to play. 'Play for a dance, piper!' the crowd called. The stamping of feet and the beat of the clapped hands quickened the piper's tempo. They danced, shouting to the piper to keep on playing. He was red in the face, panting. 'No, no, folks,' he cried, 'if it's that speed you want me to play, and to keep it going, I would need to have my bagpipes, with their own wind to give me a rest. The tune is more fit for bagpipes than for a shawm.'

Elspet Renkyne, standing by with her child, dropped upon

16

the rounded stones of the Marketgait. She recovered from her faint with the crowd around her, and was seized with a shaking and writhing. She called out, gasping, her voice deep like a man's, that a king would carry a king's hat to the tolbooth.

The child Adam English sat with her pulling hand in his. The crowd repeated her words to each other – a king would carry a king's hat to the tolbooth. They called to those still dancing to stop, to the piper to cease his playing, for a woman was sick. Some folks were saying that this was the one who had borne a child to a Cromwell trooper. The crowd looked at the red-haired boy with interest. There was talk, heard by him, that the memories roused by Cromwell's death had been too much for his mother.

The pause in the merriment sobered the crowd. Here and there a woman started to weep. Soon all the women were weeping, and some men, staring as they wept at the black gaps among the tenements, pointing to alleyways and closes where the fighting had been, where brothers and fathers and husbands and sons had fallen. A one-legged man sat upon the steps of the market cross, and shrieked about his wound in the battle, displaying his mangled stump. Through a quiet crowd, the boy English led his white, trembling mother. As they went, a few women eyed them. The boy heard whispers, conjectures as to whether or not his mother might have the gifts. Her twisting and shaking, the knowing ones said, had been like that twisting and shaking of those living folk through whose mouths the dead spoke.

The boy was hard wrought, because his mother was afraid to go outside her door lest she have a shaking fit in public. Drawing water from the well, carrying it, marketing, these were heavy tasks for a child. His mother cuddled him and wept, saying she would have to show herself again because he was too little for what he had to do. She implored him to be within call always, to accompany her always, and hold her hand. The neighbours looked at her on the stair, and in the close when she appeared for the first time for weeks. She trembled when they looked at her. In the Moraygait, at the close mouth, she pulled the boy to the wall. She said that armed men were riding there. The boy saw no horsemen. Her insistence attracted people around her, and she moaned and shook, and while two women held her from falling, she shouted her previous words about the king and the king's hat. Her threshing hand struck the wall, and blood flowed. She blinked at the blood.

'My blood will be a power in Dundee,' she said in the deep voice. 'My blood will put a rope round the neck of a bailie. My blood will become such a power as to be too powerful for so little a town, and it will go from Dundee.'

She was carried home by three men, the crowd moving behind. Women were saying that undoubtedly this red-haired one had the gift. They were reminding each other about her prophesying the dead hen's laying of an egg, and the death of Cromwell. These foreseeings had been talked about in the close, for the boy had boasted of them. Sceptics were arguing that any nonsense came true if somebody looked for it coming true, that gibberish words such as this Renkyne woman's were not foreseeings of the hen or of Cromwell's dying. The scoffers, in their arguings, were making prophecies of their own in the manner of the boy's mother.

Wedderburn, laird of the lands of Kingennie, a few miles to the north-east of the town, became chief magistrate, called provost. He wore a dented hat, its brim turned up in the old fashion – the beheaded king's fashion, some said. His horse was named Charles. The tavern debaters held that Wedderburn's choosing had been the result of pressure upon the council from men in high places. There was a saying in Dundee that in years of laird politics a laird was provost, and here was the laird for times sufficiently political for lairds. Menfolk talked about the significance of Wedderburn's hat and Wedderburn's horse. Womenfolk, listening to the men's talk, whispered words said by Elspet Renkyne, that a king would carry a king's hat to the tolbooth. For his first sitting of the council, Provost Wedderburn rode in from Kingennie with an escort in the old laird-like way, which had not been seen for long, four armed men, armed for ceremony, certainly, rather than for fighting, but a meaningful event to the arguers. Women whispered that Elspet Renkyne had seen that escort in the Moraygait three weeks before it came.

On the few occasions she went out, with her child grasping her hand, Elspet Renkyne was watched. She had more seizures. Women rushed to hear her words. They were coming to her door to hear news of their dead. She turned them away at first, but as her bonnet-making work was decreasing because of her weakness and fear, she at last accepted their money. The boy did not hear her words to those who came to the house. He was sent outside to the tenement stair. He heard the talk of the women as they came away impressed.

In the street she said this: that a young man would not lift an old man's sword, and that a king's palace was bigger than a laird's house. Richard Cromwell, son of the Protector, resigned from the rulership his father's generals had given him. In Dundee were arguings, and the women, hearing the arguings, said that this Richard must be the young man referred to by the gifted woman. Was not his father known for his fighting – the sword; did not the son prefer peace – he would not lift his father's sword; had he not retired to being a laird from being a king – the palace was bigger than the laird's house?

Elspet Renkyne, seized by her writhing and twisting while washing clothes in the Scouring Burn, said that the water of the stream was flowing the wrong way. In two weeks a storm of wind piled up the tide in the Tay estuary, and a wall of water swept into the mouth of the Scouring Burn and up the burn's course. Lives were lost, the lower lying closes of the Seagait were flooded, and the hollow of the Meadows, the public bleaching green outside the town bounds on the north, was three feet under water.

Through some eighteen months, a year and a half of

surprises in local and national life, Elspet Renkyne was saying words which when examined could be shown to have been foreseeings. More and more women came to her house. She had no way of earning her own and her boy's living now, except by giving comfort to the bereaved.

She said, just outside the ruin of that tenement where she had once lived, that Adam would not come to Dundee, but go away from it. The news was that the military governor for Scotland had marched his army southwards from Edinburgh, the same Major-General Monck of the Dundee battle. He had crossed the border, was moving on London. The Dundee men were in a fever of argument about Monck's march. The women were saying that Elspet Renkyne had foretold this. Had not the Adam, of whom she was always speaking, been a Monck trooper, probably still was?

Staring up the slope of the conical hill above Dundee, the Law, Elspet Renkyne said that a fighting name was being shouted. The people around her followed the direction of her look. Up there was Dudhope Castle. They said to each other that the exiled owner of Dudhope Castle had a fighting name, Scrymgeour, which they pronounced Scrimmager. The day came when Wedderburn of Kingennie, the provost, marched from the tolbooth over the way to the market cross to read a council decision too important for a lesser magistrate's reading, that his remote kinsman Scrymgeour, Viscount Dudhope, hereditary constable of Dundee, be listed in the locked book of burgesses as a freeman of the town and a guild brother. The crowd seethed, for this was the provost's declaration of Dundee's politics. The council, by honouring the king's man, Viscount Dudhope, was saying that it was for Charles, son of the beheaded Charles. General Monck, holding London, had already declared for a kingdom and for the Stuart, in Holland, as king. The women said that here was the crying of the fighting name.

The gifted woman said that a change would be no change

for broken down houses. The women found a meaning for these words. This Monck who had summoned this Charles from Holland was the Monck who had killed and burned in Dundee. He had killed and burned to unmake this Charles, and now with Dundee burned and Dundee men dead, this Monck was making this Charles. Let the men shout their loudest for this Monck and this Charles, the houses were burned. It was late in the day for Monck to change his mind. Could he raise the dead? Could he undo what he had done to the town? At the market cross, the council cried that the Stuarts were restored. The cheers for Monck and for the king were not so eager as the councillors would wish for. One bailie was quoted as saying that the town would have to be handled with firmness to give it a proper appreciation of what should be cheered.

Elspet Renkyne's deep voice for foreseeings cried out that the provost's seat was a cold, cold seat. The townsfolk looked for her words being fulfilled. To celebrate the new rule, the council walked the bounds, a ceremony that had not been seen by any alive. Wedderburn of Kingennie, who was for old ways, found an account of the ancient procedure and was of a mind to mark the return of an old dynasty by the return of an old custom. The provost led on his horse named for a king, then the four bailies and the treasurer, the fifteen councillors, the dean of guild and his assessors, a score of invited merchant burgesses, and the deacons and past-deacons of the nine trades and of the guildry pendicles, leaders of the craft burgesses. They walked the town's four streets, Overgait, Nethergait, Moraygait, Seagait, which met together in the wide rectangle called the Marketgait. They looked to the boundary stones, with speech-making at each of the old gateways, to the common lands at Magdalen Yard and at the Wards and the Meadows, and to the town mills on the Dighty stream. They came, at length, to the Stannergait cliffs on the Tay shore, two miles eastward of the town, the extremity of the salmon fishing rights of Dundee's royalty charters. There had been eating and drinking before the

march and during the march, and, now, to end it, was a great
eating and drinking, shouting of drunken witticisms, loud
drunken laughter, teasing and counter-teasing, jovial insults,
burgesses in merriment. The magistrates and deacons threw
pennies and food to be scrambled for by the boys among the
crowd. Adam English, the gifted woman's child, was there to
scramble with the other children. The cups were filled for
the final feature of the ceremony, were held aloft with all the
drinkers facing the river, all toasting the river, inviting the
river to drink with them. The provost sat upon the edge of
the cliff, in hollowed rocks where former provosts had sat.
He poured a tankard of ale into the water, a drink for the
Tay. They all drank with the Tay and to the Tay, laughing
with the laughing river. The provost called out that if
these rocks were the Provost's Seat they were a sight
too uncomfortable for anybody of the rank of provost of
Dundee to sit on. 'The Provost's Seat,' he said, 'is a cold, cold
seat!'

In the crowd was a sudden silence, then a laugh. It was
not the laugh that should have been for a provost's joke. The
burgesses looked, startled, at the crowd, then looked in
anger, the quick anger of drunken men.

'Their laughter will have something to do with that
damned witch and with her prophesyings,' one councillor
said. Ay, the same woman's words had cooled the town for the
Restoration, the other tolbooth men were saying. The town
needed a redding to fit it for the new rôle, they told each
other, a redding of witcheries, and ghosts, and harlotry and
republican ideas. Adam English listened to the talk of the
councillors, then turned and ran all the way home.

With six other women, Elspet Renkyne stood in the pillory at the base of the market cross. To mark her as an
adulteress, a town servant sheared off her red hair, and hung it
on the crosspiece beside her locked right hand. A minister
preached from the parapet of the cross, saying that the town
had condoned sin and the wrath of God had fallen upon the

town. The wrath would be turned from the town by the town's punishing those who were sinful.

She was fainting. The rough wood of the neck-hole cut into her throat, choking her. The town servant held her lest she die by hanging. She spoke, in the deep gasping voice. Her blood, she said, would become a power. The beginning of the power would be in water and stone. It would be heated by a hot sun and watered by pouring rains to grow in its powerfulness.

The child, Adam English, looked from the shadow of a close. The town watch had shut him in the tolbooth, and had not looked to the width of the window-hole and the slimness of the child. He had found toe-holds and finger-holds on the wall, and had climbed, to wriggle from the window. His feet and hands bled as he watched and listened. His shoulders shook as he suppressed his sobs.

The town servant unlocked Elspet Renkyne from the crosspiece. She writhed and twisted as the servant carried her through the silent crowd, which made a way and then followed him along the length of the Marketgait, into the Seagait, to a widening in the narrow street, a widening made by the battle. The boy came behind the tail of the crowd. He found a shadowed corner from which to watch.

There had never before been a witch-burning in Dundee, so nobody in the town had known how to place the faggots. A man from the adjacent Monifieth parish had come to say that he had laid and lit witch-fires. Elspet Renkyne was tied upon the standing beam above the set wood and coals. She talked, writhing. The minister preached, and his words were lost in the woman's words. The story of Dundee, she called, would be told in the story of her blood. The Monifieth man put his torch to the kindling.

'Ay,' she called out, 'the story of the town will be told in the story of my blood. The blood will go and go and go many times. The blood will return and return and return many times. In its returnings, the blood will sometimes bring back what's needed.'

Elspet Renkyne screamed in pain. The crowd shouted that this was not a fire to burn but a fire to roast. They angrily demanded that merciful gunpowder be put among the faggots. The Monifieth man threw more wood upon the fires, and the crowd were for killing him, for his wood was green and caused a great cloud of smoke. He ran. Amid the smoke was Elspet Renkyne's voice, hushing the crowd.

'The lamentation for my death,' she said, 'will be beat by hammers and sung by the voices of boy burgesses. For great men, gathered in the town, will be the lamentation for my death. A multitude will acclaim my name. I'll be seen again in Dundee, standing unburnable in cold flames.'

She sobbed, and cried for her child. He, sobbing, ran to her and stood on the verge of the fire. Women were falling all around, twisting and writhing, babbling. Elspet Renkyne was quiet. A more merciful death than had seemed likely, folks were saying, smothering by the smoke instead of burning. Men kicked away the fire, and revealed her there, smoke-blackened. A town servant seized the boy who held to the dead woman's knees.

As he was borne away, the boy heard a bailie say that the fire would have to be lit again to burn the dead witch. 'The full punishment must be carried out,' the bailie said. 'But we need some dry wood. The smoke from that wet wood is through the whole town. The smoke is in every gait and every close.' The boy always remembered what that bailie had said.

In the night was the sobbing of the child and the running of feet. He climbed up inside the chimney of the tolbooth room where the town servants had put him. He found a descent from the roof. They searched for him, and his sobbing led them to where he lay under an outside stair. He ran, dodging among the wynds and closes. When he hid again, he remembered his mother and sobbed. The men found him always by his sobbing, but always he could run from them, his bare feet silent, his boy's knowledge of the wynds undoing their traps for him. In the dawn, when the shawm was playing the start to a day's work, he darted across the Marketgait to the pillory. He pulled his mother's hair from the crosspiece, and with it, blowing in his hand, gained the Mint close, hard by the market cross, swerved through its cluttered narrowness to the ridge of the Corbie's Hill and over it. He climbed the near wall of the graveyard, moved in sharp dashes from tombstone to tombstone, climbed the graveyard's far wall, with the men's shouts almost upon him, splashed through the Scouring Burn in the Meadows, and sprinted his hardest across the open. The panting men watched him go up the slope of the eastern spur of the Law. He kept far away from the line of cottages that climbed the spur, the long village called the Hilltown of Dudhope. He went through the Dudhope Castle grounds, over the spur, down the northern decline called the cold side, through the lands of Claverhouse, crossed the Dighty water, went up the long slopes of the lands of Powrie and the lands of Tealing, and came to the Sidlaw Hills, which were no man's land for homeless ones. He had run six miles, and could run no more. He fell upon the moss and heather, and sobbed when he looked at the hair, remembering. He lay there all that day and all the night.

He went into the Sidlaw glens to hide himself. He came through a great bracken patch, and at a crossing of trails in the heart of the bracken a tinkler family were sitting. They called to him to point out the way they should take. He asked them where they wanted to go, and they said they would go where a finger pointed. They had awaited the coming of a finger. They rose and moved in the direction he pointed, and he moved with them. They told him to take his own way, but he followed. An old woman asked him where his mother was, and he wept. When he told them that his mother had been burned, they gathered around him. The old woman looked closely into the boy's eyes, holding the eyelids apart, then she took the boy by the hand, and they all moved again.

They came to a sunny slope where many tinklers sat. Adam's finger had pointed aright, and the family were pleased with him. There was much excited talk in words Adam could not understand, then a crowd gathered around him, looking at him and at the hair, the woman patting him comfortingly and drying his tears.

When, seventy years later, he told his memories of that day and of the day before, he talked of these matters as a child had seen them. He was not quite eight years old when they happened.

The tinklers' tribe name was White, a swarthy folk for the most part but with fair and brown-haired ones among them. They could speak the Lowland speech for their dealings with strangers, but among themselves they spoke gipsy words and words of that language called Irish in Dundee, the language of the great mountains lying north and west of the Sidlaws, across the central valley of Angus. They had strange stories to tell to the boy, of clan fights among those mountains to which they pointed, of broken clans wandering, of storm spirits and the kelpies of stream and hill; and, older than these, the stories of the swarthiest among them, of their forefathers having crossed great waters, of oddly weaponed warriors in battles far towards the rising sun. There was a story, older than any, of a time when a cruel god's talons had reached after man and a cold breath had frozen where it blew. The god covered all the land, the story went, crushing the land under his weight. He wrenched off the mountain tops and carried them to the plains, where they lay, keeping their secret, frightening men by their silence. The god clawed out the glens, leaving claw marks upon the rocks. Because the tinklers knew that the god would come again they were always ready to run. In mid-winter, they made ceremony. The women cleaned out the burrows and twig-woven huts which were the tinkler homes, and held the entrances against the taloned one's coming. The men were outside, waiting for the triumph of warmth over cold and of life over death, and it came in the night after the year's shortest day. The men stood around one of the standing stones to be found in many parts of Angus. They touched the stone, and went to their homes to bear the news that the days would lengthen, the spring would come, that life was triumphant over death, that mankind would survive. The boy saw that this was the same ceremony as the Hogmanay celebrations in Dundee, when women scrubbed and polished their houses, and the men, crowding round the market cross, waited for the end of the old year and the beginning of the new. The Dundee folks did not know why they did these things, but they knew, in a way, that a pillar or a steeple was necessary.

With the tinkler wives, selling the wares made in the camps, the boy went round bleak Angus, where a tree in the garden of a great laird's house was something to look at. They moved along pack-horse trails that strayed among the heathered knolls, through vast stretches of gorse and bracken and fool's-parsley, skirting the bogs and the shallow lakes of the great central valley of the country; into the red-brown villages, reduced in prosperity and population by war; up towards the mountains where in the Braes of Angus was the waste of the last Royalists' fights against Monck's men; down towards Dundee, which the tinklers would not enter, for its watchers had whips for vagrants. The women came no nearer to Dundee than the top of the Hilltown village. From there, they looked down at the place with tall houses, as they called the town. When the women asked how many people were in that spread of tall houses, Adam remembered having heard that before the battle Dundee had eight thousand people and some years after it only six. They asked him how many was that, but he did not know. One said there must be as many people as there were grains in a handful of dust. They snatched up dust to look at it and to marvel.

The boy climbed to the peak of the conical Law. On his right as he faced Dundee was the bald hump of Balgay Hill, and in the saddle between Balgay and the Law pack-horses moved on the trail from Dundee towards Coupar Angus. On his left, the long spur, where the tinklers were standing, went far to the east, split by the Dens, the gorge of a stream that had cut an outlet to the Tay. He looked down the smooth curve of the Law to Dudhope Castle on a long flat from which the lands of Lower Dudhope descended in a series of escarpments and terraces to the strath of the Scouring Burn, where in the Meadows and Wards women were washing clothes. Beyond was Dundee's graveyard, and then the line of the Corbie's Hill, round the eastern end of which the burn found a way through the pale-stoned town to the estuary.

This Dundee he saw from the Law was not Dundee as he knew it. Dundee was twisting wynds among stairs for a boy in Dundee, but for a boy on the Law it was roofs, with the square tower, called the Old Steeple, rising high above roofs, and the castle rock among roofs, and no lines of streets seen in the jumble of roofs. Across the water from the town was the long line of the Ochil spur, with a vague plain behind it. To the west of the town was the Hawk Hill in the lands of Blackness that tumbled in hillocks into the Carse of Gowrie, where the river was wide like a lake, with hills all around; to the east, the steeply stepped lands of Wallace Craigie, and beyond that the Stannergait cliffs and shingle strips, and the curve of Broughty Bay, and the long promontory with Broughty Castle on it, and sand shores further off, and Buddon jutting out where the river became the sea. Always the river, its winking gleam broken by dull ripple-less patches, sandbanks. The river was nothing to a boy in the wynds. To a boy on the Law, Dundee was a little clutter of roofs by a great river that flowed amidst hills.

He wondered as he looked down what his mother's blood was doing to Dundee in revenge for the death it had given her. He was of a mind to go into the town to see for himself what had come of her foreseeings, but he remembered the watchers' pursuit of him. In tinkler manner he cursed the tolbooth and the old steeple, rising there above the burgesses' churches. He waved his mother's hair at the town and went back to the tinkler women, down the Law spur with them, the cold side, towards the strath of the Dighty, away from Dundee.

The boy could steal like a tinkler, read a hand like a tinkler's wife. He could catch rabbits and hares, and cook his catch. He made the skins into vests and leggings to wear beneath his rags in winter. He could drink the harsh spirit that the tinklers made from heather tops. He could play the bagpipes. Except for one matter, he was a tinkler. The Whites had no cares, no complaints against Fate or those who governed. Nobody governed the tinklers. The sorners, the beggar men who also lived in the Sidlaws, talked always about bad luck or politics, and grumbled. They talked about what they would do, revolts, riots, battles. The boy was a sorner in that he found delight in thoughts about the fall of the mighty, who for him were Dundee burgesses and ministers.

The sorners' begging was not the tinklers' humble plea for alms. It was terrorisation of the crofter hamlets. In all the Lowland hills were bands of sorners, the unemployed of the towns in the vast trade depression, tramping the trails in search of work, driven from the more frequented main routes by dragoons and by the watchers of the larger burghs, finding a refuge in such remote countrysides as Angus, off the main routes. Here, their masterful begging was undisturbed. Edinburgh and the government's soldiers were beyond the great barriers of the Tay and the mountains; the Angus towns were little and far separated; the hamlets and farm clusters, on the lonely pack-horse paths, were an easy prey for roaming groups of twenty or thirty wild-looking men. The lairds, bankrupted by their support of the Stuarts and by Cromwell's fines, were in London or Edinburgh craving for court favours, or, those few at home, struggling to arrest the encroachment of the bog and the heather upon the neglected fields; they had no force, as in the old days, to deal with such intruders as these sorners, further impoverishing an impoverished Angus, where cultivation had sunk to mere

29

subsistence tilling except in the immediate vicinity of the one larger burgh, Dundee, itself in decline.

The leader of the Sidlaw sorners was one named Yeaman, a little thin, dark-faced man, with deep lines from his nose to the turned-down corners of his mouth, glistening black eyes, zig-zag veins throbbing at his temples. He had been run out of Dundee in the redding after the Restoration, a tavern talker with views to the effect that Cromwell's era of no king had its merits.

He was bitter against Dundee burgesses. When he spoke about the Dundee governance, the veins throbbed at his temples, his black eyes flashed, the lines on his face deepened. He had a phrase for Dundee burgesses – the right ones, he called them, always right and always righteous. The boy listened to Yeaman's hate, and hated with Yeaman.

The sorner orator's views shaped the views of the Englishes through nine generations. Yeaman's phrases were heard in Dundee's council two hundred years later. And seventy years after that, they were heard in the parliament at London, Miss Elspet English's scorn of 'shopkeeper mentality', of bourgeois minds, of right ones.

Yeaman's description of the Dundee burgess system was the over-simplified description of an angry agitator. In Dundee's six thousand, he said, only two hundred and thirty were burgesses. Two hundred and thirty held the town; it was their town, the churches were their churches and the God their God, the streets theirs, the air breathed in the town theirs, the river theirs. The sorners growled when Yeaman spoke. He spoke of the locked book of the burgesses, the list of the free. A man's name could be put upon the book if his father's name had been there, or if he married a woman whose father's name had been a burgess name, or if the town council wanted to flatter him (which they did not do for anyone except lairds), or if he became rich enough to own a toft of land and to be able to pay burgess fees, and then only if the council wanted him to be a burgess. The listeners laughed bitterly to this. An unfree journeyman earned half a shilling a day, when there was work for him; the burgess fees were eighty shillings. Could a worker ever have eighty shillings at once? Could a worker ever have a toft of land? If by some miracle he did gain the necessary wealth, the council would say that he was a worker, an unfree man, not the kind for the book. The locked book was indeed locked, locked against all names except those already there, and the privileges and monopolies locked in it.

Yeaman spoke of the burgess corporations. The free were organized, he cried, and the unfree should take a lesson from them. The sorners applauded. There was the guildry, he explained, the shopkeepers' corporation, with its seventy-five. A dirty bit of parchment sealed by some daft king had given to long-ago booth-keepers of Dundee the monopoly of all buying and selling for profit within the town, the right of handling and taking profits from everything that came into the town for sale and everything that went out. Yeaman was prepared to believe that if somebody asked the shopkeepers to show their parchment, there wouldn't be anything to show but a heap of dust. There were not even meetings of the guildry, except for a coming and going along the tolbooth front by members, once a year, when the dean of guild and his assessors were chosen. While there was a council, there was no need for the guildry members to meet to defend their privileges. Why? Because the council did the dirty work better than any meeting of shopkeepers could do it. The council were almost all shopkeepers. The town's constitution as a royal burgh – sealed by some other daft king! – had it that all but three of the council should be full guild brethren, merchant burgesses, with, maybe, at times, a lairdling among them. That being so, the guildry just did not bother to be a guildry. The council kept a close eye on the safeguarding of the guildry privileges, and watched out that no unfree man kept a shop, unless it was the smallest and dirtiest kind of tavern.

There were the nine trades and the pendicles of the guildry, Yeaman told his listeners. The nine trades were the

bakers, the shoemakers, the skinners, the tailors, the bon-
netmakers, the fleshers, the hammermen, the weavers, and
the dyers. The pendicles were the wrights, the masons, the
slaters, and the maltmen. They had their dirty bits of parchment, too, and only a member of one of these trades, a
burgess, could be a trade master. Only a freeman could hire
another man's labour. Only a freeman could make a loaf or a
bonnet for sale. Why, a journeyman dyer, if unfree, could
not dye his neighbour's wool for money! He must hire himself to a master dyer whose name was in the book. A journeyman mason could not, if unfree, build a shed for his own
brother and take a price for his skill. Only a burgess mason, a
member of the mason pendicle to the guildry, could take on
to build. The council looked well enough after the privileges
of the trades, too, but did not do so well as it did for the
shopkeepers, for the merchant monopolies sometimes
clashed with the trade monopolies, and, there being only
three free tradesmen in the council, the merchants won the
arguments at the council. The trades corporations were
keeping their own eye on their parchment rights, keeping an
eye on the shopkeepers when necessary, but more keenly
keeping an eye on the unfree, who might do a bit of weaving
for their own end in their homes or make bread or clothes to
sell in the unlawful markets of the unfree, the black markets
as the free called them.

Yeaman's anger against the burgesses was fierce when he
spoke, but when he ceased, he flushed and smiled to the
congratulations on his oratory and his knowledge, and his
strut was a burgess strut. The sorners, inflamed by Yeaman,
would plan their riots and battles. They would start with
talk about an attack upon Dundee. They would consider the
making and stealing of weapons, the reinforcement of their
number by contingents from the Campsie Fell sorners and
the Ochil sorners. They would be selecting committees for
bringing these plans into effect, and then would be high argument about the proper procedure of selecting a committee, with men rising to points of order everywhere. The

meetings would become interruptions of the one presiding, hints to him on the right and highly sacred way to conduct a meeting, with many long words, the meaning of which required other long words to define them. Finally, they would rise and go out on the trails to frighten the crofters. The boy, who had excitedly anticipated the raid on Dundee, would return, disappointed, to the tinkler camp, hating Yeaman, but with his heart still beating to the rhythm of Yeaman's words.

Once Yeaman, speaking from the orator's stand, saw the red-haired boy among the sorners, and called him to come up on the rock. Yeaman said that once or twice in every century war changed life in Dundee. Here, this boy, was the evidence of change, a change for the worse. Never before had the council burned a woman for witchery. Formerly, there had been some tolerance for the unfree and the unfree's beliefs in the spirits. The unfree had been allowed to live in their own way, so long as they did not infringe upon the burgess privileges. Now, the free were feeling insecure in a poorer town, and holding more tightly to what they called their rights and their own beliefs. The were afraid of the unfree. They were seeing in every move of the unfree an effort towards revolt. They had killed a harmless woman who gave comfort to the bereaved. To give such comfort was against the rules of the burgess church, the council's church with the council's appointed ministers, in which was worshipped a God who supported burgess monopolies. They would use their burgess God as an instrument to keep down the unfree. Where in Dundee was the church of Knox? Where was Knox's plan for the support of the workers by the lands of Scotland? Where were Knox's schools? Nowhere in Dundee. Only the burgess families could go to the burgess churches and to the burgess school, which had no likeness to Knox's churches and Knox's schools. Their Christ? Was Christ a burgess? Was John Knox a burgess? Christ had said that little children should be suffered to come unto Him. The Dundee burgesses had chased a child, this boy here,

33

through their streets to put him to the dirt man's service.

'No,' the boy said, interrupting Yeaman, 'it wasn't like that at all. It was nothing to do with John Knox or Christ. They burned my mother because she raised a laugh against them. The right ones did it!'

Yeaman stared.

'You're right, laddie,' he said. 'That's the reason for all their laws, to stop folk from laughing at them and to punish folk who laugh or raise a laugh. You're right!' He turned to his audience with a passion of oratory. His zig-zag veins throbbed, his eyes burned. When he came down from the rock, he listened to the sorners' praise of himself, and strutted.

The sorners talked about burning the Dundee churches, with the ministers in them. Men rose to press points of order, to argue the true way of conducting a meeting. The boy cursed the sorners who talked about riots but did nothing except talk. He did not weep, now, when his mother was mentioned. He smiled with a hard smile.

He had been four years with the Whites when, one day, a stranger tinkler asked him if he were the talked-about son of the Dundee gifted woman. He nodded, and the stranger looked impressed. 'So you're the witch's blood,' the tinkler said. The boy was startled. The blood! His mother's blood was to be a power in Dundee, to become too powerful for little Dundee. In stone and water was to be the beginning of the power. In the light of a hot sun and in heavy rains would the power grow. And he, himself, was the blood!

Next day, he left the Whites' camp. He went down the long roll of the land towards Dundee. He crouched outside the Moraygait port, and watched, fearful and, yet, eager. When dusk had fallen, he went into the town, and found a sleeping place below an outside stair in one of the wynds.

The boy knew the secrets of the nine trades and of the pendicles to the guildry. When the hue and cry was raised for him, wanted for the dirt shovelling, he hid in the burial ground, called the Houff, the foregathering place. There the burgesses of the trades met, set their guards, tyled their meetings against all who should not hear, and never knew that the boy lay amongst them. Each craft had its own place in the Houff, by the grave of some long-dead deacon of the craft, a notable whose tombstone was large. Under these great flat slabs were hollows, fallen in when the bodies beneath had mouldered, and in one or other of these the boy lay secure when the town servants poked with their halberds through the closes for him.

The entered apprentices and the newly made masters took their vows in the centuries-old ceremonies of initiation, the members discussed the guarding of their chartered rights, and the boy lay listening, afraid of being discovered by a chance loosening of the earth he had pulled up around the entrance to his hollow. There were occasions, rare but all the more awesome for their rarity, when the men of the mystic trade, the masons, performed their fearsome rites in the burial ground. The boy shivered, not because of the cold and damp, as he listened to the intonation of the oaths to keep inviolate the meaning of the ritual.

He knew the anxieties of the Houff men, dullness of trade, threats to the monopolies. The oldest member in the meetings could not remember harder times. Folks were counting their money in pennies. All kinds of hucksters were breaking in to the rights of the burgesses. Unfree men were illegally cutting cloth, making shoes, baking rolls in the secrecy of their homes and trading in the back vennels. The websters complained of the competition of the Hilltown. The weavers of the Hilltown were outside the town and escaped the dues and restrictions, but they sold to townspeople. In the town, unfree weavers were obtaining yarn outside the weaver trade and bartering their cloth for farm produce.

The boy prowled through the closes, dodging the town servants. He slept in the Cowgait ruins or in the bracken of the Corbie's Hill. In the dusk of morning and of evening, he filched his meals from the booths and from the pack-horses at the markets. In the back closes were people who would receive him at times. They were afraid of him, and whispered that his father was the evil one himself. He could tell the women their anxieties and their fears, for he had the tinkler way of listening to words and to silences. The women did not know they were disclosing their inmost thoughts, and were agape when he read the hands. His red hair had made him easily spotted by the town servants, and he had stolen a bonnet from a booth, one of the broad black bonnets worn by the guildry burgesses. He cut holes in the head-band and threaded cord through the holes, drawing the cord tight till the head-band fitted him. The broad bonnet was as conspicuous as his hair. He muddied it in the mud of the harbour. Each day he bashed it with his fist into a new shape.

He feared the terrible penalties for divulging the secrets of the masons and he feared Sarah Drummond, a ghost-raiser. She told the future, and he told the future better. She hated him, and she muttered at him and put the eye on him. He gave no concern to her eye or her muttering, but he feared that she would find some way of betraying his hiding place in the tombs. She had come into the Houff one day, had seen him engaged upon lining the hollows with bracken, and guessed his reason. He resolved that if he were caught in the Houff, he would denounce Sarah Drummond as a witch. He would know she had betrayed him. He grinned when she raised ghosts in the dimness of her house in a back-land of the Seagait. He had seen that kind of ghost in the tinklers' camps. Some of the tinkler women could do such ghost-raising better than Sarah could. They swallowed a fine linen web, and brought it up from their insides. In the gloom, after the chanting and the deep-voiced calling upon the ghosts, anything that was produced from nowhere was a ghost. Hung on sticks, shaken, the linen web was a ghost. The ghost-raiser hated him because he knew how she did her raising.

From a close mouth he watched her moving towards the men with the halberts. He had laughed at her only five minutes ago, and now she was going to betray him. As he watched, he felt with his hand among the rags that clothed him, and touched the talisman for warding off bad luck, his mother's hair, wrapped in a cloth. He called to Sarah Drummond that she had more to fear from the watchers than he had.

He ran. Looking back, he saw that she had turned away from the town servants. He laughed at her as she came past, and drew out his talisman to shake at her. She shivered. She knew that she was no witch, but she feared that the boy might be one. She had once before seen the contents of the dirty rag parcel. She hid her eyes. The boy hooted after her. He crept into the shadows as two shopkeepers passed, and shook the red hair at them. He turned towards the tolbooth, and shook the hair at it. He shook it, next, towards the old steeple. Always, when he took the parcel of hair into his hand, he shook his hate at the council and at the church.

He listened to the arguings, and observed that there was no more contentment in Dundee than before the restoration of the king and of the Edinburgh parliament. A third of the town still lay in ruins. Five little ships plied to the harbour that had been, before the wars, the harbour of forty ships, big ships among them. Half of the booths and shops were shuttered and empty. Cromwell's London parliament had spoken of Dundee as the poor burgh for which something would have to be done. They had raised a tax for Dundee, a custom on imported wine to subsidize the trade of Dundee. They had granted Dundee two fairs to be held on traditional church festivals of the town, fast days the town called them. Dundee had remained, all through Cromwell's time, the poor burgh for which something would have to be done, and still, five years after the coming of the king, Dundee was the poor burgh.

The boy was thirteen, tall, straight, swift in flight. His second winter in Dundee was approaching. He had returned from a summer's visit to the tinklers' camp in order to make his pickings at the autumn fair. The hollows under the tomb-stones in the Houff were necessary to him. He would have to deal with Sarah Drummond, lest she find a way of telling the town servants about his hiding places.

He waited in the twilight outside the manse of one of the ministers, positioned so that he had a way of escape if he had to escape.

'Minister,' he called, as footsteps came towards the door.

'What is it?' The minister was startled, and jumped.

'Don't come near or I'll run away.'

'What is it? What do you want?'

'I can tell you where there's a witch. She's raising ghosties the now.'

'Who's speaking?'

'Nobody you know. It's right. The witch is Sarah Drum-mond, in the Bailie's close in the Seagait, last stair down the close, last door in the lobby at the head of the stair. She's raising ghosties.'

The minister peered round, then entered. The boy hung about, expecting that the minister would return and call the watch to seek out the witch. Nothing happened, and the boy wondered.

The watch went by, and he hid in the shadows. A magis-trate was with the first round of the watch, as always. The boy dodged along an alleyway, and clambered to the roof of a lean-to. The watch passed under him.

'Bailie,' he called. 'I know where there's a witch.'

'Who's there?'

'Nobody you know. There's a witch raising ghosties the now.' He called out the name and direction as before.

'Climb up and see who's there,' the bailie ordered.

The boy moved fast. He was not on the roof when the man reached it. He was nearby, listening.

'Nobody here,' the man of the watch called down.

'D'you think we should have a look at this Sarah Drum-mond? There's talk of her being a witch, but you know how hard it is to get anybody to swear against these women. I'd like fine to nab a witch on my night of the watch. There's over much of this witchery.'

'If we caught her at her ghostie-raising, there'd be no swearing needed,' a town servant said.

The boy slid softly from the window ledge where he had perched, and ran, keeping to the shadows. Hidden, he watched the stair, at the top of which lived Sarah Drummond. The watch arrived quietly, and moved quietly on the stair. Women came stumbling down, and fled. Sarah Drummond came, held by the watch, fainting for fear.

The boy swore to himself in his terrible tinkler way when he learned that Sarah Drummond was not to burn. She was to be whipped through the town. The boy listened to the arguers, who said that the council had no power, by right, to burn a woman. Trial for witchcraft was a constable's trial, by Lord Dudhope. In the Elspet Renkyne affair, the arguings went, there had been no constable of Dundee, Lord Dudhope being unrestored, and the council had taken the constable's power upon themselves. The boy was angered that his mother should be burned, and this Sarah Drummond was to be whipped only. He hated the council the more for their inconsistency in the matter of the punishment of witches. He kept away from the Houff, and hid less comfortably and less safely under the outside stairs of houses. Sarah Drummond was free of the fear of burning which he had held over her. She could put the searchers to his burial ground hiding places, and was the more dangerous for his betraying her.

The boy watched the woman's trotting at a horse's tail through the streets, leaping as the whip came on her shoulders. He forgot to see that he had a way of escape. A hand came upon his shoulder. He struggled and was gripped by strong arms. He wriggled and shouted, but was held. Other town servants ran to help the one who had taken him. They carried him towards the tolbooth. He cursed and struggled. The crowd turned from the ghost-raiser's screams to the boy's screams, and crushed around him to see the gifted woman's son, the elusive laddie called English, caught, at last, for the dirt man's service.

Next day, working with the town's shovellers, he heard himself called at the market cross as having been bound to the dirt man. The calling was done by a town servant on the parapet below the unicorn on the shaft. Such an announcement, a dirt binding, was not for a bailie.

THE LILIES AND THE DRAGONS

THE dirt man was Jamie Rollo, with a monopoly, granted him by the council, of redding away the middens, the heaps of food refuse, ashes, and excrement, thrown from the windows to lie in the wynds and closes. When an accumulation of filth became sufficiently large, Rollo assessed the redding in pennies, was paid by the householders who had contributed to the dirt, and his bound men shovelled and carried their double-handed creels to the only dumping place allowed by the tolbooth laws, the foreshore of the estuary, eastward of the town bounds. To dodge the dirt man's demand for pennies, some of the vennel folks removed their own dirt. Rollo kept a close watch upon those ones, lest they infringe upon his rights by removing, for money, middens other than their own, and lest they tumble their heaps at night into the burn, or over the graveyard wall, or into another close. The laws particularly forbade dumping in the neighbourhood of the burn. Its course must be kept clear to ensure purity for washing and bleaching, to lessen the chances of flooding at the low-lying Meadows common, and to allow a full head of water to the meal mill, situated near the outlet into the Tay. Rollo paraded the banks, outside the town where the burn was the Scouring Burn, and inside where it was the Castle Burn, spying out illegal dumpings.

He watched the fleshers who cut their carcasses at the burn-side, that they did not throw their offal into the water. The offal was a valuable perquisite for the dirt man. He watched the skinners that they did not allow the lime, with which they treated their skins, to pollute the waters. In his performance of these duties that he took upon himself he was not thinking of the dangers of pollution. He was thinking a miser's thoughts about pennies, and because he was a miser for pennies his dirt policing was well done.

He was a short, thick, dirty man. Strangers, on first sight of him, took the term, dirt man, to refer to his appearance, not his work. He had no other subjects of conversation except dirt and pennies. He was the master of the boy called English and of six others, who shovelled the redd and carried it to the foreshore dump, heavy work, in exchange for a cellar in which to sleep, scraps and flesher's refuse to eat, and rags to wear; slaves, the vagrants and minor criminals whom the burgh magistrates punished by binding to the dirt service.

The boy called English could easily have escaped from Rollo but, to do so, would have meant running from the town. The foreseeings had said that Elspet Renkyne's blood would become a power in Dundee. In Dundee! The boy did not run. Moreover, he slept indoors, in conditions bad enough but out of the wind and damp. The food put before him was poor enough, but at least as good and as plentiful as he had eaten in his year of dodging through the closes. Here and there were folks who supplemented his meals by throw-him a bannock at times, remembering with fear or respect that he was the gifted woman's son. The men and youths bound with him talked like sorners about the vengeance they would take on Rollo and on the magistrates for the rags and the straw beds and the coarse food. The boy did not grumble about these matters, but he looked with hate at the dirt man, hate for a burgess, for this nearest burgess.

Lying in the dirty straw in the cellar, the bound ones coughed and spluttered. Some shouted to open the shutter of the one little barred hole that looked into a walled hole in the ground. Some shouted to keep it shut. When it was opened, men shivered. When it was shut they sweated. There would be a morning when a man would not rise from his straw.

'We'll have none of that!' Rollo would say. 'You say you're badly! We'll have none of that!' The ill man would go out to the shovelling. There were men who died in the night in the dirty straw. There was one man who collapsed across the heap of excrement he shovelled, and died there. The bodies were carried out in the creels and dumped in the sea at the place where the redd was dumped. The magistrates sent other vagrants to fill the empty straw and to shovel. Strangely, the boy called English survived these conditions, and grew rapidly in height and strength. Rollo complained, in his whining miser's voice, about the growth of this one who was always needing a larger size in rags.

Often, Adam looked towards the hills, and thought of the tinkler liberty that had been his. But he remembered the necessity for avoiding banishment from the town. In Dundee would Elspet Renkyne's blood become a power! He had been three years with Rollo when he made the discovery that the dirt man was afraid of him. As he bent over a dirt heap, the parcel of hair fell from his rags. 'Put it away!' Rollo cried, backing. 'For the love of God, put it away again. Don't look at me that way, laddie, don't look!' Adam thought much about the incident, and it was then that he recalled another of his mother's foreseeings – the blood would go and go, and return and return; in some of the returnings the blood would bring to Dundee what was needed. Needed for what? For the blood's becoming a power, he surmised.

In the smell of the refuse, the youth smelled a whiff of the Sidlaw slopes. He dropped his shovel, and sought out Rollo. 'I'm going off for a spell,' he said, 'and I'll come back. You'll say nothing to the bailies about me being away!' Rollo averted his eyes from the youth's look. Adam ran through the closes and wynds, and out among the ruins of the east end.

He gained the Dens, the gorge of the Wallace Burn, among the fields of the lands of Wallace Craigie, and followed the burn through the lands of Clepington towards its source. He went over the riggs of Claverhouse and Powrie and Tealing, keeping to the slopes, for in the hollows were bogs that could drown a man. He came to the tinklers in the Sidlaw glens. He stayed with them until the summer had faded, and went back to Dundee, browned and erect after his hill months. He came to Rollo's door. The dirt man reached for something with which to strike the youth, but stayed his hand.

'You're back, are you?' Rollo said, and said nothing more.

Adam shovelled the redd for the next ten months and never grumbled. The month of May was near its end. He came to Rollo and looked the look that the dirt man feared.

'I'm going away,' he said. 'I'll be back when the days draw in.' He pulled out a glimpse of his mother's hair for Rollo to see. 'I'm coming back, mind. If you tell the bailies I'm away it will be the worse for you!'

He went then, and Rollo could only glower after him. He climbed the southern wall of the Houff, and went through among the graves. He waded the Scouring Burn, and crossed the fields of Dudhope, westwards of the climbing line of little houses that was the Hilltown, in lands that no longer were Scrymgeour's but now Maitland's, one of a family that was in favour at court. He took the path to Glamis and the Sidlaws, where the tinklers camped. Rollo saw him once that summer, when in the Hilltown he saw tinkler women sell their wares from door to door and tinkler men play bagpipes. Adam English was among them, playing the bagpipes. Adam looked the look and put his hand into his breast in the gesture Rollo feared. 'It's all right, laddie,' Rollo said. 'Stay away till you want to come back!'

In September, the runaway returned. That night, he did not sleep in the cellar, but in the lobby of the house. He brought clean straw from the market, and spread it on the floor of the lobby, in a corner.

'I'm sleeping here,' he said to Rollo. 'It'll be the better for you if you let the others think you're allowing me to sleep here. If they think I just took this place myself, you'll have them all thinking they can come up to the house.'

Rollo saw the point of that argument. He was fiercer with the others than ever but never laid a hand or tongue on Adam. From that night Adam slept in the lobby. After some weeks he took his meals, not in the cellar, but in the lobby corner.

There was a woman servant in the house, not bound like the men who shovelled, but working for food, lodgings, clothes, and a new pair of shoes each year. Her work was hard, cooking for the men in the cellar as well as doing the housework, such as it was. She could not understand the matter of this youth's sleeping in the lobby, for she was not in the secret of his possession of a hate token. She looked at him, puzzled, became accustomed to him, passed a word with him. He was one of the dirt shovellers, bound, but he was different. After a time the food she brought to Adam was the same food as Rollo ate. Adam laughed and daffed with her, slapped her buttocks, and she giggled. She was a thin-bosomed, spindly little creature, some seven years older than the youth. He cuddled her in the corner of the lobby.

She was named Mary Lowden. One night after there had been much laughing and daffing she came creeping in the dark to him in the corner and snuggled in among the straw with him. After that she came most nights.

One named Grizel Butchart was burned in the Seagait for witchery, the only other witch-burning apart from that of Elspet Renkyne that ever happened in the town. Mary wanted a witch's bone. Women who were frightened that they might have a child wanted a witch's bone. Women who were frightened they would not have a child wanted a witch's bone. Adam went out at night, and raked among the ashes of the fire and the ashes of Grizel Butchart. He brought a charred bone to Mary. After some months she threw it away. Grizel Butchart could not have been a real witch, Mary decided.

Rollo noticed the girl's condition. This would be blamed on him, he whimpered. The bailies would find a chance in this to give the scavenging to some friend of theirs. He, a respectable widower, with a girl in his house, would be blamed, he blubbered. He would be banished for ill-living. He questioned Mary, shouting his threats. The youth, not quite eighteen years of age, was astonished when Rollo, in a cajoling voice, frightened, said that the right thing would have to be done by Mary.

'If you don't marry her they'll cut off her hair, and banish her,' said the dirt man, crafty, keeping his eyes turned from the youth's gaze.

'For that?' Adam said. 'Then it would be for that that my mother's hair was cut, just for that?'

'They'll banish you as well, lad,' Rollo said. Adam laughed. 'I'll give you a marriage before a minister,' Rollo pleaded. 'I'll pay for everything. Marry her, lad, for the love of God marry her!'

The bound man, working for food, bed, and clothes, married the serving girl, serving for food, bed, clothes and a pair of shoes. He was entered upon the church's book as Adam, called English.

'I've heard it said,' Adam told Rollo, 'that a married man can't be bound.'

'I've heard that, as well,' Rollo said. 'It looks like you'll be off the binding. I'll speak to the bailies, then you can go with your wife.'

Adam laughed at the hopefulness in Rollo's voice.

'You'll be needing a hired man,' Adam said. 'I've heard it said that you've taken on to clean out the harbour. You could never manage bound men there and bound men at the redding, on your own.' He took out the parcel of hair in an absent-minded way.

'Ay, lad,' the dirt man replied quickly. 'I've been thinking about taking you on as a hired man. But you couldn't live here in a place with bound men. You would better live in your own house.'

'I'll do that. What's the wage?' The rate of hire finally arranged between them was double Rollo's first suggestion. Adam had never handled money, and had no idea of a fair rate of hire, but he knew how to raise a miser's bid. He showed the hair.

'I would need money to set me up and see me through the first week,' Adam suggested. Rollo showed spirit, then. Adam saw that it was possible to go too far with the dirt man, whose greed for pennies was stronger than his fear of the hair. 'Money that you can keep off my wages,' Adam said, 'but not all at once, not all off the first week's wages. Eh?'

Though much of the town had been destroyed, there was no shortage of houses, for the population was falling fast. Adam and Mary took a single room in a propped-up tenement, in a Moraygait vennel.

Adam unwrapped his rag parcel, and washed the hair in a bucket. It glinted when he smoothed it.

'What's that?' Mary asked.

'My mother's hair,' he said. 'It was cut off her head in the jougs, then she was burned as a witch.' She shrank away. 'Don't be daft,' he said. 'It does no harm to the likes of you. It does no harm to anybody in itself, but it keeps me in mind to do harm to the right ones, the always right, who strut about the Marketgait and the Nethergait, in and out the tolbooth, in and out the kirks, the good folk, the right folk, strutting in their goodness and rightness when I'm a dirt shoveller!' He waved the hair from the window-hole, in the direction of the old steeple and the tolbooth. He thought about Rollo, and waved it towards the dirt man's house. 'Her blood will be greater than anyone of them. I'm her blood – and that bairn will be, when it comes!'

In the autumn of 1668, nearly two years before Adam's marriage to Mary Lowden, a great storm had blown. The range of the Sidlaws and the long eastern spur of the Ochils formed the funnel that concentrated the blast upon the Tay estuary. The neglected harbour of Dundee, already much

46

silted and banked, was filled by the storm with mud and sand. The wooden piers, rotting, fell in the wind. The stone breakwaters were torn.

Another disaster for the poor burgh. There was no other phrase for Dundee among parliament men but the poor burgh. Something would have to be done for the poor burgh of Dundee that could not repair its wrecked harbour. It was decreed that the collection taken in all the parish churches of Scotland on an appointed Sunday should go to the re-building of the poor burgh's breakwaters and the clearing of the silt.

Adam English was foreman over Rollo's bound men, who shovelled silt and carried stones. He stood waist deep in water and mud to direct the shovelling and direct the carry-ing of baulks and stones to the wrights and masons who built the new piers. Rollo tried to carry the work into autumn, but in a cold September wind two bound men died of exposure. They died standing up, held by the firm silt in which they worked. The men were dumped with the excavated silt along the eastern foreshore. Adam looked the look that Rollo feared. The bound men, after that, wheeled stones and baulks on the quay for the masons and wrights. When winter came and work at the harbour could not be done, Adam and the bound men went back to the redding of the midden heaps, and Adam did much of the dump detection that Rollo had formerly done. In April, Rollo sent them back to the harbour again to shovel silt. Adam English looked his look, and for a month the work done was that of wheeling stones on the quay. In the summer, into September again, they worked, almost naked, waist deep in the water and mud.

This was Adam's manner of life as it concerned Mary. He rose from the alcove bed when the piercing, reedy tune of the shawm sounded the call for the start of the town's working day. He pulled his filthy working-clothes over his sark and rabbit skin vest, both of which he wore day and night un-changed for weeks and months. He went out, with a shake for Mary, to rouse her. He took all his meals in one or other of the many ale-houses, as did most of the men, free and unfree. He came back wet and dirty, to the one-roomed house as the piper marched in the streets, signalling the curfew upon bagpipes. He stripped, except for his sark and vest, hung his clothes outside the window or, in wet weather, outside the door in the corridor, and washed himself in the bucket that awaited him. With a warning shout to anyone who might be below, he flung the water from the window-hole, pulled the shutter to, and, if the night was cold, jammed out draughts with rags. The routine was always the same, except that, maybe, once in a fortnight, he would be rather later than usual in coming from his work, and, when he did come, would be well pleased, humming to himself, talking about the daftness of burgesses and of Rollo in particular. Mary wondered, but asked him nothing. He had not been staying in a tavern over supper to argue, she could see. She wondered if he stole, but heard no market cross crying of thefts. On Sundays, Adam went wandering, fair skies or foul, and Mary saw no more of him than she did during the working week.

Mary Lowden's child had been born. Adam had no feeling for Mary, and thought of the child as only his. Quite often, once the baby had grown beyond the first helplessness, he would take the infant with him on his Sunday jaunts. Mary was asking if Adam could find a witch's bone, a bone of a real witch, not a bone of an old chattering body like Grizel Butchart. Adam brought her a charred bone that he got from one of the dirt slaves. Soon she was carrying another child, and she threw away the bone. Another summer was there when Mary's time came. Adam had given her no heed when she carried the child. All his heed was for young Adam, the blood, his red-haired son whose nose was broken-looking like his own. It should have been a sharply-pointed nose, but was blunt at the tip. When Mary's pains came upon her, Adam still gave her no heed. He called the neighbour woman who was to attend his wife.

'Her time's come,' he said. I'll away. Wee Adam will come with me.'

He put down money on the table. He always had money, more than his wages. Coins were found among the harbour silt at times, and he had his share of these. But he had more. He had some way of his own of getting money, and never spoke to Mary about it. He left without a word or a look to his wife in her pain.

He carried the two-year-old child on his shoulder down through Tyndall's Wynd to the quay. Rollo was squatting with his back against the packhouse wall, where Adam had expected him to be.

'I'm away,' Adam said. 'I'll be back in a week. You can do without me for that time.'

He moved off with the child on his shoulders. He went by the one other way that led from harbour to town, Couttie's Wynd that took him up to the Nethergait. He went up the Friar Wynd that some called the Burial Wynd. He left the town by the Friar Wynd port, waded the Scouring Burn and moved north-west through the pleasaunce gardens of Dudhope Castle, through the riggs of Logie, across the Dighty burn, towards Auchterhouse and the hills and the tinklers. The child, who had never seen anything but the back vennels of the Moraygait, prattled on his shoulder. The man talked to his son as he went, pointing out the wonders that they passed.

In a week he came back. Little Adam's red hair shone after a week of the Sidlaw suns. Mary had her second child, a girl, and was risen and about her housework and marketing again. Her husband gave her no heed, but he gurgled at the infant. 'Her name will be Elspet,' he said.

'It's not the name I would like. It's an unlucky name,' Mary said, afraid.

Adam paid her no attention, not so much as a look. 'Elspet, the blood of Elspet,' he cooed at the babe. Mary cringed.

Next morning he went down to the harbour and resumed

work without asking for Rollo's yea or nay. Rollo, squatting with his back against the pack-house wall, glared fearfully at Adam but said nothing. At the end of the week, Rollo paid him the full money, last week's money and this week's. Adam had only worked one week in the two, the beginning of one and the end of the other. Rollo watched for gratitude, eager for a gesture or a word from Adam. Adam took the money, and said nothing. He looked at Rollo with contempt in his look, and Rollo knew it to be contempt.

Two years after that, the third child of the name English was born. 'We'll call him for my father,' Mary suggested. 'I can just mind him. Henry he was.'

'It's an unlucky name, Henry,' Adam said. 'He had you for a daughter that couldn't keep away from a dirt shoveller. I'll get a better name.'

In the Moraygait, where it narrowed to seven feet width, a young man rode with two mounted servants behind him, a small dark handsome scornful man. A procession from the tolbooth came from the opposite direction, the bailies and the councillors, walking their slow walk. They stopped to allow the horsemen to give way to them. The mounted servants could have drawn aside, but the young master commanded them with a motion of his hand to stay as they were. The bailies continued to wait, angry but hiding their anger because this young man was obviously of some rank. He was silent, holding his place. A look of deference came on the faces of the councillors and bailies, and they moved back to either side of the street. The young man rode slowly between the two files, without a word or a smile. Adam asked of a passer-by and was told that the man was John Graham, home for a little from the continental wars, heir to the laird of Claypots, of Glenogilvie, and of Claverhouse. Adam knew the lands of Claverhouse on the Dighty, two miles north from the town. He knew the fields of Claypots with the stone keep standing among them, three miles to the east of Dundee by the hill of Balgillo. He knew best Glenogilvie among the Sidlaws where the tinklers made their camps. He looked with a smile after the heir of these lands he knew, John Graham of Claverhouse. Adam named his son John, not for a laird, but for one who scornfully insulted Dundee bailies and councillors.

After that birth, Adam never again lay beside Mary. He slept with young Adam on straw away from the bed alcove in the one-roomed home. His wife dared not come creeping to him as she once had done. His visits to the tinklers became more frequent. Every Sabbath now when he left early, he took his four-year-old eldest upon his shoulders or by the hand. Occasionally in mid-week he set out alone to walk through the early hours of the night to the Sidlaws. He was always back for his work in the morning, untired.

Mary did not directly question him, but in every anxious look was a question. He was unheeding. She bore with the situation for six months and could bear it no longer.

'Tell me, tell me,' she screamed as he prepared to leave one night, 'for God's sake, get this settled.'

'You want things settled, do you?' he said. 'Well, they'll be settled the morn, if that's what you want!'

He left, and was back soon after dawn. Always before, he had gone from the Sidlaws to his work, and she had not seen him till evening.

'Rollo will have to do without me this day,' he said. 'There are things to be done that Rollo's muck can wait for. Get yourself ready for a walk. You're going to the hills with me. One of the wifies here will look after the bairns.'

'What's ado?' she asked, frightened. She kept repeating the question as they trudged north.

He did not answer her till they were well on the way up Powrie Brae, across the Dighty.

'I'm putting you away as my wife,' he said. 'You'll not be my wife a day longer.'

She stopped, staring in fear.

'You can't do it! Adam, you would never do it. The bairns, Adam, the bairns!'

'The bairns will be all right, and you'll be all right. It'll be little different from what it has always been. I was a laddie when you came to me those nights in Rollo's lobby. I had heard the dirt shovellers talking and the tinklers talking, but I knew nothing more than their talk. I thought, maybe, when Rollo said I would have to marry you, that that was how it always came about that folk got married, and that there was nothing else to it. I was told you would have your hair cut off and be banished by their burgess rules, and I didn't want that to happen. I've seen since that there's more to getting married. It should be something you want with somebody you want, not just the touch of a lassie in the dark.'

'I wanted you,' she said. 'It was for you I came. It wasn't just for a man.'

'I've never had any feeling for you, Mary. Everything will be as it has been. You'll stay on in the house with the bairns and with me and Leeb White.'

'Leeb White, who's Leeb White? How can I live in the house with another woman?'

'You'll stay. That's all!'

She wept hysterically, but kept plodding up the hill.

'The bailies will never stand for it,' she said. 'The kirk will never stand for it. The kirk made us man and wife.'

'Bailies' laws, kirk's laws!' he sneered. 'I don't know their laws. Who are they to make laws for me?'

'They'll show you who they are.'

'No, they won't. For one thing, they'll never know. You'll never tell them. You understand? You'll keep your mouth shut. You'll have your bairns and your house, and you'll have your helper. Leeb is not proud. She'll pass as your helper.'

'A shoveller's wife with a servant,' she screamed. 'They'll laugh. God, they'll laugh!'

'Let them laugh! You understand, you'll hold your tongue?'

She kept moving onwards, sobbing, moaning.

'I'm doing the right thing,' he said.

He turned on to a trail to a crofters' hamlet.

'We need a horse,' he said. 'Don't let them see you getting into a state while I'm buying a horse from them. Mind now!'

He bargained for a horse with the crofters. They tried to pass off a broken-down animal.

'Something better than that,' he said. 'I want to do the thing right.'

He lifted Mary to the back of the horse he bought, and walked beside her, supporting her on her perch. They climbed over the Sidlaw pass at Petterden.

'What's the horse for?' she wailed. 'It's not just for me to sit on.'

'You'll see,' he said.

They came to the tinklers' camp, in the woods, a mile or two short of Glamis. The tinklers, in a clearing, amidst their twig-woven huts, were gathered as for a celebration, ragged men and women, with a swarm of sharp-faced, shambly children. They spoke strange words to Adam and he answered them in strange words. They gathered around the horse, their eyes on it. Saying strange words, making strange signs, an old woman handed Adam a knife. He lifted Mary to the ground.

'No, no,' Mary screamed.

'The knife is not for you,' Adam said. 'It's for the horse.'

He intoned strange words, pointing at Mary, at himself, and at the horse. He stepped up to the horse, pushed its head up and stabbed the knife into its neck. He ripped the neck open, and leaped back to avoid the kicking hooves as the horse fell. When its struggles had ended, he came to Mary and gently pushed her from him, saying his strange words as he did so. The tinklers, silent during the ceremony, talked excitedly.

'You're not my wife, Mary,' Adam said. 'I've put you away from me.'

'Adam, oh Adam!' she moaned.

She was left standing alone, sick and faint, but still standing. The tinklers jabbered and jumped. A girl was led from one of the twig houses and placed alongside Adam. She was

53

fair-haired and fair-skinned, one of the fair tinklers. At sixteen or thereabout, she was not yet old enough to be lean
and hard like the other tinkler women. The old woman
spoke, and the girl, solemn and unashamed, lifted high the
shapeless gown she wore, to show that she was in truth a
woman. The old one took the knife from Adam, stuck it
several times into the ground to clean away the horse's
blood, then made a cut on Adam's wrist and a cut on the
girl's wrist. The wrists were held together for Adam's blood
to mingle with Leeb White's. The tinklers danced and
capered. All this Mary saw before sickness and weakness over-
came her. This event, when written into the ledger in 1902,
was as seen by Mary, told by her son John to his children,
and so passed down the years.

In the evening when they walked back to Dundee, Adam
and Leeb supporting Mary, Adam said: 'These things you
saw were done by laws that I know. Mind that. Everything
will be the same if you hold your tongue. If you don't, you
and the bairns will have the worst of it to bear. I don't want
either you or the bairns to suffer. They're my bairns, mind. I
can feel for you, and that's why I say to you to hold your
tongue.' No other word was said by any of the three during
the journey. The tinkler girl laughed excitedly on occasion.
She was a laugher, but no talker.

Mary lay with the three children in the bed. In the corner
of the room Adam slept on the straw with Leeb White.

'You'll get on fine together,' he said as he went out in the
morning. 'Tell her to put up her hair. Tell her that women
don't go about the town with their hair hanging about their
eyes. And get her something to wear.' The tinkler girl stood
by, listening and looking, with the air of a child. 'And you
mind this, Leeb,' he said, 'you'll help with everything. Mind,
both of you, you've to get on together.'

In the evening he watched them going about their work.
Leeb was dressed in the plaid one-piece garment common to
all back vennel women. Her hair was twisted up about the
crown of her head as was Mary's. A plaid shawl for her

shoulders hung beside Mary's shawl. They talked a word or two as they worked. Adam nodded.

'It'll be all right,' he said. At that time he was twenty-three years of age, and the year was 1675.

The new breakwaters were built before the old were removed. Adam and the bound men stood shoulder-deep in the water to remove stones. Among them, Adam saw a decayed linen bag. He touched it, and heard a tinkle from within. He ordered the bound men away from the place to other work, and covered up the find. In the dusk of the long summer evening, when the work stopped, he stayed in the water. He was looking at the silver coins in the bag, holding it with both hands for it was falling apart, when Rollo came, walking out along the old wall. Rollo had wondered why Adam did not come back with the men. From the corner of the pack-house he had watched. He saw that something had been found in the stones. His miserliness got the better of his fear.

'Ay,' Rollo said, his eyes glistening, 'you've got a trove there, all right!'

Adam said nothing.

'It should belong to the master on the work,' Rollo said, 'but I'll let you have a share. You and me could have our bit, and none of us will tell anybody.'

'What about the bailies?' Adam asked, with his hard smile on his face. 'Would you not tell the bailies about this?'

Rollo's eyes were greedy.

'Adam,' he said. 'We'll tell nobody.'

'What'll my share be?'

Rollo thought.

'I'll let you have a quarter, Adam,' he said. 'And we'll never let on to anybody.'

Adam put the bag down on the breakwater stones, making it safe there. He looked through the dusk at the quay, up and down it. There was no one in sight. He waded towards where Rollo stood.

'I'm taking it all, dirt man,' he said. 'And you'll not say a word about it. D'you hear? This was foreseen. The power I am to be starts in stone and water.' Rollo's look lost its miser's intentness. He was afraid.

'I'll say nothing, Adam,' he whimpered. Adam reached up and gripped the dirt man's ankle.

'Rollo,' he said, slowly, quietly, 'you dirt man. It's time you were dead. You could never hold your tongue about this, because it's money.'

He pulled Rollo by the leg from the wall, and held him under the water. Rollo kicked, and was still. Adam dragged the body towards the new breakwater. He toiled to remove a stone while the body bobbed beside him. He jammed Rollo in the hole, and toiled to put the stone back.

'You dirt man,' Adam said. 'It's not for the money in the bag. It's not for the dirty straw in the basement and the dirty meat I ate. It's just because a thing like you is a burgess and held to be better than I am. It's time you were dead.'

He recovered the bag, gained the quay and looked around. There was nobody about. He went up to the town, and through it, zig-zagging along more closes and wynds than were necessary to take him to his destination, the Houff. In the dark, he climbed the Houff wall, and buried his trove in an old grave, in a stone pocket he had made some years before. In the pocket was a little heap of silver and copper coins, stolen from Rollo's house at intervals. Adam had long known where was the dirt man's hoard, and had known also that the dirt man could not count his money aright, so that a coin or two, carefully removed, was never missed by the miser.

That same night, Adam burgled Rollo's house, and added the savings of years to the Houff collection. There was so much copper in Rollo's chests that he had to make three visits to the house. He dodged the watch in the streets, moving silently in his bare feet, using the darkest shadows.

Nobody had known, except Adam, that Rollo had had a hoard of silver and copper coins in his house, so there was no suspicion of a theft having taken place. There was no talk of the dirt man's having been murdered. It was assumed that in a patrolling of the burn for dumps, he had fallen in, and been washed out to sea. Only Mary suspected, and she would say nothing. Adam found work at once, with the masons and wrights at the harbour; he was known to be a good labourer, of unusual height and strength, of unusual willingness to work at the roughest, dirtiest jobs, always sober, never a talker of vennel politics. When politics were being discussed, he would laugh and say that he had seen many revolutionary plannings that had quickly become debates about the conduct of meetings. He said that his politics were concerned only with doing a fair day's work and getting a fair day's rate from the master wright or mason who hired him. This talk went well with the burgess tradesmen at the harbour. They did not know how the tall, barefooted, ragged-breeched Adam English hated them for their being masters.

He never worried about how his family lived, two women and three young children in a space three paces by three, not counting the bed alcove. He could see that the children were healthy, as that word was understood in the vennels; that Leeb was washing herself, combing her hair, keeping an appearance of a town woman; that Mary, although taking care of herself as she never had done before, was red-legged, harassed-looking, and more the tinkler than Leeb. He always gave the week's money to Mary. Leeb made no objection, indeed, never noticed the handing over of the money. She was still a laugher, never a talker, and played forever with the infants.

Five months after Leeb had come, Mary spoke the first words she had ever spoken to Adam about the girl.

'What d'you do about her, now that she's that way?' she asked dully. Leeb was jumping the youngest child away from the snatches of the other two, all screaming with laughter.

'What way?'

'She's to have a bairn.' Mary had watched the girl for

sickness and langour, but a tinkler did not show these signs. Now Mary's sharp eyes could see the first changes in the girl's shape. 'Nobody else would notice it yet, because nobody else knows to look for it. You can't have my helper with a bairn without folk talking.'

Adam sat thinking, then went to his straw with Leeb. Mary, lying in the alcove, heard the whispering, but not the words.

In the early morning, Adam said: 'The dirt will do without me this day. Leeb is going to her folks till she's had her bairn.'

They went off together before the shawm had sounded. In the evening, he returned alone.

'She'll come when her bairn is born,' he told Mary. 'The church's book will take it down as your bairn.'

'How d'you think a thing like that is to be passed off?' she moaned. 'D'you think everybody's daft?'

He slept in the straw with his eldest, young Adam. On the Sundays he went away with the child, a sturdy, quick five-year old, now. 'This one has the look of being the blood that was spoken about,' Adam said of the boy. 'The others have the look, too, but not so much as this one. If I'm not the power myself, I've a mind that it'll be young Adam.'

Leeb had been gone for her full time. Adam returned from one of his Sunday trips, and announced that the child had been born. 'He's all right, and she's all right,' he added, then paused. 'Mary,' he said, at length, 'Leeb will not be coming back. She's a tinkler, and not for the town. She likes it better in the hills. Though she laughed enough here, she felt often like doing the other thing. It's her own wish. She wanted me there, but I couldn't go. One of her own kind is taking her for his woman, and that'll be right by me.'

Mary gasped.

'It's right by you?' she said. 'You took the lassie in tinkler marriage because you wanted her, and it's right by you to let another have her.'

'It's right by me!' Adam repeated. 'There's nothing in

this, only the touch of a woman in the dark. She'll grow to be like any tinkler. I saw it when I saw her after the birth.'

'What kind of man are you?' Mary asked, but was pleased.

'The bairn will come here,' he went on. 'The bairn is of the blood. Maybe it will be the one to be the power. You can say it's a motherless bairn you took in. I can see now that the other way would have been daft.'

A fortnight later, he brought the infant to Mary. 'The name's Willie,' he said.

'She let you take away her bairn?'

'What for would she want to be different? This is Elspet Renkyne's blood, and has to be here, in Dundee.'

'It's a motherless bairn, right enough,' Mary said. 'Give me the poor wee thing.'

Adam turned to his eldest. 'We'll be going no more to the tinklers, wee Adam,' he said. 'Tinklers are not for you. You're as good as anybody in the town, mind. It's time you started on learning the things that dominies teach, that making of marks and counting. If the burgesses can learn that, so should you.'

He guessed that the town's grammar school, in the vennels behind the tolbooth, would not take a barefooted labourer's son. He sought out a tenement teacher who took in some children of the better paid unfree.

'Why would a man like you be wanting his bairn to read and write?' the teacher asked. He eyed Adam's bare feet, wild hair, and rags.

'My money's the right money, isn't it?' Adam flared. 'I work hard. I don't spend anything on shoes that I can do without. I spend it on my bairns. They're as good as anybody in the town. My name's as good a name as any locked book name. Does my bairn come to you or not?'

'I'm as good as anybody in the town, myself,' the teacher replied hotly. 'If I had my rights, I would be in the town's school. Your boy will learn none the slower for not being of a locked book name. And I'll teach none the worse for my school being but a penny school.'

'You're a man after my own heart,' Adam said.

Adam continued to sleep in the straw with his eldest. Mary was never again his wife after the tinkler divorce by killing a horse. She boasted to neighbours about her good man who saved to send his children to a dominie, but the dull look never went from her face again in this life. The child who heard her sorrows was little John, her youngest, who shrank from his father.

Adam had suddenly taken to showing respect for members of the council. He touched his bonnet when he passed one in the street. Nobody else from the vennels did so, and the tall, barefooted man was, therefore, noticed by the councillors. A bailie stopped him. 'You always salute me,' the bailie said. 'I think it right that a man serving the town should be saluted,' Adam replied. Even the recognition and deference of a labourer could be pleasing, and the bailie was pleased.

'You shouldn't be getting yourself looked at by these tolbooth ones,' Mary suggested, fearing. 'It's just what I should be doing,' Adam said. 'Anybody, looking about, can see that the town will need to get a proper dirt man soon. I've got a plan to put up to the tolbooth when the right time comes. A touch of the bonnet to a bailie costs nothing. I like the right ones no more than I've ever liked them. They burned her, and chased me through the closes, and bound me to Rollo. One day it will be them that will be doing the saluting to me or my blood.'

The town had six dirt men in a year, all unsuccessful at clearing the redd. None of them had the manner for getting work out of bound men or pennies out of the closes. They were all glad to give up the monopoly in turn. The need for a new dirt man was cried at the market cross, and nobody applied. 'It's time now,' Adam said. He put his scheme to that bailie he had flattered. The dirt man need not be a burgess, he pointed out. A man who knew the way of the work could be hired by the council to make his own wage out of the redding. The town could bind men as before, and give the hired man the overseeing of them, and the feeding and managing of them, which would not be the same as giving him the custody of them, for that only a burgess should have. There should be plenty of good men, experienced in overseeing, to take on the redding on such conditions, Adam suggested. Managed well, the redding men could well take over the cleaning-up of the market place, work for which market booth-keepers had at present to make themselves responsible. The bailie was left with the impression that the scheme was his own. Adam had learned much in the years when he went round the crofts and villages with the tinkler women.

The next dirt man to be appointed was an unfree foreman of market porters. Adam swore in tinkler fashion, then laughed when he saw that the redding was unimproved and the bound men were mutinous. The porter man was out of the job in two weeks. Two burgesses, appointed on the old terms, followed, then another unfree man. Adam still saluted the council members, but cursed them under his breath. The dirt work was cried again at the cross as work for an unfree man. Adam was the only applicant. He stood in his rags, barefooted, before the tolbooth members, and they smiled upon this tall, red-headed labourer who always touched his bonnet to them. He took over Rollo's house, and the bound men.

In four days the wynds and vennels were cleaner than ever they had been. For sullen bound men and for reluctant payers of pennies, he had his frightening stare, but it was seldom needed. An easy jocularity gained pennies more quickly; a laughing, arguing camaraderie kept the workers moving. He fed and housed the slaves no better than Rollo had done, but often he sat among them at their meals, talking as one of them. He put a hand to a shovel and to the dirt creels. One of the men died, and all the redders, Adam among them, went to a proper funeral. The new dirt man dressed as before, his feet and legs still bare, his breeches ragged, his bonnet dirty and torn, his wild hair sticking from the holes in the bonnet. Nobody envied him his dirt pennies, for his appearance indicated a man who did not prosper. The town thought of him as one who in poverty could laugh, a contented man, a saving man whose children went to school because he spent nothing on himself. During that time, his hoard of silver coins in the Houff was growing. While everybody else was becoming poorer in the poor burgh, he was gaining, slowly, in the manner of the back vennels, penny by penny.

The parliament men in Edinburgh were still saying that something would have to be done for the poor burgh of Dundee and the poor countryside of Angus. Dundee and Angus were loyal to the king, they said, and should be encouraged. Parliament passed a law that all corpses be buried in Scotch linen, grown in the land, spun in the land, woven in the land. The measure was designed to strengthen the Angus lairds, whose estates grew flax, and the merchant councils of such burghs as Aberdeen and Dundee, weaving towns, on whose support the government counted against the whispering conventicle folks of Fife and Lanark and Ayr and Galloway. In Angus were no conventicles. In Dundee, the council accepted the king's mandates about bishops, welcomed the king's church decrees, made the new bishop of Brechin a gratis burgess. The Dundee council stood by the king, as always, stood against Knox's church-state, as always. In the town were burgesses who met secretly for psalms, and talked the seditious names of the old Scotch church, Knox, Melville, Henderson. But these burgesses were few, and comparatively unimportant. In the vennels, among the unfree, was argument in which the old bitter issue of the vennel folks was raised, Knox's plan, maintenance of the poor, education of the young, these charged to the lands of Scotland, the lands once held by the Roman Catholic Church and now held by lairds and burgh councils, instead of by a people's church. Knox, dead a hundred years, was not forgotten in the Dundee back-closes. The unfree of the town had been for Knox's peasant bitterness, had rioted in support of him into St. Andrews and Perth, destroying. But the Dundee burgesses of Knox's era had founded a church for the free only, a council controlled church, the first Protestant church to be constituted in Scotland, with no place in it for Knox's plan and no place for the vennel folks.

The dirt man heard the arguments, but took no part in them. His politics were the politics of the tinklers. Nobody governed him, nobody dictated to him, no decrees or mandates affected him. He had his hatred of burgesses, and no matter whether they were for a church-state or a king's state, he would hate them.

The bailie of the day marched with his piper and his drummer before him. He mounted the stair of the market cross tower, and read his proclamation. The piper and the drummer played him along the Nethergait, the Overgait, the Seagait, and the Moraygait. Where had been the old ports, the gates of the town, he read his exciting message from Edinburgh.

With the drum beating and the pipes playing in the Marketgait, the town servants with their halberds went into the closes and wynds, reciting the Edinburgh order. They called it in the Thorter Row, which ran from the Overgait to the Nethergait, and in Kirk Wynd, off the Thorter Row. They called it in the warren of vennels that led south of the town end of the Nethergait, Michelson's close, Will Schippert's close, Will Spens' close, Makkeson's close, named for men long dead. They called the order in the twisting thoroughfares to the harbour, Couttie's Wynd and Tyndall's Wynd. They called in the court named the Vault behind the tolbooth. They called in the Mint close north of the Marketgait, in Rankine's court north of the Moraygait, in the Horse wynd that connected Moraygait with Seagait. They made certain that all in the town had heard.

The order from the parliament was for the raising of men. Eighty men from the king's burgh of Dundee, ten horsemen, seventy footmen, armed, provisioned, accoutred. The long-feared Scotch revolt had begun. The Archbishop had been murdered on Magus Muir, just over the Ochil spur across the Tay. Sharp, who had gone to London to plead for the Covenant and had come back an archbishop of the church that should have no archbishops, was hacked on Magus Muir, his daughter fainting beside the body. The followers of Welch and Cameron and Balfour were risen. At Drumclog, near Glasgow, they had beaten a king's cavalry troop. They had taken the town of Hamilton. They were gathering forces and weapons. The conventicle men of Fife were marching to join the wild republicans of Clydesdale and Ayr and Galloway. Welch, the great-grandson of Knox, had proclaimed Knox's church-state. The people could depose kings, the people were greater than kings, the people would rule through their church, the church of John Knox. Hew Agag in pieces before the Lord. Dash their children upon the stones, the children of the kings and the lords, and of the flatterers of kings and lords. The people's church had been stolen from the people, the instrument by which the people were to rule. It had been made the church of the rich, and an instrument of oppression. The Duke of Lauderdale, king's commissioner for Scotland, was sending his orders for a levy of armed men to the burghs and to the feudal lairds. The Duke of Monmouth, the king's son, was posting north from London to lead the king's enlisted men and the king's levies against the revolutionaries. The council of Dundee had caused Lauderdale's order to be read, and two councillors were galloping south, having crossed the ferry of the Tay, to complain to the parliament that the poor burgh could not arm, provision and accoutre men. They would call out the town guard, as they had already ordered in an order added to Lauderdale's order, but they were too poor to do more.

The tolbooth bell rang for the summoning of the full watch, all the able-bodied burgesses, to patrol the streets and closes. Rioting among the vennel folks in favour of the church-staters was not a likelihood, but it was best, the councillors decided, to make a display of force. For the first time in the town's history, the law was called that all must attend church, free and unfree. It was an old law in Scotland, restated as a new law at intervals, most recently restated by Lauderdale in order to keep down the church-state prayer-meetings on the hills of Fife and of the south-west. It had never been put into effect in Dundee until now. On the Sabbath, the barefooted vennel folks crushed into the town's two churches, and jammed themselves around the doors, hushing their children. Most of them were hearing a church service for the first time.

The two councillors rode back from Edinburgh. Lauderdale had accepted that the poor burgh's merchant and trade corporations could not find the money for equipping soldiers. But the town guard must be called out, all the fencible men of Dundee, between sixteen and sixty, each man to parade at least twice a week for drilling, with his own weapons, and the whole guard prepared at any time to march anywhere in Angus within an hour of an emergency's being sounded at the market cross. Adam English attended his two parades each week, at the Magdalen Yard common, on the Tay foreshore, west of the end of the Nethergait. His hating eyes watched the burgesses, who were the officers, with swords and helmets, and jaws lengthened to a warlike grimness, and a suddenly acquired erectness in the old burgess strut. It was Adam's whisper, passed along the line, that drew the attention of those in the ranks to things others would not have seen, one officer's difficulty in sheathing a drawn sword, another's clumsy attempt to clean a musket, a helmet too big for its wearer and stuffed with cloth. In the disconcerting manner of men in the ranks, these back vennel rankers laughed, their faces straight, while the officers looked for one who could be seized on as a laugher. In the taverns, after the parades, the men calling for ale, imitated their officers' words of command. Each officer was proud of his ability to shout in the military way, and each officer believed that only himself had the proper voice for the slow, gutteral cautionary words and the sudden raising of the voice's pitch for the executive word. 'They think they're doing it like real soldiers,' Adam English had whispered in the ranks, starting the word-of-command laugh. 'Look at that one perking himself up for his squeal. If he orders us to turn left, turn right. That will take some of the wind out of him.'

The council had a tolbooth occasion to celebrate, and for it they assembled the town guard, lined up in the Marketgait, facing the tolbooth wall, where, for some days, masons had been insetting carved stones. The guard raised their weapons to the salute, and the provost pulled away a sheet that had hidden the carving. He spoke about the history of the town – its long-ago battles between Picts and Scots, games and stories, now, for children – its camps and forts named in words of forgotten languages, names, now, of fields around the town – its long demolished castle where Wallace had fought – its Reformation riots. The carving was the town arms, granted by the king, a pot of lilies, two long-tailed dragons for supporters, and the words *Dei Donum*, the gift of God. Adam was stirred, and found pleasure in his burgh's having a coat of arms, lilies and dragons. He pointed out the carving to his family. 'It's ours as much as theirs,' he said. 'The right ones would have you think that they're the whole town. We're as good as they are!'

Adam saw again the man for whom he had named his son John. Colonel Graham of Claverhouse rode through the town on his way to his lands of Glenogilvie. He was an honorary burgess of Dundee, who had won renown in the defeat of the church-staters at Bothwell Bridge. The town guard was again mustered in the Marketgait, to be inspected by him, every man washed, those in possession of shoes wearing them. The burgess officers had prepared carefully for this inspection; they liked such ceremonies. Graham came, riding with an escort. His inspection was a glance along the ranks, along the odd assortment of weapons. He spoke to his escort, and they turned to hide smiles. He dismounted, and walked along the length of the officers' line, with never a word for one, eyeing them as though they were the ones to be inspected. His scornful hand corrected a fault or two in the bearing of their arms. To the provost, who trotted at his heels, he said: 'Were it not for a tendency towards regularity in the lines, I should have taken this to be a Galloway hill-preaching!' He rode away, without entering the tolbooth. It was said, later, that in those ten minutes, John Graham of Claverhouse destroyed the Dundee burgess tradition of loyalty to the king.

Adam English laughed that day as Graham went across the Marketgait, a little, slight, handsome, scornful man, with black hair hanging in curls below his shoulders, a dandy. 'What does he think he is,' the councillors were saying. 'He's a killer of hill folk, a nothing trying to climb to be something.' The order to maintain and drill the town guard was still in force but, the war obviously over and the officers' enthusiasm chilled by Graham's rudeness, the number on parade became smaller, and finally was nothing at all. The law of compulsory attendance at church had been cried twice, but was never cried again. The regular church-goers had complained of the unseemliness of the crowded services.

Again the drum and pipes played for the calling out of the town guard. Cameron, the wildest of the wild whigs, had nailed up his declaration at Sanquar. The whigs were declaring war in the name of Christ the King against the usurper Charles Stuart. Colonel Graham's cavalry raided among the southern hills. Cameron was dead to a cavalry sabre. The murderer Hackston was taken, killer of Archbishop Sharp. The Dundee town guard did not parade. The officers had no keenness for a town guard now, and made an excuse of the emergency being ended. The burgesses were talking of Graham as being too severe on these Galloway folks, too anxious to do well in the sight of the king, too bloodily dutiful to the king. This was a new kind of talk for the Dundee free. Adam hated the Dundee burgesses not one whit the less for their new talk. There was one burgess he did not hate, Graham, who, like himself, was climbing to be a power, and who insulted Dundee councillors.

All Adam's children were at the tenement school now. He took pride in their making marks upon slates, the marks that burgesses could make. 'You're as good as anybody. You'll be better than anybody. It's right you should be able to do what the free can do, for you'll be higher than any of the free.' The eldest was come to an age for being apprenticed. He wanted to be a baker. The baker deacon, to whom Adam spoke, looked at the dirt man's bare legs. 'Your son can come into the trade as a learner, an unfree learner. You know yourself that he can't be a free apprentice. He can be some baker's laddie, and pick up the craft, and be a journeyman in time. It's not for the likes of him to be a master.' Adam hid his wrath. Young Adam went to a bakehouse to be a baker's laddie. 'Learn the craft,' Adam told the boy, 'and your time will come. And that baker deacon's time will come, as well, a time he'll mislike, I doubt.'

Colonel John Graham of Claverhouse came to his new home of Dudhope Castle with his bride. Maitland of Dudhope was a ruined man in the politics of the time. Graham had Maitland's castle on the Law slope above Dundee. He claimed all the ancient feudal rights vested in the possession of the castle, the policing of the burgh, the judging of malefactors, the exaction of a tribute from certain market sales and harbour imports. The council had fought against the Scrymgeours of Dudhope on these issues, they had argued with Maitland. They could neither fight Graham nor argue with him. The king's brother, James Stuart, now commissioner for Scotland, backed his favourite and dismissed the council's complaints. Graham's servants arrested men in the street, searched out the few conventicles held in houses, and stood by at the Marketgait and the quayhead to see that their master received his dues. Adam English smiled his support of this man who harassed the council, the guildry, and the chartered trades. He went to Claverhouse to tell him that the deacon of the baker trade was secretly a churchstater, and held conventicles in his home. Claverhouse looked his contempt for an informer. 'The man I'm telling you about,' Adam said, 'was on the council of 1660, and that council burned my mother as a witch.' The scorn went from the Colonel's face. 'I have a bad name in some parts,' he said, 'but I never burned anyone. Your baker will have his ears cropped for his psalm-singing foolishness, and for his woman-burning wickedness.' In his dirt scouting, Adam saw and heard much for Claverhouse's ear. He told only when burgesses were involved.

Claverhouse, by command of the king, was provost of Dundee. Those burgess families who had held hard to the council, argued that, by the law of a Stuart six generations before this Charles Stuart in London, each council selected the succeeding council and each council selected its provost. The Edinburgh privy council were unheeding of the complaint. Graham of Claverhouse sat in the tolbooth in the provost's chair, with scowling bailies and councillors around him, old royalists turned against the king by years of depression and by the king's man, Graham.

To Provost Graham, Adam English applied for the right to take over an ale-house, the keeper of which had died. A man need not be free to keep a tavern, but must be approved by the council. For the first time in his life, Adam wore shoes and stockings and breeches tied at the knee. The councillors said that this man was the dirt man and his work was well done. His leaving the redding would be a loss to the town. 'You would keep him down because he does well,' Graham said. 'I'm granting this!'

The tavern was in a Seagait close. The family moved there from Rollo's house in the year 1683, when Adam was thirty-one years old. Back vennel workmen found his place to their liking for their eating and drinking. Mary and her serving woman had had a long experience, with the bound redders, of economical cooking and catering. Adam had his quick jocularity. He never argued, but leaning over his counter, listened to the arguments – the death of Charles Stuart, his successor's Roman Catholic politics, Claverhouse's killings in Galloway during the first years of the new reign, the signs of revolt showing plainly in all the news that came from London, from Edinburgh, and showing most plainly of all in the faces of the Dundee free. When Claverhouse returned from his killing and his privy council meetings, Adam informed him about certain young men of burgess families, who had reached the age for taking the burgess oath, but had not taken it, because it was a swearing of loyalty to the throne, nor had they been entered in the locked book. The names spoken by Adam to Claverhouse were all of close relatives to members of the council of 1660, when Elspet Renkyne was burned, all except one, the son of that minister who had preached over her in the pillory and over her on the witch fire. Adam's politics were still the politics of tinklers whom nobody persecuted, nobody governed, no god or devil could frighten.

All his boys were now at trades, unfree learners, not free apprentices, John with a mason, Leeb White's son, Willie, with a wright. 'Learn the craft, and bide your time,' their father told them. He still gave little heed to Mary. John, the boy who had heard his mother's sorrows, was silent in his father's company. He was the serious one, an honest, capable boy, but silent.

Each evening before dusk, the fencible men of the town gathered in the Marketgait, to hear the reading of the arrangements for the night's watch of the defences. There was no laughing about the swords and the words of command of the town guard officers. The patrols and guards detailed for duty marched, determined men, anxious men, frightened men. Tonight the enemy might attack.

The enemy? Who were the enemy? Were the troops of Dutch William, perhaps now approaching the Tay across the North Sea, the enemy? Or the wild whigs of the southwest? Or the Irish savages of the northern mountains? Or the king's Scotch army under their generals, Lord Douglas and Graham of Claverhouse? The enemy was one of these parties, or all of them.

News came from the south. Dutch William was landed. Not in Scotland, as had been expected, but on the Channel coast. He was moving on London, slowly, so slowly. There was no news that seemed to be news. Was the king opposing the Dutchman's advance? Where was Claverhouse's cavalry that had marched to England? Where was Douglas? What was the Edinburgh parliament saying? There was no news of what parliament thought. No news of any rising of the Cameronians in Galloway and Clydesdale. No news of the Highland Irish, who hated the whigs because they hated the whiggish Campbell of Argyll. News from London now, apparently unimportant news, but it frightened further those who were frightened in the town. General Graham, Bloody Claverhouse, was Viscount Dundee. It was clear now, if there had ever been doubt of it, that Claverhouse, who called himself provost and constable of Dundee, had chosen his side in the wars. There was news that the king had fled, that he had been held by fishermen. In Adam English's tavern was argument. What kind of fools were these fishermen who could not let well alone? There would be fighting and burning because of these fools of fishermen. He had fled again. Thank God, no fools caught him this time!

Claverhouse, whom nobody could think of as Lord Dundee, was in Edinbugh with a remnant of his cavalry. It was said that he had been one of the last men to see the king, that he had pleaded with the king to fight the Dutchman. He was arguing in the parliament that was not a real parliament because no king called it. He was intriguing with Gordon who held Edinburgh Castle. He had run from Edinburgh, after climbing the rock to plot with Gordon. He had climbed the rock in full view of everyone, and nobody had fired the shot that would have eased the anxiety of the town from which he took his new title.

He was in his castle of Dudhope, looking down the hill to Dundee. God, there would be killing and burning! There was the look of killing and burning on his face as he came

71

through the town with his single troop of cavalry, on his way to Dudhope. Set guards and patrols by day as well as night, but give Claverhouse no cause to think they are set against him! He had but a troop of cavalry, but Heaven alone knew what that man might attempt with a troop of cavalry. Bloody Claverhouse, with the smell of the Cameronians' blood in his nostrils! The folks of the south-west said he had sold himself to the devil, that he could not be shot by a lead bullet. There must be something in the story. A story like that would not be told unless there was some cause. He had a witch look in his eyes, that Claverhouse!

He rode down to the tolbooth. Give him no cause to think the watch is set against him! He rode unmolested to the tolbooth. They saw when he removed his hat in the council chamber that his black curls were streaked with grey. On his face was the look of killing and burning, they said. In the king's name he ordered them to declare their allegiance to the king.

'What king?' one said out of nervousness.

With a look of killing, they said, he left them. His hat remained on the provost's table where he had sat. He rode bareheaded across Marketgait into the Overgait, up the Friar's Wynde and out towards his castle on the slope of the Law. Adam English watched him go, and saw the look of hate that Claverhouse looked at the tolbooth.

At the market cross, the new sovereigns of Scotland were proclaimed, Mary by hereditary right, William by invitation of the Estates, a frightened ceremony. Next day, the people of the town, staring up the hillsides, saw the standard of James Stuart unfurled by Claverhouse upon the summit of the Law. At Dudhope Castle, Claverhouse waited for men of the town to join him, the burgesses of once-loyal Dundee. Nobody came, nobody. With his troop of cavalry he marched to his Glen House in Glenogilvie.

The spring had come, early May of 1689. Adam English looked towards the Sidlaws to which Claverhouse had gone. He smelled the Sidlaw smell in the wind, and the smell of council blood. He remembered Claverhouse's killing look to the tolbooth.

His son, young Adam, nineteen now, tall, erect, ruddy like his father, had finished his learning of the baker craft, had been offered a journeyman's hire by his master, but had not yet accepted. Adam went to his son, and told him not to accept any man's hire yet. 'I've got something to do,' he told the young man, 'that will take me from the town – and bring me back to it, I'm hoping, bring me back with what's needed to make me a power against the right ones.' Young Adam would tend the ale-house; his baking skill would be useful in helping his mother with the catering. 'It will not take long, this jaunt,' the father added. 'A month or two, then I'll be back with a sword in my hand, Claverhouse's man, the only Dundee man to join him, a power in Dundee as he will be a power in all the land. When I come I'll keep the family safe, but there are some who will not be safe, I can tell you.'

'I'll come with you,' young Adam said. 'There are some I would like to hurt, myself.' But his father would not have that. Maybe the time had not yet come for Elspet Renkyne's blood becoming a power. Young Adam must bide his time and keep the ale-house going. He could say, if anybody commented on his father's absence, that his father was gone to help a Fife taverner who was ill. Adam handed over the key of the great chest that contained the silver coin hoard, long ago removed from the Houff grave.

'If I don't come back,' he said, 'you'll share out what's there in five parts, your mother, your sister, your two brothers, and yourself. You'll keep the tavern, young Adam. You'll not give the others their share till they're ready to use it in making their way. You'll watch that Elspet takes the right man when the lads come after her, as they will come after a lassie with that hair. You'll do well by your mother. Mind! And there's the hair! You'll divide it in four, and each of you that's of the blood, will get a strand – to keep you minding about the death the right ones gave your grandmother, and minding about what she said would come.'

He went over the foreseeings, carefully, with the young man. The blood would be a power, and its powerfulness would become too big for Dundee. The blood would go often and return often. In some returnings it would bring what was needed. The beginning of the power would be in stone and water – which had already come to pass, Adam pointed out. The power would grow in a hot sun and in heavy rain. Elspet Renkyne's blood would put a rope around a bailie's neck – which might come of joining Claverhouse. Elspet Renkyne's name would be acclaimed by a multitude. She would stand again in Dundee, unburnable, in cold flames. For great men, the lamentation for her death would be sung by burgess boys and beaten out by hammers. The story of the town would be told in the story of her blood.

He bade a casual goodbye to the rest of the family, telling them that he was going to help an ill taverner in Fife, one who had once done him a good turn. He went, at night, by a close in the north side of the Marketgait, among the gables to the Houff wall, climbed it, and dropped among the graves. The patrol moved in the Houff, and he hid from them in the shadows around one of the tombs of the deacons. He took from the hollow under the stone slab a new sword he had hidden there. He went over the north wall of the Houff, waded the Scouring Burn, and marched across the Meadows and the lower lands of Dudhope and the lands of Claverhouse. He moved in the manner of the tinklers, with the muscles of his legs relaxing in the stride forward. He reached Glenogilvie in the Sidlaws, the only man of the town of Dundee to join the lord of Dundee.

His politics were the politics of the tinklers. He cared not who was king.

Claverhouse smiled a little, looking from under his black brows, when the man from Dundee was brought before him. 'You've come?' Claverhouse said, nothing more.

All the next day mountain men, those called the Irish in Dundee, were going in and out of the Glen House, messengers from the chiefs of the northern savages, Adam was told. They looked like tinklers to Adam. The one man from Dundee sat with the men from Airlie, who had come in to join Claverhouse. Ogilvie, their lord, was held in Edinburgh, but the Airlie men of the Braes of Angus knew which side they were to take.

Word came that night from Dudhope Castle that a regiment of cavalry had been seen to enter Dundee. Claverhouse ordered a move. The little band went by Glamis and Kirriemuir, with their strength growing as they moved. They marched along the slopes of the Braes into the Mearns, also for Stuart, like Angus. By the steep pass at Cairn o' Mount they reached the Dee and crossed at Kincardine O'Neil, into Aberdeenshire, also Stuart country. Angus, the Mearns, and Aberdeenshire had always been for the king, always against church-staters and other whigs. They crossed the Spey and went through Elgin to Forres. They were a fighting force. They moved again and, when Adam English asked to where they moved, he was told to the town of Dundee. The cavalry regiment that had come to the town might be won over to Claverhouse, their old commander. News from Dudhope Castle suggested that a word from Claverhouse would win them.

There was news, too, that Mackay, the general for Dutch William, was moving on the town of Dundee. Claverhouse quickened his march to win his cavalry regiment. He chose his force, the fastest men and horses, and they raced. Adam English had his horse, and rode like a cavalry trooper. He had learned his horsemanship in the Sidlaws with the tinklers; he could steal a horse and ride it. He was thinking with relish of the killing and burning that would be done at Dundee. His mother had stood in the jougs and had been burned. He had been the laddie called English and the bound man called English. In the town guard he had had to obey orders of little right ones with swords. He was riding to be a power in Dundee.

At Cairn o' Mount, the news came that Mackay was in Dundee. Claverhouse's force went back towards the mountains from which the Irish men, like tinklers, were to come, and Adam cursed, disappointed. The mountain men had not yet arrived with their chiefs, and Claverhouse marched south by the country of Athol. Mackay moved in a slow pursuit through the Highland glens, and was mazed among them. Claverhouse marched into the town of Perth and along the Carse of Gowrie to Dundee. Adam passed the word that his tavern was to be spared in the sacking of the town.

From the Balgay Hill, Claverhouse looked at Dundee and at his own castle on the slope of the Law. He counted the chances, his small force against the Dundee town guard, desperately defending their homes. He shirked from an assault. There was no killing and burning, except for the burning out of Claverhouse's own tenants of Hilltown village, who refused to join their lord. Adam English swore in his tinkler fashion as he marched from Dundee with Claverhouse.

The force went back to the mountains. The mountain Irish were coming in hundreds. They fought with each other as they marched towards Claverhouse. They stole from the lands of rival tinkler clans as they marched through them. Like Adam, they had no politics, cared not who was king, but they hated the whig Campbells whom Claverhouse hated. They had a name for Claverhouse, black John of the battles. These men did not drill; they would train for killing by killing, their chiefs said. They murdered each other in the camp for wrongs of two centuries ago. The MacDonalds of Keppoch took a fee from the MacIntosh town of Inverness for not sacking it. Eight hundred Keppoch men who had come to join Claverhouse went home, laughing, with MacIntosh money and MacIntosh cattle.

With a force of two thousand, Claverhouse marched to conquer a kingdom for the king who had fled from it. Adam English prayed that the march was towards Dundee. The army dodged among the dark glens. When they turned from where Dundee lay, Adam swore in his tinkler way. They retreated from Mackay. They made Mackay retreat.

76

Mackay was lost in the glens. He blundered through the gorge of the Garry at Killiecrankie, into the trap Claverhouse had set for him. Mackay was caught in the valley bottom with no room to manoeuvre and his retiral through the gorge blocked by his own baggage. He stretched his three-deep line across the valley. Claverhouse's Irish came down on him from the hills. They cut through the lines towards the supplies in the gorge. They had no interest in winning a battle for James Stuart, only in gaining Mackay's baggage. Adam rode through with them, and turned to look again at a sight that had caught his eye. He moved back for a closer look, then followed the charging Irish into the gorge, his face grim and disappointed.

He went past the quarrelling Irish around the waggons, fighting each other now, while Mackay's army fled. He followed in the wake of the rout, down Glen Garry, and crossed the hills to Angus, moving warily but fast. In mid-Angus, he threw away his sword, sold his horse to tinklers, and went on, walking, to Dundee. He entered in the night, slipping through the Houff patrols.

Young Adam told him that fear was upon the town. Claverhouse, Bloody Claverhouse with his mountain savages, was coming. God help the town of Dundee, hated by Claverhouse, who had swept aside Mackay's army, and had an unopposed passage to the town, and, now, a force to capture it. Adam listened, his smile hard, to his son's account of the rumours and alarms.

'He's not coming!' Adam said. 'He's dead! What I saw him getting, there, was a wound no man could recover from. It looks as if the time's not come yet for the blood to be a power – you're sure nobody knew I was out with him?'

'Nobody knew, except myself,' young Adam assured him.

THE GALLOW STEPS IN MARKETGAIT

SEVEN years of want and of weeping came upon the town. A succession of bad summers – May frosts, June droughts, August rain-storms – withered or rotted the crops in the nearby lands from which the Dundee supplies were drawn. In the farther-off lands, the tilling was for the feeding of the crofter hamlets only, with little surplus at any time, and none in these bad harvest years. A year of dear bread had come commonly enough – one year in ten, it was said, was a short corn year – but never before had there been hungry year after hungry year, to make, at the end, famine, a year of no bread, of no fish in the Tay or the hill burns, of no rabbits, even.

With hunger, through the seven years, were the pestilences, the five-day sickness, the smallpox, the throat fever, the bowel fever and the wasting cough. The five-day sickness came with a procession of beggars from the Sidlaw Hills. The watch kept them out of the main town, but for three days they possessed the village on the hill, not now the Barony Hilltown of Dudhope but the Barony Hilltown of Dundee, for the council had bought it. When the beggars retreated, they were running not from the watchers' whips but from the danger of being infected by their own sick who were dying on the long steep street. The sickness was a shivering and a sweating, an aching of head and limbs, a fiery heat, then death. There was no cause for it except the influence of the stars, and some folks named it the influence. In every close in the town was mourning, among free and unfree, and the sound of hammers upon wood, the making of coffins. From every wynd, the funeral processions came. The few pennies were for the spirit-raisers and the seers. The old fear of the ice and of the death of the species was upon the town.

The five-day sickness went on to take its dues in other burghs. Smallpox, the fevers, and the wasting cough, which had always killed their scores now killed their fifties, through six years. A vennel orator preached that there should be quicker redding of the middens and there would be less pestilence. He vexed the town. How could ordinary dirt have anything to do with the throat fever and the smallpox? He preached of the manner of building the tenements, gable to the streets, a narrow close between one tenement and another. He angered the town. How could the manner of building have effect upon the wasting cough that was in the air itself? He cited the laws of cleanliness of the Israelites. He was driven from the town. Lice and bugs were bred of the grains of the soil. Where bodies were lice would be. The king and queen had their lice, and everyone had lice. Where stones and wood made houses, bugs were bred of the stones and wood.

In the time of the five-day sickness, in 1694, died Mary, called the wife of Adam English. She was nearly forty-nine years old and he forty-two.

John, the quiet serious one of a rowdy laughing family, his mother's youngest who had heard her sorrows, stood by the grave long after the others had gone, his father, his brother, his sister, and his half-brother. As an infant he had kept away from his father, hiding behind his mother's skirt, his brows drawn down, not in fear. As a youth of nearly nineteen, tallest, broadest and strongest of the Englishes, he was like a stranger in his father's presence, unspeaking, unsmiling. That day of the burial, when he came at last from the graveside in the Houff, he spoke.

'There is nothing now to hold me here,' he said. 'I'm going away.'

The easy-talking Willie, scarce a year younger than himself, pleaded in his manner with John, who turned his back.

'Listen to your brother, John,' Adam said. 'He's saying things you should be listening to.'

'He's not my brother,' John said. 'When I say that, I'm saying nothing against him.' His brows drawn down, he looked hard at his father as he said these words.

'You're the blood, John,' Adam said. 'Maybe it will be you to be the power.'

'A power!' the young man said. 'What's for me here? I've learned to be a mason. I'm a better mason than any of my age, and better than most who are older. But I can be nothing here, only a hired man. That's one reason, but there are better reasons than that. My mother's not here now, and there's little to keep me here.'

His father had no reply for that. Three days later, John went out, with his bundle on his back, on the western trail towards Perth. Adam and young Adam walked beside him to beyond the West Port, at the end of the Overgait. They stood on the crest of the Hawk Hill to watch him go down into the Carse of Gowrie.

'I'll be coming back some day,' he shouted as he went. 'I'll keep in mind that I'm the blood. I'll maybe bring what's needed.'

'Ay, if it's John who's to be the power, he'll come back some day,' the father said. 'He got enough from me to get him started wherever he goes. I couldn't give more to one who's maybe running away from being the power. The money is for the ones who look more like being the power she talked about.' He was silent, his eyes upon the receding figure of the son named for Claverhouse. 'Young Adam,' he said, at length, 'my marriage to your mother was a marriage made by a right one, by the rules of the right ones. I couldn't be bound by a marriage like that, but I was good to her. She didn't have to stand in the jougs in those days when that was done. She wanted for nothing in life that I could give her. What I couldn't give, well I couldn't give it!'

One, Will Auchterlonie, the son of lower burgesses for many generations back, of the wright craft, a maker of coffins, came seeking to marry Elspet English, whose hair was a talk and a staring when she walked in the streets bare-headed, as befitted an unmarried woman. Coffin makers were among the few who prospered. Adam favoured him for he was steady and prospering and, although on the list of the free, he was no right one. Elspet favoured him for he was not an ill-looking man and he could laugh and daff despite his trade. His friend was the laughing and daffing Willie English, who had been an unfree learner in the same wright yard as Will Auchterlonie had been a free apprentice. Elspet and young Auchterlonie were wed, a singing, dancing, roaring wedding despite the troubles of the times, and she went to his Overgait house, with its coffin-making cellar. As God made them He marched them, everybody said, two singing linties together if ever there were, a bonnie lassie and an upstanding, steady fellow.

At the time Adam came back from Claverhouse's rebellion, young Adam had returned to the baking, a hired journeyman. Now, in the time of the flour scarcity, he was out of work and helping his father in the tavern, where trade was poor for many men were unemployed. Ale-brewing had been stopped by the council – all available grain was needed for bread, and the ale stocks had to be carefully rationed out to customers. The tavern profits were small, but the father and son were living sparingly, and the hoard of silver coins was not lessened by them, indeed added to, a little. Young Adam was his father again, with his father's frightening look, his hard smile, his long memory for a grudge, his ambitions and hopes. He was respected – feared by some – rather than liked.

Willie had done his last months of learning to be a wright, and lived on in his master's house for bed and board only, giving his work when work came to the yard. Few masters could offer more to their journeymen, and only a young, unmarried man like Willie could accept such terms. He was a youth whom everybody liked, except in his sudden moments of anger and hate. He had his father's gift for playing musical instruments, bagpipes, viols, the shawm. It was said of him that after three looks at any instrument he could play it. Willie's humour could be cruel, but he was unlike his father in that his cruelty did not endure long, and his usual manner was one of careless and innocent gaiety. Leeb White's son had Leeb White's laugh.

A year after John's departure, Willie also left the town. The reason of his going was characteristic of him. At a pay-off, a spree to celebrate the end of an apprentice's time, the company got to talking about their prospects in stricken Dundee. 'I see nothing for it but to join up with these army recruiters who've come to the town,' Willie said. After a drink or two of heather-top whisky and the singing of rousing military songs, Willie's idea looked good to some of those present. They were daring each other to enlist. Six of them marched out to seek the recruiters. One of them went through to the end with the ploy – Willie English. Again Adam and young Adam were on the Hawk Hill to watch a going from Dundee. Some twenty men went out on the trail to Perth, and to army service. Willie was marching at the head, his bagpipes playing.

'I'll come back in my own time,' Willie had shouted before putting the bagpipes' mouthpiece to his lips. 'And maybe I'll bring what's needed.'

'Ay, if he's to be the power, he'll come back,' Adam said. 'It might be him, nobody can say, but I've always had the belief that if it isn't to be myself it will be you, young Adam. You should be getting a wife.'

'I've seen no lassie I want to bind myself to,' the young man said. 'If I did see one, I would wait till these hard times are by.'

There was talk about Scotland's own trading venture, the Africa Company. The passage of the charter through the Edinburgh parliament was cried at the market cross, and the announcement made that the company was receiving subscriptions in Dundee in an accounting office opened for that purpose. Painful pennies were being gathered together. By the Africa Company, Scotland was to be made rich. By the

Africa Company, a blow was to be struck against England which prospered under the new rule, against Dutch William, and against the Dutch from whom he came. The Scotch, in their famine and pestilences, had come to hate the Dutchman. It was said he did not favour the Africa Company. His disfavouring it was the more reason for the Scotch to favour it. Famine, pestilence, idle-set, mourning, the old fear of England and the old defiance of England, out of these was born the enthusiasm for Banker Paterson's scheme. Adam, leaning over his counter, listened to the bitter debates among his customers. He was not stirred.

There was heard in the talk the word Darien. In burgh council chambers, in the parliament at Edinburgh, in Adam English's tavern eventually, the talk was Darien, the centre of the earth's trading routes, where Pacific and Atlantic were divided by but a strip of land which could be made the great warehouse of the world. Darien was to be Scotch. The people of the scanty soil, of the rocks, of poverty, were to be wealthy. Their colony, Darien, the hub of the world, was to make them rich. In wealth they would be magnanimous, unlike the southern companies. Their Darien would be open to the world, the great free port for the world's commerce. Dutch William, the arguers said, envied the Scotch their Darien. It was good to believe that he was envious, the counting Dutchman. The tavern argument would be stopped for the singing of the scurrilous, obscene songs about the Dutchie, about his dishing of Knox's plan in the recent establishment of the Scotch church, about his murders at Glencoe in the northern mountains, about his recruiting young Scotchmen to fight his Dutch wars, about his trying to keep Scotland poor by discouraging the Africa Company.

A sailor was among the arguers one day. He was asked where was the land of Darien. He had not been there, but had been in nearby parts. 'It's hot there,' he said, 'a hot, hot sun, and heavy rains when it rains.'

'Did you say a hot sun and heavy rains?' Adam asked, staring.

'Rain!' The sailor laughed. 'Rain! When it rains there it doesn't take time to come down. Plenty of sun and plenty of rain. It's a place for things growing.'

'Growing?' Adam exclaimed, excited. 'A hot sun and heavy rains. Would power grow there?' The sailor looked blank. 'Ach, that's something you would never understand, lad!' Adam said. 'I was just havering to myself.' That night, young Adam counted the money in the chest for his father, just over seven hundred Scotch pounds, worth only a twelfth of that figure by the London way of reckoning money but a fortune for a Dundee taverner to possess.

'Have you something on your mind about this money?' the son asked.

'I'm not sure, young Adam,' the father said. 'It had its real beginning, you might say, in stone and water. It will grow, if it's this that's to give us the power, in a hot sun and heavy rains. I'll bide my time a bit, and feel surer than I am the now before I do anything.'

After more than two years of marriage, Elspet was brought to child-bed. Her daughter, Elspet, was born, and the mother died.

'My bairn is the blood,' she said as she died. 'I needn't ask you to keep that in mind, father. I know you will.'

It was a time of dying in Dundee. Will Auchterlonie had made coffins without ever understanding what coffins were. Now he knew. He was like a man who has been struck.

'I can't stay in the town where she went past in the streets, with her hair,' he said to Adam. 'I need to be somewhere away from Dundee, away from this trade I do. I've been thinking about this Darien.' He talked much about Darien to keep himself from talking about his lost wife. He found in the excitement about Darien a soothing of his sorrow.

He arranged that, if he went, Adam would bring up the child till his return. Adam remembered the man who had come to the tavern and spoken about the Darien sun and rains. It had been uncanny that the sailor should say the words he had said, Adam was thinking. The Darien expedition was being planned, and men skilled in the crafts were wanted for it.

'Young Adam,' the father said, 'it would be you, right enough, who was meant to be the power. Have you thought, yourself, of Will Auchterlonie's plan to go to Darien?'

'I've thought of it,' the son said. 'I would like fine to go.'

'It's what was meant, I'm thinking. This money grows but slowly in the chest. Put into the Company, it would grow fast, in the Darien sun and rain. From Darien, you come back to be a power against the Dundee right ones.'

On a summer morning in 1698, Adam saw the departure of the colonizing expedition. There had been competition for places in the pioneering ships, and men who were crafts-men were chosen, young Adam English the baxter and Will Auchterlonie the wright chosen among the sixteen hundred. The sad-faced Scotch were singing. The bonfires were lit. On every hill, except in the northern mountains where they knew no better, the fires blazed. The empire was being founded, the great free-trading example to all the earth. Those who had no money to invest in the empire invested their hopes and their bitterness against Dutch William. The ships went out of the Forth to the sound of the cheering on the shore.

'I'll keep in mind that it's in Dundee we're to be a power,' young Adam said as his last words to his father. 'I'll come back!'

Adam English talked in his tavern about the manner of the setting out of the pioneers.

'I envied them that were going,' he said. 'They're well away, and a good start's half the task. They're lucky. I'm sorry I missed going with young Adam and Will Auch-terlonie.'

The banker Paterson had never seen Darien, the investing burgesses of the little Scotch towns had never seen it, the investing lairds and their tenants had never seen it. The hub of the world, the warehouse of the world, its gold a talk and a stare, was in the empire of a dream.

In Dundee, Adam English talked of Darien through the saddest of the seven sad years, 1699, the year of the shortest corn. Folks crawled in the Marketgait picking up crumbs of the grain around which fights had raged. Children ran naked in the closes, their stomachs distended with starvation. The beggar hordes swarmed into the town from the sorner and tinkler camps, and the town lacked the energy and the self-interest to drive them out as it had always before driven them.

'What would I give, what would we all give to be in Darien?' Adam said. 'There's plenty there. They've forgotten us, left here in cold Scotland.'

The news came that the Darien colonizers had abandoned Darien. It was not believed. It was too much to believe that upon all the calamities this calamity could be heaped. A Dundee man back from Darien, weak and thin, came to Adam's tavern.

'I brought you this, Adam,' he said. He held out a little parcel.

'Is it true he's dead?' Adam asked. 'And Will Auchterlonie?'

'Ay, dead, Adam. Your son and Will and many more. Adam's dead at Darien. Will's dead in New York. Adam's dead of snake-bite and Will of fever and scurvy. You know it, but I thought you would like to be sure. It's good to be sure they're dead. Some are not dead, and they wish they were, some in Spanish prisons, some in the plantations. Adam, don't curse me, don't mock me, for the love of God! I've stood enough.'

'No, Alec, I'll not mock you.'

'There's not many like you, Adam. Folks who have never been further than the West Port know all about Darien. They wonder that I didn't have the gumption to pick up the lumps of gold that lie about there. They wonder that a whole army of Scotch couldn't beat Spaniards that one boatload of pirates can beat. They wonder that we didn't send home cargoes of diamonds and rubies. Adam, I'll tell you what Darien is – a bare rock sticking out into the sea, and behind it nothing but jungles and marshes. Who was it ever thought of Darien for a colony?' His voice rose in pitch, finished in a shriek. He wept hysterically.

Adam soothed him.

'You say you saw young Adam at his end,' Adam said.

'I saw him when he was near the end. He was lucky. Will had worse. He came through the time when we fought each other. Adam died easy, but Will's was a sore, sore death. Will saw the disappointment. Adam, nobody told us that the Spaniards claimed this Darien. I didn't know that they had built towns, not just settlements but towns in the land that we said was our land. They were shown our charter, but what's a charter from something called the Edinburgh parliament. We were pirates to them, the same kind of pirates as have pestered them for years. They said our king was this William. Where was our charter from him? They had the word that this William was against us. That made it certain in their minds that we were pirates.'

Adam was silent.

'I've told them at Edinburgh. They'll not listen. I was there. They weren't. But they know all about Darien. They'll know better soon enough. D'you know what that second expedition of theirs will find? There's a colony there for them to land in – a colony of graves. That's all we made in Darien – a graveyard!'

He wept again. His body shook with the sobbing. Adam, letting him weep, smoothed out a tress of red hair from the parcel. He had given it to young Adam on the quayhead at Leith.

'There's myself,' he said, 'and the bairn, Elspet's bairn. And maybe Willie, and maybe John. Are you sure of young Adam's end? You're sure he couldn't live past snake-bite?'

He rose, and put the tress into the chest beside the rest of the hair. He glowered at the few silver coins, where there had been many. Fifteen coins only, and they had all come from the linen bag in the breakwater.

'This is the beginning of the power. What was there before wasn't the beginning, for it had started before I found these coins in stone and water,' Adam said. 'This is the true beginning, all of it from stone and water. I made a mistake, young Adam! My laddie, young Adam!'

He turned on the man from Darien. 'You're sure, you're really sure he's dead?'

The wind blew with gale force from the south-west. When ships ran to sea from the insecure anchorage in the Tay, one ship attempted to beat into the estuary. Four times, four days in succession, she struggled up to the white turbulence of the bar, wrestled with it, and ran from it. Those in Dundee who were wise about weather and ships, walked the three miles east to the sands beside Broughty Castle to look for this stupid ship's fight.

'What can the master be thinking?' they speculated. 'He's better out of the river than in it in a blow like this.'

It became known that the ship was from the Low Countries, outward from Antwerp. She carried flax.

'Flax! That'll keep long enough,' they said on the Broughty sands. 'You would think he had something that was in a hurry, something that would spoil. He's got the whole sea to be blown about in, and he wants to be among the banks and reefs in weather like this. He must be daft.'

In an abatement of the storm, the Antwerp ship crossed the bar, and out from the Stannergait, a mile beyond the East Port, held to the soft bottom with every hook and weight. A pilot went out to her. He clambered up to the frightened people on her deck.

'I doubt you should keep away from us,' a Scotch voice called to him. 'We've got sickness in the ship. That's why the master has been trying to get in.'

'What's the sickness?'

'We don't know, but it's killed four already, and others are down with it. I've been thinking the now that from the look of it it might be—' He hesitated.

88

'Ay?'

'I don't right know, but from what I've heard of plague, I'm thinking our sickness might be that.'

The pilot turned and rushed for the side.

'Keep away!' he cried. 'Keep away. Take your damned ship out of here.'

'What's ado?' the man in the pilot's boat called up to him. 'Did I hear them say they've got plague?'

'Ay, they've plague!'

The boatman pulled away hurriedly.

'You're not coming back on this boat,' he called to the pilot. 'You're not coming back beside me after being among plague.'

'But, Archie—'

'I'm not to have it.' He rowed fast towards the town. 'Plague! It's a plague ship,' he shouted as he rowed.

For a hundred years there had been no bubonic disease in Dundee. There was a superstition that plague could not cross the Tay. Now it had come to the town by the Tay. Armed men patrolled the shore for five miles to the east to prevent any landing from the ship. Guns were hauled to the low cliffs at the Stannergait to drive the ship from her anchorage. They were old guns, and the one that could be made to fire did not have the range.

'He'll run for it now,' everybody said. The wind had risen again. 'He'll never hold on there.'

The ship from Antwerp did not run. She held.

'My God!' they said. 'Will nothing get him out?' On the shingly beach, men and women knelt and prayed for more wind to blow away their fear. The children danced and shouted as the wind rose. The ship dragged her hooks and weights. She drifted inshore. The crowd scattered. The night came, and the wind was a storm again.

'What happened?' they asked in Dundee in the morning. 'Was she blown out?'

'No. She's broken up on the shingle at the fishermen's houses this side of Broughty Castle.'

'Did anything come to the shore?'

'Ay.'

'Bodies, plagued bodies?'

'Ay. And worse, living folk.'

'My God. With plague. Haven't we had enough with hunger and fevers without that? The council will have to put up a bar against anybody or anything coming from Broughty.'

Armed men – the town servants and impressed harbour labourers – cordoned the fishermen's cottages beside the castle.

'Keep your distance,' they yelled to fishermen who approached. 'We'll shoot, mind.'

'There's a Dundee man come from the wreck,' one called to them.

'The pilot?'

'No, he's away. We buried his body. This is one that's just come to himself. He says he's Dundee born and has kin in Dundee. D'you know an Adam English?'

'Ay.'

'This one says he's English's son. He wants word taken to his father.'

Adam English's tavern was in a roar of discussion about the plague ship when a breathless town servant brought the news from Broughty.

'I've got three sons,' Adam said. 'No, I've got two. It couldn't be my eldest, Adam, it couldn't be him. He's lost in Darien, four years back; ay, he's lost right enough.'

Accompanied by most of the men who had been in the tavern, Adam English came from the town to Broughty. He shouted for the fishermen.

'What's his name?' he called. 'Is it Adam?'

'No, not Adam.' Some of the eagerness went from his face as the fishermen answered. He had hoped for his eldest, knowing he should not hope.

'The name is Willie,' they called.

'How is he?'

'He's all right! Knocked about a bit, but all right. There's his wife and bairn here. And another, a man, that's his wife's brother. And an old wifie that's his wife's mother. But she's far through.'

'With plague?'

'No, with the knocking about. That's them all, just the five.'

'What are you doing for them?'

'We're doing what anybody would do for folk that have come through what they've come through. We know what wreck is.'

One of the cordon shouted: 'D'you know they're plagued?'

'We know. They're folk who need help.'

Adam English looked at the guards.

'What'll you do if I go to see my son?' he asked.

They hesitated.

'We've to keep everybody out,' one said, at length. 'But maybe the order was for something else than a man wanting to see his son.'

'Maybe,' Adam said. 'Listen to this! I'm going in. If a father can't help his own son, who can?' He turned to one of the men who had come with him from the tavern. 'You, Tom, get clothes, and bed-clothes and something to eat and drink. You daren't take them to the fishers' houses there, I know that. Leave them here and get back. I'll come for them.'

Willie lay, with the others from the wreck, on a bed of grass and furze on the earth floor of one of the cottages.

'I saw you through the door,' Willie said to his father. 'I knew you by your walk.'

'This is a way of doing,' his father said. 'You've changed little, Willie. A bit more set, but the same Willie.'

'You've changed, yourself,' Willie said, 'but you're the same man though you've changed.' Willie looked up at a face deeply lined with twisted bitterness and with sardonic humour. The thin hair had no trace of red, the flat-ended nose was more prominent than it had been. 'I said I would come back, and I've come back,' Willie added. 'And maybe what I've brought is what's needed.'

They had not met for nine years, but no word of greeting passed between them. Adam sat on the gathered grass by his son's side. He had seen that all that could at present be done for the five from the plague ship was being done by the two old women of the fisherfolks, who busied themselves about the low gloomy one-roomed house.

'Ay, Willie, you've had a time of it,' Adam said.

Willie spoke of how they came to be saved from the breaking ship, by luck.

'Here's my wife. She's a Fleming.'

'One of the Flemings in the Moraygait, d'you mean? Andrew Fleming's family?'

Willie smiled in his old way.

'No, it's not that her name's Fleming,' he said. 'She's a Fleming from Flanders. You needn't talk to her. She'll not understand what you say. And here's wee Willie English. D'you know who this is, wee Willie?'

A little boy of four or five looked up.

'Adam English,' he said solemnly. 'Grandfather Adam English in Dun-dee.' The young woman beside the child raised herself eagerly, and peered at Adam.

'Grandfather Adam English, Dun-dee!' she said. The child's words had made her realize who the visitor was. She spoke rapidly, strange speaking in which Adam heard his own name. A young man sitting beside an old woman jumped to his feet, and came round the bed towards Adam, speaking foreign talk to him. The old woman raised herself a little to look, and with a gasp of pain sank back.

'My wife's brother, called Peter but in the Fleming way of writing Peter. Margriet's my wife. The name is Devint. The old one is far through, their mother.' The young man came close, his shining eyes fixed upon Adam.

'Adam English, Dun-dee,' he said.

'Dundee is their promised land,' Willie said.

'It's not much of a place to bring anybody the now, Willie. It's had a shake. Things are bad, not as bad as they were a year or two back but bad enough.'

'Maybe. These folk'll not find them that bad, after what they've seen. You can stand a lot when you've seen a war of the kind they saw. We're here because the new war was coming close to us. Anything is better than Flanders in a war.'

Willie said nothing of the plague on the ship, and Adam said nothing. The young woman and the young man wonderingly watched the faces of the father and the son. Adam gave Willie the news, Elspet's death, young Adam's death, the birth of Elspet's daughter. Young Adam and Elspet had been alive in Willie's thoughts, and were dead. Willie was silent, then gave his own news, how he met his wife, how he took his discharge in the Low Countries, and lived there, always intending to return to Dundee. They were silent, thinking of the circumstances of the return.

'You knew about the plague on the ship,' Willie said suddenly.

'Ay.'

'And you came to us here though you knew.'

'You needed help. The fisherfolk gave you help, and they were different blood. You're my blood.' Embarrassed, he rose. 'I'll go and see if the things I asked for are coming.'

'You'll be like us, now? You'll have to stay with us, and not mix with other folk till it's safe to go among them. If we've got plague coming on— You thought of that, did you?'

'Ay. I've left wee Elspet in good hands and arranged things for her just in case—' The father and son avoided each other's glance.

From outside came the hubbub of a crowd. Adam and Willie looked inquiringly at each other, then Adam went to the door. Beyond the line of armed guards, hundreds of people were gathered where before there had been a few score. They shouted their approval of Adam as he appeared, and held up what they had brought with them, food and clothing for the shipwrecked ones. Almost everyone there had brought something. The fisherfolks left their work with lines and nets, and watched with Adam. The crowd came forward to lay their articles in a heap beside the guards, then went back, cheering Adam's signals of thanks.

Adam went back to the cottage.

'It's not a bad town, Dundee,' he said. 'The folks have heard about you, and about me coming to you. They've brought things to help.'

Willie told his people. Their eyes shone. The old woman laughed a little, weakly, then cried. She slept with the tears wet on her face.

'You're right. It's not a bad town, Dundee,' Willie said after a long pause. 'I'm glad to be back home. Is it the council that's done this?'

The lines deepened on Adam's face, those of humour as well as those of bitterness.

'Would you expect it to be the council?' he asked. 'They're not so smart at helping the likes of us, Willie. No, these are our own kind of folk, the kind you expect to get help from. This kind of news goes quickly round them. No, the right folks will be getting down now to discussing how to deal with the trouble that you and me and the folks out-bye are raising.'

The crowd shouted again for Adam. He was cheered when he came. The cheers were hushed for the red-haired child Elspet to call to him.

'Will I come beside you?' she asked. She was cheered.

'No no, lassie. Stay with Meg Whittet like I told you. I'll soon be home, with your Uncle Willie and his wee laddie. You've got a bonnie wee cousin, Elspet, red-haired like yourself, wee Willie.'

A leader in the crowd came forward to shout. The heap of goods was the result of a quick collection through the vennels, he said. 'We haven't much, but of what we've got we can give something.'

'Here come the bailies and the watch,' the crowd were

94

shouting. 'They've raised the whole watch, by the look of it.' On the far side of the bay west of the cottages, a body of men moved along the top of the Stannergait cliffs. The crowd began to drift slowly in all directions, unhurriedly at first.

'You'd better be out of here when the bailies come,' Adam called. 'Ay, get going. There's no saying what they'll be up to.' The drifting of the crowd quickened a little. 'Go on, get away, all of you. They'll maybe be saying you should be kept out of the town, like me, because you've been beside plague.' Some of the crowd started to run, then all were running. The town servants and harbour labourers talked excitedly, with looks towards the approaching watch.

'Nobody went near the plague. That's right, isn't it?' They shouted to Adam. 'You can say that everybody kept away.'

Adam waved reassuringly, and waited.

The four bailies, in charge of some forty hastily summoned burgesses, tried to move their force in a military manner around the cottages. Adam smiled mischievously. 'This'll shake them,' he said to the fishermen, 'them and their daft way of walking like soldiers.' He cupped his hands to his mouth.

'Heh you, bailies!' he shouted out in a commanding voice. 'Halt your men! Halt, I say!' They stopped raggedly. 'You're too near, you fools,' Adam chided them. 'Don't you know the dangers of plague? Move further back and round to where your guards are keeping a proper line. I thought the watch would know better than that. Up on the grass there, that's about right for you.' He winked to the fishermen as the watch scampered back a pace or two before resuming their march, not now attempting to be orderly in their marching.

'Everything's fine,' Adam shouted when they finally came to a stop on the bank. 'The guards have kept everything in about. And me and the fishermen will see to it that nothing goes wrong inside the line. You can take it that if there's plague here, I'll keep it here. A town man is needed here to safeguard the town. Think of what might happen, somebody with plague getting from here to the town in the daftness of their fever, for instance.' He winked again to the fishermen, but this time with no mirth in his expression. The awful thought he had deliberately suggested in the minds of the bailies had its terrors for himself.

The flummoxed bailies talked together with little of burgess deliberation in their talking.

'The town will hold you responsible for any ill that befalls,' one bailie called. To be heavily official while howling across a stretch of sixty yards was difficult.

'What did you say?' Adam called back. He had heard well enough. 'I don't hear you,' he shouted in reply to the bailie's next shout. Everybody had to shout to make him hear. He winked to the fishermen.

The watch moved off, with no attempt at order or bearing.

'Keep well back now,' Adam shouted. 'That's right, that's fine!' He laughed with the fishermen. 'Burgesses,' he said to them, 'burgesses when they get together can only be burgesses. One by himself can be a man, but two together can only be burgesses, right folk, always right, always tolboothy and kirkie. The other folk can feel things. They felt things this day and came to show how they felt. But burgesses—' He had no words for his contempt. He spat, and ground the spittle into the shingle with his foot.

Every day there were crowds. They cheered the word given by Adam each morning that there was no sign of plague. Some of them wept; they could imagine the anxiety with which the folks in the cottage examined each other for the sickness. They quietened for the news of the old woman's weakness. On the fourth day, Willie and his brother-in-law, Pieter de Wint, called Devint by Willie, appeared with Adam and were cheered. Next day, Margriet was out with the little boy who danced as the crowd shouted. There was a long sorrowful 'Oh!' from the crowd when Adam announced the old woman's death. Next day, the crowd was vast for the funeral. Adam, Willie and Pieter dug the grave in the shingle. A hundred paces away a back vennel preaching-man prayed above the bowed heads of the crowd.

The crowd was less as the days went by, but even on the thirtieth day there were people walking to Broughty for the news and with the message that the council would allow Adam English and the shipwrecked ones to come to Dundee on the morrow. The emotion and enthusiasm blazed again. The entry was like the entry of a conquering liberator. Through the East Port the crowd moved with the cart, and howled their delight there for the re-union of Adam with his grand-daughter Elspet, for the little girl's hugging of her cousin. Tight-packed around the tavern in the narrow Seagait close, they shouted for Adam English and for the survivors until Adam came to speak, to remind them of the death of the mother and how her absence on this glad day made the gladness a strain for the others. They dispersed, mourning the old woman.

'You would have thought that somebody from the council might have shown himself.' Willie remarked. 'There's never been a day like this for cheering in Dundee.'

'Me, I never thought to see anybody from the council,' Adam said. 'This has been a day for feeling, and that's wrong with them that are always right. I'll tell you what the right ones are saying about this day. They're saying: "Have these vennel folk nothing more to do than run after a tavern keeper and his no-good son? Have they no work to be busy on?" That's them, and their way of thinking. No, Willie, this wasn't rightness, this day. A right day is a strutting day, a slow-talking day, a gratis freedom of the town for some laird they can flatter, or some such business. A right day is not a day for feelings.'

'Never mind them,' Willie said. 'We've got more to think about than them. We've got to get on with what I've brought back. It's maybe what's needed.'

What Willie had brought to Dundee was weaving skill. Margriet de Wint and her brother Pieter were weavers of linen. They wove, in the manner of Flanders, fine shirtings and bed-sheets and house draperies for the gentle. Such close cloth had never before been worked in Dundee. Willie English, trained to the work of a wright, built two looms to the requirements of the Flemings. The secrets of these looms and of the methods of the weaving were guarded from prying eyes in the town.

Willie journeyed into Angus with the product of the looms, and sold it at the houses of the great and lesser lairds. On his return journeys he picked up the yarn from those country spinning women whose even thread had been approved by Pieter.

In the long quarantine at Broughty fishing hamlet, Adam and Willie had formed their schemes to use the Fleming skill. They knew that the council and the chartered weaving craft would not grant a tradesman's freedom to Pieter. The argument that he was a foreigner would be argument enough in the tolbooth and the Houff meetings. His continental skill would be no plea to advance on his behalf. Adam and Willie in their discussions had mimicked the council manner of dismissing a candidate for entry to the locked book, and laughing together they had found a plan over which they laughed the more.

Pieter and Margriet wove at their looms in the two rooms next to Adam's shop, worked for unfree Adam and for their unfree selves, with scanty capital provided by Adam who should not have used capital in the provision or employment of looms. One named Tom Kydd, of a family that had been burgess tradesmen for two centuries, was named as the head of this manufactory. The weaving rooms were rented in his name. At the periodic examinations of workmanship by the weaver trade, the deacon, standing by the grave of a deacon, approved of craft-brother Kydd's fine Flemish cloth, a ceremony which, reported to Willie and Adam by Kydd, caused an uproar of laughter and then a solemn threatening of Kydd regarding the treatment he could expect to receive if ever he divulged the true state of affairs. This Kydd was a drunkard, and of that kind not seen to be a drunkard – except by taverner Adam, with whom he had long run a debt for drink. His family were grown up and gone from the town, his wife recently dead, and he, once a respectable, industrious father and husband, was sunk to complete ruin of character and means. Adam gave him the odd way of livelihood of being employed as a master, his name and his weaver membership to be used for the Fleming cloth in return for a home, food, and an allowance of the heather whisky which was Kydd's tipple. The scheme had been born of Adam's hate of burgesses and his hard humour. It pleased him well to have one of the right ones so degradingly in his grip.

Willie laughed with his father, but, out of a goodness of heart that his father never had had, was kindly enough, in a lightsome, joking manner, to the fallen tradesman. Willie's travelling – to deliver linen, canvass for orders, and collect yarn – was not full time work. He was the weaver's handyman, and also the housekeeper for the whole establishment. No servant was kept, for a servant would have discovered that the master was no master. Willie, with Kydd as assistant, attended to the cleaning, cooking, and care of the two children, his own boy and little Elspet. Margriet's weaving was hard work, but a lady's life compared with the water drawing, soap boiling, and dirt clearing of a housewife of the time. Her appearance and personality are not shown in the family legends, except that she was quiet, content, loved and loving, and her weaving was of a quality to give her an artist's satisfaction in creation. Nor has any suggestion come down the years about what Pieter was like, though he had a place for nearly thirty years in the family. The Devints, as Willie and all Dundee called them, come quite unexplained into the anecdotes of the Englishes, and in due time they disappear from the anecdotes as suddenly as they enter them, still unexplained, their origin, characters, place in Dundee life, all now unknown.

For three years the manufactory was not disturbed by the

local trade rules; and interference, when it did come, came not from the weaver trade but from the council, acting in the name of the guildry, the merchant body. Kydd was summoned to appear before the magistrates and dean of guild, not on any charge, but for consideration of whether or not he was infringing upon the dealing rights of the merchants by his importation of flax yarn into the town from Angus and by some of his sales of cloth.

'Consideration,' Adam said, 'I know what considering there'll be with the right ones of the council. They can't touch the ordered linen. It's according to the weaver rights to make linen that has been ordered. The craft fought the guildry on that score away back near two hundred years ago, and won. Kydd told me that, and Kydd as a free weaver can make linen for whoever gives him an order, just as a free tailor can make you a suit of clothes or a free wright build you a coffin without any merchant coming in. And is it not a free weaver's linen we're dealing with? God, Willie, if they found out the right way of things about that! On the street and at their Houff meetings Kydd looks like any well-doing burgess, and nobody could think things are different from what they look. The danger is having him go before the tolbooth right ones. He wouldn't let out anything deliberately, but he might do it without meaning to do it. They've got their heavy-worded talk in the council, and it might get him flustered.'

Willie and Adam suspected that the reason for this summons was that some merchant coveted the profits on the yarns brought from Angus and on the cloth sales to trading men from Fife and to shipmasters. The decision made was this: that Willie should go to the tolbooth in place of Kydd, as Kydd's hired man, saying his master was too ill to attend. He would offer Kydd's contriteness for unlawful dealing, done in ignorance by the hired man. It was hoped by this means to prevent the council taking a closer look into the nature of Kydd's manufactory. 'We'll be losing,' Adam said, 'but it's better to lose a little than lose a lot.' He swore in his tinkler fashion, bitter against the right ones. 'Margriet's weaving and Pieter's weaving that nobody else in all the land could do! Your work in seeking out these spinning women! Your work in getting to know these traders and shipmasters! My plans to nab Kydd! And they get the profit, wee men in this wee town, always right with old bits of parchment to be right about! If I could do to them what I'm doing to Kydd, make them crawl and cringe! We're as good as them! We're better than them, just as we're better than Kydd who's one of them. When we're a power, as my mother said we would be, they'll be nothing. We can comfort ourselves with that!'

Willie came back from the council meeting in a mood for murder.

'They were laughing and talking with one another as other men do,' he said. 'They were telling each other jokes as men in your ale-house do, the same jokes. I was outside the door, waiting to be called by them, and hearing their talking and laughing. Then I went in, and their faces were set in that heavy way for me, and their voices were changed to slowness and to their words that they use for their council talking. For me who have killed better men than they ever could be! They heard me say my say. And then one of them said one of their daft commonplaces in the way they say such things, as though it were the holy word of all the churches at once. He said: "This is the thin end of the wedge." Another said: "Ay, it is the thin end of the wedge." And another said it in the same voice, and went on to say that the ancient marketing rules of the town were made to safeguard the town's reputation for honesty and good quality in its manufactures. If the guildry kept an eye on what was used in manufactures, then the manufactures would more likely be according to the best Dundee standards. And if the guildry kept an eye on the goods going out then Dundee's reputation would not be lowered. That's the way they spoke. Think of it! They were talking about yarn approved by Pieter and Margriet, who could teach all Scotland about yarn. They were talking about linen made by weavers from Flanders where Dundee's kind of cloth would only be used for wrapping. And yet it was Pieter and Margriet and myself who were dishonest while they were the honest, the right! There was an officer in my regiment who talked that kind of heavy talk. He got the shortest experience of war of any man I ever saw. The first wee bit of a skirmish, the first excuse for shooting, and he went down with ten balls in him, all from his own men. One of these was from me. I minded on him this day as I listened to them in the tolbooth. I minded on the satisfaction when I saw him drop. Some day, one of them will drop.'

'They don't want Kydd before them? They were content enough with you?' Adam asked.

'They've got all they wanted. There was a booth-keeping cronie of theirs called Henryson there. He's to get the profits from our yarn and our cloth. He was the one who complained. They said to him: "This was the thin end of the wedge, Brother Henryson, and it was high time to bring it to our attention so that drastic action could be taken." Time is always high time in their slow speaking, and action is always drastic action. I stood there listening to Henryson being right and themselves being right. and I picked out the spot on their chests for a ball. Just as I used to stand on parade and pick out the spot on that officer's chest. He was one like them, a nothing with a nothing's words and a nothing's way of saying a nothing's words.'

'I know Henryson,' Adam said. 'He'll be pleased enough to let us carry on if we pay him his bit silver for work he never will do. Indeed, he couldn't do it. Willie, don't get up to anything rash. I'm glad enough to hear it's Henryson we've to deal with. He's easy enough and will be useful enough when we grow a bit. Keep yourself in hand when you deal with him. It'll be you to deal with him, mind.'

Adam was forming designs for an extension of the linen manufactory. The small success already gained had pointed out for him the road to that power his mother had prophesied. Listening in his tavern to the arguings, he laughed to himself, seeing his own rise and the fall of burgesses in that subject his customers debated so angrily. When asked his opinion about the union of Scotland and England, he said that a humble taverner could not form views about a great event like that. After the curfew, he and Willie talked union far into the night. For the Englishes, union meant a blow to Dundee pride and to Dundee pockets. It meant, too, money for their new linen developments, and, rather vaguely, a market for the great linen factory they would have one day. Dundee with eight thousand population had been important in Scotland. Now, with four thousand, it still had its importance, was a burgh whose burgesses could think of themselves as men of some consequence in the affairs of the Scotch nation. In the country of Great Britain what would Dundee be? A dirty little market town with the minor industries of a dirty little town. Willie had seen cities, and could tell his father – who well liked to hear it! – how little and backward Dundee really was. Dundee council sent a representative of its own to the Edinburgh parliament. To the London parliament, five burgh councils, Perth, Dundee, Coupar, Forfar and St. Andrews, would return a single member for a constituency to be named Perth Burghs, or maybe Forfar Burghs, but not Dundee Burghs. Adam yelped with delight to that.

The commercial terms of the proposed union were also gleefully welcomed by the father and son. In order to safeguard the southern wool-weaving, the raw wool export from Scotland to the Continent would be stopped. Some guildrymen, particularly hateful to Adam, were engaged in that trade, and would be ruined. The father of one wool shipper had been on the 1660 council which had burned Elspet Renkyne. 'It's funny how things work out!' Adam said. 'These little right ones sat and talked their talk about her, and now big ones sit and talk their talk about the little right ones.' The wool-weaving in Dundee, the town's main industry, would be faced with competition from the better southern cloth, for there would be free trade throughout the new nation of Great Britain. Without the protection of the

Scotch restrictions and the burgh rules, Dundee wool-weaving must decline rapidly. 'That's a knock for them,' Adam said. 'The unfree folk will feel it as well, and that's not so cheery to think on. But we'll not think on that. We'll think on the merchants and master weavers. There's more than half the council in this, and it's not the thin end of the wedge this time. This is their drastic action. And high time, too!' To balance the wool loss in Scotland, flax-weaving was to be encouraged and state-aided. The Africa Company was to be bought out by London, and the investors repaid. 'That's the money for what we want to do,' Adam said. 'It's the growth from the real beginning. It's not to be thought about as old money come back. It's new money. Say nothing, Willie, when they're arguing over their pots. It's a heated argument this. Heads will be broken, maybe worse.'

The parties in Dundee were the party of linen, the union men, and the party of wool, against union. The badges were a hank of unspun flax and a strip of ploddan cloth. Only the ploddan was worn openly. Wool had the majority, and the lust for violence. The wool men marched in the streets, high burgess, low burgess and unfree marching together. They shouted the bitter slogans of the Scotch. *Wallace and freedom, Knox and his plan, Christ's crown and covenant.* Then after some months a new cry, started by a few, swelled to an ireful roar – *James Stuart, King of the Scotch.*

'Where do you stand on that?' Willie asked his father. 'You fought for him once.'

'For the Stuart? No, Willie. I fought on the side that fought for him. I fought against the town council here, and I'm still fighting against it. They're for Stuart. I'm for whoever the other side are for. It's some old wifie in Germany, I'm told. Here's to her.'

While the Edinburgh parliament talked in the Act of Union, clause by clause, the processions in the burghs shouted for James Stuart. Big lairds and little lairds around Dundee were preparing for the coming of him they called king; Graham of Duntrune, Wedderburn of Blackness;

greater than these, Ogilvie of Airlie and Lyon of Glamis. The signals were ready for the rising, but the Stuart was not. Clause by clause, the Edinburgh parliament talked away its own existence.

The wool mob waited at the tolbooth for the news from Edinburgh. The provost came to them, tore up the Scotch flag and wept into the fragments. Orators sprang to the market cross, and called the crowd to resistance, to war with the southerners if necessary. In their speaking were the arrogance and boastfulness that poverty and inferiority had bred in Scotchmen. The decision, they called, was not one to be made by talk in a parliament, but by fighting. They were savage in their dream killing of southerners. Their oratory made Scotland's history a long series of Bannockburns. The crowd sang the old scurrilous songs about the Dutchman whose name was never mentioned in Scotland, the Dutchman who had usurped the throne of the King of the Scotch, the Stuart. A few flax men sneered. The mob turned from high politics and patriotism to the quarrel of wool and flax in a little town. They pursued the flax men. They shouted for the breaking of flax looms. They ran for axes to smash and torches to burn.

Willie English, with a loaded musket, held off the rioters from the door of the Devint weaving flat. The mob cowered back from the menace of his look, then scattered to seek an easier victim.

'Where's the watch now?' Adam was asking. 'This is a time for the right ones bringing out their burgess watch.'

'I'll bring it out,' Willie said. 'You keep the door with this gun, lest any of that wild lot come back. I'll get the watch out.'

'How?'

'I'll get it out! Never mind how. The bailies are quick enough if there's any threat to themselves.'

Adam, Margriet and Pieter, watching anxiously, saw the sky light up towards the western end of the town. The rioters went streaming along the Seagait, past the end of the close, towards the fire. Willie returned, whistling.

'The watch is out!' he announced. 'The bailies can get it out when one of their own houses is fired by rioters.'

'That's great!' Adam exulted. 'The rioters fired a bailie's house?'

'It's what everybody will say,' Willie said, 'but the fact is that I did it. It was easily done. There was nobody in the house. I just scattered the fire in his grate across the floor. This bailie was one of these thin-end-of-the-wedgers, a good wool party man. He can begin talking now about it being high time to take drastic action against the mob he helped to incite. I don't think there'll be any more trouble for us this night.'

'They lit a fire for her,' Adam said. 'It's right that they should see what fire is.'

Adam had counselled his son, Willie, to bear with Henryson, the flax dealer, but Willie had not the temperament for being meek in face of what he regarded as injustice. Henryson, for his part, saw no injustice in the free receiving their due. Not only the law, but the natural order of life, allowed that a merchant burgess should have his meed, namely the rights of a merchant burgess. What would be the sense of a man being a merchant, with a merchant's booth, with a merchant's liability to be called to the town's service, if a free weaver's unfree hired men could go buying yarn and selling cloth outside the legitimate, and deservedly protected, market for such transactions? The town would speedily become a chaos of dishonest trading and misgovernment, with nobody able to earn a living.

Willie's work for the two weavers remained as before – he brought yarn from Angus and sold linen to traders and shipmasters – but now the spindles and cloth were checked over by Henryson in his booth and a commission paid to him. The work he should have done, of course, was that of importing the spindles to sell to Kydd and of buying cloth direct from Kydd in order to sell it at a profit, but this fine yarn and fine linen business was so small that the commission arrangement, proposed by Adam, was more convenient to Henryson. It was convenient also to Adam and Willie, or it never would have been mooted. Easy money, though Willie made Henryson sweat as much as possible for it. Willie's quick, scornful tongue argued every halfpenny. He never accepted Henryson's count or measure on any deal. He called on passers-by to verify points and to laugh at the fuming dealer. He stopped Henryson in the streets, any time they met, to re-start the latest argument between them. When Henryson came to the weaving flat to complain about the impudent hired man, Kydd, well coached, said that he was pleased to have a servant who looked after his master's business. And Kydd, who liked to talk like a master, would suggest that there were other flax dealers who might like the commissions, and who might also have friends on the council. The threat always quietened Henryson, for he knew that there was no law to uphold his monopoly of these pickings. He did not know that there never would be any intention of putting the threat into effect. Adam and Willie were satisfied to have the routine of their business comparatively undisturbed; another dealer might have been more energetic, and interfered with the Flemings' secrets or Willie's canvassing and yarn collecting. Henryson was a laugh to Willie, as well as being an intolerable grievance. The dealer knew he was a laugh.

Willie filled his spare time, for a year, in the making of more Continental looms. Somebody heard about this, and the Wright trade in a Houff meeting debated whether or not it was allowable for one of the unfree to be engaged by a freeman, Kydd, for such work. Complaint was made by the chartered wrights to the chartered weavers, who, however, retorted that no privilege was infringed by a hired handyman's performing handily. The weavers were upheld when the dispute went to the council, for the weavers were the more important trade with most tolbooth influence. Almost every council sitting had matters of trade and merchandising monopolies to decide; the dyers were wroth against unfree women who took cloth into their homes to colour; two burgess musicians could not obtain engagements because unfree violers and fluters undercut them for weddings; a woman calling herself a mantua-maker was taking the bread out of the mouths of chartered tailors; one who kept a shop was not in the locked book, and should not, therefore, have a shop. The council's decisions in all such cases were for higher against lower, for free against unfree, for merchant against tradesman, for more powerful trade corporation against less powerful.

In accordance with the Act of Union, the Darien losses were repaid. Willie and Adam journeyed together to Edinburgh to receive Adam's own money, and, on behalf of his grand-daughter, Elspet Auchterlonie, the great sum her father had invested. Adam had already urged upon Margriet and Pieter the necessity of teaching their methods to others whom they could employ. He had argued that work for them was not the weaving of linen but the supervision and organization of weavers.

Pieter was of a mind to marry, and, guided by Willie's knowledge of weaving folk, the young Fleming cannily chose a wife from a family with weaving skill and weaving tradition. His wife's close kindred were the weavers whom Pieter and Margriet taught and organized into a larger manufactory, for which the Darien money was the capital, Willie's looms the machines, and Kydd, of course, the announced master. Willie made his home in this new place, a Seagait tenement, and took young Elspet in his charge, but Adam stayed on at the tavern, which would always be a reserve for the family against a failure of the weaving. 'But it won't fail,' Adam said. 'We're to be a power. I can see the day coming now. Don't be too vexing to Henryson, Willie. An ill-chosen word could spoil everything for us. And humour Kydd, for we need him. Keep him in his place, mind, for he's only burgess dirt, but let him dream away about the place being his. In time we'll be able to tramp on Henryson and every other strutting right one.'

Willie's son, young Willie, learned his reading and writing from a backland teaching man. As with his father, the town's grammar school was closed to him. He became an apprentice in the factory, Kydd's apprentice, and the weaver trade accepted him as being taught to succeed Kydd, who, having no sons in the town, could nominate an heir to his place in the locked book. He was a laughing lad, guileless, easy-going for the most part, but quick with his hands – and with his temper at times. No other child was born to Margriet, though she prayed daily for babies to the God of some Flemish protestant sect. She mothered orphan Elspet, and brushed the girl's long, thick, red hair. She was proud of her two, her son and Elspet, as they grew to handsome youth and colourful young womanhood.

The bankrupt council of Dundee pleaded for help from the united parliament. The burgesses could not think of themselves as other than a power. Two centuries ago, less than that, with a thousand spears to be raised in an hour by pealing of the tolbooth bell, Dundee had been a force against the kingdom-shaking families, against the king of the Scotch himself when need be. But the parliament in London, parliament of the new nation of Great Britain, heard the pleas as the grumbles of a little, shabby, declining township. The pleas were unheeded, except that the decaying wool-weaving trade was given the shrouds. By the new rule, the Scotch must be buried in Scotch spun and Scotch woven wool. The politics of Dundee were still the politics of looms. The flax men had lost the shroud-making, and marched protesting. The wool men marched, protesting against the protests of flax. Wool fought flax in the streets. The big lairds and the little lairds around Dundee, Jacobites, sent their reports to France. Dundee would rise, they said, for wool and James Stuart. The town was a town of whispering through the frightened years. In all Scotland, were fear and whispering. Scotland, living on careful half-pennies, feeling its inferiorities, whispered its boasts and its threats.

On an August day in 1714, died one whose death is

recorded in an everlasting jest, Anne Stuart. 'Queen Anne is dead!' people were saying in fear of what would come of her death. The weeks passed, the months, and nothing came. 'Heh, Queen Anne is dead,' was shouted with a laugh, after the Jacobites. The lairds had been ready for their true king, but the Stuart again was not ready.

Wool held the Dundee council. On that day when the word of Anne Stuart's passing came to the town, the council had paced with a lamenting piper to the market cross, and there made the announcement. A strange announcement. The bailie of the day closed his official praise of the dead woman with these words: 'Her many children have died in early life, before her. She has one close relation, her brother.' The provost should then have proclaimed the successor to the throne, but did not do so. He merely said the formal phrase which closed such occasions, but in a voice that was not formal: 'God save the King.'

'Who's the queen's brother?' the youth Willie English asked innocently.

Old Adam swore in his tinkler fashion.

'Her half-brother,' he said. 'Jamie Stuart, and that God saving of the king was for him and for wool. It looks like we're for trouble in this town.'

The German, George I, was crowned in London. At Dundee was no celebration of the event. The council's flag-waving and music-playing were for the commemoration day of the Stuart restoration of 1660. The badge for the day was an oak leaf upon a strip of woollen cloth.

'They must be sure in the tolbooth that the lairds are about to rise,' sixty-three year old Adam said. 'They would never go this length, wee men that they are, if they hadn't been egged to it by big men. They'll be thinking they've got the vennel folks with them in this, but they haven't. The wool folks of the closes have done a bit of shouting for this Jamie Stuart, but shouting is not fighting. I can see a drop for the right ones in this. Ay.'

From the north came news of the rebellion. The dirty folk of the mountains, the savages, the speakers of Irish, were out, under their chiefs. The Aberdeenshire lairds, ever for the Stuarts, were out. Angus was rising, Ogilvie with his Airlie men, Lyon with his tenantry of Glamis, Carnegie with his Southeskers.

In Dundee, one who claimed the banned title of Viscount of Dundee, Graham of Duntrune, mounted to the parapet of the market cross to proclaim James VIII king of the Scotch. The wool burgesses cheered. The flax burgesses crept away, with long faces. The unfree looked on, silent. 'What's wrong with your town, provost?' Graham asked. 'Where is the loyalty you promised, and the force you promised?' From a close on the north side of the Marketgait sounded a hoot of mocking laughter. The council men rushed, and found nobody.

A recruiting procession went through the closes, and the unfree watched from their entries and windows, saying nothing, making no move. Wool men harangued the vennels, and received no response. Wherever the procession stopped for a rallying speech, the laugh was heard and nobody could see who laughed.

A small burgess force marched from the town to join the Stuart army, which had seized Perth, and by holding Perth was holding half of the country. Dundee, with men in the fighting line, waited for news. The army was advancing towards Stirling. By taking Stirling they would take the key to all Scotland. The word came of a skirmish on the old roads of the fights, at Sheriffmuir, north of the Stirling gap. From the Dundee market cross a victory at Sheriffmuir was hailed, and the retreat of the German's supporters to Stirling. The mysterious laugh sounded from a close, and then a disguised voice, made deep and hollow, saying: 'Did you get Stirling? Is it a victory without Stirling? Why did your army go back to Perth?' Again the searchers for the laugher found nobody. In the weeks that followed Sheriffmuir, the laugh went always where the council tried to raise enthusiasm.

Everybody talked about the laugh, and everybody had a guess at the identity of the laugher.

'Willie,' Adam English said, 'stop this caper! You've got them in a state where they'll do something desperate. They know themselves that their rebellion is going badly. Their army has made no progress in two months, and the other side must be taking advantage of the time they've been allowed. They may say as often as they like that the Stuart's coming to Scotland will wake up the whole affair, but they know themselves that they're only saying it to raise their own hopes. There's no need for you to add your wee bit load to what they're carrying. If you want a hit at one or two of them, the time will come, when they know it's all up with them. Then we can both get our smack at the right ones, the burgess crawlers. Have you seen them licking round the lairds and such?'

'I've seen that,' Willie said. 'Can you blame a man for laughing?'

James Stuart rode in the Marketgait, pale, sick, unsmiling. The silent crowd watched. A few were pushing around him, lifting children to put a hand on the black-clad figure on the horse. The sick man looked straight ahead, trying not to see the sores of scrofula. His advisers had told him that this ordeal must be faced. The poor believed that their sores would be healed if they touched a king. Their jostling around him, he was advised, was his acceptance by them as a king.

They were arguing as they jostled. Was this King James a real king? They would soon know. If the sores did not heal, he was no king. Still it was a chance not to be missed. Since he was here, touch him for the sores.

He had ridden in from Glamis that forenoon, with the Earl of Mar on one side of him and the Earl Marischall on the other. A cavalcade of three hundred lords and lairds rode behind, the Angus Jacobites prominent among them, Southesk, Patrick Lyon of Auchterhouse, Stewart of Grandtully, Ogilvie. The sufferers from king's evil had moved at first to touch Ogilvie, one of a family of handsome men, thinking he was the king. The pale Stuart was least like a king of any there. He was the plainest, the weakest-looking, a cold man, shy. He had qualities, but they were not the qualities that could be shown off on horseback in the Marketgait of Dundee.

He turned his horse away, spoke to his earls. They shook their heads. No, it was necessary to remain longer, to be seen by the crowd, to be touched by them. He walked his horse among the little group who jostled each other to gain the touch, and at that moment the laugh sounded. The crowd had been waiting for it, and they laughed too. The lairds glared around, then fixed their glares upon the Dundee provost and bailies. The Stuart stood outside the tolbooth, and his supporters in Dundee formed in a file to kiss his hand. The pale hand stuck out stiffly. He smiled a wan fixed smile. As they kissed, their names were called. The sick man kept his shy gaze fixed. He winced when the laugh came again and was taken up in titters by the mob. He moved angrily towards the house of Stewart of Grandtully, at the head of the Seagait. The crowd, grinning, moved with him. He smiled his smile from a window, bobbing his head. He went from the window, and they drifted away, discussing the laugh.

That night, a January night in 1716, Margriet, clad in her nightgown, came running with Pieter and young Willie to Adam's tavern, fainting with fear. The bailies had arrested Willie, had lifted him from his bed.

'For the laugh?' Adam asked, afraid. They did not know.

Adam and young Willie went to the tolbooth. The bailies refused to allow admittance to the prisoner.

'Affronting us!' they said. 'And insulting the king! It's treason, that's what it is. Affronting us, before Ogilvie and Lyon and everybody. We've got the laugher, and he's not laughing now. It's high time drastic action was taken against disloyal folk such as this one.'

No defence of Willie could be made that would be a

defence to the bailies. All through the night, the white-faced, anxious family sat in the tavern. Adam did not try to comfort Margriet with hopes of a light punishment. He knew the temper of the council men, and the sore injury the laugh had been to their dignity. 'Affronting us!' he could hear the bailies say.

With dawn, Adam and young Willie were back to the tolbooth. Nobody had any time to see them, for the councillors were bustling around the lairds, who were preparing for the Stuart's departure to Perth. The old man and the youth saw the train move off, the pale Stuart and his three hundred. Few people were about to watch, and fewer to cheer. The councillors turned from their bowing and saluting, with set looks on their faces, the looks of men with business to do. 'You can't see him!' one told Adam. He went past, then turned and added: 'It's high time this town was made to feel that this is a serious time. We'll show them, all right. Treason, that's what it was!' He said the word treason, but his expression said: 'Affronting us!'

Young Willie, who had gone home with the little news he had, returned to join his grandfather outside the closed tolbooth door. A crowd gathered, the tidings having spread. Adam's request went back among them, that there be no demonstration, for the council were angered enough already. The folks were orderly, watching the door. The tolbooth porter came out.

'What's doing?' he was asked fifty times as he went among the mob. He went on, shaking his head gravely, but never speaking. He returned with the two town-watchmen and the town-piper. They were heatedly in talk as they approached, but to pass through the watchers at the door, they became silent. The piper nodded a friendly, but solemn, nod to Adam. 'What's doing? For the love of Heaven, piper, what's doing?' Adam asked.

'It's not for me to say, English,' the piper said, uncomfortable, evading the question. 'There's nothing I can do, or I would do it.'

In ten minutes the four town servants emerged, flushed.

'What's doing?' those in the crowd nearest the door asked.

'We're not to be hangmen of a man that only laughed,' the porter declared. 'We've told them that.'

'Hangmen!' Adam cried. 'God, they can't hang him!'

'They say they'll do it,' the porter said. He put out his hands to the crowd to indicate that he and his fellow servants were guiltless. 'They ordered us each in turn to do it, but we're not to do it! We said we were not to do it!' The four men moved into the crowd to hide themselves there, as a procession came from the building.

'You can't hang my son for laughing!' Adam called, holding up the procession's progress. In that moment he remembered words spoken long ago by the Sidlaw sorner, Yeaman: 'the reason for all the laws – to stop folk from laughing at right ones.'

The tolbooth men blinked at the crowd, and consulted together. It had been the intention, obviously, to make the announcement from the market cross, but the crowd was making no move to open a path. Standing at the tolbooth door, the bailie of the day read the formal words. 'So perish all traitors against His Majesty,' he finished. Adam, supported by a friendly arm, looked for a rush by the crowd.

The bailie had also sensed the vennel mood. 'So perish all traitors,' he said, with the official tone gone from his voice now, 'and little chance would any traitor have with the king's army so near at hand. Perth's not so far away, and these wild Irish there. How would you like some of the Irish in among you? Ay, that puts a different face on it, eh?' The foremost of the crowd moved back.

A woman screamed. Margriet came, with young Willie running beside her, tearfully pleading with her. She tottered towards the bailie, and as she reached him fell in a faint upon the cobbles.

'Do you see what you're doing?' Adam said. 'Destroying a family for a laugh or two. You haven't the power to hang, you haven't the power. Your judging can't hang.'

'There's a war,' a councillor replied. 'It's different in war!' They went within. The door opened again, for one councillor to look out at Adam, and say. 'We'll tell you when you can see him.'

Margriet lay in her room in the weaving tenement, looking up from her hurt moaning only when Adam came at intervals with the latest rumours. For three days there was no word of the council putting their sentence into effect. Folks were saying that the council had cooled down from their first anger against Willie. Others were of the view that the tolbooth would have to stand by its judgment, hasty though it was, in order to show no weakening in difficult times. It was said also that nobody could be found to do the hanging, and that the council men had at a meeting all refused to perform as executioners. There was believed to be a strong feeling developing in the tolbooth to let the prisoner off with a beating through the Marketgait. Knowledgeable ones talked about the council being afraid to send to Perth for an army hangman, lest they give the Jacobite lairds more cause for suspicion about the town's attitude to the war. Everybody became certain that the hanging would not take place, then it was learned that a man, muffled in a sack, had sought out the bailies to volunteer as hangman. 'They'll do it now,' the knowing argument went. 'They've got no excuse now for going back on their judgment. They were hoping nobody would be found to do the hanging, and now this one in the bag has turned up, and they can't get past their decision: They'll hang Willie English to show firmness, because they've got a proclamation from Perth that will need firmness to read to the town, the calling out of a levy for the Stuart.'

The family were allowed to see Willie. Margriet was carried to him in a litter. They returned to the weaving tenement, not one of them, not even Adam, able to face Willie's end. They waited. The town's noises hushed except for the shuffle of feet that went past in the Seagait, always to the west to the Marketgait. The town was deadly quiet for a little. The feet came back, and awed voices. For an hour there was only the sound of awed voices in the street, then children played again, laughed, looms clacked, the hooves of pack-horses rattled on the stones.

'They told me we would not even get him to bury,' Adam said.

The Duke of Argyll advanced northwards from Stirling, with his reinforcements, through the country the Stuart's retreating army had devastated. The king of a dream fled from Perth, through Dundee, with barely a pause there. The scrofulous of the back vennels did not jostle around the pale, shy, black-clad man. They knew from the unimproved condition of their necks that this was no king. There was no file of wool men to kiss the pallid hand. Old Adam English, stooped, weary-looking, eyed the reduced train that rode behind the Stuart's carriage, forty men not three hundred.

'They hanged Willie for laughing at that,' Adam said. 'I wonder who they got to do it. A Dundee man hanged a Dundee man for laughing at that.'

Young Willie looked up, sharply, from his grief, and the Englishes' hate came into his face. He thought of his mother who never spoke, but would only moan and put her hand to her neck.

The flax men wore their hanks of unspun flax, at last. They watched the wool men fleeing before the invasion of Argyll's Dutchmen. Families that were as old as the stones of Dundee were leaving Dundee, some for ever, with their possessions tied together. Wool was their cause in the argument of the looms of a little, dirty town of four thousand people. Flax had won in a battle of dynasties, of world movements, a battle for which both sides claimed the victory and from which both sides ran away.

In the back vennel taverns, the drinks for knowing men were free-trade rum and free-trade gin. The sign for gin was a swift upward display of the right thumb, for rum forefinger and large finger raised together, old witchery symbols. The names for the drinks, when they were named, were 'Nicol's one' and 'Nicol's two'. They induced the proper atmosphere of argument or merriment in less time and at less cost than did the ale that had been Scotland's main drink until the Union. Unlike the ale, they benefited the exchequer not a whit, the London exchequer which, according to the tavern talk, robbed Scotland to pay England's debts. Nicol's one and Nicol's two were suitable drinks, therefore, for the poor and patriotic Scotch. Nicol was one of whom to approve, Nicol the free-trader, or, as he was known to the tax-collectors, Nicol the smuggler.

On the free-trade road – which was no road, but the easy route, over the ridges and round the knolls, between Barry on the coast and Forfar town in the heart of Angus – young Willie English met Nicol whom few had met, but about whom many talked. For nearly three years, Willie had been doing the tasks that had formerly been done by his father, the rounds of the Angus spinners and the canvassing for orders, as well as his own weaving work, in which he was now of full journeyman ranking.

Nicol watched the young man who came towards him on horseback with a pack-horse in trail.

'Heh, lad!' Nicol called. 'Does your name happen to be English?'

'Ay, it's that,' Willie said.

'Man, you've got the same look and the same nose as old Adam English, the taverner of Seagait. And you've got the same laugh, now that you laugh. You'll be kin to him?' Nicol knew well who Willie was. Old Adam was one of the smuggler's agents in the town, and Nicol who had watched the young man often enough in Angus, without being seen himself, had communicated to the old man that Willie would be useful to the free-traders, and earn money by being useful. Adam had said that he would not care about arranging a matter like that with his grandson, but he had given permission for Nicol's doing his own approaching.

'I'm the grandson of old Adam,' Willie said to the smuggler. 'If you're his friend, you're mine. What's your name?'

'It's a known name to you, though my face is maybe not known. You'll have heard my name.' Nicol's thumb was thrust up suddenly, then his fingers made a V. He watched Willie closely as he made the signs.

'Ay, I take a drink when I get one offered,' Willie said. 'I'll take Nicol's two.' He made the sign for rum. Nicol produced a bottle, and offered it. 'Here's to you, and here's no tax to pay the Englishmen's debts,' Willie toasted, and swallowed a mouthful. 'I would have drunk to you by your name if you'd told me it.'

Nicol laughed loudly. He was a ruddy, hearty man, loud in his laughter. He made the signs again. 'I'm not offering you a drink this time, for you can have all you want without a second offer,' he said. Again he made the signs. 'D'you understand?'

'Man, are you Nicol?'

The smuggler examined Willie's smile for a moment, then turned towards a broom thicket. 'You can come out,' he called. Five men crawled from the bushes, dragging after them little pack-donkeys.

'I'm no more in favour of tax-collectors than is the next man you'll meet,' Willie said.

'That's what I wanted to be sure about,' Nicol said. 'I can see by your face how you stand. This is a trade that does a lot of ill to one or two merchants and masters in Dundee, the kind your grandfather calls the right ones. He was telling me that your rounds in the country made you handy for a bit of free-trading, but I little expected to meet you so soon. It would please the old man if you gave some of these right ones a bit knock, now and then.'

They all drank together, and laughed together. When they parted Willie was sworn to the smuggler. The next meeting, place and time, was arranged. Nicol, looking after the young man, did not think of himself as one who had inveigled an innocent youth into crime. He had used a little guile to engage a useful assistant, one who travelled about the country with pack-horses. Nicol was no criminal, in his own view. He was a free-trader with a business that had to keep to the less-used ways because of stupid restrictions. Willie English, riding away with a keg of gin, consigned to a Dundee tavern, did not think of what he was doing as law-breaking. All the good-fellows were free-trading in one way or another, directly or indirectly. Even the kirk ministers, it was said, showed a knowledge, smilingly hemming and hawing, of where to purchase free-trade goods.

In a month, Willie was trailing three pack-horses up from the Barry coast, an established man in the trade that he had added to his collecting of yarn. The new work did not interfere with his flax work. It was on his way, money for nothing, and those easy coins went into the chest, the growth of the power. At times Willie had the laughing mis-chievousness of his father, but not often. He was a straight-faced young man for the most part, sometimes more deter-minedly straight-faced than one of his age should be, when he looked on his mother, a failing woman, who would often sit down by her loom, her face drawn and pallid, mumbling, her hands pulling at her throat as though to unloosen a rope. As he went in the streets after witnessing one of these sudden turns his mother took, he would eye the mounting blocks outside the tolbooth, called the gallow steps because for hangings the blocks made a support for the scaffold platform. As he passed Henryson's booth, or did business with Hen-ryson, he watched the dealer, and saw him flinch from the steady stare. Here was one who had hated the first Willie. But whenever young Willie spoke to old Adam about the possibility of Henryson's being that hangman, the old man said he could not think so.

Three months after the hanging, old Adam and his grand-son had gone along to stand outside the churches, and see a new excitement, an election of a council by all the free, an event that had not been for two hundred and fifty years. Each council, in all that time, had chosen its successor, but with the wool men fled or in prison, there was no council to do a choosing, and the London government had ordered a vote. The free came to the kirkyard with their burgess tickets pinned to their broad bonnets, the shopkeepers, the tradesmen, with here and there a lairdling of some nearby estate, who, having a hat instead of a bonnet, required no other distinction from the unfree and did not show his ticket. The unfree looked on, and, as always when they looked at the occasions of the free, they found causes for laughs, this shopkeeper's fatness, that dyer's squint, a lairdling's bow-legs. The names of the new councillors were called, and the last name on the list was the name Henryson.

'Him!' Adam sneered. 'Henryson on the council! There's been many a fool there, but surely never a fool as foolish as that.'

'Henryson!' young Willie said. 'If there was anybody in the town who was pleased that day when my father died, it would be him. Some Dundee man hanged another Dundee man for laughing. It wasn't anybody on the council then for the crowd counted every councillor lined up. It would be right enough what the old councillors said – that the hanger came to them, muffled up in a bag, to say he would do it.'

Old Adam had put his hand, then, on the youth's shoulder. 'Don't be thinking of anything rash, lad!' he said. 'Don't be doing anything that will hinder the power growing.' Then, as Willie still watched Henryson, the grandfather had said: 'It wouldn't be him. You can be sure of that!' But since then, Willie had always glowered at Henryson, an accusing glower, from which the dealer had turned. Every so often, during three years, old Adam had warned Willie to be cautious, and had repeated that Henryson could not have been the hanger. Since then, Henryson had remained a councillor. After that one election by the burgesses, the normal manner of choosing the council had returned, each council selecting its successor, with the result that there was no great change in the membership from year to year.

A crowd gathered to shake their fists at the tolbooth on a spring day in 1719, no novelty in the town's history, but this time having its novel feature in that a number of higher and lower burgesses were shouting with the unfree. The council had been so unpatriotic, so renegade, as to appeal to the London parliament for action against the smugglers along the shores of the Tay estuary. The mob were in a killing mood. Then whispers went through the mob, and the mob laughed. What had been whispered was readily believable and natural. The council's plea to parliament did not have the purpose of harming free-trade, and could scarcely have such an effect. Its purpose was to remove from office the present tax commissioner. He had irritated tax-payers, such people as formed the council. His London voice had read at them long London treasury regulations, which were his only law. Even after eleven years of officials and officialese, the tax-paying Scotch thought with regret of their old tavern-bargaining with tax-farmers who had no tax-collecting jargon to deave the taxed and no absurd birch faggots in which to cut notches. They did not hope that they would be sent one of the old kind of taxman. That was beyond hope. They only hoped that they would be rid of him whom they had now, rid of the gap in his teeth where the long words of the rules bubbled and seethed, rid of the air of patient superiority, rid of the final decisive rolling up of the scroll from which he interminably quoted.

Shenston, his name was, an unhappy man, who wept for his far-away home when he was alone, then braced himself to his duty of trying to make himself understood to these strangely aggressive people. He and his kind were making two traditions: one for Scotland, dislike of departmentalism; one for the more serious-minded lower gentry of southern English, exacting attention to uninspiring tasks in the less grateful parts of the earth.

Shenston understood the council's complaint to be an indication that he would have their encouragement, and protection in direct measure against the free-traders. He and his staff, unarmed clerks, surprised a smugglers' landing on the Broughty sands. The smugglers ran, astonished rather than afraid. In the Cowgait, which for seventy years had been neither town nor fields, the pursued, recovered now from the first shock, laid an ambush. Harmless wrestling ensued, while some of the free-traders returned to Broughty to shoo away the single guard left by Shenston at the beached boat. The unfortunate tax-collector had raised a new storm. He had, the magistrates said, usurped the watch powers of the council. The Cowgait was within the burgh bounds, a royal burgh's bounds. The Englishman did not understand. Nor did he understand when a zealous majordomo at Dudhope Castle solemnly marched some armed servants through the streets to indicate that the ancient feudal rights of his master, Lord Douglas, as town constable, were being upheld against the council and the revenue officials. Both the council and Lord Douglas were now complaining to London about Shenston, and his departure was made certain. The town, free and unfree, celebrated the victory by drinking Nicol's one and Nicol's two and the barley whisky from the illicit stills of Glenisla in north Angus.

Shenston went south, glad to be going home. A wit became tax-collector in Dundee. It so happened, in an era of parliamentary corruption, that Dundee's plaint had arrived timeously. Consideration was being given to a minor problem of nepotism. A politician, a good party man, had been suggesting that the government find some office for his illegitimate son. He preferred that the office be far from London, for the young man was given to wildnesses. The Dundee post was of the correct degree of unimportance, and suitably remote. The wit, Joseph Digby by name, was to play an important part in the history of the Englishes of Dundee.

Willie met him in a strange place to find a revenue-man, the smuggler's headquarters at Barry, among a waste of sand dunes. Digby and Nicol were laughing together when Willie came.

'You'll have seen him about the town,' Nicol said when he introduced them.

'Ay, I've seen him around the last week or two,' Willie gasped weakly.

'Him and me have just been arranging things,' Nicol said. 'Every now and then he'll seize a keg or two of our stuff so that he can put it in his report, you understand. It'll save us and him a deal of worry to have things arranged between us.'

They sat talking. The Englishman was a master raconteur of London anecdotes.

'That's a lad for you,' Nicol said, when the tax-collector had been shown out by a way that even Nicol's men did not know.

'How did you get to be arranging things with him?' Willie asked.

'Nothing that I did. He came, looking for me on that bit of the shore where I go to sit by myself. That lad finds his own way about. I knew from the first word he spoke that he was all right, if that's what's worrying you. I'm not daft. I know a man quick. I have to. There's some other bits of the arrangement with him that I didn't mention to you when you came in. I've got him on the tape just the way he has me. He's got customers for us that we couldn't get ourselves, folk who want these French wines. There's money in these wines, Willie, but they're not easy to get away unless you've got somebody like this tax-collector. He's all right! Did you ever hear anything as funny as his story about the bishop's wife? And what a way he has of telling it.' Nicol laughed uproariously as he went over the story in his mind.

'Ay, a good lad right enough,' Willie said. Thinking of the bishop's wife, he laughed with Nicol.

Young Willie and Digby could not be friends openly, before the curious stares of a small town – a gentleman, as the exciseman was reputed to be, and a taverner's grandson, one of the unfree. Digby slipped round in the dark to the house above the tavern to laugh and daff with Willie and old Adam. Elspet Auchterlonie, now the old man's housekeeper, combed her lovely hair for his visits, and put on her coloured dress and the little silk shawl, said by those who saw it to be unduly gay and flaunting.

The old taverner said of Digby that this was a man after his own heart. The wit had a lively contempt for the Dundee burgesses with whom he dealt, and the old man relished it. Digby's own conversation was only jokes, but he listened carefully to the old man's love of the town and hate for the town, nodding. Digby was nodding to his own noting of points for the writing he did, at times, for the London journals. Old Adam took the nods to be of sympathy and support for himself.

'That's a good fellow, right enough,' the grandfather told his grandson. 'He knows things, that one. I've heard it said that he's doing well in his work. He can twist these right ones round his wee finger, but they don't see it that way. A smart fellow!'

Old Adam, crossing the Marketgait, watched the manner of walking of one who approached from the other direction, and turned to look when the man had passed. The man had stopped, was looking at Adam.

'It's not you, John?' Adam said.

'Ay, it's John,' the other said. 'Is it really you, father?' He hesitated on the word father.

'Ay,' Adam said, 'it's me. So you're back to the town. You said you would come back.' He saw a burly, middle-aged man, with a craft burgess appearance to him, a successful enough man. 'I'm glad to see you, John. I thought I had no sons.' To John's inquiring look, he answered that the eldest, Adam, was twenty years dead in Darien and Willie three years dead. The old man's stare was on John's face when Willie was mentioned. John did not speak, nor did he show any change of expression. To his news, old Adam added the long-ago death of Elspet.

'I'm sorry to hear of my brother's death, and my sister's death,' John said. After a long interval he added: 'I'm sorry to hear of Willie's death.' He looked with pity at the stooped old figure, shrunken into itself. 'Bygones are bygones,' he said. 'I'll be coming to see you, father. I'm back to stay here. I'm back to get what I couldn't get here before. Maybe I haven't brought what's needed, but maybe what I get here will help in getting what's needed.'

John, a childless widower, was a known man in his mason

trade. He had avoided work in the burghs where he could be only a hired man, he told his father when he came to the tavern. He had become a master in country building, around Glasgow. He was now living with the Dundee mason Cant, and taking Cant's hire. 'Only for a little time,' he said, and laughed in his quiet way. He did not explain further.

'He does well for himself in seeking work there,' Adam said when his son had left. 'Cant's old and has no sons to succeed him. That daughter of his would just be right for John. She's not bonnie in the face, but she's shapely enough, and sore needing a man at thirty-five or so.'

'I can tell you,' Elspet said, 'that it's nearer a match than you think. My uncle John is a man to look at, now that he's come to be seen in Dundee, and still with some of the red in his hair. You didn't know, did you, that Cant met John in a working they did together along the Carse of Gowrie, and brought him to Dundee as a successor in the yard and a husband for Kate? You didn't know, did you, that your John is known for his fancy masoning that he learned in Glasgow? It was that took him to the Carse for work on some big laird's house. I heard talk about it, at the well.'

Two months later John English was wed to Katherine Cant. The bride's old father asked in his own house for only a corner to dream in, and John was master. The house was in Saint Salvador's close on the north side of the Overgait near to the junction with Marketgait, an admired house, entirely of stone, built by Cant's great grandfather, first deacon of the craft when the masons received their guildry-pendicle charter a hundred years before. John, in the right of his wife, was entered in the locked book.

'So you're the first,' Adam said. 'Well, you or yours may be the power. There's no saying. You're not to be one of the right ones, surely, John?'

'I'll never be that,' John answered, his brows lowering. 'I'm a known mason, but I can only be a master here because of my wife. The right ones of Dundee and their right rules have changed little. It will soon be young Willie's turn to be put in the book. I hope he's not to be a right one either.'

'There's no fear about that,' old Adam said. 'When I look at you again, John, I can see there's no more fear of you being a right one than there is of young Willie. The Englishes don't become right! John, we've struggled out of the dirt. We're rising to be a power. An English is free, and soon another will be free. I've seen the rise. We'll mind that we're not right ones. We'll mind to mislike them.'

Joseph Digby, signing himself *Polaris*, contributing his occasional essays to the London journals, wrote about Dundee without ever stating in his writing that his subject was Dundee. He told nobody in the town about his writing, probably because his essays were of a kind that would have roused wrath had he called attention to them. He had a quick, observing eye, but wrote only to provoke a smile or raise a curious eyebrow in the London coffee houses. These were words of his:

'A carriage has never been seen for there are no roads by which one could come to my diseased, dirty, drunken burgh. The entry of a farm cart, even, is an event attended by a flock of urchins, loudly proclaiming their wonder, particularly so if the wheels be round. (Pray, *Polaris,* is it suggested that among your remote barbarians there are wheels other than circular in shape? It is replied that with a straw picked up in the market way, where lies a litter of straw, the ellipticity of the cart wheels had been measured, amid the curious interest of a large gathering, when a difference of one hand was found between length and breadth.) A farm cart's manner of movement is as limping as is that of those verses which T. ... C. ... in the fever of creation takes to be iambic pentameters. Wooden planks crudely attached to one another are trimmed to a shape roughly rounded, and wear along the grain; which statement is an explanation of the former phenomenon, a Scotch cart's bumpiness, and might be material for a metaphorical reason for the latter, a certain unsteadiness in a London dunce's lines.'

In the same facetious manner, he discussed the witches of the town. Each vennel had its seer or spirit-raiser or herbalist healer, never a skinny hag, always excessively corpulent and hearty. He noticed the custom whereby one called on a neighbour in passing to ask if he wanted anything carried. In the absence of wheeled transport an immense amount of manual labour was necessary, and by this habit it was performed gratis. A mason's stones were conveyed singly by such aid to his building site, and there deposited. A walk was not to be wasted. The provost, himself, on his way to the tolbooth would move a balk of lumber from a wright's shop to where it was wanted, or deliver an errand for a booth-keeper.

In the graveyard, the scabby brats of the vennels puzzled out the tombstone inscriptions, argued and fought over a pronunciation. Learning to read was an exciting game for the children. The walls bore the scrapes and scars of their efforts at writing. Here was a distinguishing feature of these Scotch among whom *Polaris* found himself, their desire for education. He attributed it to the Scotch poor's excessive envy of their betters.

The backward agricultural methods were seen by him, the treelessness, the run-riggs, the crude implements, the cows yoked to the ploughs. He wrote about a strange epidemic of broom. There was a belief that the broom had first come as seed on the hooves of Claverhouse's horses. The older people swore that, before 1689, none had grown in the countryside. Now it covered the knolls and ridges, and in the tax collector's first year in Dundee, the land tillers were in a panic about the amazing rapidity of the broom's growth into their strips. The winter had been mild and the broom had not ceased its growth for twelve months on end. The country folk expected a poor harvest because of the broom and the cold early summer that followed the warm winter. In Dundee the talk was of a short corn year. Faces were grave. The tax-collector's writing shows that he realized he was to see tragedy, but even in that essay he maintained his lightness of treatment. The Englishes provided him with much of his material, unaware that they were doing so. He was following what they said, and also what they left unsaid, more closely than they knew.

Willie English came before the council to be examined for his burgess ticket, as Kydd's apprentice and successor, a routine matter for the chartered weaver trade had, long ago, allowed the nomination. The council were dealing with Willie in the ordinary way of such business, when Henryson spoke: 'There's one thing. We know what this young man's father was. It's no light thing to make a man a freeman of Dundee. We have to watch out that those who get the privilege are worthy of it. You know what happened to his father in the end.'

'What happened to my father was that he was loyal to the town and the king,' Willie snapped, 'and he was hanged for laughing at those who were disloyal.'

'A hanging is a hanging,' Henryson began, and stopped, turning from Willie's stare, frightened.

'It wasn't a thing to be held against the family,' the provost said, frowning at Henryson. 'I see nothing in that but what's in this young man's favour.' The councillors nodded, and Willie was made a trade burgess.

He related the incident to his grandfather.

'It was Henryson who was the hanger. I know it,' he declared. 'He's got it on his mind. He couldn't keep his mouth shut about it, there, in the council. He did it, he did it.'

'No,' the old man said. 'It wasn't Henryson. Willie, you've got your ticket now, and we can grow without any chance of being stopped. Don't throw away the chance you've got just because Henryson can't meet your look. I tell you, it wasn't Henryson. I'm sure of that.'

Working at her loom, Willie's mother dropped, gasping,

her hand at her throat. She was dead when her son lifted her.

'That hanger hanged two, my father and my mother,' Willie said after the funeral. 'It was Henryson! I know it!'

'No, lad,' his grandfather soothed him. 'It wasn't him. Try to forget it, Willie. Your mother is better away. It has been no life for her since he went.'

In the first week of November, as always, was the choosing of the council. The names were called at the cross. Old Adam heard Henryson called as one of the new magistrates, a bailie. 'They're surely hard stuck for bailies in this town when he's one,' the old man said. As he went home he thought of something. He stopped in the street, startled by his thought.

'Willie,' he asked that night, 'if you were to find out who hanged your father, what would you do?'

'In my first kirk-going after I was given my ticket,' Willie said, 'I heard words about an eye for an eye and a tooth for a tooth, and I've minded them. It would be a life for a life.'

The old man was silent for a time, then spoke:

'I've seen five or six of my mother's foretellings come true. I've seen one come true about the blood, the one about the beginning of the power being in stone and water. When the Darien money seemed to be lost, I began again to build up the power, and the beginning was all money from the stone and water. The first beginning hadn't really been, and I made a mistake in telling myself that it had.'

Willie waited, impatient, while his grandfather walked, excited and yet hesitant, about the room.

'I've thought of another of the foreseeings,' the old man went on, 'as something that was to happen when we came to power, but I'm wondering if it isn't to happen, will have to happen, before we grow.'

'What foreseeing is that?'

'The blood will put a rope round a bailie's neck. Willie, Henryson is a bailie now.'

'He is!'

'He is, and — Willie, Henryson was the hanger, right enough. I've always known he was.'

'A hanging for a hanging,' Willie said.

'It's not to stop us growing, Willie. Mind. It has to be done, but it should be done in a way that nobody will ever find out who did it.'

'I'll wait for a time to do it!' Willie declared.

The harbour labourers gathered in twos and threes to show each other handfuls of oats. They became one group to howl. They marched in a body from their work. Through Tyndall's Wynd they shouted, in the Marketgait, outside the tolbooth. They marched in the Overgait, the Moraygait, the Nethergait, the Wellgait, the Seagait, up the steep Hilltown, everywhere shouting. They dispersed into the closes to shout. The back vennel folks looked from their windows to hear the shouts of the harbour labourers. The town servants were running to summon the bailies and councillors from their booths. The tolbooth bell was ringing the call for a muster of the whole watch, all the able-bodied burgesses. The vennels were rising to riot!

The harbour labourers had seen that the cargo they were to load on a ship was oats. Starvation was coming to the town, and yet a part of the precious harvest was consigned for export! From the closes, men raced with sticks and axes and knives in their hands. The little mobs formed a great mob in the Marketgait.

'Get the ministers to quieten them!' the councillors were saying in their meeting. 'No, get Lord Douglas's men out. They're armed. Whose cargo is it? Let the council take it over for the town. In the name of God, somebody do something. Talk'll not stop that! They're breaking down the booths and the houses of the grain merchants.'

The shrieking and wrecking were stilled by a suggestion that passed through the mob. The oats, get the oats! From Tyndall's Wynd and the Couttie's Wynd, they poured upon the quay head. Men hefted sacks and baskets of the grain. Women pulled up their overskirts to hold grain. The children snatched up handfuls. Frightened, no longer a mob but individuals, the black vennel folks scampered to hide their gains, then a mob again, for safety, they gathered to shout scurrilities but not hate at the tolbooth. They marched, singing, through the streets, past destroyed booths, damaged buildings. In the Horse Wynd, where higher burgesses dwelt, they came in the moonlight upon a sight that caused them to scamper again. A man was hanging by the neck from a rope attached to the rail of an outside stair. The stair wall down which he hung was marked by his feet as he had struggled in his death convulsions. They recognized him, before they ran in fear to their homes, as the flax-dealer Henryson, the new bailie.

THE PILLARS OF THE TOWNHOUSE

In the hungry spring of 1720, within sound of the keening for the black vennel dead, John English's first child was born, a mis-shapen girl, short-necked, dwarfish, a hunchback. Her grandfather blinked at the distorted little body and at the weeping mother. 'This one is the blood,' he said. 'It may be this one that will be the power, or the means for the power to come. Nobody can tell.'

From her first weeks, the infant, named Katherine, had the Englishes' red hair, bright red hair upon a baby's head. The old man compared the colour and the texture with Elspet Renkyne's hair. 'The same hair,' he said, 'the same as I had. This one will mind, if nobody else does.'

The hunchback was to do her grandfather's hating and hoping when he was dead, to live long through an era of change, directing the course of the Englishes. When, nearly two centuries after, the family anecdotes were dictated into a London investment company's ledger, the incidents that occurred in Katherine's childhood were related as the influences upon her early years, rather than as the circumstances in her father's life, her cousins' lives, Pieter Devint's life, and the lives of the others of that time.

Two years and two months after her birth, when old Adam was a week past seventy, John's second was born, named John, a straight, strong infant, remarkable for his quiet placidity, whereas his twisted sister was always fretful and insistent with everyone except her grandfather. John and his wife were well pleased with their son, and ashamed to own the hunchback whose hair was an added ugliness. Red hair can be beautiful and can be ugly. Little Katherine was quick to speak and quick to walk, but her speech was a grating shrillness and her gait a stumbling waddle, painful to watch. The mother was proud to display the plump, smiling boy baby, but never was seen outside the house with the girl. Old Adam would take Katherine's hand to the mouth of St. Salvador's close, and out into the Overgait, where passers-by stared at the freakish child. He would carry her when she tired. She watched at the window for his coming from the tavern, in the slack afternoons when he could shut his door and visit his grandchildren. She was excited when he plodded into sight, the one person who gave her a ready smile, who would go into the streets with her. 'A quick bairn,' he said. 'I've never seen a quicker.' When he praised her, he did not qualify the praise with pity, as others did.

She liked to hear the clacking of the looms in the Seagait weaving tenement, and to see the miracle by which threads became cloth. Her grandfather made a miniature distaff to be attached to her apron string, and marvelled at her infant's attempt to spin, exhibiting her yarn to the weavers. The future was being shaped for the family by her mother's weeping ashamedness, her father's pained indifference, her grandfather's pride in her quickness to learn, his admiration for her imitation of a spinner's actions.

Two bailies, with men of the watch, came to the linen manufactory for Willie English. They said that the constable of Dundee, Lord Douglas of Dudhope Castle, wanted him.

'It's a great honour for a weaver to be wanted to speak to the constable,' Old Adam mumbled, playing at being a senile, flustered ancient. 'It's a great honour. But he's away to Coupar Angus and then down to the Carse of Gowrie. He'll be coming over the Hawk Hill before the gloaming, in at the West Port. You could meet him there, if that's not over late for the laird.' As he spoke, he cuddled the hunchback child tightly against his breast. 'Pieter,' he called, 'here's the bailies come to say that the constable wants to have a word with our Willie. I've just been saying that he'll be coming in at the West Port before the day's out.' The child felt the tenseness of his grip about her shoulders.

When the magistrates had gone, the weaving folks gathered, afraid, around the old man. 'Listen to this,' he told them. 'None of you will say to a soul that Willie comes in from Barry this day, by the Seagait.'

He peeped from a window into the street. The bailies were gone, but two of the town servants were standing in an entry on the opposite side of the street, their eyes on the weaving tenement.

'It looks to me that any of us, trying to get the word to Willie, will be watched. Go on with your work, and don't let on that you think this is serious. If they come again, none of you know which way is Willie's way. Tell them I know, and that if I said the West Port then West Port it will be. I'll be doing what's needed. I've been hunted by the watchers, myself. None of mine will be hunted as I was, not if I can help it.' To the anxious questions, he replied that a harmless bit of free-trading, done by Willie to oblige a man, might be the reason for the bailies' visit.

He and little Katherine walked hand in hand to the tavern, at the slow pace of an aged man and a hunchback child. He talked and laughed as they moved, nodded affably to the watchers. When he and the child had walked a little way they turned to look at that kind of nothing which old men and little girls examine closely. A watcher, following them, had no time to dodge out of sight and had to loiter past.

'I was just saying that this mark in the road is like a horse's head,' the old man drooled. 'And wee Katie, here, was saying it was more like the turret of Monck's lodging in the Marketgait. What would you say, mannie?'

'Ay, it's like the turret,' the watcher said, sheepishly 'Like a horse's head, too, when you look at it.'

Old Adam went on, slowing his pace to discommode the town servant. Outside the tavern, two of the constable's men were chatting, obviously watchers, making a poor pretence of not being watchers. 'Were you waiting for me to open the door?' the old man asked. 'I'm getting done, and I take an hour or two off in the afternoon. You would be better to go elsewhere for your drink this day, for I'll not be opening for a bit yet.'

Elspet Auchterlonie was pale and flustered. The bailies had been at the tavern before going on to the manufactory.

'What do they want Willie for?' she asked. 'Is it his free-trading?'

'Two bailies and the watchers. It might only be the free-trading, and the right ones' pomp in doing a laird's bidding. But I scarcely think so. They wouldn't be posting their watchers for that. Elspet, there's something you don't know that they might be getting after Willie for. We've got to see that the family and the growing power are not broken by them. We've got to see, forbye, that Willie isn't hunted.' He lifted the child and looked into her eyes. 'Katie, you know Dave Whittet, the mannie with the ale-house like this, round in the next close? You could go to him, couldn't you? Ay, I knew you could, you clever bairn.'

The child who saw the incidents of that day, without comprehending them then, had as her most vivid recollection, a long lifetime later, Elspet's frantic search for writing materials and experiments in writing. On a square of linen, the woman wrote with a burnt stick, folded the cloth, shook it, unfolded it, scrutinized the words. 'Nobody could read that,' she said. 'What will we do?'

'Wee Katie will have to speak the message. You could do that, my quick lassie, couldn't you? Listen. You'll go out, and you'll play in the close, and then you'll go to Dave

Whittet and you'll tell him to get word to Willie, on the way from Barry, that he's not to come into the town, because the bailies are wanting him.'

On the tavern floor the child rehearsed her going out, her playing, her moving to Whittet's ale-house, her delivering the message. Her grandfather was satisfied at last. 'Off you go, my clever wee Katie,' he said.

The watchers gave no heed to the four-year-old child in her coming and her going.

'Now, you'll just tell me what you told Dave Whittet,' her grandfather said when she returned. He cuddled her when she repeated the words and what Whittet had said. 'My own clever bairn,' he said. 'You'll say nothing about this to anybody, Katie. Mind.' He took the child by the hand to the mouth of St. Salvador's close, a watcher following. The old man did not go to John's house. He was making sure that the watcher could report that there had been no communication between the watched and anybody else. When he returned to the Seagait close, a bailie was there to say that the tavern was to remain shut all that day. 'They've got their tolbooth faces on, and they're talking with their tolbooth voices and their tolbooth words,' old Adam said when the magistrate had gone.

After curfew, the same bailie came to the door. 'Your grandson hasn't come in at the West Port yet,' he said.

'No, he's not back yet. At times, he takes a day or two more than usual for his rounds. It's a pity he should be away when the laird of Dudhope wants to speak to him.'

Next morning when Elspet and the serving woman went to the well, a watcher walked near them, and stood beside them while they drew water. 'Ay, I know what it's all about,' the old man told Elspet when she returned, frightened. 'I'm wondering how they know, the constable and the wee right ones. How could they have found out, after nearly five years?'

The bailies and the Dudhope men kept their guard upon the tavern for two more days, then the old man was taken to the constable's courthouse, upon the castle rock. Douglas himself was there. Old Adam noted the constable's quickness of speech and movement, his eagerness, the absence from his expression and bearing of any pompous solemnity, not a right one's slow words, nor a right one's look of rightness.

'Read him the account!' Douglas said.

A lawyer-like man read from a journal, and Douglas watched Adam English. 'It was a funny-like story,' the old man said later. 'It was twisted up and laughing, but it was how my son Willie was hanged by a man with a bag over his face. It mentioned no names, and had no word of where it happened, but it was Dundee – you could see that – and it was Willie and Henryson. It went on to tell how the hanger was hanged, and it was young Willie that was in the story, hanging Henryson. It was all told for a laugh. When it was finished the constable was still watching me, and I let him watch. After a bit, he asked if I had understood the account. I said that I had, and it was a story about a hanger being hanged, and that a hanging wasn't to be laughed at. I said that a son of mine had been hanged, and my son's hanging had been something like the hanging in the story, and I didn't like to be reminded. I went on about my son being loyal to the king – their kind of talk – and that he had been hanged by those who weren't loyal, and some very near in blood to those disloyal ones were still in the town, and in high positions. That set two of the bailies thinking about themselves instead of about me. All the time I was the old dodderer. Nobody can answer a dodderer. I never once mentioned the second bit of the story, but doddered and doddered about the first bit. Douglas stopped watching me, and while I sat there he talked to the bailies. He thought I was too done and daft to follow his talk. He said that he had seen the journal story in London, and had been struck with the likeness to Dundee and the two Dundee hangings, Willie's and Henryson's. When the printer of the journal told him that the author of the story knew Dundee well, he had thought the coincidence was worth following. He was pleased with his own cleverness, was Douglas of Dudhope. He had no other interest in the matter but in being clever. The bailies had on their flattering faces, for a laird, and were not understanding him aright. Cleverness of that kind was beyond the wee right ones. I heard Douglas say that the old man, clearly, had no hand in it, but that the hue and cry was out for young Willie all over Angus. I felt sure that he had more than a coincidence to go by, but he didn't tell the bailies what proof he had, not while I was there. I don't think he ever told them.'

With his clever smile, Lord Douglas ordered old Adam to bring whatever word came of Willie. The old man nodded, doddering. A week after that, with two men from Nicol's place at Barry, he climbed the long slope to Dudhope Castle to tell the constable that Willie was lost in a bog on the way from Coupar Angus to the Carse. These two were the witnesses, pack-horse men, who had seen, in the distance, a man fall from a Sidlaw trail. They had reached the spot in time to save the man's horses, loaded with flax yarn and scutched flax, and had ever since been trying to trace the owner. No, there was not a doubt that the man had been drowned. 'A clever one, he was easy to fool,' old Adam said, speaking years later about that interview. 'He thought nobody but himself could be clever.' The three next went to the tol-booth, where the old man, mumbling distractedly, estab-lished the Seagait manufactory's right to the flax and the horses. 'They were easy to fool because they thought they were clever,' Adam said. 'They could never imagine that the unfree would be able to fool them. Their judging about the horses needed a great putting on of tolbooth looks and a great speaking of tolbooth talk. Men who have these faces and talk that way, have their eyes looking the wrong road, into them-selves instead of out at others.'

Only the taverner Whittet and a few of the Barry smugglers were in the secret of what had happened to Willie English. Elspet Auchterlonie and the folks of the weaving tenement mourned for his death. Even John was not told. When the hunchback Katherine was old enough to understand, she learned the truth. 'Willie might have had to hang if Douglas of Dudhope had been a different kind of man,' old Adam told the girl. 'I would have let him hang if that had been the way to save the family, but I would never have let him be hunted. But Douglas being what he was, and the wee right ones being what they can only be, the best way for all of us was to let Willie be drowned, for them, in that bog. Ay, there was a bog. These two Barry men could have taken you to the very spot. And there's Willie, happy enough in France, getting on, married with his two bairns. If he or his is to be the power, he or his will come back to Dundee. His going did nothing to take away from what I've gathered for the time when we rise to being the power. Nicol saw him away, and in France he is useful to Nicol. He's one who knows the Scotch free-trading, and he's getting on. A good man, young Willie. Not what his father was, not what his uncle, young Adam, was, nor like what you will be, Katie, but one of the blood, right enough. You never know but what, if he and his come back, they'll have what's needed.'

The Duke of Argyll, victor of Sheriffmuir, spoke in London about the haplessness of large parts of Scotland. Dundee was in his speaking. The famine of 1720 had sucked from the town the scanty, carefully gathered money capital for industrial development. Once before, distress and the bitterness of distress had turned Dundee towards the Stuart. The London parliament was giving consideration to Argyll's argument.

The aged Adam English and the hunchback child wandered among the gaps of Monck's assault, still there after nearly eighty years, cleared of their rubble generations ago, vacant lots where dockans grew and puddles formed on rainy days. The wooden-gabled buildings of the Marketgait peeled and blistered in the weather. In the back vennels, lean-to shanties propped themselves against the walls of derelict tenements that no one claimed, where dwelt the town's licensed beggars, Dundee folks with badges that allowed them to beg, whereas all other beggars were whipped. The old man had given up his tavern, and lived with John in St. Salvador's close, the hunchback's constant companion, sitting with her over her writing and reading lessons, telling her, in their walks through the town, the story of the family, instilling into her his hatred of right ones. Once in a while, a Barry free-trader would seek him out, with news of Willie in France, a great day for the old man and his freakish granddaughter, with their secret to share.

At the junction of Moraygait and Seagait, where his mother had talked, long ago, about his father, he talked to Katherine of the prophecies. 'It's not to be me that will be the power,' he said. 'It's to be the blood after me. Ay, it will come. She said it was to start in water and stone. I saw that come to pass. She said the blood would put a rope round a bailie's neck. I saw that. The rest will come. Maybe John' – he shook his head – 'maybe young John, the bairn' – he thought long, and shook his head – 'maybe Willie or his bairns in France, you never can tell. Maybe you, my clever Katie. Nobody would think so, but it's maybe you. You'll have a big say in it, I feel, and yet how could anybody believe it, my clever bairn. Maybe Elspet's bairn, ay maybe her, that bonnie wee Elspet. The fourth Elspet, Elspet Renkyne, then Elspet English, then Elspet Auchterlonie, and then Elspet Digby. She's of the blood. It might be her, nobody can tell.'

The baby Elspet Digby was Elspet Auchterlonie's illegitimate child to the tax-collector, the wit, the author of facetious essays for the London Journals. Old Adam had been puzzled by Elspet Auchterlonie's unmarried state. With her hair, her complexion, her laughing manner, she had had the young men around her, and had not chosen a husband from them. Two years after Willie's going, when she was nearly twenty-eight her laughter faltering, her looks beginning to fade, Digby had run from Dundee with his eight-years pickings from the tax-collecting and his eight-years profits from free trading. One reason for his going was that Elspet, being pregnant, was becoming over insistent in her demands that he marry her. She had been long his mistress, not the only one, she learned, for Digby's numerous associations with Dundee women were the scandalized talk of the town for months after his going. Her mother had died in the happiness of childbirth; Elspet Auchterlonie died in sorrow.

'This one is the blood. That's all that counts with me,' old Adam had said to his dying grand-daughter. 'This baby may be the power.'

'That one will only be a shame. There's his blood as well as ours in that one. I thought I was the only woman. He said he would marry me. He kept on saying it through all these years.'

'We'll call her Elspet,' the old man said, 'For the first Elspet and for you.'

'Elspet,' she sobbed. 'Elspet Digby!'

It was then that the old man closed his tavern, and his son John made a home for him and for the infant called Elspet. The linen tenement, prospering in its modest way while Dundee declined, maintained John's family through difficult years. There was little work in the town for masons. John found some repair work to do, and was a jobbing builder, without hired men or apprentices. Every month the wages of the Darien money, Adam's and Willie Auchterlonie's, came to the door in St. Salvador's close, in the hands of a weaving apprentice, the wages – not the interest – calculated by the old Scotch methods of loom's share, floor's share, wall's share, labour's share. The old man had rebuilt his hoard, and enlarged it greatly, by the payment of these wages as well as by the penny profits of the tavern. He had a separate hoard for the child Elspet, her grandfather Auchterlonie's money with its due increase. 'That bairn will be well enough placed,' he said. 'She will need nothing from me. What I have is the beginning of the power, and the one to get it will be the one that looks to me to be the one that will keep things in mind.'

He saw that the fine-weaving community in the Seagait was breaking, after more than twenty years. 'There will be little more from there to help the growth of the power,' he said.

The clan had been held together in their tenement by Pieter Devint, to whom all were related by marriage. Every Sabbath, a Low Countries God, speaking through Pieter's mouth enunciated the flax taboos. The de Wint name was Dutch rather than Flemish, and Pieter had in him Dutch blood and Dutch habits of thought. In Flanders, he had been a member of a minor Reformation sect, all the more Protestant and puritanical because of the Catholicism around it. The Dundee folks he had taken into the clan had readily adopted his faith, which required of them a hard way of life rather than observance of religious forms. But now the second generation in the tenement were inclining towards rebellion against his strict conducting of their life and work. He had no son. His two daughters had married within the tenement community, and their husbands were quarrelling about their respective rights as Pieter's successor. Another cause of contention arose when, in 1727, came the long-deferred encouragement, by parliament, of Scotch linen, a bribe, the Jacobites said, to the old Stuart burghs and counties from the house of Hanover. Dutch experts, smuggled out of the Low Countries, moved through Angus teaching the growing and the working of flax. Government schools instructed in spinning and weaving. Continental and Irish bleaching methods were being introduced. Some of the second generation in the tenement hankered after these official appointments as instructors, and were angered by Pieter's attempts to prevent their leaving the clan. Others were irritated by his refusal to allow the cheap, coarse weaving which, within the new scheme of bounties for exported linen, was making quick profits. The Devint fine weave was not for export. Even had it been, the bounty, a few ha'pennies, was but a hundredth part of the cloth's price. On the Dundee buckrams, the penny bounty was a sixth of the value. It was argued in the clan that at least a share of the weaving might be cheap weaving to earn the quick returns and high subsidies. Sitting among the wrangling, Pieter was failing, a sick man.

'There's none of the blood there now,' old Adam said, 'and except for Pieter there's nobody minds that it was for the blood that their weaving was started. It looks like I'm going to see Pieter away. There's a fright for the rest of them when he goes. What I started, I'll finish. I set their weaving going to make the power grow. When it stops doing that, there'll be no weaving for them to argue about.'

Pieter Devint died in March of 1731. While the weaving folks quarrelled, old Adam arranged for the end of the manufactory, making his last use of the drunkard, Kydd. The looms, made by the first Willie English to Pieter's designs, sold readily in that year of demand for looms. The tenement fetched a higher price than it had cost when bought in the panic year after the Union. The clan were helpless. The assertions that Kydd was not the owner were taken by the chartered weaving trade to be conspiracy by workpeople against an old man.

Adam English added to his hoard the greater part of the money obtained by the sales. The smaller portion was for Kydd, to be doled out to him weekly. 'If he outlives me,' Adam told John, 'you'll give him his shillings. If he lasts longer than that money I've put aside for him, you'll give him no more. He can go to his chartered trade. He can girn to them about how a Dundee freeman was made a Dundee slave, and he'll not be believed any more than Pieter's weavers were believed. If he doesn't outlast the money, what remains goes into the chest. Mind.'

Kydd did not outlast the money. He drank his weekly dole and starved for food, as Adam had foreseen. He was dead in four weeks. Old Adam laughed. 'We all have to die,' he said. 'I'll be going soon, myself.'

He had three more months of sitting with the eleven-year-old Katherine, who spun yarn and wove it upon a small loom that had come from the Seagait tenement. 'I've thought for long that the power was in weaving,' he said, 'and when I look at you, my clever bairn, with your lint yarn and your linen, I'm sure that it will be in something to do with wearing. The power has had its beginning in water and stone. It is to grow in a hot sun and heavy rain. Nobody can tell what that means, but I'm sure it's something to do with weaving. Spin your lint, Katie, and weave your cloth. Ay, it's in weaving the power lies. I've known it from the day weaving came into the family by the plague ship. My son, Willie, brought it, as was foreseen.'

His end was easy, in bed, where he lay for only two days, without pain of body or mind.

'This is the finish, now,' he said. 'Run and get your father, Katie, and get the hair.' When his son came, the old man said: 'You're honest, John. It's for you to see to what I'm telling you. My money is for Katie. Mind! Not because she'll be dependent, and the others will be provided for, but because she'll do what's needed to make it grow to the power. Give me the hair, lassie!' His faltering fingers divided his mother's hair into four strands. 'It's you I'm talking to now, Katie,' he said. 'One for Willie and his bairns. One for wee Elspet Digby. One for young John. And one strand for you, my clever one. Mind what I told you at the Moraygait port, about her whose hair that was. You know the things she said would come. Keep them in mind. They burned her. They hunted me. They made me shovel the dirt. They hanged my son for laughing. Mind! We must never forgive.'

'Will I get you a minister?' John asked.

'A minister! Ay, and get a Dundee bailie at the same time, then I can spit in the eyes of both kind of right ones, the kirkie right ones and the tolbooth right ones!' He laughed. 'By the bye, John, you never heard what happened to Rollo the dirt man, that time he went missing. Katie will tell you. I haven't the time!' He coughed feebly. 'The smoke from the witch-fire is in my throat,' he said. 'The wood is too green to burn my mother! They need drier wood!' These were his last words.

Dundee was poor, as all Scotland was poor, but it was no

longer the poor burgh of parliament's debates. The linen subsidy had been immediately beneficial. The eighty years decline in population was arrested. There were tuppenny pieces to spend where there had been ha'pennies.

The council looked at their tolbooth, for a century and a half their tolbooth, with masoned stones of four centuries ago in its fabric. As they looked, they were thinking not of the Dundee around them, but of the Dundee that had been a force in the history of the land. They strutted. They had shillings in their pockets. They were, in their own estimation, a force again, the Dundee merchant burgesses, and the old tolbooth was a shabby thing to house them, they declared. For them, William Adam of Kirkcaldy, architect and father of greater architects, designed a new townhouse, in the manner of Palladio.

John English made his mason mark upon the stones with which he built, old and cheap stones – the council could engage the fashionable architect to draw a fashionable design, but could not put new stone into the building. John's mark was upon the stones of the vaulted arcade with its seven arched openings and its square-sectioned piers, called pillars by the back vennel folks. The mark was upon the coupled Roman-Ionic pilasters over the central arches of the arcade, and upon the upper structure, surmounted by the slender spire. Among the first stones laid by John English the council buried a copper plate, with engraved Latin works, which stated:

Nine days from the kalends of March in the year 1732, the fifth year of the reign of George II; Alexander Robertson being provost of Dundee; David Jameson, Patrick Maxwell, Andrew Wardrope, Samuel Johnston being bailies; Patrick Hay, town clerk; and David Crighton, treasurer; the foundations of this townhouse were laid, Europe being everywhere at peace.

John wrought for seven years at the making of the

townhouse, growing old. His son, John, entered upon his apprenticeship to masonry in the last three years of the work, and at the completion was sixteen, quiet, burly like his father, with little gleam in his hair. They looked together, father and son, master and apprentice, upon the townhouse's gracefulness, and talked as masons talk, regretting that their townhouse was built in a hollow, below the level of the roadway, which John called the Marketgait and young John called the High Street. Only the building's front could be seen, for sixteenth century Dundee, even earlier Dundee, jostled upon its flanks, and the tenements of the Vault, leaning upon each other, hid its rear. They talked their masons' criticisms, but they loved the townhouse. The whole town loved it, even those who complained most about its four thousand pounds cost. The folks of the backlands, the unfree, hating the burgesses, showing their hatred by their wailing laugh against the burgess ceremony of opening the townhouse, they loved this townhouse of the burgesses. Never was stone and mortar so loved as was the townhouse of Dundee. The vennel folks claimed it as their own townhouse. The pillars was their appointed place for meetings with one another. They deserted the market cross in favour of the townhouse for their celebration of Hogmanay, the heathen festival of mid-winter, of the fear of the ice changed to joy in the promise that spring must come. They faced the pillars and looked up to the steeple, the symbol of regeneration of the species. They went singing, bearing gifts. The vennel homes had been scrubbed. What could be polished had been polished. For one hundred and ninety-three years, John English's marked stones were there, built into William Adam's shape, then was only a vast concrete square in which men stood at Hogmanay, wondering where hope was to be found in a void.

Katherine English was a hunched, dwarfish young woman who looked old, her spinning and weaving praised everywhere, but the praise always tinged with malicious pity. She taught her skill to pupils, daughters of higher burgess families, to fit them to be good wives, able to furnish their homes with fine linen. Her father had allotted, for her school, two rooms of the house in St. Salvador's close, and there she earned her own keep, and never drew from the beginning of the power, the chest of coins her grandfather had left. Independence was a necessity of life for her. From the age of fifteen she had been paying her own way by her schooling. She had gone to merchant and lairdling houses, canvassing for pupils, displaying her yarn and cloth. A strange thing for a girl to do, everyone said, but such a strange creature as this Katherine, the mason's daughter, could be expected to do strange things. 'Everybody laughs at me even if I do nothing,' she said, 'so I might as well be doing something that'll give them a good laugh.'

She commissioned her father to make a stone for the grave where he had buried old Adam. She paid a mason's rates for the work, insisted on paying from her own earnings. The old man had been put in a new grave, at her suggestion, not among the bones of Mary Lowden. These were the words she chose for her father's chiselling, odd, unfeeling words they were thought to be by all who read them:

To the memory of
ADAM ENGLISH
born 1652, died 1731, buried here.
And of his Mother, who has no grave, and of
his eldest son, Adam, lost in Darien, and of his
youngest son, William, whose place of burial in
this ground is not known.

All her life she had been apart from the rest of the family, except occasionally for an interest in Elspet Digby, who when only thirteen was being looked at by men, finely complexioned as her mother had been, her hair thick and shining. Elspet was quick in being a woman. She knew that men turned to watch after her. She made a great ado of combing her hair and arranging her shoulder-shawl. 'You know more about men than you should, Elspet,' Katherine said. 'Keep in mind that you're of the blood. Keep in mind that it might be for you to do what's needed to be done.' She told the younger girl about Elspet Renkyne's prophecies, but the girl scarcely heeded, too intent upon admiration of her own shapely, white feet or her thoughts of men who had turned to look after her. 'I'm telling you,' Katherine snapped, 'that it might be for you to do what's to be done. You should know these things that the old man told me.'

The tavern arguments of the day were about the church. John English repeated the arguments at home, his voice rising, and Katherine stared at him in surprise. 'You've got something of the old man in you, after all,' she said.

'If there's to be a kirk,' he said, 'it shouldn't be a council kirk. Knox said that the congregations would elect the ministers, but here the council chooses ministers who will see to it that God keeps in with the merchants. The services are nothing else but the praise of God's will in holding down the trades and the unfree.'

'That's tavern talk for something that's beyond the scope of tavern talkers,' Katherine said, in her sharp manner.

She went with him to a meeting of lower burgesses, followers of one Erskine, a Fifeshire minister who had proclaimed the new foundation of the true Presbyterian church. 'Do you know what this is?' she said to her father, as they sat there. 'It's my grandfather's Sidlaw sorners all over again. Revolution, that turns out to be arguments about how to conduct a meeting. Big words, and no meaning to them.' One speaker was for Knox's plan, another was for the old hard way of life, another was for the sexual and psychological abnormalities that passed among his kind for purity. 'The repentance stool should be brought out again. The harlots should be marked. The fortune tellers should be punished. Thou shalt not suffer a witch to live!' Kate was on her feet, angered but also amused. 'The Lord commands me to speak,' she said, 'to point out to you one with Satan in him, one who has been sent here with Satan's tricks of rousing you to

Satan's work. I know it is by the Lord's command that I speak. He raises my hand, and points my finger.' Her finger was directed at the zealot for the marking of harlots and the burning of witches. The meeting was hushed, everyone gaping at the man she pointed at. 'Come on father,' she said. 'We'll get out. That one has something to think about now. There are some advantages in being a wee, ugly humphy. A humphy can always stop an argument, and a pointing finger has more point to it when it's a humphy that points.'

John English did not join with the Erskine-ites, who made for themselves a secession church for the less successful tradesmen and for those among the unfree who had church-going shoes and clothes. The barefoot unfree were being sucked into their own emotional vortex which formed in the backlands at this time of argument about creeds. Men with the holy jerk spoke to mobs in the wynds. As they spoke, they jerked and danced. Christ, they said, had died to save the back vennels, not the burgess elect of the kirk. Hallelujah, praise be to Christ, whose blood washed away sins. The back vennel folks were shouting for the back vennel Christ, jerking and dancing as they shouted. The jerk meetings were not for John, any more than the Erskine-ites had been. He had ceased his attendance at the established kirk, but it was wrong, he said, to be without a church, to rear a family outside the influence of religion.

'Your father had no church,' Katherine sneered. 'But if your way of being of his blood is to be against the right ones' church, then I'll tell you a kirk for you, the kail kirk.' The minister of Tealing parish, on the way to the Sidlaws, had revolted against the government's control of the established church and the lairds' control. Glas of Tealing had been deposed from his charge, and had founded meeting houses in Dundee and Perth, attended by a few. 'Go to Glas, and you'll get a kirk to suit you,' Katherine said. 'He would be a minister for me if I needed one, but I'll not because what my grandfather never needed I'll never need. That's a man who looks happy in his religion, and doesn't cock his head to one side, nor rub his hands together when he talks to folk. He's not of the kind who call themselves the Lord's anointed and the chosen people. He's not a right one!'

The family, except, of course, for Katherine, went to Glas's meeting place to see what the Glasite faith was like. They remained as members. All were equal in Glas's church, which had been the first of the secessions after the secession of the most extreme Cameronians. There was no pulpit. Every Sunday was communion day, but communion was not the ritualistic sip of wine. It was the love-feast, the supping of a bowl of soup, the feeding of the hungry. John never questioned the simple dogma. There was an absence of rightness in this kail kirk, so called by the sneerers because of its soup.

In the streets John was hissed by a little knot of burgess youths. A crowd of back vennel corner-boys, encouraged by the burgess youths, followed the old man, jeering. They were of no church, but always ready to jeer.

'One of these kail-eaters,' they told each other. When John had entered the quietness of St. Salvador's close, they picked up stones to throw. The young burgesses looked on, smiling.

Katherine ran from the house, her little body wagging. Her quick eyes selected the burgesses as the real leaders. 'You scabby rats!' she shouted, slapping and kicking them, till they bled. They ran. 'What for do you lot want to be doing the bidding of that church-going dirt?' she shouted at the mob, the members of which drew back, then slouched away, sheepishly. 'Nobody can hit a humphy,' she said.

That little event occurred in 1744, when Katherine was twenty-four, her father sixty-nine, her brother John twenty-two, recently married by Glas's marriage ceremony. Her mother, an obscure figure in the family story, was two years dead, that Katherine Cant in whose right her husband had become a freeman of the town. Elspet Digby was eighteen, and making a stir among the men.

Dundee was grown to six thousand population, after declining to less than four thousand. The older folks were staring in wonder at the new indications of prosperity – a carter in the town, a German dancing master, the vennel women, with black stockings, going to one or other of the twelve Sabbath meetings, and, most obvious of all, the pillars of the townhouse.

It was a time of laird politics, and, in accordance with the old saying, a laird must be provost of Dundee. For the choosing of a provost, the Angus Jacobites had gathered, to gain control of the town for the Stuart cause and a port of entry for the Stuart army from France. Graham of Duntrune, who called himself by the attainted title of Viscount Dundee, had been presented for the provostship. The councillors opposed their shop-keeping canniness to laird magniloquence. They were of a growing town which provided a rising market for shopkeepers, and they had shillings to jingle. Graham was loyal to the bitternesses of the hungry years. They would have none of the wild laird of Duntrune. The Jacobites offered them Fotheringhame of Powrie, who could hide his Stuart enthusiasms. The Secretary for Scotland was watching anxiously from Edinburgh. He matched a lone Angus laird against the league of Angus lairds, Duncan of Lundie, whose colour was whig blue, against Fotheringhame, who in secret wore the white cockade. The Secretary's Dundee officials whispered the name of Lundie into council ears.

Lundie walked unescorted from his house at the head of the Seagait, that house where the Stuart had lodged for a night in 1716. In the High Street, the greater and lesser land-owners were angrily silent for him whom they called a traitor, but the town watch, drawn up along the line of the pillars, raised a cheer for the brown-clad, farmer-looking man whose face did not change as he came past the glares. In the townhouse, the councillors voted, all but three of them, for the brown laird against the brocaded laird, voting, without knowing it, for what was to be against what had been.

'The old man used to say,' hunched Katherine English

said, 'that, once or twice in every hundred years, war changed the way of life in Dundee. This choosing of Lundie starts war and change.'

One who called himself the son of the Stuart was caught and sentenced to banishment. He was but a Fife loon, David Hay, a soft, harmless creature and his court of two men and two women whom he had ennobled, in his way, were softer and more harmless than himself. Two Dundee burgesses had hurried to join David Hay's revolt, and their discomfiture was a laugh in the taverns. Because the arguers had made an end of Charles Stuart in the exposure of David Hay from Fife, their fear was the greater when the real Charles Stuart came into the tavern talk. He had ten thousand men, it was said. No, he had twenty thousand, French and Spanish. Would the government hold Stirling as in 1715, and leave all Scotland north of the Forth to the Stuart? The town was afraid.

The talk in the mountains talked itself to Dundee. Charles Stuart had no twenty thousand men, nor ten thousand. Only one ship had been seen. This was no revolt, it was but an Irish rioting, remote from Dundee. The stories told about this prince made the taverns laugh. He wore the dress of the mountain Irish, but it was of French cloth dyed with French dyes, with gold lace and linen frills. He played the games of the Irish, wrestling with them and throwing the stone, and louping burns. They laughed the more when the news was confirmed that General Cope was moving to hold all the Lowlands against the savages. Cope would show them. There were roads and forts in the Highlands now, and Cope would scatter the bagpipe-blowers before they could become a nuisance. Cope, ay, a fine general. Johnny Cope had the experience and the skill, a fine general. The arguers had never heard of this Cope before, but he was a fine general as generals are suddenly fine generals.

A fortnight's complacency was shattered. The Irish were coming down through the Athol country. They were at Dunkeld, it was said. Where was the damned fool Cope? The

Irish were at Perth, twenty miles from Dundee! The fear now lay in the possibility of Cope's being near, to battle with the Irish in Dundee's streets. At the market cross, Duncan of Lundie commanded that no opposition be made to any enemy who came, but that no help be offered. If the wild Irish arrived, the townsfolk were to do nothing to anger them, for they were men given to killing and burning. All money, foodstuffs and weapons were to be hidden. The provost and the council would remain in the town, and good burgesses should remain with them.

Young John English's wife was weeping over her four-months-old infant, named John. 'There's nothing to fear,' Katherine told her. 'Men can't get started on fighting without somebody fights them. They'll come, expecting shooting, and there'll be none. And they'll feel the relief of men who haven't been killed when they thought they might be. That's how folks' minds work. Your bairn will be all right.'

The force that came was not the feared Highlanders, but Angus and Mearns men, for whom a crowd gathered, to cheer. The laird of Kinloch was the leader, one who had walked the streets of Dundee often enough and lodged in Dundee houses. Duncan of Lundie was there, outside the townhouse, to receive Kinloch of Kinloch, and they nodded to each other like unfriendly neighbours, not like enemies in war. The Stuart man said that the Hanover man would still be provost, but under the military governorship of Fotheringhame of Powrie. At the cross, the Stuart was proclaimed king, and a reward offered for the body of the usurper, George the German. The sick man of 1716, whose touch did not cure scrofula, was James VIII again.

'Well, it's what we feared, and now that it's come, it's nothing,' Katherine said. 'If anybody should seek to put up rebels here, let me handle them.' The billeting officers found that there was a mad woman in the St. Salvador's close house, a little and ugly hunchback who gibbered about throats to cut at night, looking at the throats of the men who sought lodgings. 'Being a humphy has its uses,' she said, 'and has its fun. Elspet, when that kind of men comes, keep your legs under your skirt. I was watching you.' The collectors of the Stuart's taxes took their toll from old John and young John, but none from Kate's hoard, on which she lay, in the sick-bed of a supposed daftie.

The news for the arguers was that Cope's army had been routed by Charles Stuart, in a battle of five minutes, at Prestonpans, that the rebels were moving from Edinburgh to invade England, not by the road of the battles, Dunbar, Berwick, Newcastle, York, but by the undefended tracks through the border hills to Carlisle.

'The change will come from that,' Katherine said. 'They'll see in the south this mob of wild Irish. It will be like an army from Muscovy or some such place to them. They'll know that something has to be done about Scotland, where chiefs and lairds have power of life and death over folks. It's likely that some of the old privileges of burgh right ones will go with the privileges of lairds. The government will sort this Irish and laird nuisance that's kept us back all these years.'

'Does it not look as if the Irish and the lairds were going to sort the government?' her brother asked.

'Talk sense, John! A crowd of Irish and a few Angus and Aberdeen lairds against Great Britain!'

A force passed through the town from Montrose, reinforcements for the rebels, landed from French ships. Kinloch's men cheered the new arrivals, enthusiastic particularly for a few French uniforms in the marching ranks. Some townsfolk booed. Heads and windows were broken in the scuffling that followed, and the bell pealed for the summoning of the whole watch of burgesses to assist the governor in keeping his own men in order. Young John English was with the watch, and his wife weeping. Katherine volunteered to go to find what was doing. Nobody would touch a humphy, she said. She saw Governor Fotheringhame, for James VIII, and Provost Duncan, for George II, together on the tower of the market cross, reading the riot rules, in turn, to an amused crowd. The watch had the bored air of men who have been too long standing in line, young John among them. As she came back with her comforting tidings, an exciting stranger was peering curiously at the foot of St. Salvador's close. As she entered the alleyway, he entered, still looking about him, a youthful dandy, with kilt and stockings of brilliant green check, his short jacket of black velvet, a flurry of rucked linen at his throat and wrists.

'My God!' Kate said, in her way. 'You must be Prince Charlie himself.'

He removed his bonnet. His long hair, carefully dressed, was violently red. He said, his voice foreign sounding, his words stilted, that he was looking for the house of the family called English. Kate started to put on her mad act, then looked again at the youth's hair and nose.

'You're not young Willie English's lad?' she said. 'From France?'

He examined her. 'You are Katie,' he said.

'What are you doing in that get-up, lad?' she asked. 'That's the dress of the hill Irish, but it wasn't hill weaving or hill cutting or hill dyeing made your clothes. Is your father still in the land of the living?'

A disconcerting greeting, both in its words and subject, and the youth was disconcerted. He said that his father was three years dead, with his sister, in an infection which his father had called the five-day sickness. Kate had not meant to be unkind, and told him in her abrupt but obviously sincere way that he was welcome, being of the blood.

'The old man told your father that if he or his was to be the power foretold for us,' she said, 'he or his would come back to Dundee.'

He nodded to that, and said that he knew about the foretelling. He had joined the small expedition from France because it afforded him a chance to come to Dundee, where perhaps he or his was to be the power. He laughed as he said that, but was serious behind the laughter.

'Have you brought what's needed?' Kate asked, half laughing, half serious.

'I've brought what you see, myself, my sword, and my clothes,' he replied.

'It's maybe what's needed,' she said. 'Nobody can tell!'

Elspet Digby was at the door. From the window, as Kate had noticed, Elspet had seen them talk and smile together. 'Come away in,' Katherine said. 'There's at least one in the house would be pleased by a visit from any kind of a lad, and will be none the less pleased for a bonnie one like you. There'll be a deal of explaining to be done. Your father was drowned in a Sidlaw bog before you were thought about. It's odd that he'll have to come alive for my father, then be lost again in an infection of five-day sickness. You know the story.'

'And I know your part in it,' he said.

'I was four years old. My memories about it are mostly what I was told later. We'll leave that bit out when we tell my father. He's an old man, and his daughter has done enough already to vex him without bringing up her wild infancy.'

Old John blinked as he listened to the youth's story of old Adam's scheme, twenty years ago, to save the family. 'Well, I knew my father was gallus,' John said, 'but never knew him to be as gallus as that.' The youth laughed. Old John heard the laugh of the first Willie English, his half-brother, son of the laughing tinkler Leeb White.

'Willie English. Willie's grandson, young Willie's son, think of that!' he said. He surveyed this Willie English's clothes. 'You're for Stuart, I see,' he said. He went off into an old man's rambling reminiscence of 1689, when his father had been out with Claverhouse, and 1715 when he himself had seen the raising of Argyll's army in Glasgow.

'Willie's not interested as much as that in the Stuarts,' Katherine interrupted.

Laughing, the youth said that he had been pleased to learn that the council and kirk right ones of Dundee were against the Stuart, and he could get a blow in at them.

'You're an English, right enough,' Katherine said, 'with

the hair and the nose and the very words of the Englishes! But there's little chance of your getting a dig at the Dundee right ones. There's no fighting here. This is a grand war for Dundee. The weavers are making bags for the Irish's oatmeal, and getting paid for it. It's true the money comes from forced taxes, but there are more shillings coming in than are going out. And all the old hens that couldn't get men, have men now. There's been more dancing and singing and lovemaking in this town in the last few weeks than for ten years before.'

Elspet laughed prettily, and put on her most engaging pose, displaying her slender, rounded ankles. Willie said that he had not come all the way from Caen to Dundee in order to smile for the Dundee right ones. He would get his blow in against them, he declared. He was examining Elspet, as he spoke.

He was attached to the Aberdeen bound section of the reinforcement from France, most of whom were exiled Scotchmen. All the Highlanders, it seemed, were not for the Stuart. Some clans were raiding among the estates of the Aberdeenshire Jacobite lairds. Willie was to return to Montrose and fight against those Hanover Irish. He used the term Irish for the glen folks, in the Dundee way of speaking. He had been granted leave to visit Dundee, and had travelled south with the other half of the force from France. If he were not in Dundee to be the foretold power, he said, he would at least get a laugh against the right ones.

On his first Sunday in the town, old John and young John tried to induce him to go with them to the kail meeting. 'A church!' he said. 'No, churches are not for me.' Then, his eyes shining with mischief, he said he would have a look at the right ones in their right ones' kirk. He went alone to the town churches, in the angle of Overgait and Nethergait. There under the ancient tower called the old steeple, in rebuilt portions of the ruined St. Mary's of old Roman Catholic Dundee, were the two established churches; the South Kirk where the noted preacher Willison attracted crowded congregations of lower burgesses and the more ambitious unfree by his theological polemics, and the East Kirk, with a sparse, exclusive membership of the richer merchants. Willie watched the people entering the two churches, and chose for himself the East Kirk. He mounted an outside stair, by which he had seen the most prosperous folks enter the building. He sat in the carved pew of the councillors in the council gallery, aware of the glares directed towards him, enjoying the glares. The minister prayed, and in his prayer was mention of the royal family. Willie smiled, and jumped to his feet. 'Which royal family?' he called out. 'If you mean the German and his brood, it's time this church was cleared.' An interruption of the prayer! In the East Kirk! The congregation gaped. The minister was flummoxed. The words 'royal family' were always in prayers. No particular family had been intended by the minister, only a kirk abstraction, only words that came to his lips by force of habit. He stood in his pulpit, his chin sagging, his wide-open eyes upon the interrupter with the feared Irish garb. Willie was satisfied. He stalked out with a show of anger.

He imitated the preacher's helpless attitude for Kate and Elspet, and they laughed delightedly. 'Ay, you're one of the old man's Englishes!' Kate said. It was then that she gave him his strand of Elspet Renkyne's hair. 'Coming near a hundred years since it was cut off, but it's still got the red in it. Give it a wash in brandy at times. The old man did that.'

'You were fond of him,' Willie said.

'He was the only one who ever took my hand in the streets,' she declared, fiercely.

In the last days of his leave, Willie and Elspet were always together. They climbed the Law, something to talk about. The hill was six hundred feet high, easy enough for most people, but few of the townsfolk had ever been on the top, in Constable Douglas's lands.

'The old man was on the Law when he was a bairn,' Kate said. 'I would like to go there, but it's not for a humphy creature like me to climb up there.' Willie offered to take her up. His kilt had scared away the Dudhope keepers, and would do so again. 'You wouldn't be shamed to be with me, going through the town?' Kate asked. He laughed, and Elspet laughed with him, hastily offering her help. They lugged Kate up the long steep street of the Hilltown, amid the grins of the cottagers. He carried her along the crest of the spur to the flattened Law summit. 'I never knew Dundee was like this,' Kate exclaimed. 'The old man told me, but you have to see it for yourself. There's the old steeple, just as he saw it eighty years ago. I've passed it a thousand times, and never once has my look gone up to the top. There's the spire of the townhouse – he never saw that. Roofs – that's what he said – roofs among hills beside the river. Let me stay awhile to see it, Bonnie Dundee. I'll mind this. I'll never be here again.'

Willie English was gone to his fighting in Aberdeenshire. Elspet Digby was quiet, pale, afraid; she wept at times. Hunched Kate saw that Elspet's weeping and fear were not entirely for Willie in the northern skirmishes, but mostly for Elspet herself.

The news was that the Irish invaders of England were in retreat from Derby, from Preston, from Carlisle. They were being harassed on the south-west trails of Scotland by folks who could remember the suffering endured under Stuart kings by the church-staters, and could remember the High-land hosts who had been billeted in Clydesdale to eat up the Cameronian discontent. The rebels were in Glasgow, coldly received by the whig burgesses, then they were re-treating towards Stirling. In Dundee, again, was talk of Prince Charlie's French tartans, his lace and silver buttons, his throwing of stones like the Irish, his louping of burns. Who was he, this Charlie Stuart? He called himself Scotch, and had no more sense than to dress in Continental made imitations of the mountain Irish. A Pole, that's what he was if he was anything. What language did he speak? It would not be the Irish tongue of his army, well not an army, a mob of tinklers. Who was he to be in command of an army? The Duke of Cumberland had the experience. A fine general, the Duke.

Looking at the townhouse, regretting that it was built in a hole, old John English collapsed in the High Street. He was lying on a sick bed when Willie came back with that part of the Aberdeenshire rebel force which was being moved south to the task of holding the pass at Stirling against Cumberland's advance. Elspet cried when she saw him, and stood watching anxiously for a sign from him that he still wanted her.

'Go out, Elspet,' Kate said. 'I've something to say to Willie. It's better I say it.' The girl retired, weeping. 'Elspet will be having your bairn, Willie. Don't hang your head, man. If I know her aright – and I should! – I know which of you did the seducing. My father has brought her up as his daughter. He's a man that takes ill with that kind of shame in a family. It would be better for him, old and sick as he is, if Elspet was married when her bairn came.'

In his foreign way, he said that he loved Elspet.

'Well, that's fine. It makes everything right. Mind you, I'm not the one to feel any shame about a thing like that. The bairn when it comes will be the blood, doubly the blood. I could almost think you had to come to Dundee for that. It might be that bairn that will be the power. Nobody can tell. I wouldn't press you to marry Elspet, if you didn't feel like doing it, but I thought it was right to suggest to you that you should.'

He said that he wanted nothing better.

'She's a bonnie lassie, and with the blood in her. Everything's fine for everybody!' Kate declared.

Twenty years before, Elspet's father had betrayed his friend, Willie's father, to make a subject for wit. Elspet was wed to Willie. The ceremony, a kail wedding by John Glas, was rushed, for Willie had but three days in the town. The marriage was listed in the book of the South Kirk to make it a proper marriage, William English, son of William English, burgess, to Elspet called Digby, daughter of Elspet Auchterlonie, whose father was William Auchterlonie, burgess. The date was January 14th, 1746. When Willie marched with his contingent from Aberdeen, the Jacobite garrison of Dundee marched with them, to Perth, and south to the disputed gap. Elspet was not weeping. From the foot of St. Salvador's close, she waved to Willie among the marching men, going out, along the Overgait, by the West Port, from Dundee.

The news was of the battle of Falkirk. The Stuart's son was called Prince Charlie again in the Dundee taverns – for a day. It was said he was advancing to retake Edinburgh. No, he was retreating, past Stirling, past Dunblane, to Perth. He was a chinless dandy who had thought to win a throne with an Irish mob, the tavern arguers said. His French kilt, his louping of burns! Cumberland was a fine general. Through Dundee came stragglers from the rebels, hurrying. On their heels were the government's cavalry scouts, seeking information about the routes of the retreat from Perth, confident men whose confidence Dundee noted.

Provost Duncan and one of his bailies rode to Montrose to speak with Cumberland, who had pursued a body of the rebels along the length of Strathmore. The provost was to offer to the duke the freedom of Dundee, a burgess ticket in a silver casket. Hunched Kate English laughed, and wrote her thoughts on the matter. A hundred and fifty years later, the paralysed English, who dictated the family tales into a ledger, published her manuscript as a literary curiosity, for circulation among his financial associates. It was words spoken on to paper, a clear statement, achieved despite a remarkably small vocabulary, of the Englishes' philosophy of wrongness, the antithesis of the rightness she hated. She affirmed, at the beginning, that she was against the Stuarts, then wrote to this effect: she was aware of the provost's sincerity in his giving the freedom to the duke. She admired the provost for his conduct during the siege as much as she could admire a right one. But what he was doing was a right one's thing to do, this chasing after Cumberland. If the right ones would only get away from their rightness at times, if they would only be wrong for this hour, they might be really right for some other hour in a hundred years. If they had made Charlie Stuart a burgess – that would have been a thing to do. Cumberland was only a right one, a nothing. A song had been written by a Lothian farmer about the Prestonpans battle. It was a song the Dundee piper would be playing when Cumberland was known to be a nothing and Charlie was the something. Where were the right politicians, the right generals, the right ministers, the right provosts who were the names yesterday? They were not even names to-day. Charlie louped burns, and wore a daft French kilt. In time these things about Charlie would be things to say. Everybody would be singing about him. Nobody would be singing about Cumberland. Dundee folk would be saying, when that time came, that their town would be the better if it had been Charlie who got the burgess ticket, because there was a something in giving a ticket to one like Charlie. And there was only rightness, and littleness, and belly-crawling canniness in giving one to Cumberland. It was a shopkeeper thing to do, a thing for a wee lairdie, who was not a real laird, and for his grocer councillors. It could be said of herself that she grudged sore. She was shaped to grudge and trained by the old man to grudge. But her shaping and training had given her an understanding of things. The old man had given her more than he knew. He gave her the eyes to see the rot in rightness, and he gave her the ears to hear the lies in the right words. She was not prophesying like Elspet Renkyne, she ended. She was just saying what was what, things everybody could see if they could see things.

The news was of Cumberland's army, massed at Aberdeen, moving towards the mountains. The battle, everybody said, would be fought at one of the Spey crossings, but Charles Stuart retired with his starving men. The news was of Culloden. A bonfire blazed in the High Street of Dundee. 'Well, that's it all,' Kate said. 'Once or twice in every hundred years war changes the way of life in this town. We'll have to wait a long time and look back to see the change aright, but it will be this war that brought it about.'

Glancing cautiously over his shoulder, Willie English came in the dusk to St. Salvador's close. He was dressed in tinkler rags, his feet bare and bleeding. He sent a passing boy to the house, with the tress of red hair, to be shown only to Kate, and with the message that somebody wanted to speak to her. The boy brought the hunched woman to the shadows where Willie was hiding. 'I've nothing for beggars,' Kate said, for the messenger boy to hear. She whispered that she would meet Willie in the Houff, by the north-west entrance, and waggled away, apparently in high dudgeon.

In the dark of the graveyard, she and Willie talked. He had come with fugitives from Culloden, Angus lairds for whom rewards were on offer, young Lord Ogilvie of Airlie, Graham of Duntrune, Fotheringhame of Powrie, Fletcher of Ballinshoe, and a number of lesser Jacobites, Dundee men mostly. They were to make an attempt in a few hours to escape from the country, to France. His knowledge of France, and of the Stuart supporters there, was useful to them. He required no immediate help from Kate, only news about Elspet, whom he would not see, lest he frighten her. His wife was well, Kate told him. She did not say that old John was dying of his five months' lingering illness. Willie said he would write to Kate, and in due time Elspet could come to him in Caen. He was relying on Kate to see Elspet through her difficulties, and to send her on the journey. He gave the tress of hair into the hunched woman's keeping. He had shown it in taverns in Dundee during his first visit, and, if stopped now by the watchers, might be identified by it. He stooped and kissed her brow, then went eastward among the graves.

She never saw him again. She remembered the date of the incident because it was also the date of her father's death, recorded upon a Houff tombstone made by her brother, May 9th, 1746. The grave was that containing, until then, only the lonely bones of old John's mother, that Mary Lowden who had come creeping to the shoveller called English in the dirt man's lobby.

The latest excitement for the tavern arguers was the stealing of a fishing sloop from the Monifieth roads, by a party believed to be Jacobite outlaws. Lord Ogilvie's name was in the rumours, and the former governor, Fotheringhame. Kate held her secret. A fortnight after, the news for the taverns to discuss was that the sloop had been chased from its route by a naval vessel, and forced to put in at Bergen in Norway. The fugitives were in prison there. They were to be extradited to London. Then – they were being tried for treason in England. Then – they were sentenced to execution. Then – Ogilvie and another had escaped from the condemned cell. Kate listened to the talk. Willie's name was not given out among the beheaded or hanged. She wrote to London, and was informed that only the important had been listed. No word could be obtained as to whether or not an English was among the unimportant. A letter to Bergen, through a merchant who dealt with that port, inquired if all those who arrived from Dundee had been sent to London. It was answered briefly – all except three who were dead, drowned when the sloop had unskilfully entered the harbour, names unknown.

Elspet was not told about these matters. No news for Elspet in her condition, Kate considered, was better than the news she could be given. The child was born in late July, a boy, who was named Willie. At three months, his hair was seen to be red, the tip of his nose blunted. 'He's an English, all right,' Kate said, 'one of the blood. It might be this bairn or this bairn's bairn to be the power.' She told Elspet, then, her information about the child's father.

Elspet wailed in her manner. 'It doesn't give a lassie a chance,' she said. 'It's not right. Here I am, not knowing whether or not I've got a man.' The hunched woman stared.

Some months after that, Elspet left the house. Two young mothers together, John's wife and Elspet, made a situation impossible for both of them. Moreover, there was talk about Elspet's relations with a weaver in the Seagait. 'It's in the blood,' Kate said, 'in ours as well as Digby's. She has to go – there's no other way. She's well provided for with her grandfather's money and its earnings still untouched, and she's got the spinning I taught her. But we've got to mind she's the blood, and her bairn is the blood. It's a pity she couldn't wait till Willie was right dead or had a chance to come alive. A small chance, I'm thinking. He was a real English, one of the old man's ones. The bairn is doubly an English. We'll have to mind that!'

THE LONDON HOUSE IN NETHERGAIT

THE boy who had been named Willie English was not known by that name. He was known as Elspet Digby's redhaired brat. His flaming hair distinguished him among the three brats of whom Elspet Digby was the mother, and from all the other brats who ran in the back vennels of the Seagait.

He had hated and feared Alick Gray, his mother's first fancy-man. He whooped when Johnstone the heckler kicked and punched Gray down the turret stair. Johnston was his mother's second fancy-man, and his admiration of Johnston turned to fear and hate greater than he had felt for Gray. The first man had struck the boy often. The second man did not strike. He moved and spoke in the house as though there were no boy. He lifted his hand or foot to push aside the boy at whom he did not look as he pushed.

A woman halted the boy as he ran past in the street, a little, hunched woman whose red hair, showing at the side of the linen kerchief she wore, was ugly.

'What's your name, laddie?' she asked.

'Digby,' he said.

'Is Digby your mother's name? Elspet Digby?'

'Ay.'

'Then your name's English, Willie English. You've got good hair and a good nose, and they go with a good name. It's time you got a wash, laddie.'

The boy spoke at his home about the ugly woman.

'That humphy-backed bitch,' his mother said. 'When you were a toddler, she came pestering me to have the rearing of you. I gave her an answer straight at the end, and I've never had a word from her since then.'

'What's the names of wee Alick and the bairn? the boy asked. 'Are their names English?'

Johnston rose. Without speaking or looking at the boy, he pushed the boy to the door. Without looking, he kicked the boy along the lobby and down the stair.

The Bailie's close in the Seagait burned. The fire started in a soap boiler's shed, and seized on a rickety lean-to full of hemp and flax tow. All the boys of the town were there to see the fire, and to shout as one shanty after another was caught in the flames. The tenements blazed, and the boys danced as the roofs collapsed. Men were demolishing the shanties to prevent the spread of the fire. The boys sweated joyfully as they carried water from the Castle Burn to throw over the men.

The fire had worked back into the depths of the close. The crowd that watched moved forward into the burned-out close-mouth. The wall of a tenement, weakened by the flames, fell upon the crowd, breaking as it fell, piling upon them. Some of them staggered, fainting, through the dust that the fall raised. Men dug in the heap. The boy called Digby dug, whooping the news to the crowds who came running. They started upon the heap with their hands, shouted for tools. From the heap bodies were taken, bloody and broken. The boy whooped when he saw a body among the dust and stones.

His mother came, and he was surprised when she held him to her.

'They told me about the wall coming down,' she said. 'I got such a fright.'

He wriggled from her grip to look for other broken bodies. Ten bodies were out and three more came, a man, a woman, and a little red-haired girl. He whooped to his mother, pointing. She stared, and came forward to look at the three bodies. She made a noise as though she were to be sick, then took his hand and led him away.

'My God!' She said. 'They thought they were somebody, but nobody's anything when a land of houses drops on them.'

'Who?' he said.

'Young John English and his wife and his bairn. That was them under the stones.'

'The wee lassie with the red hair?' he asked. 'Was her name English like mine?'

'Ay ... A whole family wiped out bar the laddie. It's a true saying that you never know when it's your turn. Them that proud, and they're away just while you wink.'

'Is there another laddie called English?' he said.

'Ay, John English, the same name as his father and his grandfather. He's some kind of a cousin of yours. I was second cousin to his father, and your father was second-cousin to his father.'

'Is my right name English like the humphy-backed one said!'

'Ay.' There was a silence. She gave him a sharp slap on the ear. 'I'm married to Tom Johnston as much as any wife in the town is married to her man, mind that. If I could know aright that your father's dead I would be Tom Johnston's wife in name. It's not the thing, a woman being no wife because of a man she was with only for a week or two. I was with him so little time that I'm not even given his name in the town.' He rubbed his tingling ear. 'Here, I'll show you something,' she went on, after glowering at nothing for a long time. She opened a chest, and raked among rubbish there. 'See that. Ay, it's a woman's hair, two locks, one for me and one for your father. It's nearly a hundred years since it was cut off her head. There's them in the town that would do the same thing now if they could get away with it. She was a witch. She said that we would be big in Dundee. That's why that humphy Kate wants you. She thinks she can rear you for bigness better than I can.'

Again she glowered venomously.

'And them around here that are nothing – they don't like a woman to have good looks, the pimply bitches! It's not the likes of them I would be among if things were right. You've got better in you, Willie, than they ever had. We're better off than them.' Her voice rose in pitch. 'You're as good as anybody in Dundee. The old man told me that when I was wee, and told me always to keep it in mind. Hit them, Willie, hit everybody that thinks they're better than you! Mind!'

The boy listened round-eyed to her confused story of the family and the prophecies. In the battles and riots of which she spoke, the losers were kirk folks who looked sourly at erring women and Dundee tenement dwellers who whispered on the turns of the stairs.

He saw the dwarfish woman walking in the High Street with a boy whose hair was a sandy red. They stood to talk at the head of Tyndall's Wynd. Elspet Digby's brat crept close, and heard the woman address the boy as John. The brat slipped past them, along the arcade of the townhouse, down St. Clement's Lane to the Vault. In these jumbled courts and closes, called the Vault because here had once been a burial place, stood the grammar school. As he expected, the one the woman had called John came down Tyndall's Wynd to the school.

'Are you John English?' the brat said.

'Ay.'

'You're not the only English in the town.'

'I know that. My auntie is called English. My father's name was English but he's dead, and my mother and my wee sister.'

'There's more called English than that.' The other boy shrank from the threatening voice. 'You never knew that, did you?'

'I know. My mother when she lived said to keep away from the other Englishes.'

The brat hit with his clenched fist full on the other's face.

'That'll let you know that my mother's right married to heckler Johnston,' he said. 'It was your kind that cut off that lassie's hair, and burned her as a witch. You'll be one of these nose-in-the-air right kind, always right.'

'If it's a fight you want, you'll get a fight,' the other boy said. 'I'll see you at the Dens after school.'

'I'll be there!'

'And I'll be there!'

They parted after glaring at each other. At the head of St. Clement's Lane, the hunched woman stopped the brat.

'Let me look at you,' she said. She appraised him for strength. 'Ay, you'll beat John,' she added. 'You're doubly the blood!'

He was frighened by these words more than he could have been by a scolding. He broke from her, and sprinted in the dodging manner of a back vennel boy. Gaining the security of a corner, he stood and peeped back at the woman. She was laughing.

Willie English and John English met, as arranged, in the gorge of the Dens. They fought for an hour, with Willie taking the fight always to the other, punishing the other but never gaining the signal that he had won. The hunched woman called to them from the top of the steep bank: 'That'll be enough. I've seen it all, and that'll do.' She slithered down the slope. 'You've done well, John,' she added when she stood with them at the foot. 'You've done well. And you, Willie English, you're a bonnie fighter.'

That night she came to Elspet Digby to ask again for the boy. 'It's not for myself I want him,' she said. 'It's for the old man, my grandfather. You know what I mean.' She was turned from the door.

Without looking at the boy Johnston pointed towards him.

'How old is he?' he said to Elspet.

'Nine.'

'It's time he was doing something for his meat.'

'It's me that keeps him, not you. It's my yarn that keeps him, and could keep me and the three bairns without you.'

'Maybe, we'll not talk about that. This one is fleeing wild about the town. He could gather up the tow for me. He could learn the heckling.'

'Ay,' she said. 'He could be learning the heckling.' She rose and cuddled the boy, surprising him. 'It's time you were learning a trade,' she said.

Johnston pushed the boy to the door without looking at him, down the stairs to the street, in through a small door to the basement of the tenement. Here was Johnston's place of work. He pushed the boy against the wall, then, taking up a strike of flax, he slapped it down quickly and pulled it over the first of a series of many-toothed combs fixed on a curved-top table. This was the process called heckling. The metal combs, arranged in order of their degree of closeness and fineness of tooth, separated the filaments of the fibre. Without looking at the boy, without speaking to him, Johnston made known what was required. He pushed the boy to the table, pointed to the tow, the refuse of the process, broken and curled filaments caught in the teeth. He gathered the tow out of the combs, and put it in a basket. He made it understood that in future the boy was to do this work.

Johnston went on working. From time to time he signalled to the boy to remove the tow. As Johnston moved from one comb to the next, the boy had to clear the comb the heckler had left. Johnston worked quickly, and it was made evident, without words, that the boy's clearing of the combs must be done quickly, too. The heckler had a trick of returning with a new strike of flax to a comb that the boy was still clearing, and his displeasure when this happened was unspoken but apparent.

Speaking to Elspet in the house or to nobody at all in the heckling cellar, Johnston made known to the boy the work that had to be done. In addition to the clearing of the tow from the combs and the gathering up of tow that dropped, the boy had to tie it in bundles when it had accumulated sufficiently, run Johnston's errands, delivering parcels of tow to spinners, collecting such parcels of flax as were light enough to be carried. A quick boy was an asset to a heckler, saving time and saving tow which was sold to the spinners of coarser yarn. Johnston had recently lost the boy he employed. Elspet Digby's red-headed brat was engaged as the new boy, and the brat knew he had no cause for complaint. Only his mother's easy good-nature and shiftlessness had allowed him to run the streets till he was nine. But he missed the wild liberty and lack of responsibility that had been his. He made the most of the errands on which Johnston sent him, the instructions always given in the form of grumbles addressed to nobody. 'Does anybody in the place ever think of tying up that tow and taking it to these wifies in the Wellgait?' Johnston would grumble. And the boy was glad to hear such words for they meant air for him, light, pauses to stare, to listen to other sounds than the slapping and pulling of the flax and the grumbles addressed to nobody. There was much to see and hear.

He saw the masons and wrights at work on new houses that filled gaps or replaced demolished tenements and wooden shanties. The new buildings were novel in their rectangular solidity and their plain faces. On the fringes of the town and in the more open back-closes the builders raised compact two-storeyed blocks with an outside stair leading to the top storey. On the main streets and in the more crowded closes the new tenements were mostly narrow-fronted four-storeyed erections with a dark inner stair, starting at the ground level and rising some six or seven steps before entering the building. Until now, gables had mostly been to the streets. The builders of the new tenements erected peaks on the front walls, above the roof levels, to give the fronts the appearance of gables. But still everyone could see that these were not gables, and everyone stared.

The owners for whom both kinds of tenements were built used every rood of their ground to pack one and two-roomed apartments upon it, leaving only the narrowest possible passages for the movements of the builders and the convenience of the future tenants. Where a right of way existed they left a pend through a new block. The children clambering over the unfinished walls could step across the closes and wynds from one wall to the next. A few folk protested that the town was sufficiently huddled without this further narrowing of the wynds. They were laughed at. In a cold town, where fuel was scarce and dear, a well-sheltered tenement home was one to have. The boy who was called by some Digby, by some Johnston, occasionally Gray, saw the clearing of a gap or the demolition of an old land or shanty row. He tried to picture new lands of houses in that space, and could not. He saw the masons at work, and still could see the gap. He saw the finished block or row of blocks, and wondered what had been there before, could not recall a gap, or shanties, or a ruinous older tenement. There were people living in the new land, and they were interesting, they were to be looked at, because they were the people of a new land. And in a month, the new land was only a land, an old land, with people who were the recognized dwellers in the land, and there was no reason to look at the windows or the outside stairs.

The boy grew, and carried heavier bundles of flax and tow. In the cellar, when nothing else was to be done, he slapped waste strands of flax against the combs. Johnston rose, pushed him, held his arm and brought the flax in the boy's hand down on the comb. Johnston pulled the boy's arm and the flax was pulled across the comb.

'Some folk will never learn anything,' Johnston grumbled to nobody.

On the market days, when the farmers stood along the front of the pillars, speaking out of the side of their mouths, the boy stopped to stare. Their wives sat on the steps of the market cross, and shouted their butter and cheese to the crowd. The country girls gathered at the foot of the Over-gait, holding up their yarn. The dealers and weavers moved among them, matching threads, bargaining. There was one red-faced girl, no older than the boy who stopped in his errands to look at the admiring crowds around her. She was always there on a Tuesday, and the Dundee women gathered around to admire her spinning of even fineness throughout. 'A clever lassie,' they called her, 'a right smart lassie. See and keep these fingers of yours soft and supple like they are now, lassie. They'll make money for you, these fingers, and bring you a good man.' The red-faced girl hung her head, a country girl being praised. Pushing among the dealers and weavers was the little hunched woman whose eye the boy avoided, the woman named English. She matched yarn for evenness, and bargained with the girls.

At the government stamping office, he watched the weavers come with the cloth from their looms, to have it inspected, approved, and stamped for the export bounty. He watched them carry their stamped rolls round the booths of the linen buyers, haggle over the terms, sell or move on with their linen in search of a better price. There again, at the haggling for linen, he saw the hunched woman. At the harbour when a Riga ship came in, the bearded Baltic men humped their samples ashore, and spread them on the cobbles of the quay. The dealers fingered the flax, chewed the ends, spats out the evil taste and smell, talked. Among them was the little hunched woman, fingering, chewing, spitting.

The boy laughed at a sight at which everybody laughed, the dwarfish woman called English in a new kind of hooded cart. She drove it herself. A joke was told about her – she had been heard to say that she would be laughed at on her feet, so she might as well be laughed at on a cart while earning money. He saw her often in her cart, and ceased to laugh. She and her cart became the usual, nothing to laugh at. The talk was that she went round the country buying up cloth, yarn, and scutched flax.

Johnston was now taking in coarse fibre to heckle. It did not require his delicate touch and his long experience. The youth heckled this Riga flax. He was tired. He felt the dampness of the cellar. He was growing tall, drawn out in the heckling cellar as the flax filaments were drawn out there. He was narrow-shouldered and shaky, but his skin was clear like his mother's. Not many Dundee youths had clear skins. He hated Johnston, but he did not fear him now. He measured himself against the heckler, and smiled, pleased by his own growth. He hefted in his hand the temper pin from his mother's spinning wheel, and thought of it striking against Johnston's head.

He lay on the Castle Rock in summer days when there was nothing at which to stare, snatched quarter hours of freedom in his errands to lie there. Somehow he knew that the sun and the sea wind would make him stronger than Johnston. He looked down upon the clutter of tenements and old cottage houses. There was no castle upon the rock. There had not been a castle for over four centuries, and still it was the Castle Rock. He saw from there the changes men made in the Castle Burn. They were working to give it stone banks. Upon the banks they built new tenements among which the wynds found their own way. The youth was seventeen. He was taller than Johnston, but did not know if he were stronger.

A cow broke loose from the shambles in the High Street. Men and youths and boys waved their arms at it. Women ran, screaming. The cow, in a panic of fear from the waving and screaming, gored a woman against the wall of the building called by some Monck's Land, by some the Luckenbooths. In the sudden quietness, it trotted back to the shambles to be slaughtered. The crowd watched the woman die, the youth among them. He was pushed by Johnston who came searching for him.

'I send him to get the flax I'm waiting to heckle,' Johnston said, speaking to nobody. 'This is how he does the job. Me waiting for the stuff to heckle, and him gabbing and gaping.'

'The woman was killed by a cow,' the youth said. It seemed to him a reasonable excuse for the delay. Surely, a goring to death was worthy of standing to stare.

'There are some folk would do no work at all as long as there was something to gape at,' Johnston said to nobody.

The youth went off without any further word. He collected the parcel of flax, and humped it to the cellar. It was a heavy load. Johnston should have paid a barrowman to bring the flax, but saw no reason to pay good money for such services when he had the youth. The load had been heavier to the youth because it was Johnston's flax. He had carried it in stages of no more than twenty yards, leaning himself and his load against a wall at the end of each stumbling run. Johnston, without looking up from his combs, pointed to where the flax was to be placed. The youth, his eyes blazing with hate of Johnston, tumbled the flax on to the stooping man. The heckler went down, and the youth leaped upon him. He stamped on Johnston's face, and the blood flowed. It was not enough for the youth. His feet were bare, and did not inflict the punishment he wanted to inflict. He caught up the heavy, compressed bundle of flax and threw it on Johnston's stomach, silencing the man's screams. He pummelled Johnston's face with his clenched fist after the man had become senseless.

He left the cellar and went up to the house where his mother was spinning. From a chest under the bed he took out his best clothes, the only other suit apart from what he wore, the only other shirt and his one pair of shoes and stockings. He changed to these best clothes in the other room. His mother said nothing. She took it that Jonston had ordered this change of clothes.

'I want money,' he said to his mother. 'I've done work, and I should be paid for it.'

His mother gaped at him.

'Where does Johnston keep his money?' he said.

'You can't take your father's money.'

'He's not my father. He's your fancy-man. My name's English.'

'You'll need to see him,' she said, frightened.

'I'll see him all right!'

He pulled Johnston up the four flights of stairs, and into the house. The man was conscious now, moaning.

'I want money,' the youth said. 'Where's your money?' He

went forward, and held the toe of his heavy shoe against the man's head. 'You'll get this,' he said.

Johnston pointed to a chest. The youth took from it a linen bag, emptied the contents on the floor, and picked out four pounds in gold coins and some small silver. 'That's my pay I'm taking,' he said. He held his foot against Johnston's head. 'You know it's my pay. You know you're giving me my pay?'

Johnston nodded.

The youth turned to the other chest where the two tresses of hair were kept. He picked up one of them.

'I'm taking this,' he said to his mother. 'It's mine, this hair! The other's yours, but one was my father's, and is mine now. If I come back, I'll maybe bring what's needed!'

He left without a look to his mother. She ran after him, but he was gone from the close when she reached the foot of the stair.

The words of the men who worked with flax were old words that had in them the sounds that flax makes when worked – ripple, ret, scutch, heckle.

The men who grew flax in Angus talked the talk of a thousand generations of flax growers. Sow thickly for fibre, they said, thinly for seed. Sow in the deep plough, broken by frost, where the rain runs through the soil. The flax growers pulled their crop when the linseed bolls were forming. They combed away the seeded head from the flax sheaves, the rippling of flax. They dug holes, filled them with the soft water from streams, stood their bundles of flax straw upright in the water to loosen the gum that bound the fibres together, the retting of flax. They spread the retted flax upon grass to dry it and bleach it. They twisted strands of the straw in their hands, beat it with mells and with wooden swingle knives to break away the woody core, the scutching of flax.

The farmers of Angus were tenants of ploughgate strips, a few acres. Fifteen or twenty of them built their houses and barns and byres together, and this was a cotton, a town of cots. The land, though held in separate tenancies, was worked run-rigg fashion, in common, divided into two portions, the croft for cultivation and the outfield for the cattle, a ruinous system for the soil. A hundred people lived on and lived by a hundred acres. On the croft land there was always a place for flax, a waster of fertility the men of the cottons believed, but a crop that made work: weeding for the smallest children; rippling, retting, and scutching for the men; spinning for the women. Its seed fed the cattle and the steep water from the retting holes fed the infield. The woven flax clothed the community, and the surplus yarn from the distaffs and wheels sold for money in Dundee and Aberbrothock and Forfar and Brechin. There was money in the gossip of the women; they would spin while they talked. In the long evenings of winter they gathered in rocking parties, singing in turn as they spun. There was work and money in flax through the winter when no other work could be done.

Katherine English, the hunched woman with the ugly hair, did not wait for the country yarn coming to the foot of the Overgait. She had her cart made, and drove out into the cottons of Angus. She saw and heard much that was missed by other dealers. Her sharp eyes watched everything, and her quick tongue asked about everything. The fear, among the sorners and tinklers, of her hard stare and her hump, cleared her way. Her unworried acceptance of the risks reduced the risks. A helpless woman, with money, on the loneliest parish paths was unbelievable to those who would have liked to believe it. It was remembered by the tinklers that she was descended from a witch. She must herself have the eye, they thought.

She saw at work David Sands of Kirriemuir, at whom the weavers wondered. He wore double cloth, stitched on the loom at the proper places, for corsets. He wove and finished on the loom three shirts without seams; he hemmed and stitched them, put on buttons, worked button holes, ruffled the breasts, all on the loom. She met that weaver of

Aberbrothock who by accident first made in Angus a web of osnaburg cloth. With flax unfit for any cloth then marketable, he spun a loose yarn and wove a loose web. A dealer had seen in this the cloth of Osnaburg in Germany. There was a market for this cheap weave, and Angus weavers had ever since been making osnaburgs. She saw the girls of Kinnettles and Glamis and Logierait, known for their clean spun thread. She was in and out of the houses in the parish of Kirkden where every woman had her double-spinning wheel, and where the flax riggs were long to feed the wheels. In Coupar Angus, she saw the weavers of the coarsest packsheet, weaving quickly their rough yarn that sold in the market for three half-pence a yard.

She was for ever looking at linens and yarns. With her careful eye she went over samples of cloth inch by inch; Russian sheets, crash, sailcloth; the smooth silesias of Prussia; Hesse cloth of hemp, or with flax for the warp and hemp for the weft; ticking from Saxony; the fine Hollands; French drills and cambrics; the thin weave of the south-west of Scotland, where they pulled their flax green; the close evenness of the Ulster linen. She imitated them on her own loom or had them imitated by skilled weavers. In the farm-towns she watched the scutching and heckling. She sought out hecklers in Dundee and watched their methods. She took her nephew John English with her in her cart, and into the flax-working basements of Dundee. She talked about flax to him always, boy and youth, wherever they went and at home in St. Salvador's close. She took him down to the Riga ships. He could spin and heckle and scutch and weave, but it was not intended by her that he should be a worker of flax. The money and the power lay in employing workers, and she was eager for power, the hunched woman, not for herself, for the old man, her long-dead grandfather, for his ambitions. He had said that the power would grow out of something to do with weaving.

She had been thirty-three when her brother died, settled, it seemed, into crabbedness, thwarted, feeling herself unwanted in her brother's home in St. Salvador's close, silent at her pastimes of spinning and weaving and reading the Government pamphlets about spinning and weaving. Within a few years thereafter she had become one of the known personalities of the town, shockingly active in the lint markets, her waddling walk pointed to, her sayings quoted.

Only a fortnight after the fall of the Bailie's close, she had given her first demonstration of what the right ones were to expect of her. The mason trade met beside the grave of young John English, his wife and little daughter, to decide upon the disposal of his stock and goodwill, as was the custom when a master mason died, and had no mason heir to succeed him. Hunched Kate waddled into their meeting, waddled past the embarrassed guard.

'You can't stay here, Mistress English,' the deacon protested.

'It's my brother's grave,' she said. 'I've come to stand beside my brother's grave.'

'It's our meeting day,' he explained. 'We have matters to talk that nobody outside the craft should hear. We have secrets in the craft.'

'Don't mind me,' she said. 'Just go on with your talking. If it's about my brother's yard and tools and things you're talking, you don't need to bother. I've given the stuff to that man Blackie, the soldier man back from the army. And I've rented the yard to him, and I've seen about things so that he'll take over the apprentices and the building that my brother had taken on. All the law papers between me and Blackie are signed. I have the right to do these things for my nephew, wee John.'

'But Blackie's not of the trade,' one said.

'He's a mason right enough,' she said. 'And a good one. And he's a discharged man from the army. That's all that's needed. The new law of the land gives him full burgess and craft rights because he's served the land in war. I've given him the start he needs, and he'll pay when he can. So you see, that's it all. I'll just get down, and have a bit prayer to myself beside my brother's grave.' She flopped on her knees, and bent her head over her clasped hands. Her lips moved, and the masons never knew till long after that those thin lips had moved in mirth. They looked at her, then blankly they looked at each other. A praying, hunchback woman! In all the rules and all the rituals was no word of how to eject a praying hunchback woman from a Houff gathering of masons.

So effectively had her Houff trick worked that she used it frequently thereafter. The right ones in their solemn rightness, she had discovered, could not cope with what she called 'the power of prayer', particularly when a twisted woman prayed. There were no clichés to thunder against a praying hunchback, no way of maintaining slow and over-powering dignity when a hunchback knelt and mumbled. Twice she was summoned before the council, which met on the first occasion as the guildry and on the second as the burgh court. Each time she prayed to spoil a climax of small town pomposity. The council records for 1758 and 1761 have references to these proceedings.

Katherine English, states the first of these minutes, was warned that her methods of selling linen directly to trading shipmasters was against the Dundee marketing laws, and was ordered to pay burgess dues for the right to trade on behalf of her nephew, who would be sworn as a burgess on reaching lawful age. She gave heed neither to the warning nor to the order. 'They just tried to frighten me. It's all they can do,' she said. 'I showed them the hair that their kind cut from my great-grandmother's head before burning her. I told them their day of wee town rules and rights were past like their day of burning women and cutting women's hair. They would like to think that their Dundee law is the only law, but now there's law for the whole land that is greater than anything they can read out of their dirty old parchments. There's a sheriff court at Forfar now, not a mixture-maxture of Douglas of Dudhope and council and kirk. They know that the Linen Company is with me in this matter.

The Company are big men who don't need to bother about this burgess law and that burgess law in this town or that town, but trade in all towns. You can't make a Company a burgess, but it can trade without being a burgess. And so can I. You can't make me a burgess either. What my grandfather couldn't have, I don't want, and neither does young John. As for the sacredness of their burgess ticket! There's one of them, sitting in that townhouse, is no more a burgess than I am. He doesn't know that I know it. Themselves, they've evaded every one of what they call their rules. They know they can do nothing against me.'

An act of parliament had ended the monopolies of the chartered weaver trade. Freedom had been accorded to everyone and anyone to weave and learn weaving outside the employment of members of the old incorporation. The act had not specifically decreed that dealing in fibre, yarn, and cloth was now open to all, but the argument went that it must be so by implication, if not by statement. Otherwise, it was said, weavers could not buy yarn for their looms and could not sell linen.

The British Linen Company, founded a few years previously, with receiving offices in the main textile districts of Scotland, had read all the most liberating implications into the act. Its directors and managers were the greatest in the country, their word and attitude made laws. They had sought out good weavers, and provided them with looms to be paid for gradually by the product of the looms. They dealt with traders whom they found to be honest and did not ask them to show burgess tickets. To avoid slumps, they bought up cloth that was jamming the markets, and in doing so consulted no ancient custom of council or guildry or chartered trade. They allowed credit to burgess and unfree alike. This was the mighty organization which Kate English knew would give her support in the fight of world commerce against the narrow economics of medieval Dundee.

The bailies knew also, and, because they knew, they merely warned her, tried to frighten her – and she prayed!

The council had moved even further away from being the ruling body of a town, towards being a secret society of shopkeepers for the protection of the members and their cronies. The ancient method of council selection had not been altered in the vast alteration, following the rebellion, of Scotch procedures of governance. The powers of Lowland lairds and Highland chiefs had been trimmed, but the burgh councils remained, with their systems of free and unfree, and many of the privileges of merchants and tradesmen remained, too. The same grocery and drapery names were in the Dundee townhouse membership decade after decade, and the more energetic and more broadly-minded men, intent upon the beginnings of an international commerce, were as yet not protesting too much, except when the council directly impeded the developing flax industry. The freedom granted by parliament to weaving had, in that trade, lowered the status of the little Dundee freedom of a burgess. Many of the new men, risen from the unfree, did not trouble to ask for burgess tickets, and were sarcastically jocular about the locked book, the shadowy guildry and the chartered trades, but for the councillors and their kind the preservation of the burgess roll and of the remaining burgess monopolies were still the main business of life. The building work, the baking, the shoemaking, the tailoring, the shopkeeping of a growing, busy burgh were worth holding, and the council and trades held hard to them. They could not disallow the applications of discharged army and navy men, granted freedom by parliament, but these applications were few, for such men seldom had capital to start in business. The council could, and did, keep their burgess book locked against everybody else who looked like dangerous competition. Thus, the council and trades could only warn a woman engaged upon work that had developed beyond the little economics of a little town, but could thrash out of the town any unacceptable butcher, baker, or candlestick maker who thought he could put a hand among the clique's penny profits.

Kate's second appearance at the townhouse was made to answer the strange charge of going to law at the Forfar sheriff's court to recover a small debt. After the failure of the Forty-five rebellion, all the hereditary rights of policing and judging had been ended, such as that of the Duke of Douglas, Constable of Dundee, successor in Dudhope Castle to those Scrymgeours who had been granted the estate and the constableship in the thirteenth century, to the Duke of Lauderdale who had usurped the Scrymgeours' place and powers in 1666, and to Claverhouse for whom the king had ruled that ownership of the castle carried with it, by ancient custom, the Dundee judging. A county judge's law-learning had been substituted in 1750 for the rough justice of Dudhope, but the Dundee council did not recognize him. The Forfar sheriff's officers had frequently been chased from the town, and twice had been locked in the Dundee gaol for daring to enter the bounds in the service of the new court. The only judges who should administer law for the Dundee citizens, the council gave out, were the Dundee magistrates. Again Kate's praying dumbfounded the council. She was 'warned', after a reminder by her to the magistrates that they would do well not to bring too much London notice upon themselves and their peculiar ways.

The following year, 1762, the council issued acts and ordinances for regulating the trade and the policing of the burgh. Strongly and clearly, the document restated the medieval privileges of the shopkeepers and all the trades except weaving, and the penalties for infringement upon them. Less clearly, indeed purposely vague, were the weaver rules and the market routine for flax dealing. Kate put a title upon the copy delivered to her – *The Right Ones in Their Rightness*. At the foot she wrote this in bitter allusion to the old-fashionedness of the council – *and, be it known, that a witch shall not be suffered to live*. She hung the paper in her counting-house to raise a laugh among her customers. She continued on her course, prospering by her eye and finger for flax, her quickness of decision in a purchase or a sale, her honesty and fearlessness. Others were doing what she was doing. The purpose of the years was with them in their doing: the years made an instrument of them to fulfil the purpose of the years. The years choose strange instruments, but surely they have chosen none stranger than Kate English, a woman, a hunchback, with a lock of red hair to look at and a grandfather's words to remember.

John English grew to young manhood, tall, handsome, quietish, expert in flax. She told him her plan, a breathtaking plan to be conceived by a flax-bargainer in little Dundee. She had seen how the trade in the town was moving. The town's cheap labour could make the world's cheap linens, osnaburgs, crash, hessians. Life in the closes where the fevers raged was cheap, and the weaves that came out of the closes were cheap. The dealers of Dundee had markets for the quickest cloths, linen for packing, for tailor's stiffening, for knapsacks. Dundee used on its looms more and more of the coarsest, dryest flaxes. The linen bounty paid the profits on cheap linen; a penny bounty on cloth worth only a few pence a yard made big profits. There was fine weaving in Angus and Dundee, and Kate had her profits on her deals in these cloths, but competition was fierce in the export markets for finer goods. The growth in Dundee's flax trade, Kate saw, would be a growth of coarse weaving. The Riga ships came from Russia with the dry fibre. The supply was irregular and unorganized. She was calculating. In her journeyings around Angus she met a Russian who spoke English. He was, at the hire of the government, teaching farmers in Scotland about the growing and preparation of flax.

'John,' she said to her nephew, 'you're going to Russia. You're going to see how they grow the flax there, and how they prepare it. You're going to tell them what we need in Dundee, and get them to suit our ways. You'll find out what's the meaning of the different packings they give their flax, so that we can know what's what with the stuff. And you'll see what the chances are of working up a steady trade of their cheapest, so long as it can be spun and woven. You'll get the agencies for yourself – that's the main thing. There's a Russian I met who'll go with you to talk to the Russians what you tell him. And mind I'm putting all I have spare into this. You'll need money to fix up connections in Russia, and I've saved and scraped to get it. It'll not be like putting money into stones and mortar that can always be seen and felt, but, if you do the right thing, it'll be solid enough. I would go myself, but that would be over queer, altogether, even for Dundee where they're used to me. Mind this, you've to bring back what's needed!'

Hunched Kate was impatient of the slow movement of two years as she waited for young John's return. She tried to think of what he was seeing in Russia, but could only think of the Angus crofts and outfields with upon them that kind of Baltic bearded men she had seen at Dundee harbour. Long letters came to her from him, but she did not see the pictures in his words.

What he experienced had its effect upon the course of the flax trade in the town. This was as Kate English had planned. More than that, it had its effect upon the man who saw, and upon the course of the family named English. He saw injustice, stark misery, pain, unbearable sorrow. He saw the long trek of the serfs across the plains, amid the dust that their feet raised, men, women, and children moving to the pulling of the flax. They moved as cattle move, dull, slow, unresentful of the whip-lashes of the overseers. Unresentful? He saw an overseer stumble upon a stone and fall, stunned, beside the moving column. He saw the sudden light that came to the eyes of the moving animals. They looked for the next overseer, and he was far away. They moved the line of their march a yard or two, and they walked over the fallen man, thousands of them, grinding him into the dust with their feet. John was alone and hidden from the marchers. He dared not make his presence known. They walked at the same plodding pace throughout. The overseers looking along the miles-long column noticed nothing unusual. The body on the ground was hidden by the dust the column raised. John English had in him the blood of the hater,

Adam called English. He felt the urge to be out among these marchers, trampling the body.

He watched the working of the flax by the serfs, the dew-retting, the pool-retting, and the river-retting; the scutching by hammer, by dancing feet, by swingle knives such as the Angus farmers used. He understood the reasons for the different packings that had puzzled his aunt. These were the age-old habits of different companies of serfs, who tied bales with three bands or two bands because their fathers had done so. He saw great heaps of scutching tow and rejected straw burn with the slow, smelly smoulder of flax. He saw that the flax with the unbleached ends which puzzled Dundee, was flax that dried hanging up after the retting, held by the ends that stayed unbleached. He saw the filthy ports of Riga, Revel, Libau where men, women and children, at the loading, moved dully, like animals as at the pulling of the flax. The quays were a litter of flax refuse. He did his aunt's business in talking with the men who could organize a regular supply of fibre for Dundee. He was a changed man as he talked with them and heard their views of what men, women and children were, hands to gather up flax, mouths to eat, nothing else. He looked on the dull, patient faces of the serfs, and thought of dull, patient faces he had seen in Dundee. He thought, with a shiver, of the sudden light that had come upon the dull faces when the overseer was trampled in the dust.

He came back a man who saw in Dundee what he had never seen before. In that week of his return, the seizers came to the door in St. Salvador's close.

'A vagrant,' they said. 'There was a crowd of them tried to come in to the town, these beggars that move about the roads the now. We turned them back. We can't have them here. This one wouldn't go back. He says he's Dundee born, and he said you would swear to him being Dundee born. We didn't want to trouble you, Master English, but he's been a trouble. If you say he's not Dundee born, we'll whip him for lying and for bringing up your name.'

Kate English looked at the tall, red-haired figure whom the seizers were holding.

'Is it you, Willie, Elspet Digby's lad?' she asked. 'If it's you, you've changed from the bonnie laddie you were.'

'It's me,' the vagrant said. He held out a long hank of hair, with red gleams in it. He looked from one to another. 'Blood,' he added, 'is thicker than water. I want nothing from you. Only your word that you know me.'

John English saw in the man before him the boy whom he had fought in the Dens, the youth who had carried heavy bundles of flax and tow through the closes and wynds. He saw the serfs moving across the steppes, the broken men moving on the roads of Scotland, escorted from one end of each parish to the other, seen out of one parish, escorted by a new escort through the next.

'Yes,' John English said. 'I know him. He's kin to me. His name is English, like mine. Let him be.'

'You're right, John,' Kate said. 'Blood is thicker than water. You can get out, you watchers.'

'Mind, I meant what I said,' the vagrant spoke. 'I'm asking for nothing from anybody. I wanted back to my own town. That's all I wanted. I'm as good as anybody. I've got as much right as anybody to be here in Dundee.'

'I wanted to have the rearing of you,' Kate said, 'It's too late now to do anything about it. I can see you're far changed in health. Have you brought anything back?'

'I've brought back my temper,' he said ungraciously.

This happened in the year 1767 when Kate was forty-six, John twenty-two, and Willie was twenty-one.

Willie English, called Digby by some, by others Johnston, dug graves at Logie graveyard in the church parish of Dundee but outside the town, a mile to the north-west. It was the graveyard of the weaving folk of the growing hamlet named Lochee, one mile further north-west of Dundee on the track to Coupar Angus, and also the graveyard of the people of the new addition to Dundee, outside the West

Port. The little cottage houses of Lochee cowered together, with yard-wide lanes winding among them. The West Port houses were the same cheap, quick, plain-faced blocks as were being raised in the old town, with outside stairs and a dark labyrinth of passages giving adventurous access to the doors of one-roomed homes. A gravedigger who dug for the people of the Lochee cottages and of the West Port did not lack for work.

Willie's mother and his two half-brothers were dead of the wasting cough, and he with the same fine complexion as his mother, had coughed in the heckling cellar to which Kate had sent him. The trade he had learned from Johnston was not for him. Gravedigging at Logie, where the winds blew from the Tay over the Hawkhill, was a trade for those who coughed. It was also a trade in which to starve slowly, but Willie did not starve. For those who were not afraid of the nameless things, gravedigging offered ways of earning money other than the burial fees. Medicine was a furore in St. Andrew's College, as in all the Scotch colleges now. The students and the medical apprentices and scientific amateurs wanted corpses for study. Willie English did not bury all the dead who came to him. The body-snatchers of the talk were never caught, though there were those who said they had seen the shadows of body-snatchers by moonlight. Nobody suspected Willie the gravedigger, that laughing man, who stole corpses in the full light of day. Mourners seldom waited at the funerals for the complete covering of the coffins. They saw the first few spadefuls of earth that closed the service, and they went home. Often they returned at night and stood guard over the grave that contained no body. There were tombstones on graves that contained nothing, and rails round graves that contained nothing. Weaving folks had money at times now, and they aped their betters who put engraved stones over the dead. Willie would steal a body, and sell a second-hand tombstone to stand over an empty grave. He sold railings and other protections against body-snatchers. He hired himself out at night as a guard against body-snatchers. He sat whistling over a grave he knew was empty. He sold the coffin wood back to the wrights by devious methods. 'What a waste of good lumber,' Willie said. 'It might as well be used again.' The words were a laugh among the gravediggers. Their trade was just work to them, like any work, with sweating, cold feet and cold hands from the cold clay, and sometimes a laugh.

Willie had learned to play the bagpipes in the years when he tramped the roads. He went walking up and down, playing his bagpipes, on the road between the cottages of Lochee and the West Port houses, where he lived. He was a welcome guest at a wedding or a singing and dancing of any kind. And he was welcome when there was an arguing. He could talk well, and keep the night going. He had heard the grumbles on the roads: Highlanders driven out of their glens, their houses blazing while they looked on before moving; ploughgate tenants whose twenty strips of land had been made one farm, worked by a few where once was a village; herders deprived of their employment by the laird's enclosing of common lands; land workers of all kinds whose work was halted by draining operations and the marling and fallowing of land. It was only an arguing, but sometimes Willie's voice rose to wildness and bitterness. He had known hunger and cold and wetness and death in ditches. He showed his tress of hair while he talked.

He walked with his bagpipes blowing to Lochee to court that red-faced girl whose fine spinning had drawn a crowd around her at the foot of the Overgait, and drawn his attention when he was a boy. Her name was Annie Bowman. They were wed, and she gave birth to two daughters. Both died in that year of the dearth, 1771, when looms that had clacked so busily in the tenements, more and more looms each month, were stilled. There was too much linen, dearth because of plenty. The effects, fever in the closes, the wasting cough, smallpox, were the same as those of scarcity, of harvest failure. The gravedigger was busy in Logie Cemetery. He dug the grave for his infant daughters, and knew now what graves were. Hate was on him. A bailie spoke in the Dundee council about the complaints of the weavers and spinners who marched to shout at the townhouse. The report of the speech became twisted and warped in the hate of Willie English's mind. Willie spoke to the angry weavers. He stood on the landing of an outside stair to speak his wild words with his scorn and hate in them. He held in his hand his long tress of hair.

'It was said,' he spoke, 'that the want of work in the town would do no harm to the town. It was said that the websters and spinners would be better of a bit starve.'

The crowd shouted.

'Where was it said?' he asked. He had them in the grip of his words. 'Who said it? Was it a Russian? No! Was it a Turk? No! It was said in the Dundee council, not in Russia. It was said by Mylnefield, by that daft, stooping, skelly-eyed Mylnefield that's supposed to be better than us. Is he a better webster than you, James Penny? Is he cleverer than Willie Slatten here who can write songs? No, he's a gormless creature with squint eyes. And that's the man who tells you you're the better for a bit starve. It's good for the town, when my trade's busy, my trade of digging graves. That's what he tells you, this squinting right one.'

They were swaying to his words.

'And you let him get away with it. He's a right one. He daren't be touched. He daren't be asked to answer for what he says, because he's a right one. His mother got nipped like other women do, and had a skelly-eyed son that inherited the house at Mylnefield because he was gotten in a bed there.'

A laugh, a wild laugh. He held them.

'Are you going to stand for it, take all the insults of skelly burgesses? They are the folk that are always right. We are the folk that are always wrong. You that can weave a web! You that can number hundreds? Are you always going to be content with being wrong? If you all breathed out at the same time, the skelly Mylnefield would be blown away, and all his right folk blown away with him.'

A laugh, wilder. They were seeing this owner of Mylnefield as somebody who could be struck and hurt.

He shook the hank of hair at them.

'D'you know what this is? I'll tell you. Something that has come down through the generations in my family, a sign to each generation of the hardness and badness of them at the top. You can see it's a woman's hair. The right ones of that day stood her at the market cross. She stood with her neck and her hands in the holes in a beam of wood. Her hair – this hair in my hand! – was cut off her head and nailed beside her right hand. She had had a bairn, and the man hadn't married her. They punished her for that, and then they burned her as a witch. A bit of her talk raised a laugh against the few that should never be laughed at, the right ones. She hadn't meant to raise a laugh, but it came about that she did. Against them! Who were they? As they are now, they were then – wee shopkeepers. That's all the right ones were and still are! She was a lassie of our kind with no defence against the right ones. They said she had done wrong against them! That's the thing to think about – against them! The world is for them, this town is for them. Everybody's doing is for them or against them. The bad times we have now are to be judged by the effect they'll have on the town by quietening down folks that are beginning to shout about shopkeepers ruling. The town, that's them, not us! We were beginning to be too well-off. We were beginning to ask why shopkeepers should rule. Then, it was a wrong lassie's hair cut off. Now it's a starve for the wrong. Mylnefield doesn't starve. He's right! By Christ! Is he so right after all? Is he?'

He leaned far out over the wooden rail of the stair. He held the tress out to them. They had seen a woman in the jougs, and burning in a witch fire. They had seen themselves in the jougs, and burning. They saw Mylnefield in the jougs.

'I've dug graves for your bairns who starved and took the fevers. For the sake of your bairns, you've got to show this man he has to answer for what he says. There, over there, is Mylnefield, with his big house.' He pointed to the west. 'A bonnie house to go to, and ask him to answer in. Who's for going to see Mylnefield?'

They were shouting. He filled his bagpipes and came down the stair. He played a battle tune that he had learned on the roads. They followed up along the trail that went over the Hawkhill in the lands of Blackness, four miles on to the house called Mylnefield. The owner had no perceptible squint in his eyes, no stoop, was no gormless creature. In the mind of the crowd he was a poor thing, easy to hunt, incapable of weaving, of writing tenement songs. Wild words made him an inferior. They wrecked and ransacked his house. They would have killed him, had he been there. Playing the ferocious music of the mountain men, Willie English marched them back to the West Port.

The council talked. They were puzzled. They knew Mylnefield, and could not understand how it happened that such wrath had fallen upon him. There were puzzled councils and courts and parliaments in all Europe that year. The closes and wynds were breeding a new disease to add to the smallpox, the wasting cough, and the bowel fevers. The new disease was named discontent. It was not merely the shouting of the hungry now. There was that in it, but also the feeling that the hungry had the power to hurt and the right to hurt.

In the Overgait, Willie English met the hunched woman. She glowered and passed, then turned to call to him.

'Digby,' she called.

'My name's not Digby.'

'We'll not argue about that. Listen you, you've got your ideas about that hair all the wrong way round.'

'What are you talking about?' he asked sharply.

'I hear things in weaving sheds that the seizers or the council never seem to hear,' she said. She gave her quick look. 'But that's not the point – the old man would not be wanting a rioter. That's not what he meant.' She looked at him for a long time, weighing him. 'If you should have a strong bairn, let me know. I could help.'

She went on with her little steps, her distorted body wagging.

'They think they're somebody,' he thought, remembering words of his mother's. He watched her. 'By God,' he said, 'she is somebody, the same wee humphy, and that John as well, a good man.'

In their different ways, Kate and her nephew were, indeed, somebodies. The hunched woman no longer drove out in her cart to Angus. Men drove out in four carts to the spinning folks of Angus, Fife and Perthshire, to buy spindles for the dealing of the firm English. In one or other of the two or three Baltic ships that came to lie in the river every year was a whole cargo for which the firm English was agent. A complete shipload went out from the harbour of Dundee, osnaburgs consigned by the agents English to the West Indies, an event to marvel at in Dundee, to talk about in the Cowgait where the firm English had its office in a block of offices, and where all the dealing men were setting up offices.

Where there had been six thousand people in the year of the glen rebellion, there were twelve thousand, thirteen thousand, fourteen thousand, every year some hundreds more. Folks from the ploughgate cottons spun and wove in Dundee. Among the cottages in the Hilltown were two and three-storeyed tenements. There were tenements in the dall field to the west of Hilltown, tenements in the rose bank of Dudhope Castle, and, far removed from the old town bounds, in Dudhope's pleasaunce garden was a tenement hamlet. The old names remained; the name of a field, the names of gardens, these were the names of tenement clusters – Dallfield, Rosebank, the Pleasaunce. In the valley of the Scouring Burn were tenements. The Gaelic tongue was heard in the closes and wynds. Mackenzies and Camerons spun and wove in Dundee manufactories, sheds of a dozen looms, where weavers who did not own looms worked at day rates. There was work in Dundee. Work was a necessity in itself as much as for the bread it earned. Men and women must work. Along the roads of Scotland spinners and weavers moved towards Dundee. In a growing town, John English and Kate English of the flax firm were somebodies.

John, at twenty-eight years old, brought a wife to Dundee. She was a talk and a staring for her beauty and for the mouth-filling name she had borne before marriage, Arabella Cowperthwaite. Kate had constantly urged him to marry. She was relieved that he now had a wife but vexed by his choice.

'A beauty! Ay, a beauty,' Hunched Kate said. 'But she's a generation or two on for Dundee. We've not made our way. It's too quick for beauties. It's too quick for John's notions as well. This high-faluting whiggery is all right when the way has been made. He would have been better with a Dundee lassie with connections in the flax trade to help him make his way. This one's got nothing but her looks and her music playing. A minister's daughter, with nothing of trade or money about her, not even good health. When he was in Leeds he would have been better to have looked at the flax men's daughters there, instead of this lassie from a manse – or a vicarage as she calls it in her southern talk. And he would be better to fight the old notions in Dundee, with the new Dundee notions, instead of taking up with these new notions for all the country, if not all the world.'

The house John built was a talk and a staring, a square, London-style house at the western end of the Nethergait, in a long narrow garden that sloped steeply to the Tay. The masons who built it boasted of the straight-cut ashlar, of the two twelve-foot high pilasters at the entrance, each only two stones, and of the triangular pediment, a single stone. It was the first of such houses in Dundee. 'It's a generation on for Dundee,' Kate said. She stayed on at St. Salvador's close. 'He shouldn't be spending money on a house. This house here would have done him. The money for his house should have gone into the firm.'

The passers-by paused outside the Nethergait house to listen to the tinkling of a musical instrument that they could not remember having heard before.

'It's funny music,' Kate said, 'but if it pleases her let her play away on her harpsichord, or whatever you call it. It's all right for the south maybe where they've made their way. I don't object to things just because they're new, but I do think that this is not for Dundee. It's best for families to make their way before they sit back and play their harpsichords.'

They were somebodies, the Englishes. The aunt had a hunch, a wagging walk, ugly hair that was uglier as she aged, An egalitarian pawky brusqueness among the spinning and weaving folk of the tenements, a famous finger for flax. The nephew was a travelled man, an explorer almost, had a wife who was a talk and a staring, had a house that was a talk and a staring, and he was the friend and associate of Honest George Dempster, member of parliament for the constituency of which Dundee was part. There were those in the town who called him Dempster's accomplice, abettor, fellow conspirator.

Honest George, for whom some had other adjectives, looked with John English on the men of the roads, the dispossessed. Where a cotton of fifteen or twenty ploughgate families had been, there was now one farm. They had lived near the bone these croppers of run-riggs. The land they cropped had lived near the bone, unable to feed the sudden increase of population in the industrial towns. The towns, ready markets for the produce of fields, made the new large farms, and the new large farms, dispossessing the little croppers, made the towns. The banks were eager to advance money for land improvement; moneyed men came with money in their hands to the long-impoverished land owners. Angus lochs were emptied to make new fields and to yield the shell desposits in the floors of the lochs. Hollows in the hills were drained, from moors the peat and moss were scraped, and these hollows and moors made farm lands when treated with the marl from the loch beds. The new fields were bordered with dry stone dykes built of the scree of the Sidlaw slopes. When the scree was taken to build dykes, there were fields where scree had lain. Where a hundred folks had worked, ten worked. The ploughgate folks moved on the roads. Dempster built Letham for the dispossessed, a spinning and weaving village in his own estate of Dunnichen in Angus. They had spun and woven the flax they grew in their run-riggs. Now, they spun and wove, in their village homes, Russian flax for the firm of English.

John travelled in the mountains of the north with Dempster of Dunnichen. Where sheep live, men could not live, they were told. Where sheep live, black cattle could not live, nor the Highland horses. By black cattle and horses men had lived in the glens. John thought of the serfs in Livonia. Mountain mutton fed town weavers, mountain wool fed town looms. It was better so, said Dempster to John, who replied yes, it was better that the men of the glens should move. They were silent then, doubting, questioning the purpose of the years. Because they doubted, new villages built by Dempster in the glens spun flax for the firm in the Cowgait of Dundee.

'These notions are too big and they get too far away from Dundee,' hunched Kate said. 'The town has to make its way. You've got the old notions to fight in Dundee. You should be going after the council here. That should be your whiggery. It's needed here, not in the ends of the earth. You're no more use to the town, John, than is that son of Elspet Digby's. He's out and about with his shouting for these colonists in the plantations and their declaration of independence. A lot of good that'll do his wife when she stands in the wet and cold to draw water at the wells. There's a thing you should be after them about, the wells.'

To Arabella, wife of John English, a daughter was born, and was dead after an anxious month.

'I thought it would be that,' Kate said. 'It's not a beauty he should have for his wife.'

Cartloads of flax coming from the ships and cartloads of linen going to the ships were delayed in the High Street, still the Marketgait to the oldest folk.

'It's time that old-fashioned nonsense of markets was

cleared away from the middle of the town,' Kate said. She retained all her vigour of mind and body and speech at near sixty. The manufacturers and flax-dealers were all complaining of the High Street traffic jam. The council heard the pleas from the Cowgait. Demolishers' picks felled the ancient market cross and the shambles. In place of the shambles was erected the Trades Hall, more fitting meeting place for the trades of a prospering town than had been the Houff. 'That clearance is something gained,' Kate said. 'It shows that the Cowgait has a voice to raise. We should be getting after that council more than we do. If I was a man it's not the ends of the earth I would have my eyes on. There's plenty to look at here in Dundee.'

There were years of too much linen. There were years of harvest failure when the price of bread rose and the price of linen remained the same. Always in these years, the back vennel demonstrations were led by the bagpiper of the West Port. The red-haired gravedigger, orator in times of riot, was father of four more children in ten years. He buried them all. None lived beyond three years from birth. Only once in that time were there two children in the home together, and these two died within a month of each other. All inherited their father's wasting cough, none his urge to live while wasting. He hated. He lived for the brief periods of dearth. In the long intervals when the looms clacked, when the improved fields yielded good crops, he was but an arguer in the arguings, the gravedigger whom the frightened ones pointed out as an atheist and a talker of foreign ideas. In the dearths, he was a leader with the power to make the mobs laugh and growl.

In Virginia, New England, the Carolinas, still called the plantations, the people defeated the old privileges in riot and battle. The weavers and spinners marched in Dundee. The gravedigger of Logie spoke at the Meadows in honour of the people of the plantations. Heads were broken in the High Street and the Overgait to celebrate the gaining of freedom in the plantations.

'You'll have heard,' Kate said to her nephew, 'about Digby being lifted. It looks like he'll maybe see some of these plantations he's always getting on about. It'll be a transporting.'

'I've heard,' he said. 'Some of us have been thinking about what's to be done.'

'Some of your whigs, do you mean, with their rights of man? What would there be to be done? He's a rioter.'

'He has not been taken for rioting. The charge is their new word, sedition. That sort of rightness among those who are always right must be fought.' She stared at his use of this old phrase of the family. 'If he is to be transported for his views and his words about the American war and its result, then I and some others in the Cowgait should be transported. For that matter, Burke should be transported, and Erskine, if disagreement with George the third and his king's men is something to be transported for. George the third! He's the right one. Think of it! In this town, such people as grocer Riddoch, the councillor, are the right ones!'

'If you're getting after the council, particularly that Riddoch, you're doing something,' she said.

'I was looking at these tresses of hair,' he said. 'I thought of that poor woman long ago for whom accusation was the same as condemnation. There was no consideration of any circumstances. There were merely rightness and wrongness. To me, that has always been the point of the story you have told so often, aunt. Here is a test of whether or not there has been an advance. This man will be given no real trial, unless we see to it that he has a real trial. He will be there alone in their air of rightness, and any defence he can make will be only added wrongness. I don't know if you understand me.'

'Ay,' she said. 'I can understand. If you get after Riddoch, it'll be right for me. If you let the old ways see the strength of the new men of the Cowgait it'll be right for me. And, forbye, Digby is one of the old man's blood, doubly the blood. He's got the witch's hair. Digby? No, his name's English!'

Scared by the support for the gravedigger from John English and other Cowgait men, the council changed their charge to the anti-climax of disturbance of the peace, a local court trial. An Edinburgh advocate was brought to the town to argue all the medieval Meadows rights round to the prisoner's favour. The bailies cowered before his reputation and his Edinburgh confidence. The prisoner's ready tongue made fools of those who tried to question his evidence. He was released, and carried through every street and wynd of the town. This happened in 1782, when Kate was sixty-two, John thirty-eight, and Willie nearly thirty-seven.

'This is the best thing I've done,' John said. 'If I do nothing else, I will consider my life has not been in vain. The fact that the man was a distant kinsman of ours does not count. Nor does the fact that he may have done mischiefs that deserved punishment. The best advocate in Scotland defended a gravedigger. The air of the court was changed from an air of their rightness to our rightness that has always been wrong till now. Those who have always made good their charges against such as gravediggers were humbled and laughed at, while a gravedigger was carried in triumph through the streets, cheered by people of consequence as well as by his own kind. This is not so much the acquittal of the man who was charged, but a verdict of guilty against the right ones.'

'Ay,' Kate said. 'It's a pity it wasn't that kind of guilty that you could transport Riddoch for.'

THE TREE OF LIBERTY

WEAVERS would march for anything, the mobbing of Mylnefield, an employer's attempt to defraud them of pennies by lengthening the webs, a new infection of the holy

jerk, a protest against the dirty Highlanders who did not
sweep their closes. They marched to cheer the birth of an
heir for John English, the whig, the considerate hirer of
looms and men. Kate had talked, grumblingly, in the weaving sheds about her nephew's childlessness. The news, in
1787, after a lapse of twelve years from the first child's
death, excited the folks who had heard Kate's talking. They
were stilled in their cheering by the word that John's wife
was dying. Arabella Cowperthwaite's funeral to the Houff
was a talk and a staring. 'Too bonnie to live long,' people in
Dundee said.

'She wasn't the right kind for here,' hunched Kate said,
not to her nephew. 'Her bairn, I doubt, is not the right kind
for here. He'll be a clever bairn. You can see that. Quick, but
not the bairn we need to see us through the next generation.
We'll be making our way. In fact, I doubt wee Adam will not
be in the next generation.'

She watched the child through his early years, felt his
muscles and bones. 'Ay,' she said, shaking her head. 'I doubt,
I doubt.' His hair was pale, with dull red lights in it. His nose
had the flattening at its tip, but was not the family nose.

In these years John English was staringly silent, then recovered somewhat to an interest in the whig excitements.

'You should be getting after the council about new
streets,' Kate suggested. 'It's all the talk of the Cowgait. We
need a wide gait up from the harbour. You know how
eevrything is held back on busy days by the mix in Tyndall's
Wynd and Couttie's Wynd. The council will have to see that
these wynds are not the thing for a town that's making its
way.'

'It is a larger question than that, aunt,' he said. 'Everywhere in Britain, in Scotland particularly, there is impedi-
ment to new trade and new thought. The past has its hold
upon the present and the future. Here is Riddoch become
provost now, an insignificant man in the town's life, but he
controls the town. The thing to do is to clear away all the
past and such as Riddoch, who represents the dead past.'

'Make no mistake about him, John. He's not dead himself. He's alive to his own interests, the same Riddoch. Don't be too big in your ideas. It will be enough for the now to clear a way for that gait we need to the harbour. Two gaits would be better than one.'

He turned to little Adam, listened with sad eagerness to the boy's playing upon the harpsichord. 'He's like his mother. Don't you think he's like Arabella, aunt?'

'Ay,' she said, 'he's like her, and like you. He's your bairn and hers.'

The weavers were marching in honour of the stormers of the Bastille in Paris. The Logie gravedigger spoke in the Meadows. He was bitter in his speaking, for he had buried his eighth child but three days before. His wild words were stopped while he coughed. There was blood on the ground where he spat.

'I'll see it,' he was thinking, 'I'll see the rising. I'll see them that are always right being wrong. It can't be long now. America, then France, then us. Glasgow will rise. Ay, and Dundee. I'll live to see it. The witch's words were that somebody in the family would be a power. It could be me.'

The stone of the Corbie's Hill was quarried to build the new streets for which the Cowgait men had asked.

'There's something I don't like about this,' Kate said. 'Riddoch is not the one to see reason in the arguments that were put before him. They're on the make for themselves, that council.'

Half of the castle rock was torn down to make way for Castle Street, leading to the harbour, a way for the cartloads of flax from the Baltic ships and the cartloads of coarse linen from the looms in the closes. Gunpowder and picks tore the space for a street out of an ancient clutter of tenements and cottages just west of the Vault, a street for more cartloads of flax. One Crighton, a doctor, would not sell his house that stood in the way of the new street. The council coaxed with more money. He would sell if the street were named for him. It was Crighton Street, named for a vain man. In grass fields was built a new way to connect the Nethergait and the West Port. Vain men wrangled for the name. The street was named for a river, Tay Street.

'We're getting these things too easily,' hunched Kate said. 'Riddoch hasn't become one of your Cowgait whigs, has he, John?'

Kate listened to the tenement talk when she called upon her weavers. There was a new theme in it, the back vennel superiority, not now the whining complaints of oppression.

'Hey, you,' she called to the Logie gravedigger when she met him during one of her rounds to her weavers. 'Did I not tell you long ago that you had your ideas all wrong about that hair?' He grinned exasperatingly. 'So it's to be the sign for the revolution, is it? You'll wave the hair when the Bastille is to be captured? What's your Bastille, eh? The townhouse?' He continued to grin. 'I'll tell you this, Willie English,' she went on, angered by his grin. 'We think about that hair, as well, on our side of the family, but we don't lose our own hair in thinking about it.' She noted his pallor. 'My, you've lasted longer than I thought you would last. You'll be – what? – forty-seven. I never expected you to last to that age.'

The rising men's Whig Club had John English, the flax-dealer, among its members. They were writing to Paris, to hail the revolution. The Dundee Jacobins, society of revolutionaries, had as a leader Willie English the gravedigger. They were meeting in the Methodist close in the Overgait, giving Dundee in their arguings to the back vennels, cutting off the heads of burgesses in their arguings. The guillotine had been erected in Paris. The Dundee Jacobins were listing the victims for their own guillotine. Willie English, the orator, was coughing blood as he spoke in the Methodist close.

'The time's here now,' he said, 'what they have done in Paris we can do. There it is!' He waved his tress of hair. 'I told you it would be the signal. There'll be hair-cutting done when we get started. The password is this –"the wrong ones are right!"'

He blew into his bagpipes, and led the Dundee Jacobins out along the Overgait to the West Port, down Tay Street, along the Perth Road to the garden of Belmont House to uproot a young ash tree. The plantations had had their trees of liberty, Paris its trees of liberty. Dundee had a Tree of Liberty, the ash sapling from Belmont, planted in the High Street. The gravedigger, coughing blood, spoke the wild words for which he was known. The shout of the crowd was the shout of the mob in Paris – liberty, equality, fraternity. In the crowd's howling was the old bitterness of the town's back vennels, and the new bitternesses of men whose cottons had burned, whose glen clachans had burned.

Provost Riddoch hurried to consult his bailies, and the mob caught him in the High Street. At the bidding of the mob, he walked three times around the tree, and shouted the Paris shout. The Whig Club were looking on, unsure of this. The news from Paris was news of the terror. The provost was laughing, talking aloud of allowing the weaver lads their fun. He was whispering different words to his bailies. Bring the military, he was whispering. He was thinking of the great knife in Paris.

The revolutionaries looked for the gravedigger to lead them on the move that had been planned, the seizing of the townhouse, the announcement of the start to the new era, the back vennel era. The orator lay in one of the entries leading from the High Street. Coughing, he had fallen among the feet of the mob.

'Get out and get on with it,' he told those who had carried him into the entry. 'We've got them. We could have it all done before they're over their stupor.'

'We can't leave you, Willie,' they said. 'You're not well, man. We'll get you home. Right, we'll get him up through this close and along the back ways. Don't get worked up, Willie. It'll be against you, the way you are, if you get worked up.'

The revolution in Dundee was a laugh. Highland soldiers kept the crowd moving. The crowd, having had its laugh at the provost, was content to move, and to stop for a stare at the kilted men. In the quiet of the Sabbath, the tree was uprooted from the High Street, and thrown for ignominy in the thief's hole, the prison cell of the townhouse. The gravedigger lay dying when the seizers came for him, and they left him to die. He was buried in Logie on that day when the tree was taken back to the garden of Belmont House.

'That's what it was, their new age,' Kate said, 'the kind of dreams that a man with the wasting cough dreams. You know, dreams are what go with the wasting cough.'

'There was more than that,' her nephew said. 'In its final wildness it was maybe that, but three or four thousand don't go rioting just because one man with a wasting cough dreams.' He thought of the serfs who had trampled an overseer. 'Do you realize that Riddoch's fat absurdity, as he walked round the tree, saved bloodshed? Aunt, the signal was the hair your grandfather divided out. It's odd.'

'Ay, Willie was one of the old man's ones,' she said. 'I was havering when I said it was all wasting cough dreams. It was the old man's blood against rightness, maybe the last thing the old man's blood will do against the wee right folks. There's only you now, at fifty nearly, and young Adam.'

She listened to the six-year-old boy's playing.

'Isn't he coming on in his music studies?' John said. 'I'm thinking of bringing that man Simpson, the piano teacher, from Edinburgh. If I'm not mistaken, Adam will be a brilliant musician. I always wanted to learn to play. Music was always in the family, and he's got our music as well as Arabella's. He'll get the chance I never got.'

Kate stared, her old face contorted with disappointment and anger.

Hunched Kate English, at over seventy years old, spun scutching tow from Livonia and flax refuse from the quays of Riga and Libau. She watched the weaving of cloth with her cheap yarn in the weft, tested the cloth for strength, considered possible markets. She watched the weaving of her yarn in warp and weft. The weavers shook their heads over it. She tested it for deterioration in dampness, calculated prices.

She examined a sample of fibre, harsh and dry. She had a heckler break it down on his combs. He laughed.

'You'll never spin that, Mistress English,' he said. 'What is it?'

'It's stuff that's spun and woven in India,' she said. 'Have you ever seen the bags that hold Indian goods?'

'Ay.'

'Well, they're made out of this stuff.'

She could not spin it. She paid a woman, known for her spinning, to try it on her wheel. A yarn could be spun, but it had no strength. She had it woven.

'What is it, Mistress English?' the weavers asked.

'It's called jute,' she said.

Her nephew was travelling again. At Libau and Riga he was inquiring about the litter on the quays. In the estates where the serfs pulled and prepared flax, he was asking about the scutching tow and the rejected straw. Kate in a hired carriage drove along the Dighty Valley, inspecting the bleachfields at Claverhouse, Pitkerro, Baluniefield, and the new spinning mills at Trottick and Baldovie. The current of the Dighty was the power for flax-spinning by machinery. She examined the processes of power-spinning with eyes that could see not only what was happening but also what would happen in time. They failed with their machine to make a marketable yarn with Kate's tow from Russia. She saw they would not always fail.

The seas were unsafe. John was delayed in Russia. The Dutch fleet held the North Sea against the import to Dundee of Russian flax. There were rumours of mutiny in the navy that should have been clearing the North Sea for Dundee's trade. Looks were grave in the Cowgait for a time, then the day came when there was shouting in the Cowgait offices, shouting along the length of the street, shouting and cheering all over Dundee. A Dundee sailor had met the Dutch at Camperdown and broken the blockade, Duncan, born in the Seagait in the time when lairds had town houses in Dundee. The mob who had marched behind the gravedigger of Logie in 1793, were marching again in 1797, with another bagpiper at their head. They were marching to cheer outside the house where Duncan had been born, that same house where James Stewart had lodged in 1715. They were shouting the story to each other; how Duncan, admiral of a mutinied fleet, had deceived the Dutch, made them believe he had a navy when he had only two loyal ships; how he broke the mutiny, and broke the Dutch.

John came home with his accounts of the scutching tow and the refuse.

'Ay,' hunched Kate said, 'twenty years from now that'll be worth money. Get the information now, and it'll be money and importance in twenty years.'

Twenty years. In twenty years she would be long dead, he was thinking. In twenty years he would be over seventy, if not dead. He wondered at this hunched aunt of his who at over seventy years of age, could plan for twenty years ahead, plan for a posterity to which she would be a dead old maid. She had his son, a school-boy, in to hear the reports from the Baltic. The boy was often with her on her excursions, kept away from school to accompany her to experiments in heckling and spinning and weaving, to visit the spinning mills on the Dighty and at Kinnettles, seven miles further into Angus. When she looked on the boy's slender figure, his pallor, the ungleaming sandiness of his hair, she was afraid. He was the future of which she dreamed. She thought of his mother, dead. She urged her nephew to marry again. She had her way with him in most matters, but not in that.

'No, that one will not grow to be a man,' she thought when she looked at the boy. 'I doubt I'm wasting my time teaching him the flax. If he is to live, he should be in the new side of the school, not among that Latin and old nonsense, not plastering about with that piano.' In the house in the Nethergait was the first piano to come to Dundee.

The boy spoke enthusiastically to the old woman about the composer whose music he played.

'When he was only five he played at the Austrian court, and the Empress took him on her knee. And he played everywhere after that, in Paris and London and everywhere, and all the generals and admirals and dukes and kings clapped their hands when he played. He was very, very famous. He was the most famous person in the world.'

Her old eyes lit up for a moment.

'Play that thing again, that thing by this Mozart.' He played, and she nodded to the tune. 'Did he make money out of his tunes and his playing, this Mozart?' she asked.

The boy shook his head. 'When he died there was nobody at his burial, and it was in the burial ground for the poorest people. It was a shame for the town of Vienna and for everybody.'

The old woman cackled maliciously. 'They would never understand that kind of famous in Dundee,' she said. 'I sore doubt it. It would need to be money power for Dundee. The old man said it would be money power!'

'Your grandfather, auntie?' he asked.

'My grandfather,' she said, 'ay, him. The only one that smiled to me when I was a bairn, the only one who would be seen taking my hand in the streets. Play your tune again, Adam. I got your father to name you for my grandfather. He could play the bagpipes and the fiddle, the old man.'

She never argued with her nephew about his schemes, his attempts at education of the weaving folk, his raising of funds to treat the sick of the back vennels. She argued with Dempster of Dunnichen, when he came about the house. There was a new phrase, in Dempster's long list of whig phrases, electoral reform. She laughed at his new phrase as she had laughed at the others. It had the whig vagueness of meaning that had always made her laugh.

'You're havering, Geordie,' she said. 'It's a funny thing to me that you whigs who know just how much power of water or steam you need to drive a mill, think you can change the world by having a daft done man, a king in London, write his name on a bit paper. Man, there's not enough power in that to spin one inch of yarn. You're blethering, man. What's the good of talking about the future happiness of mankind? Neither you nor me nor anybody knows how to make folk happy. Look at me, a humphy twisted creature. What would you do to give me happiness? If you could straighten me out, would you do it? If you made me straight, would you be sure that you were giving me happiness? I've seen lots of straight folk that had no happiness. And I've seen myself having some – sometimes. You can't legislate happiness, Geordie.'

'Katherine,' Dempster said, 'you are very wise in many things, and very stupid in others.' This was not a quarrel, it was a Scotch arguing. 'Happiness can be legislated, and will be. What you say has truth in it, but not all the truth. It is possible to remove injustices. It is possible to deliver mankind from some of the servitudes. It is possible to bring about an increase of freedom, of equality, of brotherliness.'

'There's no use debating with you,' she said. 'When anybody says a six-pound spindle of three-tie Livonian, anybody else who knows these words knows what is meant. The words can be taken into the court and a contract can be judged by them. But nobody could try anything on your words, Geordie. They've no fixed meaning at all. They're havers. Jingles for orators, to make speaking easy for orators, to keep them speaking. An orator is a good orator if he can keep talking, so you've had to make your sentences and phrases that roll out easily and can come in anywhere in a speech. That's what your freedom and happiness are – words for orators.'

Dempster nodded.

'Katherine, you're right, but again not wholly right. There are matters which can be stated only in words devoid of concrete meaning. I know that my phrases seem to be clichés to you, but they are understood by many people as signifying ideas that cannot be exactly defined. Words and thoughts are different things. Words are a means for trying to express thoughts. They do not always do so.' He was silent, watching her, watching the future. 'Katherine, some day women will be on the platforms, trying to express their thoughts with words. They will be more practical than men. They will talk about bolls of oatmeal or pounds of butter while men talk some vague phrase about the feeding of the hungry. They will talk about baths and soap while men talk about cleanliness, and about specific diseases while men talk about ill-health.'

'Ay,' she said, 'and they'll be talking of getting men like Riddoch out of the council and parliaments. They'll not talk phrases like the widening of the suffrage nor the reform of the legislative assemblies. They'll just say that men like Riddoch are thieves.'

'It's a cruder argument, but no better because it's crude.'

'Man, I'm not speaking in your platform figures of speech. When I say thief I mean thief! Have you ever wondered how it is that a wee grocer's shop can draw in the money that allows Riddoch to make such a display of wealth. He and his cronie Guild go about as though they were dukes. Over wee and fat and shopkeeper-looking for dukes, but you know what I mean. Where is the money coming from? Did you know that before Castle Street was built Riddoch the provost sold some town land to Riddoch the grocer?'

'No, I didn't.'

'Because the council is run by Riddoch for Riddoch. Only his cronies are on it, some of them only laddies. They can rate you and me to build Castle Street. We hear none of the townhouse talk nor see the townhouse accounts. You talk about the suffrage, and the rights of man, when you should be talking about Riddoch the thief. You don't need new laws to deal with Riddoch. There's plenty of laws against theft.'

'Are you telling me, Katherine, that Riddoch sold this town land to himself then sold it back to the council for the making of the street?'

'I'm telling you that. It's been going on under your nose. Riddoch who's in the best place to see the way the town grows is getting to be a man of means by his land deals that nobody knows about. I'm ready to believe that he held most of the land in Crighton Street and Tay Street. We were all a bit dumbfounded when these streets were opened up. We wondered at Riddoch doing that. Now you know.'

'Are you sure of this, Katherine?

'I hear things that others don't hear, hints. A man in your position could get it proved.'

Dempster considered.

'It is what we're fighting against,' he said. 'These things are the reasons for electoral reform. This is but one example of what is happening all over Britain. The country will awake soon. I was startled a little at first, Katherine, but, when I reflect, it is but a detail in our general argument.'

'Ach!' Kate said. 'You whigs! Why is it that this thing that my grandfather called rightness can never be dealt with in a straight way?'

To the house in the Nethergait she brought engineers who roughed out plans for a harbour fit for the growing trade of the town, and for a water supply, a hundred wells instead of the six or seven that supplied nearly thirty thousand people. 'If I was a man I'd have Riddoch out and hanged as a thief,' she said, 'in order to get on with these things we need, water and a harbour. It's a man's world. A woman can do nothing.' Yet, with all her scorn of the old ways, she could not sleep in a bed that was not a lumpy wool bed in a bed recess. She had always slept in a recess. When she came to live in Nethergait house after Arabella's death the builders had been brought back to make a bed recess.

Carried in her sedan chair through the streets of Dundee, she would stop her chairmen in order to shout at the councillors, leaving a townhouse meeting.

'What are you doing about a new harbour, Riddoch?' she would yell. 'What about some more wells in the town? You've got the same pipes and the same wells in this town of twenty-eight thousand as you had in a town of six thousand.' The hunched woman who could not sleep in a bed unless it was in a recess, taunted the councillors with being old-fashioned. 'Dundee's not a wee grocer's town now,' she shouted.

Women to whom she gave spinning work excused themselves for delays because of the inadequate water supply of the town. They had to stand for hours at the wells to draw water, they said. They had to walk nearly half a mile to draw water, some said. Kate knew the excuses to be good excuses. She listened to the quarrels in the water queues, shaking her head angrily, grumbling with the grumbles of the women. She appointed herself a judge of queue rights, shouted at those who attempted to crush in before their turn, called for preferential treatment for those who pleaded sickness at home or other valid reason for requiring water quickly. 'A shame, a black burning shame,' Kate said of the water queues. 'Good spinning time thrown away.' She urged upon her nephew and Dempster that in water was a subject for the speech-making. They spoke of water, and she was angry because water, it seemed to her, became an abstraction, a phrase in the whig phrases. 'Havers!' Kate said. 'Water is what clothes are washed with and soup is made with. Rights of man! Havers! What they need is water for their work. It's pipes that are wanted, not blethers! Give them water and give them a right way of redding the dirt, and you'll give them things they'll appreciate. D'you not know what the life of these women is, standing in every kind of weather for water? D'you know what a birth is in these tenements, when they need plenty of water and are dependent upon neighbours for bringing water or on the bairns who get shoved aside at the wells? In this house we have to keep a laddie for nothing else but drawing water. He has to be a fighting laddie. That should give you some measure of the expense and waste of time and temper.' She was out in the early mornings to watch the dirt men at work, as they shovelled out the running excrement from the pits in the closes. They wheeled it to the smelling heaps which they built in the streets prior to the dirt being carted to the river. The smell of Dundee, hanging in the back lands where the sea breezes never blew, was the smell of the dirt that soaked into the beaten-earth streets from the dirt heaps. Kate shouted and shook her head at the grinning dirt men. In the speeches of her nephew, dirt was mentioned, and Kate chided him for making dirt an abstraction, a whig phrase.

She halted her chair to look at a passing cart loaded with flax.

'Heh, you!' she shouted at the carter. 'Ay, it's you I mean. Who's that bairn you have with you on the cart?' She pointed at the little boy who sat beside the carter.

'He's my sister's bairn,' the carter said.

'Who's your sister?'

'What is it to you who she is?'

'It's maybe a lot. Keep a civil tongue in your head, man.'

'She's in the spinning mill at Douglastown up near to Glamis. She looks after the bairns in the mill.'

'Ay, ay, ay. But what's her name? Was she married to get that laddie?'

'Of course she was married. You think because you're in a sedan chair you can talk the way you like.'

'What's the name?'

'English is the name.'

She looked at the child, at the red hair and blunted nose that had drawn her attention to him. She signalled to her chairmen to proceed.

'Would you say I was right in calling that bairn a healthy, sturdy bairn?' she asked them.

'A healthy, sturdy bairn, ay, he's that.'

She was carried to the Westport, to the tenement where the gravedigger of Logie had dwelt. She called on a woman she had once employed.

'Did Willie English have a bairn that lived?' she asked.

'D'you mean him that was called Digby?'

'Ay, him, the Tree of Liberty man.'

'Ay, he had a bairn. He never saw it. It was born seven month after he was dead. I don't know if it lived. None of the others lived, and that one is likely dead. The mother was old to have a bairn. She left here to bide with her folks, but somebody told me she went into the mill at Douglastown.'

The old woman looked at the slenderness and ungleaming hair of her nephew's son. 'This one'll not grow up,' she said. 'If he does, he'll play his Mozart that Dundee will never understand.' She sat thinking of the wedding celebration she had seen in her youth, Willie English to Elspet Digby. 'That laddie is doubly the blood,' she said. She was calculating, planning. Two days after she had seen the child on the cart, a hired carriage took her by the turnpike, past Tealing, past Glenogilvie to Glamis, then by the new Glamis-Forfar road to Douglastown in the parish of Kinnettles. She asked to see 'the wifie Digby or English or whatever she calls herself.'

Annie, the wife of the Logie gravedigger, heard the hunched woman's plan, to take the child, educate him, train him. They sat in the living quarters of the children and old women who gathered up the rove in the spinning mill. They sat by the fire where, under Annie's eye, the cauldron of porridge boiled for the next meal of the orphans and the done old bodies who worked for porridge and a sleeping place.

'I'll be glad to get out of this,' Annie said. 'It's over heavy work for me. I'm not young, near fifty, over old to have a bairn to run after and to work for. He's been in the burn twice, nearly among the water wheels. I let him go with my brother in the cart that goes round this way from Dundee.'

'I didn't say you,' the hunched woman said, 'only the bairn. You'll stay here.'

The mother stared.

'Make up your mind,' Kate said. 'I'll need to be getting away.'

'My God! You wouldn't do that, separate a mother and bairn.'

'I'll away,' the hunched woman said. 'I was offering him a chance in life. I couldn't do what's needed to be done with him if you were there.'

'You said you had nothing much to give him, only a training. Would you take him from his mother just to give him that?'

'I've put a long, hard life into work for the future, and the

213

future will get the benefit. He could be the future and get the benefit. There's what you would call wealth as it is, but it's nothing to what's needed. And mind you, what there is is not money you can handle. It's trading connections that you need to work at. And there's trade knowledge, the most important thing. I could teach him to work at that.'

'You're an old woman. How could you teach him?'

'I'm seventy-eight,' Kate said, 'but I could live years yet if I saw something to live for.'

She was at the door. The mother was thinking of the water-wheels and of the life of the orphans of the mill.

'You can have him,' Annie shouted. 'Oh, God, you can have him, you can have him.'

'What d'you call him?' Kate said.

'Dyke, David for right. He should have been Willie after his father, but the first one called Willie didn't live, and I thought maybe it wasn't a lucky name.' She wept, saying in her weeping: 'Oh wee Dyke.'

'I'll be going,' Kate said. She took the five-year-old child's hand. 'You'll come with me in that nice carriage, bairn, eh?'

'Wait,' the mother called. 'There's this for him.' She held out a faded, decaying hank of hair.

The running boy in the Nethergait, the boy with the flaring hair, the blunted nose, the long stride, was noticed. He was a boy to look at, to ask about. 'Who's that laddie that comes from the Englishes' house to the school?' they asked. The sour ones, looking upon his health and his energy, sneered that his father had been the republican, the Tree of Liberty man. Those who looked with delight upon a loud-shouting boy, remembered his father's oratory and bag-piping.

'He'll do things, that laddie,' they said. 'The old woman'll keep him away from the Frenchy notions his father had. She'll knock that kind of thing out of him, if he's got any in him. We know now what Frenchy notions are. We didn't know when we laughed about the Tree of Liberty. Man, they tell me that the tree is growing bonnie at Belmont. I never thought it would live. It looked sick for a year or two.'

Frenchy notions now signified not the Paris slogan's equality but Napoleon, the name of terror. They laughed about the little white-faced Corsican, showed their fear by laughing. No, they said, it could not be Napoleon who won the battles. His generals won them. An upstart Corsican could not win battles. The red-haired boy, long-striding, ran past in the Nethergait. They looked after him. Strange the flax firm had been connected with that gravedigger who was the republican, the rioter. The boy ran past to the town school beside the churches. He learned subjects that were old Kate's idea of education, commercial arithmetic, geography, not the medieval scholar's Latin of the old side of the school where pupils were whipped for speaking in their own tongue. Long-striding, the boy ran from the school to the Nethergait house to talk flax with hunched Kate.

The ancient woman was the wonder of the town for her vigour and activity. She had ceased her visits to the Cowgait office some years before, but now resumed them, and appeared almost daily to terrorize over the clerks. Now it was David who came from school to meet her there, and to listen to her talk about how the flax trading was run, to finger flax, to be introduced to clients and weaving men. He sat beside her on a carriage or on a double sedan chair, and had the landmarks of the family's story pointed out to him.

'It's a far changed town,' she said. 'There's little in it now that was here when I was a bairn. There's the old steeple, and Monck's land, and a cottage here and there and some tenements in the narrows of the Moraygait and in backlands. And there's myself, no iller to look at now than then. Ay, and there are the burgess thieves, showing themselves now as thieves.'

She showed him the place in the Seagait where Elspet Renkyne had been burned; the remaining part of the harbour breakwater where the bones of the man her grandfather had murdered were still locked; and the site, long built over, of her grandfather's tavern. Pointing eastward along the Tay at Broughty Castle upon its promontory, she told her grandfather's tale about the plague ship that had brought the weaving trade into the family.

The old woman did not know that the boy was meeting his mother. John English had sought out Annie, brought her from her mill drudgery to her folks, and allowed her the small income that made her no burden upon them. Her son David came out to Lochee, and listened to her stories about his father and his father's forebears. He fitted his mother's tales to those of old Kate, and saw the course of the witch's blood.

When he was eleven he attended his mother's funeral. Kate allowed that. The old woman looked at him sharply when he returned from Lochee and saw the tear stains on his face. 'We can't have this,' she said. 'You're the old man's bairn, nobody else's.' She spoke about flax to him. He sat with his eyes upon her, excited about flax, and she nodded in satisfaction.

Young Adam at sixteen had gone to London for advanced study of the piano. Kate had laughed and raged, horrible in her laughter and rage at over eighty years old, but the youth and his father had taken no heed of her.

'They'll never understand that kind of bigness in Dundee. It's not what Elspet Renkyne meant,' she shrieked at John.

'Let the boy do what he wants to do,' her nephew said. 'He will not make a flax man, that's sure enough.'

Adam returned on vacation after six months. The old woman sat listening, hour after hour, to his practice. 'Would it be this kind of power right enough?' she muttered repeatedly. 'No, it couldn't be. No, no, no!' She screwed up her aged eyes to peer at his pallor and slightness. 'He won't live!' she said.

A melody swelled to overtop all majesty, hesitated, and broke into tragic triplets.

'What's that?' she asked, excited, for music could excite her.

'It's the largo e mesto from a sonata written by Beethoven.'

'I don't know what you're talking about,' she said. 'Speak plain language, can't you?'

'I'm sorry, aunt. Musicians speak in those terms. In plain language it might be called slow and troubled.'

'It's troubled, right enough, and it's different from that Mozart of yours. It shows the change in the way of life. Who did you say made the tune?'

'Beethoven, in Vienna.'

'God, are they all in Vienna? Is he famous, too, and without money? Another one for the paupers' graveyard in Vienna, eh?' After a long pause, she added: 'Play again, Adam, play your troubled bit with the new way of life in it.'

She surprised her nephew by suggesting that young Adam should do a piano-playing in public. She, herself, arranged for the hire of the largest room in the Trades Hall. She named the guests to be invited, flax men and councillors. She listened to Adam's rehearsals, and selected his programme, choosing what seemed to her to display a pianist most obviously. 'Put in the slow and troubled one,' she said. 'They'll surely see there's something in that.'

At the recital, she watched the audience. She was anxious for the recognition by Dundee of Adam's gift, eager for signs of recognition. She was angry that none was shown. Among bored, politely strained faces, only one or two faces looked up, startled into intentness for a moment. The applause was cold. The type of comment was this: 'Ay, it's a fine thing to be able to play a musical instrument. You're welcome in any company if you play. There were two fellows at the Freemason's lodge last night, and you should have heard them scrape a tune out of a fiddle. There's nothing I like better than a musical evening.' The old woman scowled as she listened. 'That decides it,' she said. 'Just as I thought. I wanted to be sure.'

The freight and insurance charges of ships that entered and left the Tay had to pay for ships and cargoes captured by the French. Looms in the tenement houses were idle. Weavers marched in the streets, shouting. Nelson destroyed Napoleon's battle fleets at Trafalgar, and released British naval ships for convoy duty. The marchers cheered for Nelson, and wept for Nelson. Now they would weave, they said. They learned that flax work was more than the heckling, spinning and weaving of flax. There was the clerking of flax, adding of figures. Looms had been idle because flax was dear. Trafalgar had halved the shipping costs of flax. Flax was cheap, and looms were idle because it was cheap. Cowgait dealers had been wealthy men with stocks of dear flax. Cloth merchants who gave out work to the tenement looms had been wealthy men with stocks of dear flax. The price of flax was reduced to a half, a third, in the panic of the clerking of flax. In the Cowgait men added figures, and found no answer they could think of as a correct answer.

For hunched Kate English, flax had never been ledger entries, but always fibre for spinning and weaving. Her nephew had seen the fields where the flax grew and had sailed on the seas over which the flax floated to Dundee. He had been held in Russia once by the fear of a Dutch fleet that never sailed out of sight of the low Dutch coasts. The adding and subtracting in the office of the firm English had the right answers. The boy David English saw the Cowgait frenzy. He looked at white-faced men passing him, turned to look on their despairing stoop, heard shots with which some of them ended their lives, and the screams of those who found hanging bodies.

The old woman, cackling at intervals over the failures of other firms, made flax lessons for the boy out of the trade crisis, talked forever – and never bored him – about the firm English, the future, steam-engine spinning, tow for cheap yarn, the jute that the East India Company was trying to market but could not. He no longer went to the school. 'You just need school to start the habits of reading and writing and counting,' she had said. 'In the office you'll learn more than dominies know.' The clerks in the Cowgait office spoke of the boy as the 'young master', and 'Master David'.

Young Adam, back again on vacation from London, paler, his hair even less gleaming now, had scarcely noticed the boy David. Suddenly he was enthusiastic about him. Adam had heard talk about David's orator father. 'Listen to this,' he said. 'Your father spoke these words, David. Listen to the thunder rolling in them and the sudden flash of lightning in the vowels.'

Old Kate looked at Adam in anger. 'So it's words as well as music,' she said. 'Havers! Plastering the wind! It's not the kind of power that was meant.'

The Czar was Napoleon's friend, and flax was dear. The Angus and Fife fields bloomed blue with the flax flowers. The southern shore of the Tay, across from Dundee, was a seven miles hillside of flax. The new farmers, farmers of two hundred acres worked by ten men, had not until then grown flax, a waster of fertility, a crop that required preparation by many hands before marketing. Now the price of flax paid for lost fertility. The spinning mills of the hill burns and the few engined mills in Dundee were sending men to the fields to ripple, rett, and scutch. Dundee's sail-cloth was needed for the fighting ships. The youth David English listened to the old woman's talk of flax in war. The clerks bowed to him, flattered him, who knew so much about flax, their Master David.

Young Adam, twenty-one now, still studying, and quite often earning some money and applause by playing in London salons, looked at the glass case that contained two smouldering tresses of hair. He had often heard the story. There was no sleeping hate in him to be roused by the sight of the hair. He thought only of the woman who had stood in the witch-fire with her hair shorn. He made verses of Elspet Renkyne's grief. He sat by his piano and made a tune for the verses.

'A song!' Kate cried in high excitement. 'There was a song in what Elspet Renkyne said. Great men were to gather in Dundee and hear laddies sing the lamentation for her death. Sing your song, Adam.' She listened. 'Ay, it's a good song! It's a lamentation for her death. Burgess laddies were to sing before great men.' She hirpled about the room, talking to herself. 'My God!' she suddenly cried out. 'A piano has hammers! A piano has hammers! The witch said that hammers would strike the lamentation for her death. Adam, keep at your playing, keep at it. Your playing could maybe bring great men here. What else is there that would do it? It's likely enough to be you that will be a power. What is it your father allows you? Eighty pounds. Well, I'll make it up to a hundred and twenty. Keep on!'

Thereafter, Kate would sit often by the piano, thumping down the keys. 'My blood will be a power in Dundee. My blood will become so much a power that Dundee will be too little for it, and my blood will go from Dundee.' She muttered the gibberish over and over, trying to find an interpretation that indicated Adam. 'Ay, Adam is too big for Dundee and has had to go to London. That's what was meant. No, the blood was to be big in Dundee first, and that would mean the bigness would be seen by Dundee.' She watched the wires quiver. 'Hammers, hammers!' she exulted. 'And a song!' Her quavery voice tried to sing the song. 'But, first, Dundee should see that he is big!'

For weeks at a time she would return to clarity. David, a tall, robust youth, his hair flaming, his nose like her grandfather's nose, listened to her flax talk and to the practicality of her views on local politics, the necessity for better shipping facilities, for better water supplies, for easy reform of the council by treating Riddoch and his gang as criminals instead of political opponents. The ageing Riddoch was provost every alternate year with one of his henchmen in the chair when he was not in it. 'David,' she would say on these occasions, 'it's to be you that will be the power. It's in weaving. It's to be you that will get after the right ones. I've thought of young Adam at times as being the power, but when I think again, I see it's not to be him, even if he lives. It's weaving, and it's you or yours. I've seen us rise. I've seen the growth of the power, but we're not yet nearly big enough. Money, David, money! They know that kind of power in Dundee. There's to be big money, big power from weaving in this town, with all the changes in weaving that are coming about and all the changes in money-getting. Go for the money, David. What I've given you is what you need for the times ahead. John doesn't believe me, but I know. If he holds you back, you'll have to go on without him and without the rest of the blood. But always mind of the blood!'

She came to the age of ninety, an event. A Cowgait deputation came to show their respect and admiration for one who dated back to pre-subsidy linen and had seen the beginning of industrial Dundee. It was one of her daft days. She hit the piano keys and shouted about hammers.

News came from young Adam in London. He was to marry one named Alice Greenacre. He asked, very diffidently, if his father and grand-aunt would continue their allowance to him in this change of circumstances. The old woman astonished her nephew and seventeen-year-old David by her enthusiasm. 'Adam will get to bigness the quicker if he's got a wife and bairns to work for,' she said. 'You'll write, and tell him that he'll get a hundred and fifty out of the business every year. And he's to get married at once. Who's the lassie, did you say? A music-teaching lassie, teaching somebody's bairns. Well, she can get bairns of her own and teach them the piano – with hammers!'

Alice Greenacre had no relatives, it turned out, and Adam brought his bride north for the wedding. The hunched old creature, with a glint in her crazy eyes, examined the girl closely, looking for health and fitness to bear children. 'There's more to her than you would think at first look,' Kate said to the girl's face. 'There's a good body there. You'll get a bairn as quick as you can, mind! You'll stay on here to have your bairn. I want to see it. Do you hear that, Adam! Give her a bairn, then you can get back to your hammers, but not in London. You've got to be a power here first, and they've got to see that you've a power. I was talking to some in the town. They're wanting you to teach their bairns, and some of them want you to play at their as-

221

semblies, some of these that are getting up a bit with wives that are even more up a bit. There's a house in my mind that's just right for you and your music.'

As it happened, Adam had been considering just such a course. A London training would command good fees in this growing Dundee, whereas it was nothing in London.

Hunched Kate, first of anybody, saw the earliest signs of pregnancy. English, the name, the family, the firm, the future. She watched, and nodded to herself. 'She's bearing it well,' she said. 'There's good blood there.' She scowled at the son born to Adam and Alice. 'He's wee,' she said, 'but firm and straight.' She held a finger to the infant's tiny grip. 'Hold on!' she said. 'We'll see if you can hold on,' She raised the child a few inches by his own grip upon her finger. 'Ay,' she said, 'you can hold on. It might be you that was meant to be a power. Nobody can tell.' She went away, laughing and muttering. The child was named Adam, to humour her, not for his father, but for the first English.

The Czar who had been Napoleon's friend was Napoleon's enemy. Flax was cheap. The weavers, wondering, shouted in the streets. In the Cowgait offices, men added and subtracted, wept into their sums. The firm English had its losses, but losses they could meet. The farmers of Angus and Fife met in Dundee to shake fists at the Cowgait offices. Never again, they swore, would their fields grow flax which wasted fertility, and which required expensive preparation for a market that might be a panic market while the crop was being grown.

Napoleon's conscripts of a united Europe moved across the flax fields of Russia in 1812, advancing, retreating. The looms in the tenements were idle for lack of flax. Too much flax, no flax, dear flax or cheap flax, the looms were idle. The weavers were cursing flax and all who dealt in flax. Soldiers cleared the streets. The riots of the tenement dwellers were not now to be shrugged at by councils and parliaments. French notions, guillotine, Marat, Robespierre, Napoleon, these were in the vennel riots and vennel oratory. Clear the streets, shoot to kill, arrest the leaders, transport them.

Aged ninety-two, the ancient woman was done at last, completely dottled, bedridden. She could not be made to understand the news that the stooping, haggard John English brought to her, that his son was dying. Adam had collapsed, sprawling over the piano keyboard. Hunched Kate raved deliriously about hammers. They made no attempt to tell her of his death when it occurred, and his burial beside his mother in the Houff.

The old woman lay three months, horrible in her twistedness. The family, mourning for Adam, gathered around her bed for the last minutes of her long life. Something of the old brightness came to her eye.

'Where's Adam?' she asked. They were silent, and she did not comprehend the significance of their silence or of their black clothes. 'Tell him to keep hard at his piano playing. The hammers, the hammers!' Alice sobbed, but the dying woman did not understand. She made out David. 'Mind about the cheap tow,' she said, 'and mind about that Indian plant – what is it, again? – jute. Mind about jute!' She went into a long rigmarole about the witch's prophecies, confused at first, then reciting them exactly as her grandfather had told her eighty years before. 'The old man took my hand,' she said. 'Nobody else would take my hand.'

She sought out David in the mist.

'Mind about the right ones!' she told him. 'Mind about the wells, and the harbour! Go after the right ones. Mind! It will be you that will be the power. You were the reason for your grandfather, Willie, coming from France to be nabbed by Elspet Digby's clear skin and her white legs. The first Elspet had white legs, the old man said. Money, money! Weaving will bring the power. I've seen us rise. It's funny – when I was a bairn our rise was shown by two names in the locked book, my father's and my cousin's. And now the further rise is shown by our names not being among the burgesses. We're above the locked book, as high above it as we were once below it. But we're not high enough yet. We're not the power yet!' She coughed. 'It's the smoke,' she said. 'The old man told me that their wood was too green.'

She struggled with death. They turned their glances away from the writhing and grimacing. David motioned Alice from the room. This was not for her, so near the time of her second birth.

'Humphy, wee humphy!' Kate shrieked suddenly. 'Humphy for all that time.' She wept, and died weeping.

THE STREET OF REFORM

An infinity of field-patterned knolls and hollows, of distant mountains, of silver river and grey sea, of racing clouds, and in that infinity – there, below! – a puny clustering and a puny straggling of roofs, a thing that a hand could cover, the town.

'I've lived seventy years in Dundee before seeing Dundee aright,' John English said. 'I've always wanted to be on the Law top, and I've always put it off till another day. As you had to come, David, I had a mind to come with you, and I'm just in time in deciding to get up here. Every day from now, that climb will be one day more impossible for me. I felt on the spur, there, that I wasn't to manage it.'

'I had to come?' David said. 'I'd never have thought of it. You asked me to come.' He had that kind of build and that kind of face that make a man look much older than his years in youth, and much younger than his years in middle life and old age; tall, lean, large-boned, large-featured, handsome but not attractive, uncommon, his hair gold in the high lights and deep crimson red in the shades, his nose thin, high-bridged, and abruptly flattened at the tip. 'I had to come?' he repeated.

'This day you had to come here,' the old man said. 'September the sixteenth, in this year of 1814, your birthday. There's a letter for you, David. The words on the outside will tell you why you had to come.' He held out a large sealed packet. 'Read it by yourself. I'll sit here and get my breath and my legs back.'

On the cover of the letter these words were written:

Go to the Law top to read what's inside. You will be standing where my grandfather stood when he was a laddie and where I stood with your grandfather and your grandmother, both of the blood, Willie in his Frenchie kilt and Elspet. When you look around you will be seeing things that will mind you of the blood. It will be well for you to be thinking of the blood when you read.

A twisted corpse had been mouldering these twenty-one months in the Houff, but Kate was alive. Her quick crackle of a voice spoke. Her heavy pen-strokes recorded the words of her speaking. Her tongue licked up a blot. The young man stared at the words, hearing the words.

'Open it, David,' John said. 'You needn't bother about me. It's for you. I could have given it to you in the office, but I liked the idea of taking it up the Law. You would be expecting something to be told you this day.'

David nodded. Certainly he had been expecting something to be told him, had been impatient for its being told. He broke the seal, glanced, a little fearfully, at the contents; a legal parchment and a letter in that same determined handwriting as had been on the cover. He moved away from old John to read:

Since you're reading this, it means that you're in good health on your twenty-first birthday and that John is alive and well and that I'm dead. You would have been reading something different had things been otherwise. You know I'm to make no will, but everything is arranged in lawful way.

The law-paper with this letter is the arrangement made between John and me. I can tell you better than it can, in my

225

own words, what you get. First, there's three hundred and odd pounds in Geordie Dempster's bank, and the bankmen there have my lawful leave to give you the money. I kept a separate accounting for fifteen old shillings in my grandfather's chest. They were the beginning of the power and they came out of stone and water. I made them take big risks in trade but they always gained, and now they amount to that money in Geordie's. Mind where it came from at the start.

Then there's my share in the firm. John and I have arranged between us that his share and mine are a half to each. In giving my half, I've got to mind all the blood. When I mind on John, I mind that he has his half, and so he needs none of mine. When I mind on you, I mind that you are doubly the blood and in the weaving. When I mind on Adam and his, I mind that maybe there will be something in this piano-playing, nobody can tell. And so it will be two-thirds of my share to you, and one-third to Adam and whatever bairns he has. I fear it will be his bairns that will get this I'm leaving, not him. Making that arrangment, I'm paying no heed to whose son Adam is and what he or his will get in time. I have to mind all the bairns of the first of the name English. Maybe Adam and his will never get anything from John, nobody can tell, and Adam has to have something of his own now, not just his father's charity.

Now, you understand, none better, that the firm is not something that can be divided up and eaten. It has to be worked at, and you've got the training to work at it. One-third part of the profits after allowing for reserve and working capital will be yours, one-sixth part will be Adam's or his family's, and one-half part will be John's.

There is nothing else for me to leave except some money that is an added reserve for the firm or for the purpose I will tell you about now. It is eighteen hundred pounds. If you should give up your third share of the firm that money is yours, and it buys all your rights back into the firm for John and Adam. You have six years to make up your mind about that. If you're going to stay, the money will go into the firm's assets. It can be used by the firm during the six years, but only in a way that will keep it as money.

Everything else I made from the firm went back into the firm, particularly in these war years when things are hard, with markets opening and shutting before you can wink, and other firms going down. They are hard times for everybody in Dundee, but the hardness and the times themselves are making a big change in the trade. That change will more than make up for the bad days. That is a matter you and I talked about and I don't need to say more. John does not see the change as you and I see it. I have been thinking a lot about John and his ways and that is why I made the arrangement about the eighteen hundred pounds. It might seem a bad bargain to take eighteen hundred for a third share in the firm, but it might not be such a bad bargain to you. It's all to the good that the money you would get by leaving the firm is so little. Its littleness will keep you from being too quick in leaving. Mind, there can be no more given you out of the firm for your third share than this eighteen hundred. The law-paper has arranged that so there's no getting past it.

When I made this arrangment I had in mind John's age and Adam being a useless man when it comes to flax. It might come about that for years you will have everything to do in the firm and only a third part of the say and a third part of the profits. That will anger you. Well, an English is the better for having something to anger him, and I have kept that in mind. An angry English is the more likely to do what is needed to make the power grow. I know you, and I know that whatever you do will be the best for my grandfather. What you have to do is be the power, you or yours, for it is in weaving, not in pianos, I'm nearly sure. And you have to get after the right ones. You will not sit down and deliberate on what is best to be done for my grandfather. No, no. You will be thinking thoughts far different from that when you decide, but your thoughts will work for the old man who took my hand when I was a bairn.

Mind, the power is to grow in a hot sun and heavy rains. And mind, the hammers are like enough Adam's piano hammers. They will beat out the lamentation for Elspet Renkyne's death, and burgess boys have to sing it before great men gathered from afar in Dundee. Her name is to be acclaimed by a multitude. She is to stand again, without burning, in flames that are cold. The blood is to become a power in Dundee. It is to become such a power as to be too big for little Dundee and is to go from Dundee, but before that there will likely be times when the blood returning to Dundee will bring what's needed. It has happened before and is to happen again, maybe many times, maybe a few times.

That last paragraph was wavery and indistinct, a senile woman's writing. The date and the signature which followed were strong and clear, as had been all the writing before the last paragraph, but it seemed as though the strength and clarity for the signature had been achieved with an effort of will: 'September the sixteenth, 1811. Katherine English.' Finally, with a return of the daft sprawl, these words: 'Grand-daughter of Adam called English.'

John was peering round, expectant of some comment coming from David. The young man said nothing. He stared down at Dundee. He saw the old steeple above the Overgait and Nethergait roofs. He looked for the other landmarks above the roofs, picked them out in order to avoid John's eyes. The clock spire of the townhouse above High Street roofs, the pale stone spire of the nine trades kirk above the roofs of Cowgait offices, the derricks of jib-loaders above harbour roofs, the draught funnel of an iron foundry above new roofs in the Wards, the thick columns of smoke rising from the engine houses of four spinning mills.

'Have you read the legal agreement?' John asked.

David did not answer. He read again. 'September the sixteenth, 1811.' Three years ago exactly! The hunched woman had written her letter on his eighteenth birthday!

John still waited for some indication of how David was

taking the arrangement of the firm's structure. The young man folded his letter, placed it with the parchment in the cover, put the packet into the breast of his coat. He came towards John, pointing down at the town as he came.

'That's what Riddoch is provost of,' he said. 'If he and his cronies could hold their meetings here on the Law, there would be a deal less pomp in their walk and their talk. A pickle of roofs that two waves from the river could drown!' He sat down beside John, his look still on Dundee. 'Now, what way would it be that the first English came, that time he ran from the watchers, when he was a laddie?'

'Did the letter tell you how the firm was to be from this day?' John asked.

'Yes, it told me.'

The old man waited again.

David pointed. 'See, he would come out of the Houff, there, straight down from where these Highland soldiers are drilling at Dudhope Castle Barracks, and up the slope through where that mill is, in Dallfield, and past the back of the weaving sheds in Rosebank, and he would cross the ridge just between here and the top of Hilltown.'

They sat in silence, then John said: 'A hundred and fifty-four years ago! If you want to talk about that, David, that's what we'll talk about. You know, the change in this view from then till now has been almost all in my life-time. A tree was still something to be looked at when I was a boy. Balgay Hill was as bare as the Law is now. I saw these roads being made, the Coupar-Angus road, there, through between Balgay and the Law. Lochee was a few cottages, then. The Forfar road, there – King Street coming out from the jumble of roofs around the Cowgait corner, then Princes Street, then the open road to Forfar. ... Just there where the Princes Street houses end at the Dens, I fought your father. Take your eye down the slope, along the Dens, till you see the road crossing the gash. Yes, there. That was the place for boys' fights. They would have to go into the culvert itself to fight there now. ... And, there, the Arbroath road going off the Forfar road. Aunt Kate was one of the first to make regular use of these roads, when the first trees along their edges were just beginning to be planted, and the first fields were being dyked. You wouldn't have seen this view then as you see it now. What gives it the look now is the fields.'

To see the full spread of the field-pattern, they moved around the rim of the depression in the Law summit. John talked of the change in Angus. There was much of his dead son's love of sounds in him, and he lingered on the Angus parish names, hard and clean as the hill lava, rich as the valley soil. Barry, Monifieth, Monikie, Murroes, Strathdightie, Tealing, Lundie. These, the nearer lands were fully tamed to beauty; birches and elms in clusters on the knoll tops, in lines by the roadside; yellow and green squares of ripe corn and pasture and potatoes; brown squares of September ploughing, close climbing furrows, curving with the swell of the fields, whorling around the knolls. Names to roll on the tongue, these Angus names, to roll in the mind. Glamis, Newtyle, Eassie, Nevay, Rescobie, Kirriemuir, Cortachy, Tannadice, Oathlaw, Careston, Fern, Dunnichen, Inverarity; in these farther-off lands hidden by the Sidlaws were the same disciplined beauty as in the nearer lands, and beside it the unkempt beauty of the last cottons, where the high-ridged askew lazy-beds of the run-riggs wandered among bogs and stone outcrops and vast wildernesses of bracken and fool's-parsley. Among the groomed beauty of the new farms and the tinkler beauty of the old farms was the ugliness of those lands in process of being disciplined; the mud bottoms of the drained lochs, the scars where broom had been uprooted and moss scraped away, the raw lines of ditches and drains, the humps of lime and marl, the black ruins of cottons.

'In all my life-time,' John said, 'there have been homes burning in the country-side and homes being built in the town.' He and David had come in their slow walking around the Law summit to where they had started.

'Progress hurts a few to benefit the many,' David said, gazing down on Dundee.

After a long hesitation in which he looked several times from the young man's face to the town below, John spoke. 'David, you were going to tell me how you feel about becoming a partner of the firm, weren't you?'

'I haven't examined the law-paper yet,' David said, sharply.

A hurt expression came on John's face, and his figure drooped suddenly. 'I'm glad to be a partner,' the young man added quickly. His words sounded dry and harsh.

'There is one other change in Angus that has been made in my time,' the old man said, slowly. 'There are the water mills for spinning along the Dighty behind us, and in the Sidlaws, at Friock and Kinnettles!' On the word Kinnettles was a faint accent, and his eyes moved to David as he spoke the word. 'More progress, but perhaps the orphan workers in these mills do not use that word. Perhaps they have other words for their prison-like life, just as the run-rigg folks have words, other than progress, for the burning of their homes.'

Fifty-two years went by before David understood, fifty-two years before he knew the implications accented into that name of an Angus parish, where his mother had made the soup and porridge for mill children. That day on the Law, his twenty-first birthday, failing to understand, he said: 'These country mills have not long to go, now. One steam-engine in a Dundee mill will turn more spindles than all the hill burns of Angus. Look, that foundry down there is the biggest change of all. Machines and engines made in Dundee for Dundee's kind of work! Dundee has been moving only slowly to the new way of the spinning and weaving industry. And the reason was the lack of engineers on the spot. Now that we've got the Carmichaels and their foundry, the spinning mills will go up in the town as quick as you can count them. And that means a quickening in the proper organization of weaving, too. Our way just now is dying out, this collecting the cloth from weavers working for themselves in their one-loom cellars and rooms. There will be more weaving sheds and factories with the weavers working for hire. It's the only way by which the trade can grow and the town grow. The firm should be in production, in a mill and a factory.'

'So you've told me – often,' John said. 'I haven't made any reply that really expresses my point of view. I'll make it now. You're a partner now. I'm not arguing with you, David; keep that in mind while I talk. A long time ago I went to Russia, and I saw a sight that is always with me – a long line of serfs trample an overseer into the dust. My sympathy was with the serfs. When I returned I saw the look of these serfs upon the faces of some Dundee folks. In recent years I have seen that look become even more common in the town, as weavers and spinners lost their independence. A weaver's life or a spinner's life has been a hard enough life all my time, but for most of that time weavers and spinners have been folks with something of their own to make, something of their own to bargain over. The word for them was manufacturer, one who made something with his hands. That word is coming to mean an owner of a factory, where folks have no pride in making and they have no selling to do of something they've made. I've worried about my place in the trade. I was glad, when I began to see the way the trade was moving, that my son was finding a life for himself away from flax.' He halted there, pained by that memory. 'I have no great ambitions in flax now. I keep in mind that my grandsons may want to be flax men when they grow up, and such ambitions as are left in me are for them, to maintain the firm for them.' David stared. Most of the work for himself, he was thinking, all of it as John aged, for one-third of the profits, in a firm that was for John's grandchildren! Was that better than being a hired man, was there independence in that? 'I believe,' John was saying, 'there is still a good living for the firm in the old ways, the encouragement of the independent weavers, even of the hand-spinners to some extent. We have good markets for that cloth and for that yarn, and I don't see them disappearing as readily as you seem to think they will. I am all against the firm going into mill owning. No doubt we could raise the money, but I will not be a serf driver.'

'How can you see it as serf driving?' David cried. He named some of the Cowgait men. 'Are they serf drivers, your own kind of whig?'

'The look is on the faces of the mill women, and it was not on their faces when they were hand-spinners. It's on the faces of the men and women in the weaving sheds, and it's not on the faces of most of those who weave on their own. I know, David, I know that there are few serf drivers in the Cowgait. It's the thing itself that makes serfs, not the men who run it. I shouldn't have said it. I know this new way has to go on increasing. I know it is the Cowgait men, these same men talking about mills and factories, who are running our dispensary and our poor reliefs and the poor schools. I know they'll do their best for Dundee, but the new way will make serfs despite them.'

'You admit it's coming,' David said. 'It's the only way Dundee folks can go on living, by the proper organization of their work. They're better in mills and weaving factories than on the roads. The organizing will go on whether our firm is in it or not, and it will be a good thing for the whole town. The town can't stand still in these days. It has to grow to live at all, and only by the new ways can it grow. The firm would be hurting these folks, as well as itself, by not taking a part in the organizing. We're well placed for helping to organize Dundee and to make it grow. The way to look at it is that we're hindering Dundee folk in their getting a living, if we don't join in.'

John stared for a long time at the town. 'Dundee will grow?' he said, at length. 'Well, maybe you're right in saying it will grow. If it does grow it grows on its one economic advantage. Heaven help Dundee as it grows! And Heaven help it when its one advantage is in rivalry with some other coarse weaving district that has that same advantage, only more so!'

'What d'you mean? What's the one advantage you talk about?'

'A town with a narrow hinterland of fields and beyond that bare mountains,' John said, pointing down, 'a town without coal or other source of power and without an easy access to raw materials for manufacture.'

'These are its economic disadvantages. What is this economic advantage you speak about?'

'It shows itself in the legends and memories of our family,' John said. 'A town battered in a siege, years of poverty in a battered town, the flax and wool fights for ha'pennies, the meal riots, a subsidy that was a politician's bribe, the low greed of Riddoch and his kind, the small ambitions, the self-satisfaction with mean attainment among little right ones. I'll tell you in one word what is the economic advantage of Dundee. Poverty! A tradition of cheapness – that's what we've got. Nothing else but that!' He paused, and the anger that had been mounting in him cooled. 'Remember, David,' he added, 'I wasn't arguing with you. What I've been saying and the way I've said it was not against you. I'm from the quiet side of the family. We've always been quiet, except for Kate, and she had her humph. We think plenty though we're quiet. We can be Englishes, too!'

He started to move down the hill, feeling carefully, in an old man's manner, for footholds. David put out a hand to help. Grasping David's hand, holding to it, John stood on the slope. 'Down there where the road crosses the Dens, I fought your father,' he said. The words were a plea, not a threat. He smiled up to David, above him on the slope. David's smile, in return, was hard and one-sided.

David English had been born to hate such men as Riddoch, provost of Dundee, reared to hate such men. He had his full share of the Englishes' capacity for anger against rightness. He had, too, his own feeling of disappointment. In the ledger of English anecdotes, the description of Riddoch, one of the few right ones to be named and described in the ledger, is David English's characteristic venom, a frustrated man's invective, remembered eighty years after Riddoch's death and thirty years after David's.

In youth and middle life, Riddoch had been fat. Now, in 1814, in old age, when the bulging beefiness had melted away, his over-stretched skin hung in dry folds on wizened face and withered frame. He had been heartily loud and confidently aggressive. Now, bleared eyes looked out from the deadness with the greedy suspicion of a miser, and, dripping saliva, a lipless slit in the deadness mumbled the defensive platitudes of caution. This monstrosity was dictator of the Dundee townhouse; only creatures of his were allowed to be councillors, and their part in the council business was an acquiescent nodding. His ability to dominate lay in his stupidity. His only interest was self-interest, and that he held to be the interest of the Dundee community, even the national interest. His politics, the meanest kind of negative toriness – down with everything novel, all novelties being jacobinism – were a witless man's toadying to what he conceived to be the wishes of the higher orders, such as Angus lairds. His religion was disapproval of all beauty, and he required of the kirk ministers that they preach no other god and pray to none other than that ugly god whose chosen people were a small clique of Dundee shopkeepers of Riddoch's selection.

The ancient Dundee institutions, formed centuries before in faith and hope to serve the nobler aspirations of Dundee, had for long been degenerating, having outlived the times for which they had been formed. Alexander Riddoch made of their decay an evil corruption. With the craftiness of stupidity, he used the burgh's chartered rights and the chartered rights of the guildry and the trades to maintain his grasp upon the local governance, which became for most of those in it only a defensive association of shopmen and small trade-masters, and for Riddoch and a few close associates a means to wealth. These few were not immoral, but amoral; they did not have the cleverness to know right from wrong; their gains were, to them, a normal and natural result of their being in the townhouse, and while they kept secret the methods, even from their fellow-councillors – who might want a share! – they made no attempt to hide the riches.

Riddoch's dirty little grocery at the head of the Seagait drew no more than a few pounds a week. Riddoch's house in the Nethergait was the largest in the town, and Riddoch, flaunting his fortune in Dundee's face, regarded himself, with the sincerity of a stupid man, as a model of integrity and public service. A fifteenth-century law stated that a Scotch burgh council had the selection of the succeeding council; a fifteenth-century division of the classes held that, after the lairds, a few shopkeepers and master tradesmen were counted as the free people, and indeed, as the only people who need be counted; and Alexander Riddoch, grocer, guild brother by right of being a property owner and having paid eighty shillings for grocering privileges, was provost of Dundee, where were now no lairds.

In the townhouse Provost Riddoch spoke: 'During the war we were over-busy in keeping an eye on the unity of the nation. We were seeing that it wasn't broken up by these jacobins we've got about the town. And we were over-busy, too, in the matter of seeing to defence against invasion – for Boney might have landed, though he thought better of it! And so we had lots of things to do in connection with the volunteers and with the troops at Dudhope Castle and with the raising of men for the navy. It was because we were over-busy on these things that were so needing to be done, that we had to let other things be neglected a bit. It is high time we saw to them, for they are now much needing to be done. There's been a slipping in of unfree men to free privileges and it's high time it was put a stop to. Keep our own fish guts for our own sea maws, I say. Two in particular came into the town when everybody was busy on the war, and without let or hindrance these two have set themselves up in work that could be done by free hammermen. If these two are to be doing hammermen's work, they should be applying to the hammermen trade for admittance. They should be ready to take the tests of the trade, and to abide by the decision of the tests. And if they do pass the tests, they should apply to us for freemen's rights, and abide by our decision as to whether or not they are fit men for freedom. We have got to get back to the strict rules of well-regulated work in the town. Things are lapsing badly we can see, now that we have time to look about us and see what has been going on.'

The flax men, walking to and fro in the Cowgait, talked about the steadying of fibre prices, about an improving demand for cloth, about the readiness of the banks to finance mill building, about the Carmichaels' new steam-engines, the Carmichaels' new spinning frames. They talked, flushed, about Riddoch's reference to the brothers Carmichael. Did Riddoch not know, they asked each other, that the Cowgait had invited these West of Scotland engineers to Dundee. Ignore Riddoch, the older flax men were saying. He had only been blustering to his servile councillors to keep them servile, they said. If it did come to a strict interpretation of the trade rules, then the Carmichaels could pay the small fees and be burgesses, some were saying. A few pounds expenditure and the writing of names in a book, there was nothing more than that in this freedom. These older men of the Cowgait were nodding their derision of Riddoch's freedom of the town. Yes, let the Carmichaels be in the locked book if that would shut Riddoch's silly mouth.

Younger flax men were around David English. 'The feudal system of fleshers,' he was saying in reference to Riddoch's rule, 'the divine right of drapers, and the gross greed of grocers! Contempt is not enough. Doing nothing contemptuously will not hurt Riddoch. Doing something contemptuously is what's needed, doing something he could understand as contempt!' He was silent, thinking, then he laughed. He talked quickly, and the young Cowgait men laughed with him. 'It must be done this week if I've to be in it,' David said. Only a few days remained before his setting out for Russia. He was going there in order to organize a supply of the scutching tow and flax refuse which John had looked at seventeen years before. The new spinning frames could make a serviceable yarn with this cheap fibre, called codilla. 'Mind,' David finished, 'We're not to tell anybody about this till after we've done it!'

Six young flax men appeared before the council at the next townhouse meeting. They were all men of imposing height and appearance. They wore their best clothes, and had groomed themselves well. One was there for his ability to mimic a dandy's flourish of a quizzing glass. They announced themselves as Cowgait men anxious to lay before the council a matter of supreme importance to the town, and after some delay were admitted. In the manner rehearsed by them again and again, they solemnly ignored the staring councillors and, standing in line before the provost's chair, examined him sternly.

'Well, and what can I be doing for you, gentlemen?' Riddoch asked. His bearing towards men in well-cut clothes was always that of a little grocer.

Loudly and clearly, David English read from an important looking scroll. He and his accomplices had spent several hours in giving the scroll an appearance and wording to hold the council's attention.

David read to this effect: James Watt, creator of much of the country's prosperity, had, as a young man, opened an instrument-repairing shop in Glasgow; from certain unworthy elements in the Glasgow community had come demands for the closing of his business, and the driving of Watt himself, one of the great figures in all Scotch history, from the burgh. The famous genius resisted these ruffianly intimidations, and because he did so his shop was burst open by a mob, his stock stolen or broken up, and he himself put in danger of his life.

Riddoch nodded sympathy when he heard the words ruffianly and mob; it would be these low jacobins, he was thinking.

David read on: Only by the kind offices of Glasgow University, which allowed the world-renowned scientist and inventor to come within its walls, was Watt allowed to carry on his labours, destined to be such a great benefit to humanity, and, particularly to the burgh of Glasgow.

Riddoch nodded his patronizing approval of Glasgow University.

David continued: In this burgh of Dundee, a selfish and unthinking mob of low scoundrels had uttered the self-same threats against citizens of the highest repute and skill, citizens whose labours might well be of the same importance to the Dundee community as had Watt's labours been to the Glasgow community.

'I am not to have such jacobinism!' Riddoch declared. 'I'll have the watch out, and keep them in about! Who are these low ruffians?'

'They are the same kind of low ruffians as were the low ruffians in Glasgow who broke up James Watt's shop!' David intoned. 'Oh, by the by, provost, you seem to have a drip at the end of your nose!' All the deputation leaned forward with anxious concern, looking at the provost's nose. He hastily brushed his hand across it.

'No,' said the one with the quizzing glass, 'no, it's not away yet.'

'Perhaps the provost would like to blow his nose,' another remarked. 'It is quite all right with us, provost, if you care to give your nose a good blowing.'

'Perhaps,' David said, 'the provost does not have a handkerchief. Perhaps he would like to borrow one.'

The provost blew his nose after, rather helplessly, holding out his handkerchief to show that he had one.

'Ah, yes,' David said, 'the names of these rogues! The names in Glasgow were the hammermen's trade incorporation. The rogues in Dundee who threaten the Carmichael brothers are the hammermen incorporation and the grocer called Alexander Riddoch!'

With careful gravity, the deputation marched slowly to the

door. They turned to look at the speechless provost and council. 'You have another drip at your nose, grocer!' David said.

Next day, David left Dundee on his Russian journey. Riddoch had made no move against the young Cowgait men of the deputation. It was known that, in his first anger, he had ordered the town watchers to go out and arrest the six flax men. But he had rescinded that order within a few minutes, before the watchers could leave the townhouse. 'It's not so easy to lift these Cowgait ones,' the provost was reported to have said. A crowd cheered David off on the ferry – on his way to Leith, a laughing crowd, not the lowest vennel dwellers, as crowds usually were, but the higher workmen type. 'Dundee needs a provost who can keep his nose clean,' the crowd were shouting. Already, they had shouted it at the townhouse and at Riddoch's house. The bell had rung for the calling out of the full muster of the town watch. The burgesses assembled, and they were laughing. 'Yes, Dundee needs a provost who can keep his nose clean,' many of them were saying. The Cowgait men smiled as they walked and talked at the Wellgait corner. 'We should be active against this Riddoch,' they were saying. 'There's no need for all this negotiating we're doing with him about harbour control. No satisfaction can be gained from negotiations with such people as Riddoch. The Cowgait should control the harbour. The Cowgait requires that the harbour be efficiently run. As these young men have shown us, it is not enough to be contemptuous of Riddoch. We will have the harbour! Who is he to stop our having it! We'll go direct to the government! No need to negotiate with a dirty little grocer with a drip at his nose!'

David English was gone a full year. His organizing in Russia was retarded by the unexpected resumption of the long war. It was three months after the battle of Waterloo before he returned to Dundee. He heard the roar of riot as he came across the river by ferry. The vennel folks were out. They howled that while bread prices were rising wages were falling. The new corn laws, they called, would starve the poor of the towns. They wailed their protest against the new spinning frames. In the mills, one woman tended a machine which could spin more yarn than twenty women with twenty spinning-wheels. Women who had been hand-spinners were weavers now, in new weaving factories, working for women's rates while men weavers walked the streets.

'The further cheapening of cheap Dundee,' old John English told David when the young man came to the Cowgait through the shouting throng in the High Street.

'It's hard for them,' David said, 'But work for everybody is coming. The town must prepare itself for that day even though the preparation makes today a difficult day for some. The firm should be in production. The larger mills will soon be organizing their own supply of fibre from Russia. The larger weaving factories will soon be organizing their own supply of yarn from mills.'

'There will always be work for agents and dealers,' John said. 'I've said before that I will not be a serf-driver.'

'You prefer these folks should have no work to their having the work you could organize for them,' David said.

'Welcome home, David,' old John replied after a long pause. 'This is no time for an argument, surely.'

David heard the news of the town. The Cowgait had gained control of the harbour, and were already engaged upon plans for vast improvements. A large group of burgesses were in revolt against Riddoch, who, however, by means of the co-optive system of selecting the council could still retain the townhouse dictatorship. The long moribund guildry had been revived by the burgess revolters, and the almost moribund nine trades, too. The guildry had the right, by old parchments, of nominating one council member, and the nine trades of nominating three members. These rights had not been exercised for many years, two hundred years in the instance of the guildry, it seemed. Some of the Cowgait men had become burgesses. They thought no more of the name burgess than they had thought before, but they wished to be in the burgess fight against the co-optive council. They held that the old trade and guildry charters could be used now as instruments against Riddoch.

'It's odd the way things are shaping,' old John said. 'The old parchments used against rightness.'

David laughed to that, then – 'Against rightness?' he said. 'Riddoch is nearly finished, but there will be rightness after him. I don't intend to become a burgess!'

'Nor I,' old John said. 'Nor most of the Cowgait. The Cowgait does not need to dabble in this old-fashioned nonsense. The burgess fee is up to ten pounds. That's Riddoch trying to keep out the new men. He knows they don't put any value on his silly freedom for its own sake. It gives them no trade privileges that they didn't have without it. Those flax men who are becoming burgesses want only the bit of political force that goes with the name. Riddoch believes that ten pounds will be more than they'll be prepared to give for that.'

Old John talked about one called Cobbett, an agitator for electoral reform.

'It's coming,' John said. 'Electoral reform will finish the Riddochs who are all over Scotland, and in England, too.'

'A king's signature on a bit paper,' David said. 'D'you remember who said that about this reform thing? Ay, her! This Cobbett you talk about sounds to me like a tory. That's tory talk, all that ranting against machines and against the new ways of farming. It would be funny if your own opposition to mills and your electoral reform turned out to be toryism.'

'It doesn't matter what it's named,' John said. 'I know, now, that I'm not the same as those new whigs in Dundee. Most of the burgesses call themselves whigs now. I called myself a whig when it was dangerous to call oneself a whig. If these burgesses, now shouting against Riddoch, are whigs then I'm no whig. These men are getting into the new rightness that has come with the new ways of industry. It's still the rightness of little right ones, still a strut, still low ambitions, still the Dundee-ness of Dundee shopkeepers.'

David remained only a few weeks in the town, then moved to Liverpool for a venture he had thought about in Russia. The export of Dundee linen was done mostly through the agency of Liverpool dealers. Liverpool was a world market for all British weaves, cottons, woollens, linens. David's plan was to set up a Liverpool office by which direct contact could be established between Dundee and the buyers of Dundee cloth. To that he obtained John's ready consent.

Before he went he saw old John demonstrate the English opposition to rightness, a quiet man's demonstration but as definitely of the family as had been David's townhouse ploy. A mob of vennel folks raided some High Street shops. The burgess watch pursued the raiders along Moraygait to the Cowgait, and there some of the mob took refuge in a narrow pend leading to a back-square of offices and warehouses. The men of the watch, armed with sticks, flushed by the chase, muttering their threats against jacobins and dirty tenement dwellers, were preparing to charge into the pend. The Cowgait men, among whom this unexpected excitement had come, stood looking on.

'We'll get this lot,' the watch were shouting. 'Get them good and hard. It's the stick they're needing.'

Old John moved to the pend mouth, and stood there, blocking the way to the watch.

'There are womenfolk and bairns in there,' he said.

'Get out of the way,' some of the watch shouted.

'That pend is a place for killing if you go into it with your present tempers!' John said.

'They broke into shops in the High Street! They need the stick! Get out of the way!'

One or two of the flax men moved to old John's side. After a few seconds hesitation, other flax men joined these few at the pend mouth, and stood there, chatting casually. Only John looked at the watch. Many of the burgesses threw down their sticks ashamedly and turned away. The others shouted for a little while at the flax men, then, their tempers cooled by the delay, moved off sheepishly.

243

In the next four years, David was comparatively infrequently in Dundee, some two months in each year. On these occasions he was with the family in the Nethergait house but not of it. The company there, nowadays, was always writers and musicians: Tom Hood, a boy poet sent from London to live with Overgait relatives and breathe Tay air for his cough; journalists from the two Dundee newspapers, the whig *Advertiser* and the tory *Courier*, violent enemies in their columns but good friends, it appeared, when not writing the savage politics of the period; William Lyon Mackenzie, a revolutionary pamphleteer, a draper's assistant, speaking wild words about forming a working man's nation in Canada, a nation without laird traditions or burgess traditions, with honour for skill in work and respect for the dignity of labour. David English glowered silently from a corner. The talk here seemed to him to be about nothing. Music-playing, verse-reading, absurdly impractical schemes like this Mackenzie's Canada and old John's equality between man and man. It seemed to David that the two children, Adam and John, were being reared on wind plastering for a flax office. Neither of them had ever been shown a hank of flax as the fibre that paid for all their tuition in fiddling and piano-playing.

'Without me, there would be no money to pay for all this plastering,' David told John at last. 'While I am gaining new trade for the firm, you are losing old trade. The firm hasn't advanced a ha'penny's worth since the old woman died. I was right. We should have been in production. I should have been in production myself. I should have got out years ago. I'll get out now. The larger part of the work is mine, but the firm is yours. When you leave off, your grandsons will take up your control. Their training for it will be fiddle-playing!'

'David,' John said. 'If you go now the firm might finish. I'm coming on for eighty. Young Adam and John are but little boys.'

'Oh, you realize that, do you?' David said. 'I also have my sentiments about the firm. I've stayed on because of them.'

John suggested an arrangement that until the boys were taking their full place in the firm, David would receive one-half the income and would be an equal in management.

'It is not enough,' David said. 'You should be retired, John. I'll stay on if I'm given complete management.'

The old man was nodding. Alice, Adam's widow, had listened in silence to the argument.

'Wait,' she said. 'My boys are their grandfather's heirs, as well as being part heirs of Aunt Katherine. On their behalf, I must refuse to allow this. It can only lead to dispute. I want them to be spared that. Your manner just now does not promise a pleasant future, David.'

'Do you want them to have a firm, at all?' David asked.

'That is maybe not so important,' she said. David stared. 'We do not consider flax as being of the highest importance!' Alice added.

'Yes, you're right, Alice,' John said, breaking the long silence that followed Alice's remark. 'David, you will have to leave the firm. You can't stay after this. You know the terms!'

'I know them!' David said. 'Eighteen hundred pounds! I should have taken it five years ago when I first learned about it. I should have been in production! Have the legal papers drawn up and I'll sign them!' These were the last words he was to speak to John.

Two days later as David came from a lawyer's where he had signed away his share in the firm, the aged Provost Riddoch emerged from the townhouse with some of his councillors.

'Heh, you!' Riddoch called. 'Ay, you, red-haired English. I've something to say to you!' The old man was aflame with senile anger as he shook his fist at David. 'It was you that started this. You were at the bottom of all this. Everybody laughing at me, at their provost. Everybody trying to get at me. The government in London inquiring into me, law courts in Edinburgh inquiring into me. The free of the town trying to get me out, and the unfree – jacobins – shouting that surely I'm an argument for their reform! It was you started it! And that old humphy-backed woman put you on to it, her that used to shout at me long ago. Long ago, ay.'

The provost wept.

'I'm a man of integrity,' he said. 'Forty years and more of public service. It was you that started it. Well, you'll have a different provost soon. You'll find out if he's a man of integrity! You started it with your long words about James Watt! It's you to blame!'

David listened to the whole tirade, then, without a word or a smile or a look, went on his way.

The last of the long line of town-pipers had a cheery tune for his rousing of the folks to the start of the working day. A tune of victory it was. The old time, the good time, fought the present time, the bad time, and the good time won. Yes, the good time won! The victory tune of the good time was sounding, making you dance, a laughing tune. *Hey, Johnny Cope, are you wauken yet?* It was that song a Lothian farmer had made to celebrate Prince Charlie Stuart's win at Prestonpans. The Dundee folks, rising for their mill and factory work, were whistling it as the piper played. Ha, Johnny Cope hadn't been awake. Johnny Cope, the general for the bad time, had slept in, and the good time, the old time, had won. The present time had lost, the bad time! Louder than the piper's tune, a steam-whistle shrieked, the first steam-whistle, shrieking down the last town-piper. That was not a tune to dance to, the tune played by a machine. The old time? What was it like, that old time, the good time, the time that Dundee weaving and spinning folk thought about, a time back in the past, a time ahead in the future, with cheery tunes?

The mills spun the cheap codilla for weft. Cheap Dundee was cheapening itself to live in the age of cheapness. The mills spun codilla for warp. The trade of the world, growing, wanted packing cloths, the cheapest weaving of the cheapest weavers. Dundee would live cheaply, grow cheaply, weave cheaply. Dundee had always lived by cheapness. Dundee was inured to cheapness. Dundee could make the cheapest packing cloths. Ay, though Dundee had to import the fibre and import the fuel, Dundee could do the cheapest weaving! Even though, after a century, the government had ended the export subsidy for Dundee cloth, Dundee could weave cheaply enough to retain its trade and expand its trade! There was work, now, for everybody in Dundee. The population was rising by a thousand in each year, Angus folk and Highlanders.

There were wonders to be seen in Dundee. A wonderful thing called a steamship moved on the river, the new ferry. A wonderful thing called gas lighted the newest mills and the newest factories. Navvies were digging a tunnel through the Law for a wonderful thing called a railway.

The weavers were marching, shouting, not the dirtiest vennel dwellers but the skilled men. 'Reform!' they shouted. 'One man, one vote! Equality!' Old John English spoke on the platform of the reformers, about Cobbett, and serfs.

'It's out of this demand of the working men that the improvement will come,' he explained in the unsure Cowgait. 'I haven't long to go. I hope I see the coming of reform. It's all I want now!'

David English had returned to Dundee after a five years absence. He had been doing agency work in Liverpool of the kind he had formerly done for the firm English. Standing with the Cowgait men, he avoided meeting old John's look. 'I left the firm in order to get into production!' he said. 'I've wasted five more years. I did well enough in Liverpool, enough to keep me but little better than that.' He invested some of his money in a heckling shed, and the Cowgait wondered that such an astute flax man as David English should do so. All the Cowgait men were saying that machine heckling would be the next development in the industry, and would put a finish to hand-heckling. The hand-hecklers, the workmen with the highest skill, were difficult fellows to organize into the new system. They were an ungovernable lot, with their new trade union, and their sudden strikes. It was not known that David's interest in heckling was not in hand-heckling. In his shed an engineer was working to perfect a heckling machine. He had analysed the movements of the heckling men, and had found that what had seemed to be one process was really three processes. He was building machines to copy the shoulder work, the elbow work, and the wrist work of a heckler's arm.

An East India Company agent lectured to the flax men in a Cowgait office. 'This is jute,' he said. 'These are the cloths that this fibre can make. This is what the native Indian weaving makes of jute. You've seen it often. A gunny sack. This is what Abingdon, in Berkshire, makes of jute. In Abingdon, this weave is only a raw material to be dyed and worked further.'

David English examined the Abingdon weave closely. 'Mind about jute!' the hunched woman had counselled him. A cheaper fibre!

One of the Cowgait men questioned the East India Company agent. 'Can this jute grow in Scotland?' he asked. 'What we need most is a fibre that grows here.'

'I'm here to sell you produce of India,' the Company agent said, laughing. 'Jute will not grow in Scotland. It grows only in India, in Bengal and Assam, nowhere else. It needs a hot climate and a wet one, sun and rain.'

'The power is to grow in a hot sun and heavy rains,' David English thought. He smiled at the thought, and dismissed it. but it recurred many times to him during the next few days. Jute, a cheaper fibre! The hunched woman had planned for jute!

The Cowgait did not give much talk to jute. A few were experimenting with it, and David watched the experiments.

'It needs a lot of handling, this stuff, in the working, but at the price it can bear the expense of a lot of handling,' one knowledgeable flax man said.

'You think it will come, Neish?' David asked.

'It will come,' Neish said. 'I'm sure of it. Watt is carrying on with his trials of this jute.' The Watt he named was another Cowgait man for whose views David had a high respect.

The Cowgait men crowded into a Wellgait shed to see a demonstration of a new heckling process, by machines. David was there, looking as though he had been struck. The process shown was not the one he had been financing. He could see that these demonstrated machines worked on the same principle, but worked more efficiently. When he visited his own shed he found the engineer sobbing like a child. 'I've heard about it,' the engineer said. 'It's the same thing, and they've got it perfected first. It kills the heckler's skill, but it kills me, too!' David fingered a hank of jute in his pocket. He remembered that the blood would go many times from Dundee, and in some of its returnings it would being back what was needed.

David was missing from his place in the Cowgait. Nobody knew for sure where he had gone, but Neish and Watt, with whom he had talked so much about jute, conjectured that he had accepted an offer made to him by the East India Company. David, they told the incredulous Cowgait, had been corresponding with the Company, trying to induce them to give him a living while he studied jute. They had actually offered a small clerkship, first in Abingdon for some months, then in Bengal. 'What can he be thinking about?' the Cowgait said. 'He had good prospects here if he had cared to apply himself to starting an agency. He knows the flax trade inside out. This jute caper will get him nowhere. Jute, that stuff!'

These incidents happened in the year 1824 when David was nearing thirty-one. Old John was eighty. His grandsons, Adam and John, were fourteen and eleven. The hunched woman was almost twelve years dead.

Old John, living to see reform, was straight and alert, the wonder of all the Cowgait, struggling to hold to his flax agencies and his linen merchandizing: old-fashioned English, they called him, with his deals among the independent home weavers and his continued buying of hand-spun, country yarn. Old-fashioned English, a queer old survival, born in the infintely distant year before the glen rebellion. Old-fashioned English, a radical in politics and a tory in industry. Eighty years of age, eighty-one, eighty-two, eighty-three, eighty-four, eighty-five, and still alert in body and mind, more than ever a wonder, more than ever a queer survival from a story-book past.

Reform, reform, reform! The tenement folks were marching. 'It's theirs, this reform,' old John English said. 'It belongs to the working people, and when the time comes for reform the credit will be theirs, as the fruits of reform will be theirs. These townhouse burgesses don't understand what's happening. Their co-optive council is going, and they don't know it. The end of these Scotch burgh councils will be the great reform. Parliamentary reform is of the first importance, of course, but local electoral reform will be the great event in Scotland. The end of right ones!'

A government pledged to reform was in power in London. Reform, the government said, would be the vote for all payers of ten-pound rents in the burghs. 'It's not so good as we expected, but better than nothing!' old John said. 'It will make a change in the Scotch burgh councils, a vast change. Elected councils instead of co-optive councils. Yes, the end of rightness!'

A dispute in the Dundee council was taken to parliament. One who was not a burgess had been sent to the council as representative of the revived guildry. The council had refused to have him as a member. How could he be a guildry man if he were not a burgess?

'This is the last antic of the burgess council of Dundee,' old John said. He laughed when parliament decided to end the Dundee council dispute by means of an election. All property owners were to have the choosing of the new council, not only the burgesses. 'The Cowgait should show their power here,' John said. He was surprised that few flax men were interested. 'We have the harbour to attend to,' the Cowgait said, 'and we have our infirmary and orphanage.

250

And there's our Chamber of Commerce. These are institutions of our making. We want none of this townhouse. Also we want none of this working men's reform. The operatives are difficult enough to manage without these political excitements!'

The issues of the council election were little right issues. The men elected to the new council were all men who had been in previous councils, some of them in Riddoch's council. In their first townhouse meeting, they raised the burgess fee from ten pounds to twenty pounds. Old John English shook his head, puzzled and hurt, when he heard of that. 'The fee should be coming down,' he said. 'It shouldn't be going up. If reform is to be worth while, this thing called the freedom of the town should be of no value at all.'

The old man was suddenly looking his age. The Cowgait commented on his shrunken look. He was pitied by the flax men. Ay, they said to each other, he had been among the first in the Russian trade, biggest of anybody in it. When Dundee imported three thousand tons of flax, the firm English had handled more than half. Ay, long ago, before the war, the firm English imported a shipload for their own use when the whole import for the town was carried in two ships. And now, when twenty thousand tons of flax were unloaded in the port, the share of the firm English was less than five hundred tons. The Englishes had been in at the start of the tow trade, said the Cowgait, organized the tow trade themselves almost, but let it slip. No shame to the old man. Ay, he must be coming on for ninety. Wonderful how he had managed to hold on long enough for his grandsons to take over. Good lads, particularly that older one, Adam, but inexperienced yet. The other would not be a flax man, the one called John, but Adam was good. The firm English had been unlucky with such a long span of years between the old man and those to succeed him. There had been the tall fellow, David – an unfortunate quarrel that had been. He had looked for a time like becoming one of the big men of the trade. Where was he now, that David English, a bitter man, a difficult man to deal with, too ready and too smart with sarcasm?

Old John muttered to himself, always seeing serfs. The expressionless, animal faces of serfs looked up at him when he sat on the platform at the reform meetings in Magdalen Green and the Meadows. He drove in a hired carriage in the reform processions, and, looking back at those who followed, saw serfs, moving on the plains to the pulling and the preparing of the flax.

A crowd of incomers came up Castle Street from the dock. They were from the far north of the country, Sutherland folks, driven out in the clearances to make way for sheep, driven first from the inland glens to the coast, then from their scarcely built homes there. They moved in Castle Street as driven ones move, their heads down, listless. Old John stood up in a carriage waving his stick. 'Trample him, trample him!' he yelled. He tried to dismount to join the serfs in the trampling of an overseer, and fell on the roadway.

He could not, after that, be allowed out in the streets, to be looked at and laughed at. He sat by his window in the house in the Nethergait. The processions of the reformers went a quarter of a mile out of their way that they might be seen by him. 'Ay,' the weavers said, 'he watches out for us. He was one of the first reformers, in the days of Geordie Dempster. Give the old man a wave as you pass, old John English.'

Gunpowder cut a path northwards through the Corbie's Hill, the low lava ridge that stretched behind the Overgait and the High Street. The picks of the demolishers razed old tenements on the High Street front, older tenements and cottages in the backlands, tombstones in the eastern end of the Houff. There was argument about the name for the new street. The tory wags suggested Mortgage Road and Bond Street. They said that the payment for all the digging and blasting would cripple the town's finances and the trade of the town. In the Meadows, to which the new street led, the foundations were laid for the new burgess school, to be named not a school but, with dignity and sonority, the Dundee Public Seminaries. The tories had another name, Bog Academy. The Scouring Burn could be hidden underground, they said, but it would be flowing still, making of the Meadows a bog to swallow up the town's money.

Lava rock, bog soil, old stonework and plaster, Houff memorials and bones, these, the debris of the blasting and excavation, were dumped along the river and made a new shore in which a new dock was scooped. There was argument about the name for the dock. Call it, the tories said, Ruination Basin where the finances and the trade of the town were sunk.

In a glut of linen, looms and mills were idle. At the meetings of the whig orators, the mob howled for the suffrage reform which parliament was debating. The idle looms were an argument for both the tories and the whigs. Too many reforms were silencing the looms, the tories said, too many schools, new streets, new docks, new money-spending notions. The looms were idle because there were not enough reforms, the whigs said. The mob howled for the whigs. The bill, the whole bill. Reform, reform, reform.

The news from London was of the bill through the Commons. The mob in Dundee marched, cheering. Mobs were marching in every town. The news was of the defeat of the bill in the Lords. The mobs howled for the bill and for blood. The wild men of the Clyde were risen, the tavern arguers said. A day was named, the arguers had it, for the revolution of the Clydeside republicans, arming under old flags preserved from the long-ago days of Welch and Cameron, shouting slogans that the men of Drumclog and Bothwell Bridge had shouted – maintenance of the poor, education of the young and ignorant, government of the people by the people. The news from London was of the passage of the bill. Ring your bells, Dundee, Glasgow, Bristol, Leeds, Manchester, all the burghs, ring your bells! The day had come, the golden age had begun.

The new street had a name, Reform Street. The new dock

had a name, Earl Grey Dock, named for the Prime Minister of Reform. The shouting crowd marched past old John English at his window.

'They're cheering the bill,' he was told. 'It's passed, electoral reform, a great widening of the franchise. Don't you understand? The reform bill!'

He was listening to an argument between hunched Kate and Dempster. They were sitting there by the fireplace where they used to sit. 'A signature on a bit paper!' the hunched woman was saying. 'There's not enough power in that to weave an inch of flax.' Old Honest George was nodding, as he always nodded to Kate. 'Legislating away injustice, legislating away the bad habits of the past,' he was answering her. 'The people of this country with the vote, think of it, Katherine. The instincts of the people being allowed to function. The instincts of a nation can't be wrong.' Kate was laughing her cackling laugh. 'By God, Geordie, she was saying. 'You know that they can!' They were both laughing. 'Their wishes can be wrong, in some matter of an hour or a day, but not their instincts, Katherine. Their instincts cannot go wrong. I have the last word, this time Katherine.' Laughing she said, 'No, no! You don't. Instinct is a word like your other words, Geordie, an orator's word, meaning nothing. And as for your reform, it'll be this – an occasion of rightness, with the right flags flying, and the right bands playing, and the right ones marching in all their rightness.'

Old John listened to the argument. Strange, he thought. They should not be there. They were dead long ago. Reform, yes reform. It had come. He had lived to see reform. The moment of clarity passed. He laughed with hunched Kate and Dempster.

A great procession of celebration moved along the new street to see the laying of the foundation stone of the new school. The watching tenement-dwellers cheered for the new school and for reform. The procession moved back down the new street, with the crowd cheering for reform and the street of reform, down Castle Street to the new dock. A silver plate was sunk in the water, enthusiastically inscribed in townhouse language, oddly punctuated and capitalled:

On the Day, set apart by the People of the United Kingdom of Great Britain and Ireland, for a grand national jubilee, in celebration of the disfranchisement of the rotten boroughs – the enfranchisement of large and flourishing towns – and the general extension of the Suffrages of the People, in the Election of their Representatives in the House of Commons: His Most Gracious Majesty, King William The Fourth, King; The Right Hon. Earl Grey, Prime Minister; this Wet Dock, named EARL GREY'S DOCK, in Honour of the honest, zealous, eloquent, long-tried, and consistent Advocate, and now triumphant Leader of Reform – One of the Works, Authorized by a Statute of the British Parliament passed in the eleventh year of the reign of George the Fourth, vesting for ever the Harbour of Dundee and its revenues in Trustees popularly elected – was Founded, in presence of the Harbour Trustees, the Magistrates and Council, the Guildry, the Nine Incorporated Trades, the Fraternity of Masters and Seamen, the Three United Trades, the Commissioners of Police, and the other Public Bodies and Societies of the town; And also in presence and with the assistance of the ancient and honourable Craft of Free and Accepted Masons, by the Right Honourable George Lord Kinnaird, Grand Master of the Grand Lodge of Scotland: The odious system of self-election of the Magistrates and Council of the Burgh having been abolished, by Parliament, in 1831, and William Lindsay, Esq., elected by the suffrages of the Burgesses, and holding the office of Chief Magistrate of the Burgh. Thomas Telford, James Jardine, and John Gibbs, Engineers; and James Leslie, Esq., Superintending Engineer of the Harbour. August 9th, 1832.

Old John English, allowed to be abroad on that glorious day, sat in a hired carriage with his family, his daughter-in-law Alice, his grandsons Adam and John. The crowd remarked on the blunted noses of the Englishes. The two young men kept up a run of conversation as for a fractious child, to hold the old man's interest.

'Why are they cheering, Adam?' he said.

'For reform, grandfather. You remember, the great reform bill is passed.'

'Yes, yes, of course, reform.'

'This is Reform Street, grandfather.' Humouring him.

'Are all these people celebrating the reform bill, Adam? It doesn't seem right. There were five reform men in the town once.'

'Yes, and you were one, one of the first five. The new school is well situated, grandfather, don't you think?'

'Yes, very nice. A new school – and a new harbour, did I hear someone say? Yes, a harbour. What about the new wells, Adam? There should be wells. And there should be a new way of clearing away the redd. Aunt Kate wanted new wells more than anything. Surely they haven't forgotten her wells.'

The young men, glancing at each other, resumed their brisk calling of his attention to the dignitaries in the procession, but he would not be quietened.

'There is something wrong,' he said. 'This is not what I meant by reform. The people lining the street are cheering, and that is as it should be. But they should not be cheering a procession of burgesses. The burgesses should be in hiding. It is as Aunt Kate said – the right ones in their rightness. This is all it has come to. What was wrong becomes right with the rightness of the always right.'

They pacified him for a moment.

'Who is that?' the old man pointed a wavering forefinger towards a carriage.

'Mr. Neish. You remember Mr. Neish, the flax broker? And Mr. Watt, the linen merchant.'

'Yes, I see Neish and Watt. But who is that beside them in

the carriage. Surely it is David. Older, so like his father now. His father stood in the court in that very attitude, a smaller man, but with the same way of standing. That was the best thing I ever did. A vennel orator was freed in a right court. Adam, is that David?'

'Yes, grandfather. I omitted to tell you that David is back in the town.' The omission had been no accident. The old man must not be excited. 'That is his wife beside him, the little woman.'

'He has not come to visit me?' old John complained.

'He will come, grandfather. He informed me he would come.' A lie. Adam and David had met. David had snubbed the young man and passed on.

'What does he do, Adam?'

'He is from India. He is trying to interest the spinners in jute. I fear he is having little success. It's coarse stuff, this jute, a joke in the Cowgait. Only a few like Neish and Watt take jute seriously.'

The old man stared with his rheumy eyes. He was in his own travelling days, talking of his triumphs with flax. They let him ramble, glad that his interest had faltered from David and from wrath against the right ones.

'Jute, it might not be such a joke, this jute,' the old man said, his wandering mood past. 'Aunt Kate had it spun and woven. But there should have been a processing of the fibre before the heckling. Perhaps the time has come for it now. Aunt Kate had a way of thinking about what was far ahead in the future.'

A line of tenement children moved with mock pomposity alongside the carriages and marchers, their faces twisted to a caricature of the self-importance of those in the procession. The old man rose, his gleaming eyes upon the children.

'Trample him,' he shrieked. 'Trample him!'

Everyone watched the Englishes' carriage where the old man was held in his seat. The procession stopped. The English carriage was turned out of the route and the crowd made a lane for it. It moved along the Nethergait.

'Jute,' the old man said, his gaze on young Adam. 'Yes, we

will talk about this jute. We will experiment. We cannot further cheapen Dundee, so we must cheapen the raw material Dundee uses. Good flax, then poor flax, then tow, and then what? Sunna fibre? Or some new use of cheaper hemp? Or jute? Yes, why not jute?' His eyes closed, wearily, 'What am I saying?' he added, after a time. 'Flax, hemp, jute! Work, work, work! For serfs, work for serfs. Trample him! Trample him!' All the way along Nethergait he shrieked for the trampling of an overseer, and through his last week of life, sometimes shrieking in pain under the feet that were trampling himself.

He had lived to see the reform he had preached, they said in Dundee. He must have died happy in the attainment of reform, they said. How appropriate that he should struggle through those last difficult years of his life to see reform and die in the year of reform. The whigs followed the coffin of the orator of reform, the flax men followed the coffin of the man who had been first in the trade.

David English was not present in the long funeral procession. From an office window he saw it pass. He was the man who knew about jute, as old John had once been the man who knew about flax. He had seen the growing of jute and watched the carriage of jute on the rivers of Bengal, the selling of jute in Calcutta, the baling of jute, the shipment of the long dry fibre which was a laugh in the Cowgait of Dundee. The office from which he looked down upon the funeral was a single room in a block of offices in the new street, Reform Street. David, at thirty-nine years of age, was, with the despised jute, carrying on the Englishes' bitterness, the Englishes' ambitions and the Englishes' hopes.

THE ARCH AT THE QUAY

ON the higher flats of the great plain of Bengal, the mallow grew, the plant of jute. The Hindu dancers danced the dance of jute in the ceremonies of their religion. The dance was older than Hinduism, as old as the fears from which Hinduism had grown. The waving arms of the dancers were the long waving stems of the plant. The dancers fell and their fall was the cutting down of the mallow. Lying upon their faces, they covered the backs of their heads with their hands – the mallow lying in water-filled pits was retting. The dancers stood erect, their arms circled in the motions of slapping the mallow stems upon water to remove the outer bark, circled to scatter the stems over the water surface.

David English had seen the dance of jute, the first European to see it and to fully understand its allusions. He was in Dundee with the knowledge about jute of a man who had gone so far into the study of jute as to have seen the dance. The few Cowgait men who talked about the possibilites in jute must talk also about David English, linking his name with this new fibre.

The price of raw flax was rising. Lesser men of the industry experimented with jute of which the cost was less than a half that of flax tow. The methods of jute spinning and jute weaving, they found, were long and laborious, wetting and mangling of the long dry fibres before a yarn could be made, starching or sizing of the rough yarn before a cloth could be woven. 'It's scarcely worth the trouble,' they were saying. David English sought out these experimenters, demonstrated to them the Indian tricks of spinning and weaving, advised them about the qualities of jute to use. He was gaining nothing by it except recognition among the men who would rise if jute rose, those lesser men who could become bigger men only by change. The established flax firms were amused by the experimenters and by the uncouth weave produced by the experiments.

David English was dressed like a Cowgait man. He was earning little, but must look as though he prospered. His wife kept herself hidden away in their home on the northern slope of the Hawkhill, a low-rented house, once alone in the fields, but now closed in by tenements. The Hawkhill weavers stared at the top-hatted man who came through their closes on his way to and from his home, the dandified husband of the shabby woman whom they saw at the well, waiting her turn for water like any tenement wife.

'They say he's a jute dealer,' the weavers said.

'Jute, that stuff! He'll make nothing out of jute. No wonder his wife is the poor thing she is. He'll not have his lum hat long if it's jute he's selling. It's as hairy as a gooseberry, that jute, and stiff, and dry, and unbinding. What a stuff it is!'

Westward in America were the plains that grew wheat, the dry grass lands for cattle herds, the mountains with gold in them. The waggons moved westwards, people on the move, driven by the old fears, of the ice, of want, of death of the species. The roofs of the waggons, homes with wheels, were canvas from Dundee. The sacks and sheets that hung around the waggons were the osnaburgs and hessians of Dundee. It was said in Dundee that reform had brought work and wealth. Fire swept along the New York quays. Canvas and sacks burned in the sheds. The burning made prosperity in Dundee, as the word was understood there, plenty of work, and shillings for it.

The labour recruiters went into the village market places. They spoke of the work in Dundee, of the need for spinners and weavers, of the shillings that could be earned for spinning and weaving. Nodding away the insecurity of the country parishes, folks nodded to the promises of the recruiters. Families with daughters were wanted. Folks nodded to the call for labour, and moved to Dundee where daughters were hands to earn, not mouths to feed.

Storms swept across the Russian plains in the summer of 1835, and the flax was broken in the wind. Jute began to make its way in that year of the flax crop failure. Into the wefts of the Dundee cloths were woven yarns with jute in them. The Cowgait dealers kept their jute transactions secret. The linen merchants kept secret their buying of cloths with jute in the weft. David English did not profit by these deals. Those who used jute fraudulently could not do business with the one man in the town who called himself a jute dealer. A few small spinners were making all-jute yarns. One small factory was weaving all-jute hessian. David English's trade was with these few. He moved among them with his knowledge of the Indian working of the fibre, of the different qualities of crop from the different Bengal districts.

'You're in the wrong end of the trade, English,' one of them said to him, the one manufacturer of all-jute cloth in the town. 'Jute will come into its own in time, but I can see now that there'll be little in it for you as a dealer. It looks to me that the buying of the fibre will be done through the London market. I take it that you don't have the money to bring a shipload or two to Dundee.'

'You're right in that,' David English said. 'I haven't the money for it, and, moreover, there's no call yet for anybody doing it.'

'You'll just be doing agency work with the London men, buying on commission for the spinners here? There's nothing much in that, English, and there won't be much in it for a long time.'

'I'm beginning to see it. I didn't think of jute getting its first foothold by stealth and fraud.'

The manufacturer regarded David English for some minutes.

'You know, English,' he said at length, 'you and I would get on fine together. You know the jute, and I know the machines. I think we're coming near finding the process we need for the softening of the fibre. You've been in that just as much as I have been. I'm getting my jute hessians sold now, as you know. It makes bags that hold together as long as bags need hold together. There's little money in it, but it's keeping my place going. English, I could do with a bit capital and I could do with a man who knows. Were you thinking of going into a partnership?'

David stared into the past where the hunched woman sat, into the future, where a power was growing in a hot sun and heavy rains. 'Give me time to think,' he said. 'I've always wanted to be in production!'

He was back in two hours. 'I've done all my thinking,' he said. 'We're partners.'

The firm called English & Henryson was founded. English's great-grandfather had murdered Henryson's great-great-grandfather a hundred and seventeen years before. The new partners laughed together over the long-ago story that the hunched woman had told to a boy at her knee. 'If I see you with a rope, I'll keep out of your road,' Henryson said. 'You never know but what that kind of trick is handed down in a family.'

In English & Henryson's, both partners worked with their twenty workpeople, women and boys mainly. Henryson did the setting of the spinning machine and of the eight hand-looms, and walked among them, his own overseer. The factory, in the Chapelshade, on the rising ground northward of the Meadows, was a long, one-storeyed building with a tarred wooden roof, too weak for its length, sagging in the wide spaces between the rafters. David English arrived each morning in his tall hat and Cowgait clothes, performed the office work, then changed to workman's rags for the mashing of the fibre in water tubs, to soften it, and the pulling of the yarn through basins of thin starch, to smooth its rough hairiness for weaving, work worth only a labourer's fee had it been done by anyone else, but of the highest value to the firm because it was done by a partner, one who held himself to the monotony and squalor of the work by his hates and hopes. Now and again, when the stocks of mashed fibre and starched yarn were large enough to keep the little factory in employment for some weeks, he went out for orders, searching for those who wanted the cheapest cheapness. The work he brought to the firm was for odd consignments of cloth and little parcels of sacks. 'I'll take anything that's work for us,' he said, 'anything that keeps us moving and keeps our work-folk with us, gaining experience.' He and Henryson toiled far into the summer nights on the most menial tasks, sack-sewing even, saving wages, because their small chancey output and their low prices allowed little margin of half-pennies. They looked at their sagging roof. 'Let it hold,' Henryson said. 'God let it hold!' They had a small reserve, some of David's money, but it was for development of their markets and their machines, not for roofs.

The larger linen-manufacturers of the town were unconcerned about the dirty little jute factory in the Chapelshade. They were engaged upon the next great development in their own linen production, the application of power to weaving. Hand-loom weavers in the tenements and in the basements were idle. They marched, men and women, shouting against the new power-looms. They had boasted that the heavy linens of Dundee would never be woven by engine-driven looms. Now, in power-loom factories one weaver tended a machine which could do the work formerly done by six weavers. The shouters who had shouted for suffrage reform now shouted against reform. What was it, this reform? It was the burgesses' reform, not the reform of the workers. The workers would have their own reform, their own charter, would make parliament their own. They hissed the whig orators, sang obscene songs about the phrases of the whigs, the brotherliness, the freedom.

They had a name to shout – William Lyon Mackenzie, leader of a working man's revolt in Canada. David English, listening to the shouts in High Street, remembered a young man who had argued in old John's Nethergait drawing room, argued for a working man's country, without burgesses, without lairds, without traditions, Canada, William Lyon Mackenzie's Canada, where that same William Lyon Mackenzie now led an armed revolution, was defeated, had a price on his head. The burgesses were saying that Dundee was indeed well rid of that bitter little Mackenzie who was in the shouts of the Dundee marchers.

In the Cowgait, the flax firm English, not among the first flax-dealing and linen-dealing firms of Dundee but still with its importance, lived by that trading which only an old firm could do, agencies for a few Russian estates, the buying of hand-spun yarn for special weaving, and the supply of cloth to the oldest-established markets. Young Adam English, ambitious, was not content with the trade of an old firm. He loved the daughter of one of the mill owners, was loved by her and accepted by her people, but it seemed to him that there was a hesitancy in her love and their acceptance. His ambitions were sharpened by the hesitancy. He remembered his grandfather's words about jute – that it should not be laughed at. Adam had high capacity for business. He saw that jute, the fraudulent fibre whispered in the Cowgait, would not always be whispered, but would take its place in Dundee. The failure of the Russian harvest had set the manufacturers and dealers to think, and to be afraid. Many markets competed for the world's flax crops, an expanding demand for a supply that could not easily be expanded. Russia was spreading over Asia, towards India. In the future there would be war with Russia, everybody said. Jute, Adam said, was an answer to the puzzle of the limited flax supply which might be stopped by war, and an answer to the problem of a further cheapening of cheap Dundee.

He went to London and Liverpool to study the jute markets and to make contacts with brokers and merchants. He wrote to his brother John:

It is my opinion that we shall have no difficulty in entering this business of jute dealing. There will be little in it at first, but it will become important. Grandfather said we should be in it. Our great-grand-aunt thought of jute when it was even more absurd than it is now. I find that the market is as yet a small one, and noisily new. Its shipments from Calcutta are as regular as the nature of the fibre permits, its being a light cargo that shippers do not care to carry alone. So much for jute just now! I am to travel to Yorkshire tomorrow in order to inspect some new linen processes in Leeds, and it is my intention to sail from Hull on the 6th by the Dundee steamer 'Forfarshire'. I shall give you a fuller report of my travels and contacts when I come home. I promise you a lively account of my meeting with that Tom Hood who was a visitor to the house when we were little boys, and of my piano and violin playing for him and his literary cronies. They were astonished when I told them that you are immeasurably superior to myself. 'Two musicians of that merit in Dundee!' Tom Hood said. 'Why, I thought the only music you knew there was the jingle of silver!' It is now I am grateful to our dear mother for her music lessons which give a shy, silent Scotchman a place among these brilliant talkers.

September 7th, 1838, the keeper of the Longstone Light on the Farne Islands, off the Northumberland coast, looking out to the stormy dawn, the end of a night of storm, the start to a day of storm, saw a broken steamship upon rocks a mile away. The *Forfarshire*, tossed in the storm of the night, her boilers ruptured, her fires extinguished by the leak from the boilers, had been thrown by the seas on a Farne reef. The after end in deep water was wrenched off by its own weight. From the wreckage left upon the reef, eleven survivors crawled and through the wind of the night, among the spray of the seas, held to the rocks. Adam English was among them. They saw the light-keeper's answer to their gestures for help. At the base of the light two figures moved, launching a little boat into the storm, a woman's figure and the keeper. Those on the reef had prayed for help. They prayed now that the man and the woman by the light would not attempt help, only two of them, one a woman, their boat a helpless thing. William Darling of the Longstone Light looked at the mile of water between him and the wreck. 'We'll ne'er get there, Grace, I doubt, but we should be trying something when folks are in that plight. I'll take the fore oars, and you'll take the hind oars, Grace lass.' Grace Darling and her father moved into the headless storm, and were forever names in the gallantry of the seas.

Adam English came home to Dundee, carried in a litter through the crowds who talked of Grace Darling. He was home to die of the exposure on the reef. His reports of jute markets, of the gay evening with Hood, were never spoken. His funeral was the mourning for the fifty Dundee lives lost by the splitting of the *Forfarshire* upon the Farne rock, and it was the sad acknowledgment of the courage of the keeper and his daughter. Hundreds followed the coffin, moving between thousands in the route to the Houff.

David English, watching, remembered that this corpse going past in the street had been the infant who could hold on to the hunched woman's finger. For a moment he was of a mind to fall in with the funeral procession, or to visit the Nethergait house in order to offer what comfort he could to the bereaved mother. But his look tautened again when he thought of her dismissal of himself, seventeen years before. This was the boy for whom she had opposed David's claims to dominate the firm. Seventeen years? David had been important in Dundee, and now he was a masher of jute fibre, a starcher of jute yarn, with no position in the town, living sparingly. 'This is the end of their flax firm,' he said to Henryson. 'The other one is a violinist and pianist with no taste for business. He would be well advised to get out of it now, before he begins losing. The goodwill and connections would sell for enough to set him up in something that would keep him going. I should be sorry, but I'm not.' He was planning even as the funeral went by. 'Henryson,' he told his partner, 'I've thought of something. This talk about the flax Englishes' connections brought it to my mind. They provide coffee bags for Rotterdam. I'll take our stuff to show in Rotterdam. I believe we could get bags made of our jute into that trade.' He laughed. 'It would be doing young John English a service to cut him out. He would know the sooner that he should quit the flax business. Make me a stock to peddle round the coffee merchants, and give me the lowest prices you can offer. You don't need to try and compete with flax in appearance for this. These bags have to be frankly jute. I know what these Rotterdam men will take. We'll spend a bit of our reserves on this trip, but I'm sure it will be worth it.'

In Holland, David spoke of the coarseness of his sacks as a merit. They could hold coffee beans, and be thrown away. What more did flax or hemp do, at one-third more cost? The Dutch coffee-importers nodded. They were buying and selling coffee, and sacks were but an overhead expense to them. David English came back to Dundee with a regular trade opened for the factory.

'Jute is an honest fibre now,' Henryson said. 'We're away, David! Do you know that the softening process has been found? Ay, the whale oil and water softening, in the batch. It will cut a lot of the hard work you've been doing, and give you more time for canvassing. If we could just get rid of that long, dirty way of starching the yarn. It takes money and time. We'll get the right yarn out of jute yet without that plastering about. When we've got it, we'll know we're on the road to be big.'

'Ay, we'll have that in time,' David declared. 'Meanwhile we have an assured income from jute at last. It's not much, but it means we don't have to scrape for ha'pennies now. I'm taking my wife out of that Hawkhill warren. It's a good year for me this. I didn't tell you there's a baby coming.'

'That's fine!' Henryson said. 'It's a good omen. By the by, there's a bit news for you. Young John English has closed his flax business. He's a music teacher now. I'm told he's doing well enough. You'll be glad that he didn't wait to get this knock, your getting his Rotterdam sack trade for jute.' Henryson looked queerly at his partner, whose hardness he was beginning to understand. David only laughed.

David English's new home was one of the old houses of

the last century's rising men, on the Forebank, east of the long slope of Hilltown, a cheap house because it was out-moded now, but still pleasantly situated in its own strip of green. He was forty-five, his wife thirty-seven. She was a daughter of the clerk with whom he had lodged in Abington during his eight months there. She had shown her love, her worship, of him, and his resentful loneliness had made a worshipper a necessity of life to him. Twins had been born to them, but had died while he was in India, without his having seen them.

His excitement for the new birth was more than the normal excitement of a father. 'This one might be the power,' he said. 'I know it's nonsense, that superstition in my family, but it could be made to come true. No, I'll be the power. I'll grow with jute in the hot sun and the rains to be a power.' He held his finger to the infant as hunched Kate had once held hers to a baby. The child's tiny hand fastened, and he raised the child by the strength of its own grip. With a laugh David English named his son Willie, grandson of the bagpiping gravedigger, whose Tree of Liberty was now a spreading ash at Belmont House.

In an autumn of hot drought, in 1840, the springs in the Law dried, and people fought till they bled around the few wells of the town. A half-witted woman struggled in the crowd at the Ladywell and could not obtain water to quieten her fevered children. She led her staggering family to the well. 'They've got the bowel-fever,' she screamed. 'Let them get water!' The crowd scattered, and the brood of half-wits held possession of the well that fed all the other public wells of the town. They died beside the well, while the crowd watched from afar. 'The town will pay for this,' the crazed mother called. 'It'll pay for not having water for my bairns when they were dying.'

A small spring in the yard of English & Henryson's factory maintained a flow during the drought. The housewives of the nearby tenements peeped enviously in at the gate on their way down the Chapelshade slope to the fights at the Lady-well. David English saw their glances towards the trickle.

'We could let these people take water from here,' he said. 'I'll send a laddie round the houses to tell them. Once our tanks are filled each morning, the spring runs to waste. It might as well be helping these folk.'

At the end of the drought the women showed their grati-tude by a presentation of gifts to the factory partners. The newspapers reported the happy little ceremony, with a sen-tence or two that David English had said about the necessity for neighbourliness. His words were talked about in a quarter he little expected would be interested in words of his.

'I've been asked to stand for the council,' he told Hen-ryson a day or two later. 'I had what is called a deputation of public-spirited citizens call upon me last night. They flattered me in their silly manner about what I said to these women, as though it had been a feat to talk for two minutes. They have the admiration of fools for anybody who talks. Their great art is public-speaking, as they call it, and they've dis-covered me as a public speaker. Their spokesman, in a speech he had learned by rote, urged upon me, as he said, that I was the type of right-thinking, far-sighted and enter-prising man for the council.'

'It wouldn't do jute any harm,' Henryson said, thought-fully. 'It would make folk talk about jute, and it could do with some talking. Forbye, jute could do with a man in the townhouse to watch out for any impediments that might be put in jute's way by the council.'

David stared. 'Surely you understand me better than that?' he said. 'To me their deputation and their words – public-spirited and enterprising and far-sighted – were an insult. They took that report of what I said to these wifies as being their own kind of soothing platitude. They actually assumed I must be a burgess. Would they go to a flax manu-facturer or to one of the Cowgait dealers with their urges? No, they would be treated with contempt. But they come to me, because I am taken as one of their little right ones, among shopkeepers and such. Is jute to be regarded as being in the same class as their baking and haberdashering and grocering?'

'Whether we like it or not, jute is wee, Dave. It'll be big in time. Right now it needs just that kind of talk a good jute councillor could get for it. There's no reason why industrial men shouldn't be in the council, flax or jute.'

'There's every reason, man,' David snapped. 'The Cowgait has always been outside the council. The little right ones tried to hold down the Cowgait, and failed. And flax grew too big for the townhouse, and could look down on it. You've scarcely ever heard of a flax man in the council. Once in a while there might be one, but only for a single term, then out of it, disgusted by the words and views of right ones. The harbour was won away from the townhouse cliques by flax, but flax had no ambitions to win the townhouse itself from them. The townhouse tradition was a thing to be laughed at by flax, and still is. Despite this thing called suffrage reform, the same kind of right ones are in the council as in Riddoch's time, not thieves now, but with all the little squabbling for little positions. Flax is not ambitious for their bailieships and councillorships. Neither is jute. Jute should not be little and right. It can't afford to be. It can't afford to enter the oligarchy of small minds and small aims. Why, the clumsiness of the townhouse debates is the laugh of the town! They can't even use their own canny, right phrases without unintentionally insulting each other. Their meetings are a series of unmeant insults and apologies which further insult.'

'If it's the way you think, Dave, there's no more to be said about it. I don't just see these little right ones of yours as you see them. It's right enough that the best men of the town never seem to be in the council, but I don't see why you should be so up against council folk.'

'Because I've been watching them for nearly two hundred years, ever since they burned a witch in 1660. You know what I mean if you've listened aright to the stories I've told you about my family.'

'I still don't understand,' Henryson ended. 'I'm sorry in a way that you're not considering it, Dave. It might have done jute a bit of good. You would make a grand candidate with your height and red hair and with that beard you've taken to wearing. And you've got the words for winning in this election. It will be a water election, after that mad woman's bairns dying at the Ladywell. If you were in the council, there would be one whose insults wouldn't be unmeant.' David laughed to that, then was silent, thinking. His thoughts made him laugh again.

Henryson came to David with a newspaper account of a speech given by one of the candidates for the coming election. 'That's one of the fellows you would have been against, Dave, had you thought to stand,' Henryson said. 'He's been getting on about an unfree man being invited to oppose him. It'll be you he means. He thinks that it's a lowering of the dignity of the townhouse for you even to have been asked. It's a matter that I thought was finished with, but this man doesn't think so. He's all for the locked book, and the last bits of privileges that go with the freedom of the town.'

'Freedom of the town? Are they still using these words?' David said angrily. He read the report. 'Henryson, I'm going to these people who invited me to stand. This fool was talking about me, right enough. He's in the ward I was asked to contest. I'm not with any clique, but I'll use one of them in order to get the chance to make this blob of rightness sorry for himself. The old woman told me to go after the right ones. I got my one smack at Riddoch, but the Englishes need to have more than one smack.' He glared at a phrase in the newspaper. The speaker had referred to the Tree of Liberty in Perth Road as the symbol of democracy.

David English entered upon the election with no politics, no views for or against local progress, only the hate. He had been born to hate, and trained by the hunched woman to hate. His natural tendencies towards scornfulness were forced to exaggerated growth by his fall from flax prosperity to the dirtiness and hard labour of jute. Henryson, looking up at him on the platform, smiled to see that his hair and beard were not faded and streaked with grey. David English's middle-aged redness had been dyed to gleam as in his youth. The tress of Elspet Renkyne's hair he held in his hand had been dipped in the same dye.

'This hair,' he said, 'was waved as the signal for the rising at the time the Tree of Liberty was planted. My father waved the hair, and started the rising. You know that tree, in a garden along Perth Road. It is not now the tree of humble back-street folks. It is the tree of the right ones. It is mentioned in all their speeches as a symbol of the thing they call democracy. It is pointed out to strangers as an historical relic that reminds the town of bad old times before there was democracy. The impression given is that the tree was planted by shopkeepers, as an example of that enterprise of which they continually boast. I've just told you who gave the signal for the planting – my father, who was a gravedigger.' The crowd yelped their delight. 'Let me tell you the kind of grievance these people had who rose in wrath at that time. That was the bad time, remember. There were not then the great benefits we all share now. For instance, in those days women had to stand for hours to get water. Sometimes there were fights at the wells.' In the crowd's laugh was a growl. 'The town council was led by a knave – we did not have the benefits of democracy then! – and that knave would not give the town an adequate water supply. In those days, too – I saw it myself as a small boy! – the redd was piled openly in the street, and shovelled by men with their legs bare to the thighs. Think of that – their legs bare to the thighs! Nowadays, when we have democracy, the redd is shovelled openly in the street by men who wear sea-boots. There is the benefit of democracy clearly shown – in those days the dirt men had bare legs, now they have sea-boots. Let me tell you another benefit. Much of the redd was then thrown away into the river. Now it is all sold for fertilising the fields, and brings five thousand pounds every year to the town. That money, no doubt, is spent in giving you the benefits of democracy. Do you know that redd is next to flax as a trade product of

Dundee. You can see the great democratic benefit that arises today from the open heaps on streets as compared with the small benefit of the same heaps in my father's time.'

The chartists had gathered at this meeting, as at all other election meetings, to howl the speaker down, to seize his platform and use it for advocacy of their People's Charter. They laughed with David English. In his resentful sarcasm they found the expression of their own resentments. They had no votes to give him, but they gave him their roaring applause. They were for the most part the poorest vennel dwellers, dirty, diseased, out of work in the adjustment of the flax industry from hand-looms to power-looms. Marching through the town, shouting for maintenance of the unemployed, for full manhood suffrage, for a people's parliament, they shouted also for David English, who like themselves hated the right ones.

The main opponent in the ward was the very caricature of all that David derided, old burgess pomposity mixed with paralysed embarrassment, malapropisms and mispronunciations, unfortunate timing of the stalest platitudes, the whole town's butt for a hilarious fortnight, each one of his meetings an uproar of delighted savagery. He spoke first on the hustings on election day, and, during his speech, the chartist bagpipes played for the dancing of the vennel mobs. Not a word of the speech was heard. David came up on the platform, and the chartists hushed for him. His election address must have been the oddest ever heard in Dundee – the laughing man on the platform, his dyed hair and beard glinting, telling the family anecdotes against burgesses. He waved the strand of hair. Puffing out his cheeks and his belly, he strutted, imitating the slow-speaking of his opponents.

'My claim to be elected,' he ended, 'is this – that I am not a burgess, not a guildry man or a bonnet-maker or a baker. All my opponents have put forward their memberships in the burgess cliques in support of their candidature as though these were distinctions. My distinction is that I am not one of these fellows. Nobody, so far, in the council but has been one. Nobody, so far, could be a councillor without being one.'

The chartists had toured the different wards of the town to demand from the candidates a statement of their policy. They did not howl the question at David. 'There's a man with a policy,' they shouted. He had none, and did not claim to have one. He was against right ones. In the other wards, the chartists proposed their own mock candidates – usually half-witted street singers and beggars. But there was no such proposal at the hustings where David stood. He was elected in the show of hands, with each of the voteless vennel folks, men, women and children, raising both hands, and demanding that the bagpipes be counted as voters on the score of being full of wind like many of the ten-pound electors. Little more than half-way through the roll-call vote, confined to the few hundred lawful voters, David English had sufficient votes to put him on top of the poll. The unfree voters were solidly for him, and even burgesses were naming him as their man. The chartists played their funeral march for the defeated, then charged the platform to break it up for their bonfire.

The council talked of a water supply to be brought in pipes from a hollow in the hills at Monikie. Would the council provide the water or would a company? The company's plan was for water to be delivered where a profit could be taken from it, water for the houses and factories and shops of those who could pay the company's price; all others would stand for their water at the old wells. The newspaper reporters noted down Councillor English's quick scorn, and made it the drama in their reports. There was no constructiveness in his speeches. He waited for the motives of his fellow-councillors to disclose themselves, then leaped into the argument with furious wit. His phrases were quoted by the tavern talkers: 'Dundee's ten thousand Rebeccas at the well,' 'the terrible disease of company water on the brain,' 'to talk of water is not necessarily parish pump politics.' He reminded the council of the half-witted woman at the Lady-well, and of her threat that the town would pay for the thirst

274

of her dying children. His purpose was to raise a laugh against a superstitious councillor. The back vennels talked, the believers in magic and witches. They looked for a fulfilment of the mad woman's words.

A smoulder of rubbish became a flame in the council controlled churches, four churches together under one tower, the old steeple. For lack of water the churches burned. The great tower stood as it had stood through many burnings. 'She meant this fire, that wifie at the Ladywell,' the vennel folks said. 'These daft ones know the things that nobody else knows. Davie English knew there was something in what she had said. What a man he is! That's their burgess kirks away in smoke. God surely couldn't have been looking after His own chosen ones this time.'

The shocked council ceased to argue, and hastily decided for council water, the quicker way of obtaining it. Parliament approved of the Dundee council plans, drawn up by highly-paid experts, lawyers and engineers. 'Well, you get your way with the water,' Henryson said to David. Everybody gave the credit to Councillor English. 'Not my way, the hunched woman's, old Kate's way,' he said. The housewives ran after him in the streets to pat his back.

In the council, a newly-appointed water-bailie stood up, red-faced and mumbling, to announce that the town's water plans had made no arrangements for raising the money to pay for the water. 'I'm not to blame,' he whimpered. 'It was the experts that forgot.'

'Did your experts forget to take their fees,' David interrupted, 'since they are so forgetful about money? Who were your experts, anyway? Burgess lawyers, and burgess engineers! Their qualification was not that they knew about pipes or knew about law, but that they were in your absurd locked book. You argued for them against better names submitted to you. You said it was a good thing to have men who felt the responsibilities of freemen. These privileges of burgesses have got to cease. This is the lesson the town needs on this matter of these business rights of the free. Experts! Experts in rightness! Had you consulted the real experts – the women with the buckets – you would have learned that water is not obtained without labour and cost. I'm wasting my time here!' He strode out. The prospect of the coming of abundant water had made him the hero of the mobs. The fading of the prospect made him all the more a hero. 'There's Davie!' the crowds shouted. They held up their children to see Davie's hair and Davie's beard and Davie's loose-jointed walk, like a tinkler's walk.

Thereafter he attended the townhouse meetings comparatively rarely, when an occasion arose for an attack on the last burgess privileges. The newspaper reporters smiled to each other when he appeared. 'Here he comes to jump on another of the right ones,' they said. The Englishes' phrase, right ones, was now used by all the town. 'Have you heard Davie's latest?' the tavern arguers asked each other. 'He gave the right ones something to think about.'

The council debated whether or not the honorary freedom of the town should be given to Cobden, Lancashire leader of the Anti-Corn Law League. 'No,' the tories said, 'He is only a low agitator, a rouser of mobs. The name Cobden is no fit name for the locked book, no name to put beside the honorary burgesses of the past. Cobden is a nothing!' The whigs screamed for Cobden. Councillor English rose, and the exchange of townhouse insults was silenced. Nobody could guess which side he favoured. His vote and the votes of those few who always followed him would decide the issue.

'We are told that the name of Richard Cobden is not a great enough name to be honoured by the council,' he began. 'It may be so. Compared with the names of men we might honour, Cobden's is probably a little name. It is that kind of name the council has always noticed, the easy name to notice, the name in the news. In a little while, it will be out of the news, and then will be time to decide whether or not Cobden is a great man. Very few of the names of today turn out to be names of tomorrow.' The tories beamed upon this unexpected support of them, but the smiles vanished as Councillor English continued. 'But I do not oppose the granting of the town's freedom to Richard Cobden. Whatever be his fame tomorrow, it will at least be equal to that of most of the honorary burgesses in our locked book. I feel that those of you who extol the greatness of past burgesses, have not taken the trouble to examine the list. I have, and I found little distinction there. Admiral Rodney is there, and Admiral Duncan is there, names in the day's news that are still names, but the others, one would think, could only have been selected for their complete unimportance – obscure politicians, unsuccessful generals, and Angus lairds in abundance. Their names signify, now, no more than that the councillors of those various times were fools, flatterers always of the wrong men. If Cobden is nothing, he is a suitable name for your locked book. If he is actually a something, then it will be a pleasant change for the town to have a something to honour. I will vote for him on both counts, that he is maybe nothing and maybe something.' The whigs looked more cheerful, now. 'The advocates of free trade are smiling,' Councillor English went on, 'the supporters of world free trade in cotton, world free trade in flax, world free trade in corn. There is little merit in their enthusiasm for free trade. They live in a town which imports fibre and exports cloth. Their self-praised perspicuity in supporting free trade is nothing more than the simple ability to see which side their bread is buttered on. It requires no high-souled intellectuality for a man to try to preserve his own ignoble skin. These same shouters of Cobden's slogans, so wildly eager for a repeal of the Corn Laws and a lessening of tariffs, are as wildly anxious for the continuance of the absurd restrictions upon Dundee grocering, Dundee baking, Dundee butchering, Dundee slating, Dundee masoning. Behold them – the supporters of Cobden, the butchers, bakers, masons, slaters and grocers of Dundee! The free traders! Yes, let them have Cobden, the orator of free trade, in that locked book which is the symbol of trade restriction!'

277

Even the excitement of the long-threatened split in the Church of Scotland was used by Councillor English to bait the burgesses, and to call attention to their chartered monopolies and privileges. Sunday, May 18th, 1843, one-third of the ministers of the establishment walked from their churches with their congregations, and on village greens and town streets formed the Free Presbyterian Church, free of laird's patronage, government influence, town council dominance. This was the Disruption. The kirk quarrels of the previous century had been small things compared with this, only secessions which had left the establishment intact. In Dundee the event was particularly noteworthy. The council were the owners of the rebuilt churches under the old steeple. The ministers were council employees. St. Andrews Church in the Cowgait was partly owned by the nine trades. This great new dispute was closely linked in the town with the disputes about council rule and trade rights. Of nineteen Dundee kirk ministers, eleven were in the dramatic departure, forswearing their sure stipends and positions for the uncertainty of income and uncertainty of place in a church that had freedom but nothing else. Rich and poor, burgess and unfree, left their pews to follow their ministers into the streets, while the churchless mobs gathered to howl their approval.

In the townhouse, the event was feverishly debated. Some councillors and bailies had been in the walk out, and some had been in the minority who remained in the pews. David English grinned, maliciously satisfied, at their bandying of seventeenth-century slogans and their rival claims to be the true followers of John Knox. This was the start to a long word-warfare which through some twenty years was, for most of the council, the main business of the meetings, involving the town in interminable lawsuits and its treasury in a bankrupting expense. Councillor English's contribution to that first argument was his most ferocious attack upon the local trade restrictions.

'You have quoted John Knox against each other,' he said.

'Let one who is for neither of your churches now do some quoting. What I have for you are not the Knox sayings that you know, but they are the sayings that were known to his first followers. They were the foundation of the Knox church, which in this town was never seen as a living church because burgesses killed it before it could be born here.' His quotations were the bitter Knox of the peasant revolt and the vennel revolt. Councillor English adroitly turned each quotation against the burgess system and against the monopolies. 'There is Knox. Quote these things that Knox said,' he finished.

Into the town's discussion of the Disruption came discussion of David English's attacks upon the burgesses. A John Knox who was against Dundee bakers and grocers was in the tavern arguments, with remarkably up-to-date remarks, some genuine, some invented by Councillor English, in support of freedom for Dundee trading. The voices of trade members were raised, now, in the arguments, saying that in this age of freedom there should not be the tag 'unfree' for the great majority of the people of Dundee, and that the free competition of bakers was a better safeguard against bad baking than any twenty-pound right to baking monopolies could be.

The flax industry was adjusted, now, to power-looms. The chartist shouts were silenced by shillings for work. In a spurt of trade, country folks and Highlanders crowded into Dundee. The men from the north were no longer called Irish, not even by the oldest. The word was required for the first trickles of immigration of another people, the Irish from Ireland, a sad folk.

A growing town grew by its own growth, railway work, harbour work, plumbering for the gas-lighting of the main streets and the factories, digging for the company water, tenement-building, furniture-making, clothes-making, work for dominies, work for music-teachers, work for grocers and drysalters, work for printers, work for the lame who knocked up the workers to a six o'clock start to work, work even for the oldest women who attended to the babies of the young mothers in the mills. In the growth of the town beyond its old bounds was work for dirt men.

There was work for whalers. The ships lay in the river in March while the town feted the crews. The drunken whaling men were cheered off at the harbour, amid flying flags, everyone singing while the heroes fell into the dock and were fished out. From the river at night came the sound of the songs as the ships lay awaiting the sobering of the crews. In June they came back from the sealing, announcing the extent of their catch by cannon fire. The sailors, glamorous figures, were met at the quay, drank with everybody in the taverns, sang, fought, were wild in their love making. They were off again to the whaling within days, drunken, singing, falling into the dock, singing in the river at night. Their trade had declined after the introduction of gas-lighting, but, in the rise of the new fibre, jute, whaling rose. The town was importing more and more jute each year, a thousand tons, fifteen hundred, two thousand, three thousand. A small industry as yet, a small import compared with flax's forty thousand tons, but growing. Whale oil softened the harshness of the long, dry jute strands, and the whalers sang.

English & Henryson's factory had a roof which did not sag. It had a brick-built extension in the rear to house sixty hand-looms. Henryson was experimenting with power-weaving. 'No,' he was saying, 'not until we get rid of that starching of the yarn. We'll keep building our reserve, Dave. We would need to be bigger to make power pay.'

The girl queen, Victoria, came to Dundee, in 1844, on her way to her mountains in the north. She came through an arch at the harbour and heard the welcoming roar of a growing town in a boom. The provost read his official flattery to her. She was frightened by his nervousness, and wondered why he should be nervous of herself, so little and so plain. Nervousness in the presence of Albert, her handsome, tall, clever husband, she could understand, but the provost was not nervous of Albert.

'Thank you, my Lord Provost,' she said, stammeringly.

He gaped. He had been royally recognized. 'Did you hear what she called me? Lord Provost?' He asked his nearest councillor. 'It's a great honour for Dundee.' That nearest councillor was Councillor English, with his hard, sideways smile. He had not sought to be returned to the townhouse after his first three-years term had ended, but at the hustings had been proposed and re-elected by acclamation.

'The little woman was excited, I think,' he said to the provost. 'She mistook the smell of Dundee for the smell of Edinburgh.'

'What d'you mean? The little woman? D'you mean Her Majesty?' The provost had no words with which to be loyally dignified, other than the townhouse clichés. 'I'll not stand for Her Majesty being called a little woman. I am not to have it. I'll not take it lying down.'

'If she's not to be a little woman,' David said, 'I'll propose at the next meeting of the council that our monarch be King Victor, eight feet tall by special dispensation of the Dundee bye-laws.'

After the visit, the council talked as to whether or not the queen had intended to raise Dundee's status from a town to a city. Did not Dundee have a population of well over sixty thousand? Was it not increasing? 'Perhaps,' Councillor English suggested, 'the queen was not considering the size of the town, but the size of the man. I can well imagine her, as she looked with awe on our chief magistrate, saying: "This is surely not a mere tuppenny ha'penny provost. This is a lord provost!"' The tenement folks repeated Davie's lastest. The provost was a notably fat man.

Parliament was inquiring into the monopolies still held by the locked-book free of the Scotch burghs. 'A lot of Englishes will get their own back now,' David said. His townhouse speeches, always given lengthy reports in the local newspapers, were quoted in the London debates. Passages were read from the letters he wrote to members of parliament. In the council now was support for his venomous assaults upon those who still held hard to the burgess rights. The more skilful masons, slaters, grocers, bankers and other such small masters were calling for the competition in which their skill would prosper. The old privileges protected incompetence, they said. They, too, were writing to parliament men.

'It's the end of their burgess trick,' David said to Henryson. 'Because of their monopolies a Henryson hanged an English and another English hanged that Henryson. Now when there's the growing firm of English & Henryson, their locked book is far behind the times. The new law when it comes will make their freedom of the town less even than it is. After parliament has done with it, there will be in it only the empty-sounding name of burgess, and that will go soon, in the way the burgess privileges went.'

The parliamentary act which ended all the last vestiges of the old burgh privileges was a comparatively small parliamentary event in the month of that big parliamentary event, the repeal of the corn laws. But in Dundee it was, to the marchers in the streets, of equal importance. Shouting for Premier Peel's free corn, they shouted also for the tearing up of the ancient charters, and for David English. He laughed. 'The hunched woman should have seen this,' he said. 'Soon, in the council, I'll propose that the fee for a burgess ticket be reduced to ten pounds for anyone who wants a bargain at a bargain price. In due time, I'll move that the fee be five pounds. There are still a few laughs in this burgess business. It will come that only the honorary freedom will be left of it, a ceremonial honouring of people in the news.' He had none of the feeling of a man who has striven for a reform and been successful. He had given expression to the hate to which he had been born and to which he had been trained, nothing more than that.

At the harbour more and more jute was being unloaded; four thousand tons in a year, five thousand, seven thousand.

In a trade slump, jute held its own, even gained by its cheapness. The lowest vennel folks, those who worked only in the height of the booms, were shouting again for the charter, for maintenance of the unemployed, for the blood of the moneyed men who, by gambling in railway stock, had, in some incomprehensible way, put Dundee weavers and spinners on the streets. When the chartists marched, the town watch, all the special constables, marched alongside them with heavy sticks. The vennel folks had a name for these years of their marching – the hungry forties, as hungry for them after the repeal of the corn laws as before.

At the Quayhead, masons were building the royal arch, the vast memorial of the queen's coming to Dundee, erected in the place of the wooden arch through which she had stepped. That provost who had received her – for one rapturous moment a lord provost, David English said – had raised a subscription to build a lasting reminder of the event. The year was 1848. The trade depression was at its worst all over the trading world. In Paris, Berlin, Buda-Pesth, Warsaw, the mobs rioted; the grand eighteenth-century kings everywhere were being replaced by nineteenth-century kings, dowdy and small. That year, the small, dowdy, plain Victoria had to be smaller, dowdier, and plainer.

The revolution day for Britain was known. The chartists' petition was to be presented to parliament and signal the hour for the revolution. In Dundee, the unemployed were shouting in high excitement, awaiting the day and hour. The name of Davie English, the friend of the poor, all the better a friend for being rich, was in the shouts, the chosen leader. He had never identified himself with chartism in any way, but the mob held him to be for them and for the great petition. A worried council meeting discussed police arrangements while the mobs streamed from the vennels into the centre of the town.

The chief commissioner of police, head of the burgh watch, drew Councillor English aside.

'We know their plan. They're going to wreck the royal

arch. After that, they're to force the Houff – to bury a family they say has starved to death. What's your part in all this? They're shouting your name.'

'They'll be shouting many names as well as mine. You don't take Cobden to be a vennel rioter, do you? Will you let me speak to them?'

'Would you be going to quieten them or to rouse them more than they're roused already? Your kind of speech might set them in a blaze.' He examined David. 'This is between us, mind. The provost doesn't know. Listen, they're shouting for you!'

Councillor English appeared among the mob. They who had cheered Victoria four years before were hooting at her arch. He climbed on to a cart at the harbour entrance. The crowd howled. He quietened their howling with his raised hand. He was smiling. 'I hear that you don't like this royal arch,' he said. 'Well, I'm with you in that. I don't like it myself. It's an ugly thing, as ugly as the flattery of the queen when she came ashore here. It's stupidity in stone. Just look at what the pigeons think of it. When it comes to showing scorn for the arch, the pigeons can beat you all.' White streaks sullied the new stonework. The crowd laughed. 'Now that I hear you laughing,' he went on, 'I can talk to you about serious things. Have any of you ever had your heads broken? Do you know what it is to fall among the feet of a crowd, and get trampled on? It's what's going to happen if you folks don't have more sense than the watch has. The town's relying on you to give these fellows no encouragement to begin breaking heads. Look at this wee fellow here.' He pointed. 'He would have no chance of standing up in a crowd that was getting its heads burst open. Nor would this one, nor this one, nor you, nor you, nor you over there. The feet trampling on you! Just think of it. You've done fine up to now. You've marched like the decent men and women you are, and you've made your grievances known, but will it do your wives any good if you men get your skulls cracked? Will your bairns be any the better off if you women are walked on by somebody's hob-nailed boots.' They were thinning even as he spoke, becoming individuals, not a mob. For the last obstinate knot, he raised again the laugh against the royal arch on which the pigeons perchèd, and against the right ones who thus celebrated a little woman's presence for an hour in the town.

The mob applauded the pigeons for each new streak of white. The Dundee revolution was a laugh. Next day the news was that the great London revolution had also been a laugh. It was said by the vennel folks that Davie had saved them from being massacred by the watch. All others said that Councillor English had prevented a battle that would have damaged property and cost lives. His scorn of the right ones was quoted in the taverns. The royal arch was, thereafter, always a laugh.

In that year, 1848, the depth of the depression, the jute import was ten thousand tons. English & Henryson's took their full share of it. Power-looms and more spinning-frames went into the extended factory in the Chapelshade slope. They came from a flax factory which had failed in the collapse of the railway gambles. The firm's carefully garnered reserve provided only the smaller part of the new capital. The larger part was David's secret fund. 'I've told you,' he said to his partner, 'about the money that was found at the harbour, long ago. Fifteen coins of that remained from the Darien investment, and were the real beginning of the power. The hunched woman got these actual fifteen coins among what she inherited. What they grew to she left to me, three hundred pounds. What that has grown to in my time is enough to make up what we need now. We don't have to borrow. That money is lucky money. I've held it out of the firm, waiting to be sure. I'm sure now. It's funny – the witch said that the power would have its start in stone and water, and grow in a hot sun as jute grows.'

Henryson fitted the flax machines for jute. New processes for heckling and spinning provided yarns that engine-driven looms could weave. A hard twist in the spinning made the starching of the yarn unnecessary.

Ten thousand tons of jute in a year, ten thousand five hundred, eleven thousand, twelve thousand, thirteen thousand. The growth of the town was a growth of jute. Flax recovered from the dullness of 1848, but did not rise above its previous peak.

The population of the town rose, by jute, to seventy thousand, to eighty thousand. Work for masons, plasterers, slaters, house-wrights. Ugly tenements to build for the increasing poor, ugly villas for the increasing middle orders, ugly mansions for the increasing rich. Ugly chimney stacks to build. New churches to build, the ugliest product of the ugly era. The church of the Disruption, the Free, competed for worshippers with the Establishment, the Old. Wherever the Free built a hasty, cheap kirk the Old built a rival kirk, hastily and cheaply. The eighteenth-century secession sects, now joined together, built, hastily and cheaply, in rivalry to both Free and Old.

In the council, the church disputes of the period were almost the only subject of discussion. David English, still a member of the council, seldom attended at the townhouse. When he did attend, his purpose was to laugh or to raise a laugh. His status was now far above that of most of the members. They tried to flatter him. They would have made him provost. 'No,' he said in one of his most venomous speeches. 'Provost of Dundee! Two thirds of the council could fill the place so much better than I can do. They all have the traditional manner for it and the traditional appearance for it. It needs that kind of face a shopkeeper acquires through years of shopkeeping. It needs the subtle touch of one experienced in weighing sugar or of unrolling flannel.' He accepted a place on the magistrates' bench, however. He accepted with a laugh and a jeering glance to another councillor who had wanted this bailieship, and who would have had it if Councillor English had declined, as Councillor English had always done before. Bailie English performed none of the duties of his position, an unorthodox gallus bailie. To the vennel folks he was the only magistrate. Their name for him was no longer 'Davie' but 'the bailie', and it was so all his remaining years though he was a bailie for only one term, and thereafter always refused to be a bailie again.

In the Cowgait, David English and Henryson were beginning to be men of the first consequence. Jute had made its way into the Cowgait. Jute and Flax talked together, pacing slowly together at the Wellgait corner, almost equals; Jute somewhat aggressive, somewhat noisy, somewhat impatient; Flax, slightly patronizing, slightly more formal in discussion than need be. Flax laughed with Jute about David English's townhouse sneers. An odd fellow, yes English was odd, Flax was saying, odd to bother his head even to the slight extent he did about the council type of people. But funny, yes laughable, yes his insults were laughable.

'D'you mind when you mashed the fibre in tubs, Dave?' Henryson said. 'D'you mind when the Cowgait laughed at us? What a change!'

'Nothing to what is to be,' David said. He was in his sixtieth year, but looked less than forty with his upright gait, his dyed hair and beard. 'When the war comes, jute will grow like a mushroom in the night. We're ready for it. War with Russia! Something that has been talked about for twenty years!'

His son was fourteen, the wonder of all the teachers in the Public Seminaries for his mathematics.

'This counting will be useful in the factory office,' the bailie said.

'I would like to stay at school a little, then go to college,' the boy pleaded.

'The power is in jute,' his father replied. 'I'm not so young. I'm beginning to wonder if, after all, I'm to see us reach the power. If I'm not to be the power, it will be for you to become the power. The witch's words were nonsense, I know, but it's for us to make them come true.'

He read a newspaper announcement of the forty-year-old John English's wedding to an Edinburgh woman, a musician. 'I had forgotten about them,' David said. 'They were the important Englishes. Now, even their only kin forgets them.' Thinking of the course of the family called English, he thought of their graves. The descendants of Leeb White, he reflected, had only one mention upon a tombstone, the first English's memorial which named the first Willie English. He sought out the unnamed grave of his father in Logie and over it put a monument, worded in the manner for which he was known, the gallus manner:

> Buried here is William English, 1746–
> 1793 an orator.
> He was at the assault on the mansion of
> Mylnefield in 1772, in the bread riots
> of 1781, and the planting of the Tree
> of Liberty in the High Street of Dundee
> in 1793.
> Also eight children of the above, all of
> whom died in infancy.

David's mother had been buried in the grave of the family from whom she came. He could remember her funeral. He raised a stone over the grave:

> The Bowmans lie here, a Lochee
> family, good weavers. One of
> them, Annie Bowman, who mar-
> ried William English, orator,
> suffered that her child might be
> spared the life of a spinning mill
> orphan.

David moved to a new house in the Perth Road. The tenement folks liked their friends of the poor to be rich and imposing. 'That's the bailie's,' they said. 'A fine house!' The bailie went past in Nethergait and Perth Road, in a new carriage. He was one of the carriage-owners of the town, now. 'There's the bailie!' the folks said. 'That's his laddie, young Willie. And that's his wife. Man, I scarcely knew he had a wife. A quiet soul she looks! It's said that a big bright flame will put out the wee flames near it.'

The bailie heard of the birth of a son to John English, the Nethergait music teacher. 'It looked for a time that they would be the side of the family to make Elspet Renkyne's crazy words come true,' the bailie said. 'There's that baby and you, Willie, in this generation of the family. It's jute that's the power, not flax or music.'

There was a saying in the town that he who put a tombstone over an old grave should leave space upon it for recording another burial in the near future. The monumental masons had further work to do upon the stone under which the bagpiping orator lay. They carved these words:

Also
Agnes Woodman, 1803–1854, wife
of David English, the only surviving
son of the above William English.

'She had only a month or two of her bonnie house in Perth Road,' Dundee commented. 'A quiet woman! They say she lived only for her laddie.'

The bailie looked at his son's unweeping misery.

'You need something to do, Willie,' the bailie said. 'You'll come into the office right away. There's work there to take your mind from this.'

'My mother wanted me to go to college,' the boy said.

'You need work, lad, and the excitement of the growth of jute. Willie, d'you know what this Crimea War means to us? Dundee will take thirty thousand tons of jute this twelve months, to substitute for Russian flax that can't be got. And forty thousand the next year. You'll be there to see us grow to a power.' The boy continued to stare ahead. The father watched the son's red hair, his blunted nose, his tallness, the gallus bailie's son.

'Your mother saw jute start in one room in Reform Street,' the bailie said.

THE JUTE FORTRESSES

WHEN he dictated the Englishes' stories to a clerk in his employ, Sir William English, slowly dying, lingered upon that brief period of uncrippled manhood that had been his, his few weeks of love, his year of high adventure, the odd series of causeless events that led to his tragedy. His financial triumphs, for which he is known, were scarcely mentioned in that part of the sequence of anecdotes which dealt with his own times. His own story was as objectively told as were those of the others in the family, with their reminiscences of these surprising years gathered in among his own.

He was seventeen. He decided while looking at the river that he would try to swim to Fife. His lively friends hired a boat to follow him, and he undressed and dived. Now he was talked about and pointed to as himself, not as his father's son. He would select a passer-by in the street for kindliness of face, stop him, jabber in a language suddenly invented, making frantic gestures for aid with his hands. The passer-by would ask questions to try and make sense of it, suggest all sorts of recourses for what was apparently a foreigner in some distress or other, would be gesturing as frantically to make himself understood, while a crowd gathered to grin. The gallus Willie English! He would enter the Overgait taverns and stand drinks to the drouths in exchange for their singing of bawdy songs. He would accost girls in the street, laugh and daff with them, yank whoever accompanied him into an hilarious hour of girl chipping.

Most talked about of all his exploits was his patronage of one McGonagall. The hand-loom weaver McGonagall was an Irish half-wit of a remarkable kind, an entertainer in the more raucous pubs with Shakespearian recitations, the fun of which lay in his solemnly bathetic improvizations when his memory failed him. McGonagall pestered all the best known men of the town, ministers, councillors, employers, for testimonials of his acting skill and his elocution. He had come often to the bailie's house, and had been chased away by the servants. Willie found the long-haired, cloaked McGonagall weeping in the garden.

'Genius, sir,' McGonagall said, 'is never appreciated. When I am in the cold grave, they will build monuments to William McGonagall, tragedian. Come away, come away death, and in among the cypress trees let me be buried.'

Willie's eyes shone for mischief. In an old quarry among the back lands of the Overgait was a penny theatre, a geggie, where a family by the name of Giles performed *The Murder in the Red Barn* and such melodramas. For a few pounds the Giles theatre and the Giles family were hired for the presentation of *Macbeth*, with the half-wit in the title rôle and also as Macduff. Willie decided that the combat between the king and the thane of Fife would be more interesting with McGonagall fighting himself.

The performers, the patron, the young bloods who came at the patron's invitation, even McGonagall himself, had to battle through a crowd to enter the geggie. The show was all that Willie had promised himself and his friends. It was given three times in the course of the evening, a different rendering each time. The crowd cheered and whistled for every line from the half-wit. The combat was a riot of cheering and whistling as McGonagall leapt from one side of the stage to the other, thrusting as Macbeth, parrying as Macduff, finally stabbing vigorously from the right and dashing to the left to take the stab, and fall. In the second playing, he mistimed the fatal blow, and the play had to end with Macduff dead, after the tragedian had risen from the boards to argue the point with the audience.

Thereafter McGonagall was paraded round the houses of

the bloods to recite and to act. The combat scene from *Macbeth* was repeated often, until outdone, at Willie's suggestion, by the smothering scene in *Othello* with McGonagall as both the Moor and Desdemona.

'I wouldn't worry about Willie, Dave,' Henryson said. 'It's all just harmless wildness. You must have been a right wild one yourself when you were his age. Or, if you weren't, it was because that old humphy woman could hold you in about. Why should the gallus Dave English be worrying because he's got a gallus son?'

'I get a laugh out of it, too,' the bailie said, 'but I still am worried. I feel all this amazing talent for rowdiness and mischief comes out of resentment.'

'About your making him come into the jute when he wanted something else?'

'Yes. I've spoken to him about some of his tricks. He just says that one who has to do with jute all day needs some fun in the evenings. He says it with a kind of look that I don't like.' The bailie sat silent for a time. 'It's a funny thing that families that get on a bit seem to take to wind-plastering. There's a life in jute for anybody. If he got at jute the way I got at it ...' He was silent again, nodding to his thoughts. 'He'll go to Calcutta. That's the way for him, if I know him. The blood will go and come back with what's needed.'

The youth looked upon the proposed journey as a ploy, greatest of all his ploys, talked eagerly of it. He was not enthusiastic about jute, but was about the novelty of an Indian voyage. Once he had turned eighteen, it was arranged, he would go. The younger the better, his father said; eighteen was an age for quick assimilation of knowledge and experience. David talked of the jute fields, the boats on the rivers, the bazaars, the Hindu spinning and weaving. Willie was ready to sail when news came of the mutiny of the native troops in the Indian army. The study of the source of jute by the son of jute was delayed.

Out of devilment, he visited one of the Saturday musical assemblies in the Nethergait home of John English, the violinist. He knew that his father would be angered. He was prepared for one of his peculiar escapades, whatever might suggest itself in the course of the evening. John saw him, an unexpected member of the audience, dangerous. The youth sat quietly. There was in him some talent for music, the talent of his side of the Englishes. He had had piano tuition in his childhood, had progressed rapidly as with every study, but now preferred to play merrier instruments, mandolines, bagpipes, tin flutes, musical bells. The music played by John English, his wife and the more advanced pupils, was a new experience for Willie. It appealed alike to his ear and to his quick brain. The rippling arm muscles of a girl pianist held his eye. At the end, he thanked John in his own likeable way, said he would come again, departed whistling a melody that had taken his fancy. He glanced towards the girl with the beautiful arms. When she left the house accompanied by her brother, Willie was waiting with a hired carriage. He had taken a chance on the girl having a longish walk home. He had judged that she was in the class that walked rather than rode. The brother's presence did not disconcert him. He had expected she would have a male escort, and had hoped for a brother, bored with a family duty.

Next day he announced to his father that he would like to resume music lessons.

'What is your caper, now?' David English said, watching the wild glint in his son's eyes.

'No caper at all. I heard music I'd like to know more about.'

'Where?' The father stared, suspecting.

'At John English's school of music.'

'You were there!'

'Yes.' His apparent innocence was disarming. 'I'd like to study under him.'

David English rose, his face working.

'You know that I don't want to recognize these people in any way. Nothing would please them better than to be noticed by me.'

'I don't think they care a damn.'

'I'll have none of your impudence, my lad. Listen now! You won't go there again. Understand that!'

'You talk at me for rowdiness, then when I propose to do something quiet, you kick up a row.'

'That's not the point. Remember, you will not go there.'

'I'll go. I've no quarrel with John English.'

'If you do, I'll come for you!'

Willie sat in the Nethergait drawing room on the next Saturday evening, watching the light on the smooth arms of the girl. A servant beckoned to John English from the door, murmured to him, and John signalled the youth. Willie's father had come for him; an angry father, the servant had reported.

'Please don't let there be a scene,' John English whispered. 'I know your father dislikes me. I was a child when that family quarrel happened. I have done nothing to earn his dislike.'

'There won't be a scene,' Willie said. 'I didn't think the bailie was as gallus as that, to carry out his threat.' He smiled, squeezed John's hand comfortingly, the youth of less than nineteen in command of a situation that frightened the man of near fifty. He left, and did not call again at the music school.

John English was relieved, and forgot the flutter that the youth's coming had caused in the quiet Nethergait house. His pupil, Mabel Broadfoot, the girl with the rounded elbows, was to play in a concert, her first appearance apart from the Saturday evenings in the school. He was there to encourage her before the performance. In the excited Broadfoot party that arrived, father, mother, brother and the girl, was Willie English, at one with the others in his nervousness for the girl. She played well, and, standing for the applause, looked at Willie and only at him. John English glanced at the youth beside him. Willie was not applauding. He was too moved to applaud. His eyes were wet with happiness. This, John saw, was honesty. The gallus Willie English was in love. The girl bowing on the platform was, quite under-standably, one whom Willie English could love. The crowd were clapping their hands for her littleness, her neatness, her modesty, her goodness, her pretty excitement as she smiled down to her lover. The Broadfoots were nodding along to Willie, good folks, accepting his happiness into theirs. They must know, John was thinking, that this was Bailie English's son, but there was no servility in their manner to him, no flattering of him. Willie must have more to him than gallusness. He had a place with these Broadfoots, and it was not accorded him for his station and his wealth.

The Indian mutiny was ended. The jute plains had not been affected. Soon, David English decreed, his son would make his delayed trip. The bailie had fully decided on the trip for business reasons now, not merely as a cure for wildness. Willie was past nineteen, nearly twenty. It seemed to his father that he was acquiring repose and a sense of responsibility. He showed no wild exuberance about the proposed voyage as he had when preparing for it almost two years earlier. For some time there had been no new reports about his scrapes. He was growing up, the bailie said. Then the talk in the town about his courtship of Mabel Broadfoot talked its way to his father. The bailie said nothing about the matter to his son, but the plans for the trip were hastened. David English announced to Willie a departure in three weeks.

A Calcutta agent, home on leave, arranged the details of the equipment necessary and accompanied Willie round the shops. He found the young man apathetic. Willie made few suggestions, asked few questions. He was ill with un-happiness. Calcutta was six thousand miles away. He was in love, with all the fears of youth in love. He could not believe that he was worthy of being loved. A year, perhaps two! She would be sought after by lovers. He would not be there to offer his adoration. By such thoughts young love makes itself unhappy.

A week remained before the parting.

'Father,' Willie said. 'There is something I'd like to tell you. There is a girl. She is the girl I want to marry.' It was not easy for a lad of nineteen years to speak of his love. He had thought of asking Mabel to become engaged to him. An engagement accepted by her parents and his father would make the separation bearable.

The bailie did not reply.

'Father, will you allow me to bring Mabel to meet you?'

Willie waited. He was kept waiting.

'Surely you are old enough,' the father said, at last, 'to understand that my reputation in the town can be harmed by what you do. You could have kept your pursuit of girls out of the kind of place it seems to have blundered into now.'

'I don't understand, father.'

'You understand well enough. I'm not going to ask you who this girl Broadfoot is. I know. I have taken steps to find out. One very interesting point I discovered was that she is a pupil of a certain music teacher, and that fact threw a new light on a little argument you and I had some time ago. In a town where there are hundreds of good-looking wenches who would play about with you in your manner, you go chasing after one who is so stupid as to take your attentions seriously, introduce you to her family, and they further introduce you and talk about you as Mabel's young man. That's what I complain about, your getting yourself talked about and getting me talked about. Don't you realize that these Broadfoots are the kind of people called respectable who are not accustomed in their simple-mindedness to your type of philandering? Don't you realize that I occupy a public position? I said little about your Overgait beer-house adventures or about your teasing of that poor deluded McGonagall. But I am putting my foot down now.'

The method of attack made reply difficult for a youth of nineteen, shy about his love.

The bailie strode from the room. He scarcely saw his son in the next few days. The Calcutta man reported that all the arrangements were completed, the full equipment delivered.

'Damned lucky to have luggage to travel with,' David English said. 'I had to wear the same woollen suit through the voyage when I went. Two crossings of the equator! I knew what prickly heat was. I couldn't afford proper clothes for India for three months. How is he taking it now, do you think?'

'No better,' the Calcutta man said. 'I can't understand it. Well, maybe I can to some extent. I was rather sweet on a girl myself when I first went abroad, and the going was a bit of a tragedy to me – for about a week or so.'

'For about a week or so!' David English repeated. 'Yes, a week or so! Did he tell you about the girl?'

'I've seen her. We came upon her yesterday. It wasn't easy to get him away from her.'

It was late that evening before David saw his son. He could guess where Willie had been.

'Hadn't you better cease these visits to the Broadfoot people?' David English said. 'Haven't you been talked about enough?'

Willie did not answer. He knew, as youth does know, that experience was taking advantage of the inarticulacy of youth.

'I spoke to you,' his father said. 'I said that you have been talked about enough. Your visits to these people must stop.' He paused, then added: 'A shopkeeper's daughter! That kind were once considered above the Englishes!'

The bailie, long practised in putting others in the wrong in a dispute, had made a mistake and knew at once he had made it.

'So, that's the reason for all the indignation,' Willie said. 'Mabel is not of the right social class. You are the bailie, you are the jute man. Jute! Damn jute! It's the stuff coal-bags are made of. That's what you and your other jute men are – coal-bag makers! I've never wanted to be one of your jute men. I want it still less now.'

He rose and went towards the door. He stopped before a glass-lidded cabinet upon a small table.

'Look!' he said. He took the tress of hair from the cabinet. 'What about the wrongness you're always boasting about? You're just another self-important jute lord, just another bailie, a right one!' He threw the hair upon the table, moved to the door. 'Your witch's hair!' he added. 'If it doesn't bind you to staying out of the ranks of the right ones, it needn't bind me to go to your Calcutta and bring back what's needed!' He waited, shaking, looking towards his father, then fled.

He walked the central Dundee streets, Crighton Street, the Quayhead, Castle Street, High Street, the Overgait, Tay Street, Nethergait and was back to Crighton Street to repeat the circuit, and again to repeat it. There was in this the despair of youth, and also the conscious melodrama of youth. When the earliest taverns opened, he entered one. He ate greedily of the free bread and cheese in the bar. He slept, with his drink unfinished. He awoke after four hours. The bar tender and a number of customers were grinning at him.

He wandered up the steep slope of the Hilltown, deciding that he should not try to see Mabel but going always towards the shop. He knew she was there in the forenoons. He decided he would not enter it, but entered. He bought a handkerchief, made that his excuse to her mother for the visit. He did not ask for Mabel, but lingered in the shop. In order to linger he talked, with awkward pauses while he searched for something to say. He would go before Mabel appeared, he determined. He stayed, talking clumsily. She came in from an errand, frightened when she saw him, but happy. She made another errand a reason for their going out together. He told her about the quarrel. They walked to the top of the Hilltown. She bought the bread for which she was out, and, carrying it in her basket, went east into the countryside of Clepington with him. She wept for sorry and for happiness. They were together all that day in early summer, lovers, unhappy together, happy together, heedful of nothing but that they were together. They ate the bread she had bought.

It was dusk when they came towards the tenement where the Broadfoots lived. Her father and brother met them.

'Your mother's in a fine state,' Broadfoot said to the girl. 'Get home to her! Go on, run!' She ran . . .

'What have you been up to?' Broadfoot questioned Willie angrily. 'You know we liked you. We thought you meant right by Mabel. Your father's been here, looking for you, and what he said sent us out to look for Mabel. A nice reputation your father gives you for daffing with girls. And now you're out all day, till night with my Mabel.'

Willie could not answer.

'What have you been up to?' Broadfoot asked. 'My God, if you've done anything to her, I'll kill you, you that we took into our house.'

Willie knew no words to explain.

'Ay, I thought so,' Broadfoot said, fiercely, after staring at the youth's ashamed confusion.

He and his son moved in upon Willie. He dodged the father's rush. The son closed, and held long enough for the father to use his belt. He struck for the face, and the weals rose. Willie threw Bob Broadfoot aside. He would not fight Mabel's father and brother. He ran from them, sick with sorrow.

He drank in a Quayhead pub, sitting among whaling men, back from the sealing and due to get out in a few days for the whale fishing. Drunk, he became one of them, louder, more obscene than any.

'Ah! Who is this I see before me?' a voice said deeply. 'Is it? – yes, it is, it is my patron, most noble of men.'

'Ah, my beloved McGonagall,' Willie said in his drunkenness. 'My actor, my Kean, my Garrick, my discovery and mine alone. Be tragic, my tragedian, for tonight I would hear tragedy. I am a-sorrowed, my good William. Nay, nay, let us be merry for tomorrow we die. Comedy, my good comedian. Let there be laughter. Your masterpiece, William, your death of Desdemona.'

Laughter, more laughter, drinks for everybody, songs,

recitations from McGonagall, who, sober, half-wittedly crafty, collected the change from the money Willie threw down.

'And why, pray you, my good McGonagall, waste the sweetness of thy voice upon the works of lesser men. This Shakespeare, beside the glorious dawn-like effulgence of McGonagall, what is he? A poor player, sir, who struts and frets his hour upon the stage and then is heard no more, a tale told by an idiot full of sound and fury signifying nothing. Why, my McGonagall, do you not yourself produce immortal verse for your immortal gift of elocution?'

The pub shut. Willie went with the singing whalers to drink in the home of one of them. In the morning, their stock of alcohol exhausted, they trooped to the pubs again. McGonagall sought them out.

'Sir,' he said, 'I am a poet. Something said to me, "write!" I looked for a subject to write about, and there I saw the Law rising majestical. I wrote.'

His long hair had been combed in a different manner, more becoming a poet, McGonagall thought. Willie and the whalers shouted for silence. McGonagall read:

Most beautiful it is for to see
The beautiful Law Hill near to Dundee.
It is a very beautiful hill as all no doubt will agree,
No matter whether you look at it from Dundee or Lochee.
On the top there is a flat part
And the way there is too steep for a horse and cart.
Many young lassies and lads go wandering up the Law
And they declare it is the most beautiful sight they ever
    saw.
On one side when you look down is Lochee,
And on the other side is the beautiful city of Dundee,
And then there are the Sidlaw Hills of which the highest is
    Craigowl,
And, when you see it, with amazement you howl.

Laughter, more drinks for everybody, the change for the

poet McGonagall. He had more efforts to recite, it seemed, a prolific poet. The approaching voyage of the whalers had inspired him.

The whale is the largest fish in the sea;
With this all who have seen one will agree,
Because the whale is no less than thirty feet long,
And, I venture to say, in making this statement I am not
    far wrong.

When the whalers dash at the whale with their spears
The mighty monster sees them and under the water it
    disappears,
And when it comes up again they nearly have a fit,
But quickly they stick their harpoons into it.

The whale is chased for its whalebone and its oil,
Which makes a terrible smell when it is brought to the boil,
At the whale oil refinery, on the banks of the silvery Tay,
Not far from the station of the Arbroath Railway.

Everyone who entered had to hear it. A whaler, fighting drunk, argued that harpoons could not be called spears, even by McGonagall. The poet had to run, the only one sober enough to have given an account of what later occurred.

The crowd around Willie kept changing hourly. The whaling ships were leaving one by one. The drunken mate of one of them came, making a last hour search for men to fill up a crew.

'I'll join you,' Willie said drunkenly.

'Can you write?'

'Yes.'

'Write your name here. What's your name?'

'McPherson!'

'Where d'you come from?'

'Glasgow – in the Trongate.'

'You'll need a kit, good thick serges and woollens and a

tarpaulin coat and seaboots. See that he gets a kit, Alec. And see that he gets aboard! Here you, McPherson. See that? That's your first month's pay. You're on our crew. You know what it means not to come on a ship you've taken pay for, I suppose.'

'Yes!'

Wrapped in his new outfit of clothes, Willie English was carried aboard the whaler he had joined. In his hazed mind, before he became completely unconscious, had been a belief that he had cunningly outwitted fate in becoming McPherson of Glasgow and escaping the confusions of Willie English of Dundee. A witch had him tangled in her hair, he was muttering, in her old hair and in strands of flax and jute.

The aches of hard work lessened the agony of remorse and of love. The deep sleep of utter exhaustion was relief to torn emotions. Willie English worked, watching for the signals of those who ordered work, listening for their cursing shouts. He held to ropes for which the gale in the canvas wrestled with him. In a change of wind the ship made use of her steam, and he shovelled coal in the ship's bottom. He ached. He thought none of these men knew of his aches. They cursed, pushed him to more wrestling with the gale, to shovelling, to scraping the foul-smelling blubber holds. He hated them, savages, disgusting in their eating. He held his eyes away from their food bolting, their open mouths showing blackened teeth, gaps in the gums, and the food they revolved with their tongues.

One turned from his slobberly eating, and patting Willie upon the sore shoulders said: 'You're doing fine, lad. There's only one way to get through the first week, and that's to keep at it when you think it's killing you.' They all looked at Willie in appreciation. They had been watching to see what he would make of ship life. 'Ay, he's doing fine,' they said, spitting food. 'There's things to come you'll not like lad, cold and wind, and maybe worse. We don't like the thought of them ourselves, but we know they have to be faced.' They nodded, looking at him. 'Ay,' one said, 'but if you face them they're not that bad, after all.' They laughed. 'They're good if you face them. You feel yourself somebody,' one said. They all agreed in that. 'That's right, a whaler's somebody.' They had no words to tell him or anybody of the pride they found in labour and privation, but he understood. He liked these men. He averted his eyes from their spitting and eating, but suddenly he liked them, liked the ship, the *Lucky Scaup* named for a bank in the Tay, 270 tons, sail and steam, manned by sixty-four, master George Gellatly, heading north-west to pick up Cape Farewell.

The cold was in the wind. His fingers would not close upon the ropes. He made them grip. He wrestled for the rope with the wind that blew cold. The pains were in the small of his back, in his thighs, in the stretched muscles of his arms. The cold bit into his pains.

'That's it,' one of them said, pointing. 'That's Cape Farewell, Willie.' He was given his name. Now that the headland had been seen, pointed to, it was out of the talk. The talk had in it, now, the name Disko Island. Steam and sail, they moved along the western coast of Greenland, past the fiords. Willie saw in the distance the ice over Greenland, the great ice cap of his ancestors' fears, and of his own fears.

The ship crept closer to the Greenland coast, anchored within sight of a settlement.

'I give you two hours,' the master shouted to the clamouring men. 'If you're longer away than that, I'll leave you there.'

'Are you going ashore, Willie?' Dargie, one of the older men, asked. 'I thought you would want to stretch your legs. Would you like to give me a hand with some digging and planting? It'll keep you out of the mischief these others are thinking on. Ay, even in a wee bit out-of-the-way placie like this there's mischief, the usual kind for sea-going men.'

Willie nodded, intrigued.

'It's a kind of flower I'm after,' Dargie said. 'I always get some here if we stop, and keep it growing aboard. It's great for the scurvy. Some laugh at me, but let them laugh.'

Dargie pushed Willie past the crowd of Eskimo women

awaiting the landing from the whalers' boat, led him beyond the village, and searched among the rocks on the mountain slopes.

'This is it!' He pointed to a flowering plant. 'Look for that, Willie!'

It was easily found. Whenever there was a dirt pocket of any size in the mossed rocks, the plant grew. Instructed by Dargie, Willie dug up the strongest roots and the earth around them. Dargie filled a sack.

'Grand for the scurvy,' he said. 'Some of them think that a five-months trip is not long enough to get the scurvy, but I've seen them get it bad in two months. It's the salt meat, some say, that gives you it, or the hard tack, others say. I don't know who's right, but I know that these plants keep it away. I'll tell you something. If you get that you've got a notion for a turnip, come to me. Ay, a turnip. Man, I've seen chaps near mad with longing to get their teeth in a raw turnip or an apple or a cabbage stump. This flower is what you want if you get notions like that. I've told them, but they laugh. You've seen their teeth, Willie? Maybe I should say, you've seen their gums where they should have teeth. Look at this.'

He opened his mouth wide. His teeth were dirty and uneven, but few were missing.

'There's not many whaling men with a mouthful of teeth like that,' he boasted. 'And this is the bonnie wee flower that kept my teeth in. Let them laugh. I've got teeth, and they've got none. D'you know what happens when you've got scurvy? Your teeth fall out. Your gums get sore and soft, and out drop your teeth. I've seen men die of scurvy, a hell of a death.'

The master drove a flock of Eskimo women on the ship to their canoes. There was a bite in his orders to the crew. He lined up the men, and, with his two mates, arranged them into boat crews, a skilled steersman to each of the eight boats, a skilled harpoon gunner, a reserve for each of these key jobs, lance men for the kill, oarsmen selected by grades of strength to equalize the pulling power. 'Out with the boats! Come round, you boats on the port to the other side. I want to see you all together. You're going to row. Ay, you're not so quick and ready to pull as you are at some things, eh? Race out to opposite yon point and back again, and make it a race. No swinging in the wind. I'll be watching.'

The men roared as they pulled oar. A race. They made it a race, shouting jovial insults to other boats. Willie pulled, panted for breath, but pulled. They were all panting in the boat, winning the race. They lay on their oars, winners, proud, a good boat's crew.

'Ay,' the master said, 'I'll need to split you champions up among some of these other slowcoaches. You can pull, McPherson, I see.'

'What for would he not be able to pull?' somebody called. 'That's no McPherson, that lad. That's Bailie English's son, Willie English who swam the Tay.'

The master gaped at Willie.

'The bailie's son!' he said. 'You're a long way from your Dundee jute.' He laughed. 'Well, there are no jute lords' sons on the *Lucky Scaup* when it comes to work, mind.' The sight of the youth's strained expression stopped the master's chaffing.

The ship moved northwards in Davis Straits in a wide lane between the ice-covered land and the sea ice, using sail or steam as the winds shifted. The aches were gone from Willie's muscles. The aches of love and remorse were not gone. 'That's it,' one said, pointing, 'that's Disko Island.' There was no island. There was a long stretch of ice higher than the frozen inshore water, lower than the ice mountains beyond.

The talk was of Swartenhook now. 'That's it,' they said, pointing. It was, as was all the coast, ice that Willie could not distinguish from any other ice. The lane of water had closed, the ship had to search for a way at times. The master was in the crow's nest, his telescope turning round the horizon. There was an alertness among the men.

'There's one of them,' the master howled. 'After it, lads!'

Willie had been waiting for the 'There she blows!' of the whaling writing. Everybody moved. Those below on the sleeping watch rushed on deck. The boats were splashed into the water. Everybody, after some tumbling about, was in his place in the boats. 'Where is it?' the men called. Willie had expected some careful traditional routine for this occasion. Instead there was a confusion of argument. 'Look, there! Where? There's no whale at all! He dreamed he saw a whale!' Finally, they had the location. The boats raced. Willie pulled with the rest. His boat went ahead, and he could see the men in the other boats, straining, silent, the steersman and harpoon gunners tensed, watching ahead. He could not see his own gunner in the bows, nor where they were going. His own steersman was tensed, watching ahead, his face expressionless. Then suddenly the steersman's eyes sharpened. He showed his teeth. 'She's up again,' he said. 'Pull! We'll get her. Never a word or a sound, now.' He held up a warning hand, slowed the rowing, quietened the rowing. Anger showed in his face. 'She's down. Hold to your oars. Quiet now, never a word out of any of you!'

'There she is!' somebody said, pointing. Willie's oar dipped with the others. The boat came round with the first pull, moving in a wide curve. Willie saw the whale. There was a thin, scarcely visible vapour above its head, not the water stream of the illustrations of the accounts. A boat near to the whale was creeping nearer. Its gun fired. 'They've got her!' The whale went under at once. 'Pull!' shouted the steersman. The boat sped, parallel with the course of the scarcely moving boat that had harpooned the whale, raced ahead, turned with its gun levelled. The oarsmen held against drift. Willie was able to look round. A flag flew from the successful boat, and the others were racing towards it. They waited. The steersman watched ahead. His eyes lit, and he nodded. The boat edged forward. He timed their silent rowing with his hand. His face tightened. His waving hand was clenched suddenly. The firing of the harpoon gun threw the boat back into the water. 'Got her!' the steersman said with fervent satisfaction. The boat moved, drawn by the whale. They moved slowly, rowing only enough to keep the line from tautening too quickly and to give steerage way. The boat that had first harpooned the whale moved level with them. The other boats moved on the flanks. Willie could not see the whale when it rose. He saw the lance-throwers poised in the other boats as they prepared to throw. He heard the happy oath of the lance-thrower in his own crew. The whale raced. Tight ropes smacked the water. The boat was hauled after the whale. Everybody was suddenly shouting, cursing. For two hours they fought the whale, skill of rowing, skill of steering, skill of throwing matched against the whale's bulky strength. There was danger when they moved in for a throw. Willie saw fear once in the steersman's face. The man's hands were useless, then he laughed and steered.

The whale lay dead. 'An easy kill, that,' they said. 'The easiest kill I've seen,' veterans were saying. 'I don't care to start with an over easy kill.'

With blubber chunks and bone in her hold, the *Lucky Scaup* cruised for two days with the master on the watch with his telescope. He came down from the crow's nest, and the ship moved on a northward course. The water lanes were narrow. A man was in the crow's nest using the telescope, not for whales but for a clear way to the north. Willie learned that this was nothing unusual. The ice was as they expected to find it. The talk was of Devil's Thumb. 'That's it,' they said. 'That's Devil's Thumb!' To Willie, it was the same landscape as always, ice. They cruised in a great area clear of ice, and saw no whale. The course went on north. 'It's bad now,' Willie was told. 'We've to cross Melville Bay, a bad bit. Some years you can't get a way through it. We'll be glad to see Cape York.'

The ice closed in on the ship, high hummocked ice. The water was sticky with ice scum. Willie hid his fear. He saw that others were afraid, and not all of them could hide their fear. The ship groped for a passage. 'That's it,' one pointed.

'That's Cape York. That's the worst, Willie. You've done fine!'

The course to be followed was shown to Willie on charts, scarcely ever used for reference by the officers. The *Lucky Scaup* was in the vast Baffin Bay, the centre of which was solid ice with lanes around the coasts. They had entered the bay by Davis Strait, hugging the eastern shores for the lanes there and for the east side fishing. Now they must keep to the Greenland coast into the furthest north recess of Baffin Bay, near to the 80th parallel, fish there and come south by the lanes along the western shores of the bay, Ellesmere Land, Devon Land, Baffin Land, fishing the inlets until they came to Cumberland Sound in the south of Baffin Land, their last fishing ground. The season for the large whales there was the last weeks in September and the first in October.

Northwards. Smith Sound was ice like everything else, but recognized by the men. They fished, and had a small whale there. Southwards, with pauses to cruise in Lancaster Sound, Pond Inlet, Home Bay – a long pause there, for it had a reputation for whales. They found nothing.

Willie felt tired, and was breathless after exertion. His bones ached, but not with the same ache as in his first weeks on the ship. He awoke in the night to anxious brooding about Mabel, and could not sleep again. Hour after hour the same frightening thoughts turned over in his mind. For the incessant salt pork and porridge he had no appetite, but was hungry. His dreams and his thoughts moved from Mabel to food, fresh vegetables, fresh meat, milk, fruit. He remembered Dargie's talk of scurvy. He had pictured himself tearing up a turnip from a field, and biting into it, Dargie's symptom for the early stages of scurvy!

Dargie took him to where the plants grew in their native earth in the ship's stern. The flowers had withered, but the stems and leaves were green.

'They laugh at me with my flowers growing here,' Dargie said. 'Here, eat this!' He broke off one of the fleshy stalks, and handed it to Willie. 'Eat a bit every day for a day or two, and you'll feel fine. I know.'

Willie's hand reached for it eagerly, and he ate greedily.

'You've got the sense to let your body know what it wants. You're used to food that would be funny food to these other chaps, Willie, and you see nothing much wrong with eating this plant. The others get the scunner if they even think of eating anything out of the ordinary. They'll laugh at you as they laugh at me. I'll tell you something. The whole bunch of them has scurvy, most of them worse than you. But it's a common thing to them, and they keep on working through it, and they'll get home in five weeks before it's got a real grip, and it'll disappear if they get away from salt meat and hard tack or whatever it is that the scurvy is in. Watch them. They're slow in their work. Look at their grey faces, and their sunk-in eyes. Some of them have the bleeding gums, and some have the scurvy bruises. They'll keep going on, but there's not one of them is the man he was.'

For a few days Willie ate the green stems and leaves of Dargie's plants. He slept well, could face the fo'c'sle meals again.

Into Cumberland Sound, the last fishing ground. They had only two small whales for their two thousand miles voyage to the whaling waters and their three thousand miles search of them. Their hopes were in the famous luck of their master. George Gellatly had never failed to get a paying catch in twenty years. He was in the crow's nest, his telescope turning. Day after day, and never a whale. They found a giant, put one harpoon in her, and lost her. 'Ay, it's a bad trip,' they were saying. They were less glum, less argumentative. They were resigned to a bad trip. After all, bad trips were in the job. 'Our women will be in the mills this winter,' they were saying. George Gellatly kept cruising, kept his telescope turning. They saw two other whalers, sailing vessels, heading for home. The men smelled the cold. 'Time we were out of here,' they said. For days after, the *Lucky Scaup* searched the waters. A deputation of men went to the master to ask if he was remembering the ice at the mouth of the sound. 'We're going home now,' he said. 'It's a bad trip, and nothing more can be done.'

The ship turned through the lanes. Willie was shovelling in the ship's bottom. He saw that the other shovellers had stopped, were looking at each other.

'Anything wrong?' he asked.

'We're just wondering. The engines have stopped, and this is no place for sail if you've got engines.'

One went above, and returned pallid, mumbling.

'The ice has barred us in,' he shouted. 'What'll my wife and bairns do in Dundee?'

'Be quiet, you,' a veteran said. 'It' bad, but it's not as bad as all that. I've been twice iced in and came through it. It's not the first time a whaler has wintered in Cumberland Sound. There's meat in the ship, and firing. We're victualled and coaled for a year. We'll be here for a winter, but we'll live.'

'What about my wife and bairns? They'll think I'm dead. What'll they live on?'

'It's happened before, and it'll happen again. They'll be all right. Did you ever hear of an iced-in whaler man's bairns starving? I've had it twice, so I know.'

In a corner where he thought he was unseen, the veteran was sick with fear. Willie saw, and knew he had seen courage. He went above. The master was among the crew.

'It looks like we're here for a long spell,' the master was saying.

'Ay,' they were saying. 'It's all right, Geordie. We're not blaming you. You had to hold out for whales. And the ice is a day or two earlier.' The master nodded, relief in his face for their naming him Geordie, not Mister Gellatly.

The agony of love and remorse seized upon Willie English.

The veterans comforted those, most of the crew, who had never before wintered in the north. Cumberland Sound would remain clear of ice, they said. The ship would have a snug anchorage in the shelter of high ice on shore, or if it had to run would have sailing room in the hundred miles wide inlet.

'We'll be home by the end of May,' the master said. 'We'll fish the bay now, and have a catch to take home. We'll miss only the sealing, but we'll have the first whales to take in next year and get extra money for early whales.'

They searched Cumberland Sound and found whales, the giants for which the sound was known. Their holds were packed in a week. Ice formed on their hands and faces. The winter was coming upon them. The master, in the crow's nest was looking for shelter from the fury to come. He went out in a boat to examine inlets. He tested the ice walls of the inlets for stability, tested the water for currents, tested the bottoms for secure holding. They edged the *Lucky Scaup* into a creek. The ice walls rose above them higher than the masts. They fastened the ship to the sea floor by the anchors, by cables to the ice. 'We'll be fine here,' the master said.

'What about scurvy?' Willie asked Dargie. 'You say they have it now. It will become worse, I take it. Dargie, I must come through this. I must get to Dundee. There's somebody there. Will we get back?'

'Some of us will die, Willie,' Dargie said simply. 'I've told you it's a terrible death from scurvy. Those who know are worried about it more than about the cold.'

'Can nothing be done? Does your plant live through the winter?'

'I couldn't say, lad. I believe it could be made to live. It's not a plant that grows in a season from seed. With nursing it might be kept green, and even if it does die down, the good might be in the roots. I don't know. What's on your mind, Willie?'

'Can we get it here?'

'Ay, I expect we could.'

'Dargie, we'll have a search for it, and try to keep it alive in the ship. Will you go to Gellatly with me?'

'I'll come if you like, but, mind you, they'll laugh.'

The master smiled incredulously.

'I've heard before of Dargie's plant. There's a few believers in it. It's the best pub argument we have. But, man, how could a plant kill the scurvy in salt pork?'

'The lime juice they carry in the navy seems to kill it,' Willie said. 'I think myself that there must be something in lime juice that counters the pork. Maybe Dargie's flowers does the same. It helped me when I was sick.' They talked.

'Right, we'll have a look for it,' Gellatly allowed. 'Don't say anything to the men about the hopes you put in it. They'll laugh at us. If it wasn't you, English, I'd have nothing to do with this daftness. You can say you're collecting the stuff for botany. I've heard of folk who did that.'

In a sheltered little glen, they found the plant, and filled a boat with it and the earth in which it grew. The master was fussy about the effect of damp dirt on his woodwork, but finally granted a place where there were the warmth and light that Dargie wanted.

'We've got to get them to eating it,' Willie said. 'I'll find a way.'

The wind of the Arctic whistled across the top of the ice walls, a wind solid with snow. Sheltered from the wind they kept the decks clear of snow. If it lay an hour, it froze and had to be chipped. They were faring well, plenty of food for all, good fires burning. Willie had induced a few to chew an inch or so of the plant stems at meals. Soon all were eating the plant, greedy for it. They admitted nothing, but were obviously the better.

'I'm keeping them working while they can,' the master told Willie. 'We're coming near the time when you daren't put your nose into the air. I'm depending on you when the time comes, English.'

'For what?' Willie asked.

'For keeping us lively. If we once stop talking, we'll not see Dundee. They tell me that in the pubs before we came away, you were a talking, laughing lad. There are one or two others, talkers and laughers. We'll need all the laughing we can get.'

'I was drunk then.'

'You'll have to raise laughs now when you're sober. There's some drink, but only a ration for every day, and heavy drinking for when things get bad. A spree's too precious up here to be used for everyday raising of hearts. They'll be cast down a bit when Hogmanay comes – if we see it! We'll use the drink for times like that. Right, get laughing!'

Organizer of morale, Willie collected the musical instruments aboard, a set of bagpipes, a fiddle, a tin whistle, but found nobody capable of doing more than pick out one tune or two. He, it appeared, was to be chief musician as well as chief talker and laugher. There was molasses to put the bagpipes in condition, and resin for the violin bow. To give himself something to do, to take his mind from the love and the remorse, he arranged a programme: of discussions, music and ploys of his own peculiar kind, dramas to be acted in the McGonagall style, and tests of strength, weightlifting, wrestling. The cold gripped. In the wind were daggers of ice. For days on end everybody was imprisoned below. The four-foot thick wood of the bows held out the winter, kept in the muggy warmth of men crowded together.

Willie learned the songs of the whalers, working songs of the sea, tenement songs, bothie ballads of Angus. He played the fiddle to their singing of an interminable account in homespun verse of the guests at a barn dance held in the town of Kirriemuir. New verses in the crudely carnal manner of the original were added with each singing, until everybody on the ship was in the song. They sang of that short-sighted man who had once mistaken a cluster of wind-swept boulders for seals and stalked them:

Jock Taylor saw the couples sitting out the reels;
He went and clubbed the lot of them; he thought they
    were the seals,
At the ball, the ball, in the light of the morn,
It wasna what they came for, to be clubbed among the
    corn.

One of the crew had, on an occasion years ago, become sentimental about an Eskimo woman and was discomfited to learn in rhyme that his mates had not forgotten:

Willie Lonnie, he was there, with drink an affie mess.
He brought his lass from Greenland, and she was a great
  success.
At the ball in the barn, Willie's lassie was the belle,
The country lads they like them fat and like them with a
  smell.

They talked of the tenement poets and the ploughmen poets, talent new to Willie. There was one of whom they spoke, Peter Livingstone, in the Deershorn Close in the Hilltown, whose latest song, heard by some of the whalers before the departure from Dundee, became a favourite.

'We'll keep that one for our New Year celebrations,' Willie decided 'We'll sing it no more now.'

He played them, in his own way, bits of melody from Schubert and Mozart. They were enthusiastic for these, once they became accustomed to them. 'Bonnie tunes,' they said. Mozart, *The Ball o' Kirriemuir, Drunken Sailor*, an imitation of McGonagall's combat, strathspeys, reels, an argument about Dundee's religious sects or Dundee's politics, these were all in the entertainments. When the weather allowed they shovelled and chipped on deck and came back ready for more singing, playing and arguing.

Dargie had reported the fading of the plant. The time came when all the green had disappeared. The root was still living. As Dargie had surmised, the plant was a perennial.

'It's done its work,' Willie said. 'It was nearly four months before the scurvy got started on me. Four months from now will see us into March. Don't use the roots. We don't know but what they're poisonous.'

'Ay,' Dargie said, slowly, 'four months from now will be March. Four months!'

With arguments, fiddle-playing, singing, and the con-

tests of strength in the mugginess of the fo'c'sle, they with-
stood the Arctic. They came to the old celebration of
Hogmanay, the promise of spring to come, of deliverance
from the winter, of life for themselves and for mankind.
They were thinking of the tavern jaunts of the folks at
home; of the women cleaning their tenement homes, poli-
shing, scrubbing; of the crowd around the pillars of the
townhouse, yelling the New Year in, breaking their empty
bottles upon the stones of the pillars, setting off to first-foot
friends. The wind shrieked above the *Lucky Scaup*. They
listened to the wind as they thought of home.

'I can't stand it,' one shouted. 'Nothing but snow and ice
and cold.' The men were rising, their eyes wild with longing
for home.

'English, play or talk! I'll get the drinks round!' the
master said.

The fiddle and the bagpipes were beside Willie for such an
emergency, but he could not think of a tune.

'Let me get above!' the madman was shouting. 'Ay, I'll
freeze. It's better to freeze!'

A tune blew itself into the bagpipes, a wildly rhythmed
song of the Aberdeenshire bothies. Willie speeded the tempo.
They were staring at the pipes and the piper. They smiled,
they stamped their feet. The madman stamped his feet, sat
down. 'Hooch!' they shouted. 'Go it, Willie.' They were singing:

> Sarah, she ran to the barn door,
> And she let oot an affie roar.
> She tripped on the midden and fell on the boar,
> At the mucking o' Geordie's byre.

> The boar, it loupit ower the dyke,
> Right into the midst o' a waspie's byke,
> Oh wasna that an affie fyke
> At the mucking o' Geordie's byre.

The auld wife she was bending doon,
And the soo got kickit i' the croon,
And its heid gaed into the wifie's goon,
    At the mucking o' Geordie's byre.

They cheered the arrival of the drinks. The master announced midnight. The year 1860 had come. They shook hands, shouted greetings. They sang the New Year song written by the tenement poet, Livingstone:

A Guid New Year to ane an' a',
    O' mony may you see,
And during a' the years to come,
    O' happy may you be!
And may you ne'er hae cause to mourn,
    To sigh or shed a tear—
To ane and a' baith great and sma'
    A hearty guid New Year.

O' time flies fast, he winna wait
    My friend for you or me,
He works his wonders day by day,
    And onward still doth flee.
O wha can tell gin ilka ane
    I see so happy here,
Will meet again and happy be,
    Anither guid New Year?

Now let us hope our years may be
    As guid as they hae been;
And let us hope we ne'er may see
    The sorrows we hae seen;
And let us hope that ane and a'—
    Our friends baith far and near—
May aye enjoy for time to come,
    A hearty guid New Year.

'The worst is to come,' the master whispered to Willie. 'January and February. I'm watching the ice on the creek walls. There's none forming yet, but the next two months are the months when I'll have to watch with both eyes, if I can get up to watch. Play to them, and I'll get the booze away. Over much booze is as bad for them as none. You have to watch that they get merry but not tearful. What a way of doing if they got tearful drunk!'

Once again in January the drink had to be hastily put round. Willie and the drink saved a panic of home-sickness and sickness for lack of women. Talking, singing, playing, they were through January.

'I've picked a champion anchorage,' the master said. 'I'm going to put it in the charts, once I get a blink of sun and a bearing or two. You'll give me a hand, English. It's a figuring job. If we can get it in the charts, it'll be a godsend to us or to somebody else. There's never been a wintering like this. Not a man lost yet. You've done fine, English. I'm letting you name this creek for the charts.'

Willie's first thought was to name it for Mabel, but he thought again. 'Call it Elspet Renkyne creek,' he said. His laugh was hard.

'It's a funny name. Is it a woman?'

'She was a Dundee witch,' Willie said, 'burned in the Seagait.'

'It's not so bad a death as cold,' Gellatly remarked, laughing. 'I wouldn't mind being on a fire in the Seagait, this minute.'

There was hope for the men now. They lived by hope through the terror of February in Baffin Land. Only on two days in the month were they on deck, working at the shovelling and chipping. The load of snow had lowered the ship's freeboard to inches. 'If we hadn't been out of the wind, we would have sunk,' they were saying. 'The snow piled even on the deck because we were out of the wind.'

They were into March. 'It's daylight,' they said, 'real daylight.' Their faces were darkening with scurvy, their eyes

317

receded into their faces. Willie felt the terrible melancholy upon him again, could not sleep, could not move without breathlessness. The hope of seeing Dundee went from all of them. They had come through January and February, and feared April and May. Willie drove himself to the bagpiping and fiddling, but they sat glowering, could not be stirred to hope.

'Will your plant be growing on the land?' Willie asked Dargie.

'No. These Arctic plants grow quick when they start, but it'll be May before they start, I'm thinking. What about the roots?'

'No, we'll hold on.'

'We can do it, Willie. The scurvy will not get a grip in time to kill more than one or two. You and I will get through it, I think, but I know some that are not to see Dundee.'

'I have to get through it!' Willie said. The thought of Mabel kept him alive in the next week, torturing thought, but holding him to a determination to live.

Working on the slippery deck, giddy in his scurvy sickness, he fell on his back upon an iron chain. He could not rise. The men lifted him to his bunk. Though ill themselves, they had sympathy for his hurts. They gathered around him, feebly attempting to rouse him out of the depression of scurvy, aggravated by his fall.

'If we believe that the plants will grow, they will grow,' Dargie told Willie. 'If you believe hard enough, your belief comes about.'

He came one day in high excitement to the bunk.

'Our plants are showing green,' he said. 'The touch of heat they get has made them think it's May. That stuff grows quick. In three or four days we'll be right.'

Turnips had been in the dreams of the men before they had tasted the plant. Now their dreams were of the thick stems and leaves of Dargie's flower. They snatched at the small portions put down beside their plates. In a week they were well, sure of salvation, singing, stamping their feet, but

Willie still lay in his bunk. They were gentle in their nursing of him. He was improved in general health, his spirits lifted, but he could not walk or even move his legs. 'You'll be right in a day or two,' they said. 'This kind of thing just needs rest.' Dargie was grave, but did not tell Willie of the reason for his gravity.

In late April came a blink of the sun, and they cheered. May, the month for return to Dundee. They left their anchorage, and steamed in the sound. They searched for an opening in the ice across the mouth. They found lanes. 'Wait!' the master said. 'There's no saying what these lanes lead to, if they lead anywhere.' They waited, steaming slowly along the ice. The ice lanes widened. They were free. They had not lost a man, a miracle of Arctic wintering.

The *Lucky Scaup* went through the ice jumbles and ice scum to the open waters. They sang as they worked. Homeward bound, and with whales. The carpenter made a litter which allowed Willie to be on deck, sitting up to watch the waters going past the ship.

They saw Scotland and sang. They came south to the Tay. They fired eight guns at the Tay bar to announce their home-coming with eight whales. Laughing, singing they came by the channel. The mill and factory whistles of Dundee were sounding for the *Lucky Scaup*. From the shores of Angus and Fife, flags and handkerchiefs waved. The Quayhead was a black mass of folk, a white flutter of handkerchiefs, a coloured flutter of flags. For the *Lucky Scaup*, for her crew, home and with whales. The welcoming roar of Dundee came to them.

They came by the boats to the Quayhead. The men's women and bairns were lifted over hundreds of heads. The crowd's roar was silenced by the sight of Willie, sitting in his litter. 'He'll be all right,' the whaling men called. 'He just needs a rest. He had a fall.' The crowd howled again.

'Everybody safe! Nobody lost!' The words went back through the mob. The miracle was cheered.

There was news for two of the crew, the death of a wife,

the death of a loved child. The stricken men stood among the singing and shouting. A band was playing. Youths were struggling with each other to have a hand in carrying the whaler men. They raised Willie's litter gently, and moved with him in the procession forming behind the band.

'I'll tell your father, Master Willie,' a man shouted. 'I know your father. I'm in the mill. I'll give him the word.' He ran, and others ran with him, at once kindly and obsequious, keen to be the first with good news, the more keen because it was good news for the jute lord bailie.

Willie was carried among the singing and the band playing and the free drinks. He held to this last moment of his adventure, and ever afterwards remembered his thoughts. Never again he was thinking would he know exhaustion, but never again know the sleep of exhaustion; never again know fear, but never again know relief from fear; never again know cold, but never again know warmth after cold. He did not suspect that soon he was to know a more terrible fear than the Arctic fear, a more gripping cold, an exhaustion of soul. He laughed as a whaler laughs, open-mouthed. He sang as a whaler sings, unashamed of loudness.

The crowd had cheered for the ship, for everyone of the crew, for each of the eight whales. They asked for another cause to cheer.

'Cheer the creek where we were kept safe,' Willie called. 'Cheer Elspet Renkyne creek!'

'Elspet Renkyne creek!' the mob shouted. 'Elspet Renkyne.' A multitude were acclaiming the name. Willie laughed, then he thought of Mabel, and was suddenly sober and anxious.

He saw his father come through a lane the crowd made for him, his father and Broadfoot. David English's hat was in his hand, and his hair and beard, no longer dyed red, were white for sorrow.

'You've come back, Willie. We never thought of your being with the whalers,' the bailie said, an aged man, stooped, mumbling. He saw Willie's look towards Broadfoot. 'Mabel is all right, Willie,' he added, 'she's with me, and her baby Elspet. You didn't know you had a daughter, did you, Willie?' There was a return of the former alive look to his face when he mentioned the child.

'I'm glad that Mabel and I have a baby,' Willie said, after staring silently.

Men lifted the litter to the carriage on the outskirts of the crowd. They ran with the carriage, struggling to have a hand on it, as it moved along Nethergait. It outpaced them, and they stood cheering its going from them.

Willie sat in his litter in that room where he had quarrelled with his father a year ago. A year! Mabel came to him with her child. He hugged them to him, weeping as she wept. Outside, a noise that had been growing was suddenly a hubbub of noise. Willie caught some of the words in a tumult of words. The mob had heard of his singing and playing in the Arctic. They were calling for him. Bagpipes started to play, rising above the voices, hushing the voices. The tune was *The Mucking o' Geordie's Byre*. His body tried to sway to the wild rhythm, but could not. He realized then his grasp upon Mabel was not a young man's desire for a young woman. He was afraid, and cold, and tired. He knew he was a cripple, paralysed, a useless man for a woman. He thought bitterly of that old family legend, the prophecy to the effect that the blood would go and return, and bring what was needed.

Jute, a dying murmur on the lips of hunched Kate English, a frightened whispering in the Cowgait, an argument in the taverns, a shouting in the markets of London and Liverpool; a whirring of spindles, a clacking of looms, a roar of spindles, a giant clatter of looms, of the engines for looms; growing, growing to a crescendo of shouting, roaring, clattering, hammering; the wind in the sails of ships with jute, the sirens of steamships with jute, with people to batch jute and spin jute and weave jute and calender jute; the rattle of wheels on rails with jute and jute-workers, moving to the clamour and babble of the town of jute.

The American civil war made a boom of jute in Dundee.

It was the greatest of all wars for the size of its armies, the bitterness of its fighting, the number of its dead, the length of its supply columns, miles after miles of jute sacks, miles after miles of jute and linen equipment for soldiers. The blockade of the southern states was idle-set for cotton-weavers, but work in Dundee, the making of jute substitutes for cotton cloth. Destruction in Virginia, Georgia, Maryland, Pennsylvania, decay in Manchester, Preston, Paisley, Glasgow, these were the building of Dundee from a town to a city.

The profits of the war raised masses of masonry in all parts of the town, jute factories. The stone, carefully cut and laid, was the even-textured Kingoodie stone from the Carse of Gowrie or the stone of the Angus quarries, cream-grey with hints of red in it when the sun shone. Viewed down the long slopes and steps of peaked roofs, the square lines and wide windows of the new structures held the eye.

The labour recruiters spoke in Ireland of the vast new mills and factories in Dundee, of the work there, the shillings, the security. The fare from Dublin to Dundee was two shillings for adults, a shilling for children. You brought your own food, if you had any. You brought your own blanket to wrap around you as you slept in the hold, or, if unlucky, on the deck. The ragged, starved Irish streamed up Castle Street and Crighton Street from the harbour. They were in the fabled land of clothes and food and boots. They forgot the voyage, beam on to the Atlantic swell of the Hebrides, through the tossing Pentland Firth. They gaped at the massiveness of the factories to which they had hired themselves. They swarmed into the oldest, dirtiest closes, renamed by the tavern wags, in contempt, Mulligan's Maze, Sligo Fair, Tipperary, the Bog. These Irish were the greater part of the two thousand a year increase of Dundee's population in the long boom of jute, to a hundred thousand people, a hundred and ten thousand, a hundred and thirty thousand, a hundred and forty thousand, and on, rising.

Dundee grew, an unplanned conglomerate of drab oldness

and drab newness. The songs of Ireland were sung in the streets, homesick songs. The voices of the small-boned, dark singers were Irish. In a year, singing the same songs, they were singing them in the voice of Dundee. The little medieval Dundee had made its thousands of Scotch incomers people of Dundee, and it made Irish into Dundee folks, with the quacking-mehing words of Dundee. The four-flighted tenements marched in ranks up the spurs of the Law, along the length of the spurs, down towards the valley between the Law and the Sidlaws. The farm-house word for a northern decline was the name for tenements beyond the Hilltown crest – Coldside. The Scouring Burn was not a stream, but a tenement street. The escarpments of Wallace Craigie were hidden by tenements built against the steep rock faces, three storeys in front, six storeys at the back.

In the older part of the town, four centuries jostled together. The warrens of Monck's time remained, with the eighteenth-century outside-staired tenements squeezed into Monck's gaps. The squareness and straightness of new structures, built in clearances, were distorted to fit land lots measured in feudal times. Gables of new tenements stared blankly high above cottages. The cottage chimneys rose on brick stilts up the tenement ends to find a smoke draught. The clearances were few. While ancient outer walls stood, a little plastering and carpentry kept the inside habitable for years to bring pennies in rent. Buildings in which not even the poorest Irish could live were still serviceable as warehouses and as workshops for the minor industries. When they were falling they were propped up, an investment in the future, to be sold for the increased space prices of the future.

The central streets seethed with spenders of shillings. On Tuesdays, the farmers stood along the front of the townhouse watching the exciting town that made farmers fat. They talked out of the sides of their mouths, as Angus farmers had always talked. They spat, lifting up their great whiskers to spit. On Saturday afternoons, the ploughmen strode into

Dundee, to the Greenmarket on the Quayhead, a centuries-old Saturday fair of vegetables, fruit, quack medicines, witcheries, the festival of laughter where the country lads joined in sex horseplay. Happy Dundee of the booms, where happiness grew with the growth of tenements and mills! There were shillings for the Scotch starved for centuries, for the starved Irish. In the smell of Dundee they died, forty of them to every thousand in a year, but always the Scotch and Irish had died fast. In the boom the fears were conjured away, the fear of the ice, of the death of the species. Dundee laughed, the Scotch and the Irish laughed often, the peoples who had laughed seldom.

The accumulation of wealth which the war had brought to English & Henryson's was in one of the squarest, widest-windowed of the vast fortresses of jute. David English, white, stooping, but still capable of gallusness, looked with his partner on the building of the factory.

'We'll need a name,' Henryson said. 'You can see both the Sidlaws and the river from it. I was thinking that maybe a nice name like Sidlaw Factory or Tayview Works would be right.'

'Too ordinary,' old David said. His devil's smile came to his face. 'She said the blood would be a power. It was gibberish, but we've made it happen. She said the growth of the power would take place in a hot sun and heavy rains. It was a crazy woman's talk, but the growth was jute. She said she would be seen again in Dundee, standing, unburnable, in cold flames. Henryson, some of the new jute and flax places are having statues put on them, James Watt, Minerva the spinning goddess, and such. We'll have our statue – no, a carving, one of these low relief carvings on the front, above the main doorway – a woman in a witch-fire. You know the story of Elspet Renkyne.'

'It's a funny thing to have on a factory.'

'It is. That's the point. It's away from the usual. People would talk about it. It would be a story to tell to buyers. Our agents could hold the attention of possible customers with a story like that. And if the name had a connection with the story, so much the better. The Elspet Renkyne Factory – no, that's too odd. The Witchfire Jute Works. That's it. Batching, dressing, spinning, weaving, calendering, all together in the Witchfire Jute Works.'

They watched an Edinburgh sculptor at work upon the carving. The old market cross was there, with its six octagonal steps forming a base for the tower from which rose the shaft with the unicorn upon it. A woman stood in the jougs, her hands and neck in the holes of the crosspiece. Her hair, shorn from her head, was nailed beside her right hand. The stumps of the Moraygait port's archway were there. A woman sat with a boy, and pointed among the ruins of Monck's assault. The old tolbooth was there. A woman lay upon the ground, and a crowd danced, for joy that Cromwell was dead, to the playing of a shawm. Set in the triangle of these three lesser carvings, was the great carving of a woman among stone flames. A sour-featured minister, a right one, preached, his finger pointing pompously to Heaven.

'There's the beginning of my line, Henryson,' old David said. 'And it ends after two hundred years with little Elspet, the only grandchild I can have. We'll have no celebration for the naming of the works. Let the masons build this into the front, and when they've finished, it's there, without any pulling away of sheets or any speech making.'

In an office built on to the Perth Road house, Willie English worked with accounting clerks at the more abstruse mathematics of the firm, the investments in shipping to bring the jute from Calcutta, the bargaining for the harvests of great areas in Bengal, the rise of new markets for cloth, the decline of old ones. He had himself suggested that this be his work. His father, allowing him his whim, had started him on small matters, and had seen that Willie's schoolboy flair for figures was now a great talent for finance. In four years he had made himself indispensable to English & Henryson's. 'Willie's the new kind of man in the town,' David said. 'He knows about money as I knew about jute, and as you knew about its spinning and weaving. He's the future's man. Jute cloth and ships and even wheat are to be by-products in the great money industry, produced as a side-line in the making of money.'

Willie had settled to a way of life. Dargie was his legs, he said. The former whaler was always near. His superintendence over an elaborately artificial routine, of wheeled chairs and hoists and inclined planes, made it appear simple and natural. The first despair past, Willie and Mabel found reasons for some measure of contentment. They had Elspet, a laughing, red-haired little girl. They had the excitements of Mabel's piano-playing, and of Willie's odd hobbies, which brought entertaining visitors to the house, shy ploughmen from the country with songs of their own composing, tenement poets with their verses, roaring Arctic voyagers with whaling yarns. There was laughter again in the Perth Road house.

On the lower slopes of Claypots, west of Broughty, and on the Camphill, behind Broughty, rose the new homes of the jute millionaires. On Sunday afternoons the tenement-dwellers walked to Broughty to stare in awe at the mansions in the making. The mill and factory folks argued the greater grandeur of one employer's house against another's. 'Henryson's is the bonniest of them all,' declared men and women and children of the Witchfire Jute Works. They were proud of Henryson's extravagancies of architecture, the useless towers and cupolas, the buttresses that supported nothing, the whirligigs, the whamwhoozles. 'It's a pity the bailie doesn't build one. He would show them something in the way of houses. He'll not be feeling like it, him having only poor Master Willie to come after him. It's a true saying that you can't have everything.'

Old David, seventy-three years old, read the announcement that Alice English, who had been Alice Greenacre, was dead, aged seventy-seven. He stared into the fire where his memories burned. He talked to Mabel about the other Englishes, who were still her music teachers, asked her about the dead woman. 'Won't you come and visit them with me?' she asked. 'They speak to me about you. John remembers you from his childhood. The boy is proud of your success.' He was startled. 'The boy speaks about me?' he said.

He went with Mabel, and sat in the drawing-room where he had sat at hunched Kate's feet, recognized pieces of furniture that had been there fifty years ago, the table where he wrote the flax words that the old woman dictated, the stool he had fallen against. He felt for the little dent in his brow where the gash had been. He looked from the window down the slope of the garden where he had played. He had bathed in the water that flowed at the bottom of the garden. Now, the river was a quarter of a mile distant, across rails and shed roofs.

John's thirteen-year-old son, grandson of the dead woman, pale in his mourning, sat with his father and old David in the first carriage at the funeral. The old man, watching the boy's profile, saw an English, blunted of nose, a ruddy gleam in his dark hair. This was his kin, the relationship two centuries deep in the dust.

He came by the front entrance of the Witchfire Jute Works to his counting-room, and looked up at the carving. 'The boy is an English,' he said. 'The hunched woman said I was to keep the others of the blood in mind.'

He called again at the Nethergait house. The sound of music came from upstairs.

'Tell your master and mistress to go on playing,' he said to the servant girl. 'I should like to come and hear them, if they will allow me.'

They were in a small room that he knew, differently arranged from his youth, when it had been filled with flax samples. As he entered, he had motioned to them to go on with their playing. He listened, admiring the woman's quick light hands on the keys, the dexterity of John's bow. An air that he had heard before came into their music. The sound

327

of feet, a sad moan. Why, he wondered, did he think of the feet of a crowd and of a woman in distress.

'It is the suite I made of my father's songs,' John said. 'You won't think it strange that we should be playing so soon after her death. You understand this was very dear to her.'

David nodded, understanding. 'There was a tune in it, towards the end.' He hummed a few bars. 'Will you let me hear it again?' A crowd, a woman's sorrow, a fire! He knew now what it was, Adam's song, inspired by the hair of Elspet Renkyne. He remembered hunched Kate's excitement. 'A song!' she had cried out. 'There was a song in what Elspet Renkyne said. Hammers, a piano has hammers!' He told the story. 'At first,' he said, "the old woman was angry because Adam drifted away from her flax to music. Yet, here's the music alive when the flax is dead.' He nodded over his recollections. 'John,' he said, timidly almost. 'I could be of assistance to your boy. He is coming along towards the time when he will be thinking of his future. I can help. I do not like to think of the family's long connection with the trade of the town just fading out. Your side of the family gave me my chance. I'm afraid I have not shown much gratitude for it.' He stopped there. He had suddenly understood the significance of a parish-name spoken upon the Law on his twenty-first birthday. Kinnettles! Where his mother had been a mill hand! Where he himself should have been a mill orphan! 'The Englishes should be all one family – the blood!' he said, staring. He groped for words, and there were none. 'Would your boy be interested in an industrial career?' he said.

The boy's hero in the family was his great-grandfather, John said, one of the first Dundee men to go to Russia. Young John, the father and mother argued with each other, was musical, but not the type to make a professional musician. No, certainly more fitted for business. He was clever at the school. David was pleased with their simple pride in the boy. He saw that they had not understood the full implications of his offer, and on that score, was the more pleased with them. 'Young John could come to Willie's office, now,' he said. 'His education need not suffer. We have been thinking of bringing in a tutor for little Elspet. We could get one who could also teach your boy in the afternoons. Willie will be glad to have him, I know, and the work is worth learning. It's become the most important work in the firm.'

A glass case on the stairway held his attention as he was leaving.

'There were two tresses of hair in this,' he said.

'They were so faded,' John said. 'They were burned long ago, but we don't forget them. We have the song.' He pointed at the case. 'That is the original manuscript of the words and music.'

The old man snapped his fingers, laughing.

'Before great men, gathered in Dundee,' he said, 'burgess boys are to sing the lamentation for her death, and hammers are to beat it. A poor, pained woman's craziness, but her craziness has come to pass in other matters. It will come to pass in this. Great men, undeniably great men, not the names of the day, not just the right politicians, or the wonderful preachers, or the jute lords, or the lairds!' He was flushed with the excitement of his thoughts. 'Yes, it will come to pass!'

THE PIERS IN THE RIVER

THE mobs had marched in Dundee to cheer for the victory of Lincoln and Sherman and Grant in America. They did not know that the war had been their shilling shower. They marched again, to shout their complaints and threats at the townhouse and at the jute lords' houses. Trade depressions, after trade booms, were the industrial century's short corn years. The tenement folks flocked after the Liberal orators who had the cure for idle-set, compulsory education.

A new buyer of jute came into the market, the Prussian army, with orders of miles after miles of jute sacks, miles after miles of webbing. The Scotch and the Irish housewives laughed again on Saturdays, moving, with a rattle of shillings, down the long slope of the Hilltown, down the Welgait, jamming the decrepit narrows of the Moraygait. The ships queued in the river for berths, to unload Irish immigrants and raw jute, Dundee ships, manned by Dundee crews, with sails of Dundee canvas, or engines from Dundee's foundries. The town's industrialists made trade advantages out of the town's economic and geographical weaknesses. Their workers and their fibre must be imported, and their sacks and sheeting exported. Let the importation and exportation be done in Dundee-built, Dundee-manned ships to balance the town's economy, to provide work for skilled men as well as for women and boys. The jute profits built ships and docks and foundries. Willie English juggled with his figures and young John watched him, learning the money industry.

For a year, various committees in the town had prepared for a novel excitement, the visit of the British Association with the great men, undeniably great, of old David English's scheme to make gibberish become a prophecy. Dundee astonished the scientists with its strutting provincial confidence of the middle orders, its slinking destitution of the poorest vennel dwellers, its fifteenth-century methods of clearing the redd, its advanced factory organization and factory buildings, its mill schools where mill-owners themselves taught reading and writing to the rove-gathering and sack-sewing children, the barefooted women at the street wells, the Saturday night drunkenness in the Overgait where an Irish priest kept better order than all the police could do, the modernity of the medical methods in the charity-maintained infirmary, the full-sized *Courier* newspaper for a halfpenny, the horrible driving of cattle to an open-air slaughtering, the rows upon rows of well-thumbed books in the first free public library in Scotland. Here was a town incredibly old and incredibly new. The scientists, in their turn, astonished Dundee. After the preliminary ceremonies of rightness, as old David called them, the biologists, chemists, physicists and astronomers talked about the evolution of man, the nature of the universe, the structure of matter, the weaknesses of un-controlled industrial competition, staggering theories even when not fully comprehended, words to anger the stupid, to silence the intelligent, humbling words, shattering the com-placency and self-importance of a town cut off until now from the main streams of thought. Old David laughed maliciously through all that week.

For the first time, Dundee had an exhibition of pictures, which, as David noticed with his eye for such effects, were carefully catalogued and hung in accordance with the social precedency of their lenders, the Belgian king's picture first, then a British royal duke's, then marquises' contributions, earls', viscounts', barons', baronets', knights', then misters in descending order of wealth.

'These magnificent art treasures made a tasteful setting,' the entertainments committee report had it, 'for the numer-ous soirées, concerts and assemblies with which the dis-tinguished visitors were regaled.' In that setting, the voices of burgess boys sang and hammers beat the lamentation for Elspet Renkyne's death. The concert arranged by old David was local music, verse, and drama. Adam's song was per-formed by Mabel at the piano and a choir of youngsters from the Public Seminaries, now beginning to be called the High School, each singer selected for his being of a family in the old locked book. In the background, raised above the choir, was acted a mime of Elspet Renkyne in the jougs and on the witch-fire. John's suite made from Adam's melodies was played by John and his wife, the Hilltown poet Liv-ingstone's songs were sung, and other of Willie's discoveries appeared with tenement poetry and a tenement playlet, crudely cruel in its vennel irony. David had brought an Edinburgh producer to the work of making the most of the concert, for the delight of the scientists and the confusion and discomfort of the right ones.

The town's guests were trotted round the show places in and around the town. They came, on the last day of the visit, to the Witchfire Works, in a crowd, eager to see more of the strange old fellow who had provided the best evening of the week. He presented each with a booklet, bound in jute – probably the first use of the fibre in bookbinding. It was titled *What You Will Remember In Dundee*, a collection of photographs. Not the usual views of Broughty sands, the Tay from Balgay Hill, the castle at Claypots. David English's selection of what would be remembered was indeed the memorable – the interestingly historical look of the stairturrets of new tenements, the shabby but merry Saturday crowd at the Greenmarket, the dirt men shovelling the redd from one of the waterless thirty-seaters in the streets, the camera's cruel catching of a robed procession of magistrates in a moment of ludicrous pomposity, a fight by drunken women at the dockside, children's arithmetic studies chalked on the walls of filthy vennels, ragged washing hanging on ropes from slum windows. With each booklet was a folder, new from the printing, short quotations from the speeches and lectures of the week. Among the world-shaking pronouncements of the scientists were inserted the gaffes of the Dundee right ones:

'When we look upon these wonderful paintings, we realize the purpose of art – to make us better subjects of our gracious Queen.'

'Dundee's enterprising drapers, of whom I am proud to be one of the best known, have assembled large stocks of souvenir goods, Scotch tartan and other fashionable gifts at a moderate price, for our celebrated guests – and I am not one to deny their celebration, although they are not engaged in the famed commercial pursuits which are the chief glory of this enterprising age.'

'Never mind what all the professors say about the age of the world. What does the Reverend Mr. Wilson of the United Presbyterian body in Princes Street say about it?'

The Americans were buying jute cloth again. The Prussians continued their buying, increased their buying of jute as they prepared for war with France, increased it further as they drove French armies before them. Dundee was in a craze of growth, frantic buying, feverish selling, plastering, masoning, hammering, loading, unloading, rail-laying, levelling hillocks, filling hollows. The dirt men scowled at the trenches in every street for water pipes. Alongside the stair-turrets of the tenement were being built privie turrets, one water closet above another, called W.C.'s by the prim, each to be shared by only three or four families. The pulling of a chain would wash the redd into the river. The turn of a tap in the tenement homes would bring sweet water from the hills.

David English had his final outburst of gallusness. He was seventy-nine, as melodramatic in appearance with his stooping frailty and his whiteness of hair and beard as he had been in his years of ruddy erectness. The personification of malevolent scorn, he seemed, as he addressed the council for the last time, his lined face contorted to an aged man's caricature of a sneer, his thin hand raised as though to strike, his bony finger pointing around the chamber, seeking out the councillors for condemnation. His speech was as well-prepared as ever; the replies to anticipated interruptions were rehearsed, as were the sudden furies of words, the sudden slowings, the silences.

The occasion was the last townhouse meeting before the 1872 election. In all the elections for thirty-two years he had been the dominant figure, even though, after his first, he had taken no part in the contests, never canvassing, never making an address to the electors nor circularizing them, but never suggesting that he did not want to be nominated. This time, in his first sentence, he announced his retirement. The words he chose for the announcement were characteristic:

'We all have to die. Soon I will be dead. I ask, therefore,

that those electors who are of a mind to nominate me for the coming poll and those who are of a mind to vote for me to refrain from doing so. They will be nominating and voting for one who has no chance of seeing more than a month or two of the coming council's three-years term.' He smiled his jeering one-sided smile. The newspaper men were in a lather of writing. 'The bailie's' last appearance in the townhouse! The sketch of the bailie's townhouse career, with re-quotation of his many jibes, an account of the rise of jute, the story of his son's whaling adventure and of the *Lucky Scaup*'s return from an Arctic wintering, all these were ready for the day, and now was the day!

'I have been thirty-two years a councillor. I leave a better council than was the one I came to. It is better because I can see, looking around this council, a few who do have the good of Dundee at heart, whereas in my first council I could see none.' He named these few, his aged eyes searching them out, passing over the others who glowered as his look went by them. 'These I have mentioned are men of some distinction in Dundee life. Their being here is recognition by the town of their distinction. As for the rest, they have no distinction except that easy distinction they save sought for and intrigued for, namely, membership of the council. It is a distinction they prize though it is mocked at by all the town. It is the only distinction they are capable of attaining to, and they can attain to it only because of the continued survival among their kind of an evil tradition.'

Members were on their feet, protesting. The old man waited. When the shouting had spent itself, he went on as calmly virulent as before.

'I hope that the reporters have taken note of the interrupters. The electorate will, no doubt, be interested in their names. Let me remind you that there is a long-established custom in this chamber whereby the speech of a retiring member is heard without disturbance. It is one of the customs worthy of being retained. Other customs are not so worthy!'

Again he waited, keeping them wondering.

'The council to which I was first elected was, notoriously, a bad council. Six years before, there had been a remarkable change, outwardly, in burgh rule, a change even more revolutionary for Scotland than had been the parliament suffrage reform of two years previously. The closed governance by small and unimportant cliques had apparently been ended, and we had open nomination to the council and open voting by all the payers of ten-pound rents, a small electorate but vast in comparison with the few shopkeepers who had previously held the power of electing the council, that is, electing themselves. Outwardly and apparently, I say, these changes had taken place. In actuality, there had been little change. The evil tradition still lived. The machinery of nomination still remained with the cliques. I was nominated in error. I was then of no consequence in industry and had no place in town life. A deputation came to me to ask me to stand for the council because I was of no consequence, because I was believed by them to speak their speech, because I was taken to be one of their own kind. I was elected to a council in which I was surrounded by that small-minded, low-ambitioned, self-satisfied kind, the people who called themselves burgesses. The town had sixty thousand population. It lived then as now by yarn spinning and cloth weaving and by the world trade in these manufactures. Yet its council was drawn from men who lived by local trading, and the world trading interests, both of employers and workers, were completely unrepresented, except by myself, if I may be said to have represented anything or anybody. The men in that council were exactly the same type of men as had held the council in the era of closed rule. That was the revolution, the great deliverance! Throughout my years in the council, the same kind of men have been here, and most of the time I have been in a minority of one. This last council is, except for these named few, the same kind of men as ever. Why, after two great reforms of Scotch local government, is it so? Because the evil tradition lived and still lives? It worked two

335

ways. It made council membership desirable to that small section, and it made council membership anything but desirable to everybody else. The historians write of 1832 and 1834 as the great dates, but I who have seen one burgh council at close range and have followed the workings of other Scotch councils, say that the revolution only begins now. I have seen the beginning of the revolution. Having seen that, I can go. These few men I have named are the beginning of the revolution. Election to the council is really becoming free and open. The name burgess has been laughed out of use. Remember, you few, this is but the beginning. There is still the tradition, holding to its wicked machinery for nominating inferior candidates, nominating them because they are inferior. It is able to hold to it because self-respecting ability still remains aloof from the scorned townhouse. You few know how easily these men of the tradition can be beaten at the polls. They are jokes to the electors, who regard an election as a time for laughter, laughter at the stuttering stupidities uttered on the platforms by these creatures. But in that laughter is the strength, in a sense, of these fools because it makes the townhouse cheaper than ever, and makes it more difficult to enlist such men as yourselves in the public service. Gentlemen, you few, I confess I have never had any other object in my public life than that of raising a laugh against the right ones in their rightness. I see in your presence here a better way of puncturing their pomposity.'

He waited, turning away from the councillors towards the reporters.

'The council of thirty-two years ago almost brought plentiful public water to the town. Almost! The town's demand for water was such that even the council had to listen. The water did not come. The evil tradition, showing itself in incompetence and in back-scratching concern for its supporters, turned away the water, and the councillors argued for years the trivialities of pew-rents and the trimming of churchyard grass until the town was bankrupted by that absurd quarrel. That, too, in years when Dundee grew

336

rapidly without any control by the council which was engaged solely upon that little right dispute. Today I have seen another council in a glow of self-praise for its being the council that has taken the first measures to give Dundee the water it so much needs. One councillor, even more foolish than the others, has said that this council will always be remembered with gratitude as the council that brought water. But the town will not give you much credit, believe me. Most of you have been long on the council. Do you recall your water speeches of ten or twelve years ago, you who were on the council then? Courteously I call them speeches! Let me remind you.' He quoted from half-a-dozen newspaper cuttings in turn, pointing to the men who had spoken these words that he read.

'The circumstances were different then,' they cried.

'Yes, the circumstances were different,' he went on. I'll tell you where the difference lay. Why is Dundee now to get water, and why couldn't it get water before? Is it that the patient suffering of the town's women at the wells has at last gained the sympathy of these councillors? No! That suffering is no more noticeable today than ever it was, and is no more pitied by these men than ever it was. Is it that the warnings given by the scientists in their meeting here some years ago are at last being taken to heart by these councillors? No, with silly catchwords they tried to answer the scientists then, and still deride, in the know-all manner of utter ignorance, the improvements urged by doctors and public health experts.'

He listed the catch-phrases, pointing as he spoke.

'Why then is it that Dundee is now to obtain water? I'll tell you. Because the right ones, whose one interest is self-interest, now see that in this matter the general good will further their counting of ha'pennies. They have grown rich, in their little way, by the growth of Dundee. They have become convinced, carefully counting the ha'pennies for and the ha'pennies against, that further growth cannot take place without certain public improvements. Water has become right, with all the trappings of rightness, the self-approval of little right ones, the dinners, the after-dinner stutterings, the royal duke. Well, in Glasgow, it was a royal duke. Here it will be an Angus laird, but that will be large enough rightness for Dundee's right ones. Dundee is to get the right public improvements. I warn the town that it will not obtain water so quickly as would be liked. The water of rightness requires not only the digging of trenches and the laying of pipes. It requires also the little arguments of right ones, the little back-bitings and back-scratchings. The estimate is that water will be supplied in five years. The town may reckon on nearer ten years, because water of rightness will be the slow water of incompetence. I have named men who are truly sincere for the public good. They will try to hurry Dundee's water, but they are few.'

He waited.

'There are other public improvements – so-called – which this council prides itself on having started. The little right ones are to have a bean-feast of public improvement of the right kind – with the ceremonies of rightness. It is unfortunate for Dundee of the present, it is even more unfortunate for the Dundee of the far future that the destroying and building to be done in the next few years are to be done by rightness. The few will be attempting to save what is interesting and beautiful from the destroyers. They will be attempting to add interest and beauty to the new structures. But the evil tradition will be working against them, and defeating much of their effort.'

There he faltered.

'If there is a Dundee in the far future,' he said, almost as though to himself, 'without a hinterland, without coal, without an easy source of raw material for manufacture—.' Old John English, reformer, was speaking on the Law summit to the youth David English. The council members and the reporters stared as old David havered about that long-ago argument on the hill above Dundee. 'Sentimentally and romantically, old John believed that the town has but one

338

economic advantage,' David said. 'Without sentiment, without romance, my son believes it. I didn't believe it then when I was a youth. I don't believe it now. In time there will be a new way of life, and new views of economy, for which an absence of coal, of metal, of a trading hinterland will be unimportant. It will be important that Dundee has the location for a good place in which folks can work and live. It could be a grand place for folks to live in! It shall be!' Some of his hearers applauded. He glowered at them. 'I'm not speaking your little right talk!' he snapped. 'Don't mistake me. I'm speaking the opposite of your rightness!'

He steadied himself, recovered.

'A digression, a memory that came into my head,' he explained. 'Let me finish. You think you will be remembered with gratitude by Dundee. I was suggesting that you would be remembered only as the men who delayed water until water and rightness mixed together, but, come to think of it, you will not be remembered at all. Who remembers councillors and bailies of Dundee? Most of you have your names as the names of streets, and even while you are still alive, in public life, the names are the unmeaning, undistinguished names of streets, not of men.'

He spoke directly to the reporters. 'Remember to print the names I gave you,' he said. 'These few signify that my years in this townhouse have not been entirely in vain. I see something I can call success for myself and for all the Englishes since the first one.' His finger stabbed towards the condemned councillors in turn. 'Right ones, little right ones! You would still burn a witch if an Angus laird would open the ceremony for you. Likely enough you will burn a witch before your tradition is done with.'

He moved with an old man's slowness from the council chamber. Outside he stopped to laugh. 'A hundred and fifty years ago they hanged an English for a lot less than that,' he said to the townhouse porter.

He had used all his fire, it seemed, for that final display of the Englishes' wrongness. He was a done man for the remaining two months of his life, seldom seen in the town or in the factory. He sat beside Elspet for her lessons, interrupting them with an aged man's mumbled marvelling at her growth and her quickness. Mabel played for him the Elspet Renkyne song. John and his wife told him their side of the family stories, and he re-told them to his grand-daughter. His end was the slow, almost painless death of old age. He suffered only a few seconds, gasping for breath. He was thinking of the hunched woman's end, it seemed. 'It's as though the smoke of that fire was still through the town,' he said, 'in every gait and close.' He died at the same age as had died Adam called English a hundred and forty years before.

The funeral was a fitting one for the gallus bailie. The family had arranged for quietness, but the longest procession ever seen in the town walked behind the coffin, mill and factory folks in their working clothes, the women and children barefooted. They crowded the jute lords and the councillors away from the Logie grave. There was no religious ceremony. The diggers waited, uncomfortable, for a clergyman's signal to shovel the earth upon the body. 'It is as he wished,' quiet John English said, apologetically, to them. 'It's quite all right to go on with the burial.' The stones and turf rattled upon the coffin wood.

The newspaper obituaries and the speeches at the Chamber of Commerce said of him that he had been a power in Dundee.

American railroad builders wore jute overalls, received their wages in little jute pokes, slept on jute palliases in bunks separated by jute screens, drank in saloons made of jute stretched on frames, saw girls dance on stages curtained with painted jute, died and were buried by the trackside in sheets of jute. Work and shillings for Dundee.

Picks and crowbars felled the ancient taverns where four centuries of history had been drunkenly debated. The old houses of the lairds, now become the dirtiest vennels of the Irish, were carted as rotting stones to the riverside to push the water back. Placards covered the crumbling walls of the High Street, the Moraygait and the Nethergait: removal sale, demolishing sale. To replace the low-windowed, low-doored shops of old Dundee, the new and larger premises of the placard announcements were rising, storey on storey.

The four-flighted tenements spread northwards, over the lands of Clepington, eastwards, farther into the lands of Wallace Craigie. The gorge of the Wallace Burn was seen only in lengths of a yard or two, in mill courts, the steep banks dammed across to make reservoirs for mill boilers. The Dens was the name, not for a gorge, but for a long street of tenements and factories. The tenements spread west. Hawkhill was a tenement street. All Blackness was tenements and factories and warehouses and suburban villas. Where had been the winding Coupar-Angus trail was a winding double line of tenements ending in a great blob of tenements, Lochee.

Willie English calculated with his pupil John, who was recently returned to Dundee from an American voyage of discovery. Much of the development of Dundee had come out of the American west. The wheat prairies and the cattle lands of the United States had always been within the environment of the Dundee millionaires. Dundee, without metals, without coal, without an easy source of raw materials, without a trade hinterland, was already fully capitalized, Willie said, over capitalized, perhaps. He listed the threats to Dundee, seen by him but scarcely apparent as yet to others, jute manufacture in India, talk by Continental politicians about subsidies for jute weaving in their own countries, rumours of new methods of packing. He looked for a field for investment of the Englishes' profits, made mostly in America, and found that America was the field. The western tendency of Dundee's wealth was, in his instance, quickened by his necessity for exciting activity.

'You went from Dundee and brought back what was needed,' Willie told young John. 'I once went away from these family legends. I brought back what was needed – my paralysis!' His face was taut as he spoke.

In India, where jute grew, the factory industry for spinning and weaving jute was gaining every year in size and experience. Machinery men and clerking men, trained in Dundee's ways, were in India, which paid them a hundred times the wages of Dundee. They were organizing the power looms, the engine-houses, and the offices of Bengal jute factories. Some of the Dundee jute lords were saying that they would have to enter the Indian industry in order to have some control over the developments there and safeguard their holdings in Dundee. They were not yet afraid of India. The expanding trade of the world, they said, could take all of India's sacks and all of Dundee's. Willie was not one of these. The distaste he had had for jute in his youth remained with him. He was selling out his jute interests at the high prices of booming prosperity. His money was building prairie towns and prairie railroads, clearing land for American farms, buying the tools for American farmers. He was calculating not only for his own investments but for those of others, founding, while barely aware of the course of his own thoughts, the investment companies associated with his name. In the town were a few calculators like him, making a new tradition to add to the old Dundee traditions.

In those years when Willie sold out jute, with Dargie silently watchful behind him, Elspet grew to young womanhood, her mother's daughter, little and gentle. The passers-by in the street looked after the carriage in which she sat. 'A bonnie lassie,' they said, and told each the well remembered story of her birth, when her father was believed lost in the Arctic, the gallus bailie's gallus son, the grey-haired man in the wheeled chair, now, to be seen on sunny days in his Perth Road garden.

Every month through the long boom of jute had, as Willie said in the English way, its display of confidence, its civic occasion, the first flushing of a new sewer, the first bullock killed in a new slaughter-house, a new elementary school for the new compulsory education, a new hospital, a new prison, a new lunatic asylum. The dignitaries presented to each other golden keys to open doors; spoke the ritual of public platform worship of Victoria, the little goddess of the growth of towns. The occasions found their poet.

> Then the band started to play, and the brilliant procession
>   formed up.
> To the amazement of all it was led by a playful pup.
> As the procession passed along, the spectators made a great
>   din,
> When they saw the well-known public citizen, and shouted
>   out—that's him!

> When they arrived at the new poorhouse, Sir Joseph gave
>   an address,
> Stating how useful this magnificent institution would be
>   to the poor in distress.
> There followed the opening ceremony at the nurses' home,
> Succeeded by a visit to the Provost's to partake of
>   lunch-e-on.

The voice was the voice of McGonagall. Ever since his discovery that he was a poet, he had been writing occasional verses for the sprees Willie English provided for whaling men. Now he became a poet in spate, pouring forth a rhythmless flood of bathos, singing the occasions in his own crazed caricature of the language of the occasions. His heroes and heroines were the local eminences, this eloquent preacher, that public-spirited philanthropist, that remarkably enterprising draper. He sang them in their hours among the headlines, their tapping of foundation stones, their munificent gifts to the town, their funerals.

> Amongst those present at the interment were Mr. Marjori
>   banks, M.P.,
> Also a noted ex-Provost from Bonnie Dundee.
> Besides the Honourable W. G. Colville representing the
>   Duke and Duchess of Edinboro,
> While on everybody's face was depicted sorrow.

He had sent a copy of one of his poems to the Queen, and, from the clerks who dealt with such manifestations of loyalty, had received the usual curt acknowledgment of the manuscript's receipt. He took this to be royal recognition, headed his penny broadsheets with a crown and the letters V.R., and underneath proudly proclaimed himself: 'By royal appointment, poet to Her Majesty. Also to the nobility and gentry.' He visited Balmoral, 'among the bonnie Highland floral,' to present himself to Victoria. A reception by laughing servants established his absurd pretensions more firmly in his mind.

Willie English collected the poet's broadsheets. They were of a type to appeal to the strange humour of the Englishes.

McGonagall sat on the damp grass of Magdalen Green. A pestered shopkeeper had at last given him the pieces of wrapping paper he had begged. On them he wrote his latest masterpiece, inspired by the most inspiring of Dundee's inspirations, the two-miles-long bridge, the engineering marvel of the age, the symbol of Dundee's confidence in a future of shillings and security. For eight years the making of the bridge had been Dundee's talk and staring. Thousands had picnicked upon Magdalen Green to watch the building of the piers in the river, the laying of the viaduct, the crossing by the first train. Everyone in Dundee knew the times of the trains on the bridge. Everyone looked for the plumes of smoke and steam appearing upon the Fife end of the two miles, a thin dark snake breathing fire, crawling towards the criss-cross of girders in the bridge's central stretch, wriggling among the broken light of the girders, speeding on a wide curve to the Dundee shore. McGonagall rose, stiff and shivering, sure that he had the gift of prophecy as well as that of poetry. He had written this:

Beautiful Railway Bridge of the Silvery Tay!
With your numerous arches and pillars in so grand array,
And your central girders, which seem to the eye
To be almost towering to the sky.

The greatest wonder of the day,
And a great beautification to the River Tay,
Most beautiful to be seen,
Near by Dundee and the Magdalen Green.

Beautiful Railway Bridge of the Silvery Tay!
That has caused the Emperor of Brazil to leave his home far
    away,
Incognito in his dress.
And view thee ere he passed along en route to Inverness.

Beautiful Railway Bridge of the Silvery Tay!
Which will cause great rejoicing on the official opening day
And hundreds of people will come from far away,
Also the Queen, most gorgeous to be seen,
Near by Dundee and the Magdalen Green.

Beautiful Railway Bridge of the Silvery Tay!
And prosperity to Messrs. Bouche and Grothe, the famous
    engineers of the present day,
Who have succeeded in erecting the Railway
Bridge of the Silvery Tay,
Which stands unequalled to be seen
Near by Dundee and the Magdalen Green.

Beautiful Railway Bridge of the Silvery Tay!
I greatly fear that you will fall one day,
For as I look at you I do say
That your central girders are not strong enough and will give
    way
And that will be a most awful sight to be seen
Near by Dundee and the Magdalen Green.

McGonagall came to Willie English in the evening. 'My
patron, most noble sir,' he intoned gravely. 'Alas, alas! The
scurlish printer! The druggist knave! Money, money. A
curse, sir, only a curse! The printer asks money to print the

deathless work of William McGonagall, poet by royal appointment. The druggist, a mere seller of medicine, tells William McGonagall that sitting on wet ground brings its own punishment. He offers no relief for the pangs of piles unless paid filthy money. I thank you, sir. Your name will not be unknown in the halls of fame, McGonagall's patron.' Willie tore off the last verse. 'It is McGonagall's words,' the poet protested. 'All that McGonagall writes should go forth in print to the world. You say not this closing stanza. For five more shillings, sir, mere lucre, William McGonagall will bow to your wishes. I thank you, sir. McGonagall, poet, thanks you.'

Young John, twenty-six, and Elspet, nineteen, were in love, shy in each other's presence, their love undeclared. The lovers climbed the Law, a public park now. Tomorrow they would be parted. The girl's father had opened a London office, where John would be in charge. They looked down on Dundee, the little old steeple among little roofs, little spires and towers among little roofs, little chimney stacks among little roofs, a small confusion of roofs beside a vastness of river which flowed in a vastness of hills. The bridge was a thin thread of black across a shining immensity. The lovers made their love known to each other, these two children of Adam called English, dirt shoveller, she the child of Leeb White, tinkler, he the child of Mary Lowden, dirt man's serving girl; she, the child of Elspet English of the lovely hair, of the coffin-maker Willie Auchterlonie, of the laughing Willie English whose laughter was his death, of the fine-weaving Margreit de Wint, of the hanger Willie English, of the exciseman Digby, of the fine-skinned Elspet Auchterlonie, of the smooth-legged Elspet Digby, of the Paris-kilted Willie English, of the bagpiping orator Willie English, of the Lochee spinning-girl Annie Bowman, of the jute lord David English, of the silent Agnes Woodman, of Willie English who went with the whalers, of Mabel Broadfoot with rounded arms; he, the child of townhouse mason John English, of Katherine Cant, of John English killed in the fall of the Bailie's close, of reformer John English, of Arabella Cowperthwaite who played the harpsichord, of Adam English maker of songs, of Alice Greenacre, of violin-playing John English. They were in love. The present and the future were for them. The past was dust, the dust of dead Dundee, dust yards deep down to the first dust of men upon the boulder clay.

That year, 1879, the past now, too; these lovers upon the Law, in 1879, the past; that black thread across the river, the bridge, the past. A night of rejoicing for the Englishes was a night of fear for the town, Sunday, December 28th, 1879. Young John had come north for the Hogmanay holiday. He and Elspet announced they were to wed. This uniting of the two sides of the family, Willie declared, was an appropriate occasion for his own news. John's parents would want to be near him. Mabel and himself would want to be near Elspet. Moreover, the family's work was entirely in London now. Yes, he could bear the discomfort of travelling, he assured them. 'The blood has become too great a power for little Dundee, and it goes from Dundee,' he added. They played and sang to celebrate these two excitements. 'There remains only the writing of the town's story in the story of Elspet Renkyne's blood,' Willie said. 'Before I come to my end I will do the collecting together of the legends and memories from which the story can be made.'

Outside was storm. Poised between the liquid blackness of the firth and the cloudy blackness of the sky, the long Ochil spur in Fife was solidly black. In the darkness of water and sky and land, lights floated, a line of little squares of light, a train upon an unseen bridge across an unseen wildness of foam. Mingled with the wind's triumphant shout, the shriller voices of fear were heard. The lights of the train fell in a cataract of light from blackness in which they were visible to blackness which hid them. The moon hurried across a sudden rent in the blackness of the air. The clouds it passed were as solid, as hard-edged as the hills. The polished waves in the river shattered themselves against piers which carried no central criss-cross of girders. The moon pushed on against the wind into the blackness of the sky. The river was black again, the hills were black. A few wayfarers peered into the blackness, afraid to believe what had been shown to them in these few moments of the moon's appearance – the wrecked bridge, the wrecked confidence.

McGonagall, bedraggled by the storm, came sobbing to the Englishes. They shouted that he was welcome, that everybody was welcome in their celebration.

'I, William McGonagall, poet, should be also William McGonagall, prophet,' he wept. 'I saw it, the inspired eyes of McGonagall saw it. For five shillings, a mere five shillings, I threw away the vision I had seen, and the prophet is not known to be a prophet.' They did not understand his babbling. They sang and played, letting him weep.

THE END